REVOLUTION

Dean Crawford

ISBN: 1499115822
ISBN-13: 978-1499115826

Also by Dean Crawford:

The Ethan Warner Series
Covenant
Immortal
Apocalypse
The Chimera Secret
The Eternity Project

Atlantia Series
Survivor

Independent novels
Eden
Holo Sapiens
Soul Seekers

Want to receive notification of new releases? Just sign up to Dean Crawford's newsletter via: http://eepurl.com/KoP8T

"A people that wants to be free must arm itself with a free press."

George Seldes

1

They were closing in on her.

She could hear them as she scrambled up the frozen hillside, her threadbare clothes drenched with moisture spilling like diamond chips from the foliage clogging her path. She looked up through veils of mist at the trees towering into the sky, then risked a quick glance over her shoulder.

Terrific mountain ranges smashed across the horizon, their ancient heights draped with blankets of snow, and far below the silvery thread of a river reflected the dawn sunlight.

Deep, insistent barking haunted the valley. She recognised the breed from the sounds they made: North–Caucasian Volkodavs, a giant Kavkaz mastiff. Completely fearless, they were trained to hunt bears and wolves. Or humans.

She plunged onward through ferns and bracken as her breath sawed in her throat and the chill air numbed the tips of her ears and nose. A thick tree root grasped for her ankle, the satchel that she protected under one arm almost falling from her grip as she stumbled. It briefly came undone to reveal a sleek, black object that seemed far too modern to be in her grasp. She staggered back onto her feet, closed the satchel and forged onward.

The barking of the dogs competed with the shouts of men echoing through the forest behind her. Their voices conjured memories that reeled through her mind – vehicles charging through the grey dawn, burning buildings, thick coils of smoke filling the streets; the dogs, the cackle and thump of machine guns, cries of terror and pain and confusion. The chorus of mankind's hymn of war.

The trees thinned as she fought her way through a brittle tangle of thorn scrub and staggered into a clearing, surrounded on three sides by the forest and with an open ridge ahead of her.

She hurried across to the ridge and looked down into another valley far below. Fields of frost–hardened earth spread into the distance across a barren, icy plain. A scattering of old barns stood beside a farmhouse, distant figures toiling in the fields. Biting her lip to stop it trembling, she judged the distance to the farmstead against the sounds of pursuing men and animals. Too far, *much too far.*

Twigs snapped amid the trees close by, curses and shouts following. They had flanked her, coming in from both sides as well as from behind. A dizzying wave of panic flushed like ice water through her. A fallen tree caught her eye, dominating the edge of the forest, its bulk entombed within coils of frozen vines. Lunging toward it, she knelt down and buried her satchel deep within a cavity in the decaying trunk.

Backing away from the tree, she returned to the ridge and stared down at the quiet little farmstead, the serene view more bitter–sweet now than she could ever have imagined.

'Arretech! *Arretech!*'

The man stumbled out of the forest nearby, the ugly barrel of his AK–47 assault rifle pointed at her. She froze in place as though a part of the forest and fought to keep her expression neutral.

The soldier kept the weapon trained upon her as the sounds of men and animals echoed ominously across the clearing, camouflaged shapes moving like demons through the trees. The soldier glanced to one side, and a smile twisted across his skeletally thin face.

Hordes of troops broke through the forest and into the clearing, pointing and shouting at her. Her legs emptied of strength as though hollow, her throat thick with loathing as she watched. The dogs were leading them, each animal restrained by two soldiers holding thick leashes. The animals glared hungrily at her, catching her scent and spouting dense clouds of breath from huge chests. She counted six dogs and perhaps fifty soldiers armed with various types of machine guns and pistols, all moving to surround her in a loose ring.

A silence enveloped the clearing, until the only sounds she could hear were the breathing of the dogs and the muted patter of countless water droplets falling through the trees to drench the forest floor. The troops watched her with silent, sullen expressions. Slowly, the ring of soldiers parted and a tall man walked between them, his shoulders bearing the epaulettes of an officer. She shrivelled under his gaze as he approached. Obsidian eyes observed her without emotion from beneath thick brows, thin lips framed by a heavy jaw dense with grey stubble.

'Salut,' he said softly.

The girl's vision jolted as the world toppled over before her, and it was several seconds before she realised that she had been struck. Blood dribbled from her split lips and lined her tongue with a metallic tang. White pain ripped across her scalp as she was yanked by her hair onto her knees, the officer glaring at her from inches away.

'*Voul Americanis, niet?*' he asked, and then in distorted English. 'Yes, you are an American. Always you appear where you are not wanted.'

The girl did not reply, her skin taking on the pallor of the frosty earth. The man held her for a few seconds and then thrust her back into the dirt. She looked at the ring of soldiers as she lifted her bruised, bloodied face.

They returned her gaze with neither excitement nor shame, the brutality of conflict having long ago scoured them of their humanity.

The officer casually lit a cigarette as he looked down into the valley, watching the villagers tending their fields. Several of them were looking up toward the hills, and he guessed that they had heard the barking of the mastiffs. The girl watched as the officer drew slowly upon his cigarette, then turned away and gestured to the soldier who had intercepted her.

The soldier lunged forward, pinning the cold metal barrel of his assault rifle to her forehead as he squeezed the trigger.

'Belaye! Wait!'

The soldier scowled before reluctantly jerking his weapon away from her. The girl turned to see the officer staring thoughtfully at the village below.

'They will hear the gunfire,' he murmured, and then turned to two of his lieutenants. 'Bind and gag her.'

The two men hurried across, grabbed her roughly and bound her wrists with cords that wrenched her skin before gagging her with a length of coarse leather. Satisfied, they backed away. The impassive ring of soldiers stirred, their eyes hungry now. She trembled both from the cold and the fear that scraped at the lining of her stomach as the officer leaned down to bring his face level with hers, his features quivering with exotic excitement. The smell of stale tobacco smoke wafted across her face as he spoke.

'Many a foreigner has vanished in these mountains,' he whispered. 'The bears, the wolves, the wild dogs, we are all prey when out here alone.'

She recoiled as the officer regarded her with his sullen black eyes and licked his lips, taking a long pull on his cigarette before dropping the butt and grinding it out with his heel. He straightened and walked toward the circle of his men.

'Unleash the dogs.'

It took a moment for her to comprehend what the officer had said. Bright tears burst from her eyes as she gazed imploringly at the handlers, who had not moved and were staring blankly at their officer. The watching ring of soldiers also looked up at him as though confused. Some of them began backing away as though distancing themselves from her fate. The officer snatched his pistol from its holster and screamed at the handlers.

'Unleash the dogs!'

She scrambled to her feet with a muffled cry and staggered away toward the ridge as fast as she could with her awkward, half–bound gait, fleeting visions of her family flickering like ghosts through her mind. The dogs snapped and snarled as their handlers fought to loosen their ties, and then she heard all six of the beasts lurch in pursuit of her with a broadside of deep barks.

The soldiers stood paralysed in a rictus of horror as she ran from them, screamed for help through the gag as she looked over her shoulder at the dogs pursuing her in a roiling cloud of muscle and fur. Behind the pack, the officer stood with his pistol drawn, his features shining with primal excitement as the mastiffs bounded up and launched themselves at her.

In a flash of movement she glimpsed one of the watching soldiers cry out and raise his rifle, aiming and firing a single deafening shot that shattered the frigid air. Something slammed into her back with the strength of a fallen angel and the world spun around her as she fell, the back of her head jarring as it smashed onto the unforgiving earth.

The mastiffs scattered fearfully from the sound of the gunshot and hurried back to their handlers. Through blurred vision, the girl saw the officer turn and fire his pistol in one fluid motion. The bullet hit the disobedient soldier squarely in his chest and hurled him backwards into the foliage nearby. His body shuddered and then fell still as the shots echoed in endless symphony into the distance.

She lay silent and still, her eyes closed now.

There was no pain from the wound, and yet she knew that the deep numbness enveloping her must surely be a terminal embrace. The sudden silence of the forest around her seemed filled with a dense pall of shame that hung over her captors. She sensed the officer stride past her to look down into the valley. She could hear distant shouts, the villagers already running toward their farmstead for their own guns. But she knew they would be too late.

She felt the officer kneel down beside her and savagely tear the fabric of her clothes. For one terrible moment she feared that he was not yet finished with her, but then she felt him place a pistol in her palm and stand. His voice broke the silence as he pointed at the dead soldier nearby.

'Strip him of his uniform and leave them both to the peasants.'

There was a flurry of activity nearby in the bushes, and then in sombre silence the troops moved away from the lonely clearing, the sound of their boots and the dogs fading. She managed to force her eyes to open and saw the soldiers vanishing like ghosts into the forest, some of them casting glances back over their shoulders until, finally, she was alone.

Lying paralysed on the cold earth she saw the forest above her fill with twinkling stars and galaxies of light before plunging into a darkness as deep as time itself.

***

2

London

Megan Mitchell tried to jog in a straight line and ignore the loathsome jolts of pain grinding around the interior of her skull.

The sun had just risen over the glassy surface of the Thames as she ran beside the embankment, the towering edifice of Big Ben and the Houses of Parliament looming through a light mist hovering above the water. She squinted up into the powder–blue sky as she plodded miserably along, struggling to contain the bolts of nausea churning through her stomach.

She jogged the same route every morning and for the same reason. From Tower Bridge, along the Embankment past St Paul's Cathedral and down to London Bridge to cross the Thames and make the return journey. By the time she returned home the headache and nausea would have faded, the pungent film coating the back of her throat vanished and the poison purged from her veins for another day.

She wore headphones like the other runners who passed her with brief nods of greeting, but no music played within. Megan wore them only to deter others from attempting conversation and ruining the silence of her unsteady rhythm.

The gothic towers of Tower Bridge loomed before her as she accelerated for the last leg of her run. She could see the ranks of pedestrians and cars streaming across the bridge toward their offices, banks, warehouses and restaurants, and she smiled grimly. She was no longer one of them.

After sprinting the final hundred yards she finally slowed, regaining her breath as she turned left through a large and ornate archway with the legend 'St Katherine's Dock' emblazoned around its circumference.

The Yacht Haven of the marina was filled with pearly–white vessels glistening in autumn's morning light. Megan could see a number of shops and restaurants around the marina, opposite the Dickens Inn and the Clock–Tower. The development was one of London's most exclusive and was dominated by a row of Penthouse suites, toward which Megan jogged.

As she moved she cast her eye across one of the largest vessels in the marina, a sleek blue–water yacht with *Icarus* written in delicate script across her stern. She had not taken her out for a few weeks now. Maybe she'd head south for Spain, when winter finally descended.

Megan checked her watch as she walked into the foyer of the apartments. She ignored the elevators and instead walked up the steps two at a time, both to warm–down from her run and to avoid the possibility of narcissistic chatter with the other residents. Emerging onto the top floor, she walked to the end of the corridor and her own apartment.

She swiped her resident's identity card through the keypad beside her door and keyed in her pass–code.

The apartment was bright and airy, sunlight streaming in through broad windows where the Thames glistened in the distance like a sheet of beaten silver. Megan strolled into a large living room, pulling off her T–shirt and tossing it onto a leather couch.

As was her habit on every Monday, she checked her answering machine. There was rarely a need to do it more frequently as nobody really called any more. For this she only had herself to blame. *There's nothing and nobody out there*, she reminded herself. A small winking light told her there was at least one message waiting, so she pressed a button and listened to the warbling electronic voice as she performed the *Shotokan* karate form, moving through the defensive and offensive postures as she listened.

'You have four – new – messages.'

'A bumper harvest,' she murmured to herself as she punched an imaginary enemy in the face and drove her knee up into his groin.

'First – new – message; Megan, it's Monday morning and it's Harrison once again. If you think I'm going to stop calling then you underestimate my tenacity. I've got assignments all over the world, and any one of them is yours when you're ready.' There was an awkward pause. *'Hope you're okay. Speak soon.'*

Megan smiled briefly as she touched her toes.

'Delete.'

'Second – new – message; Miss Mitchell, it's Sarah from Zurich Associates, just letting you know that your transactions went through as discussed. All deductions have been made for you, registered with the Inland Revenue and cleared. Thank you again for choosing Zurich Associates to handle your financial contracts. Good–day.'

'Delete.'

'Third – new – message; Hey Megan, it's Tom from the office. I finally got your new number from Harrison, just wondering if you want to go for a drink and..,'

'Delete.'

Megan took off her trainers and walked toward the bathroom.

'Fourth – new – message; Er, hi, I hope I've got the right number here, for a Megan Mitchell.'

Megan stopped walking and glanced at the machine. The voice was American –Brooklyn, if she recognised correctly.

'I'm sorry to make contact so abruptly, but I have a real problem and I don't know of anyone else who can help. I got your number from the GNN office in Manhattan. I.., I don't know if I wanna talk about this on the phone. I'm here in London right now.'

Megan blinked in surprise, staring at the machine as the voice went on.

'I've booked a room at the Marriot and will be here until the 24th. I couldn't get any more time off work than that. I couldn't get an address for you, but I understand that you live near Tower Bridge. I'll be in the Hunter's Lodge in Rookery Street every day from noon until three. I hope you can arrange to meet me there – it's quite literally a matter of life and death and I have nobody else to turn to.' There was a long pause. *'Thanks in advance for your time, Miss Mitchell.'*

Megan glanced again at her watch. It was the 24th. She unpinned her pony–tail and shook out her long blonde hair before turning toward the bathroom.

'Delete.'

***

3

Megan Mitchell would never have set foot in the Hunter's Lodge were it not for the smoking–ban enforced in the United Kingdom. Before the law had come into effect it had not been possible to walk through most London pubs without night–vision goggles and breathing apparatus, the narrow corridors of the ancient inns turning their confines into a swirling miasma of tobacco fog. Now, the low ceilings were no longer stained nicotine–yellow and the pub smelt uncharacteristically clean.

Megan checked her watch as she walked inside: just after half–past twelve. She briefly eyed the liquor bottles behind the bar before ordering a coke and looking around. A few aged locals sat huddled around a fruit–machine, and a couple of Japanese students scrutinised a map at a nearby table. Megan scanned the booths further down, deeper inside the Lodge, and almost instantly caught the eyes of a man watching her from a table opposite the booths. Middle–aged, wearing a blue shirt and with a heavy leather flying jacket hanging over the back of his chair, he couldn't have looked more American if he had tried. Megan strolled across to the table.

'Brooklyn?' she asked the man.

'Right on,' the American smiled, his apprehension vanishing as he extended his hand. 'Frank Amonte – thanks for coming Megan, I appreciate it.'

Frank gestured to the seat opposite and Megan sat down.

'I don't know what I can do for you,' Megan said cautiously. 'In fact, I don't know you at all.'

'I know,' Frank said, raising an apologetic hand, 'and I'm real sorry for all the cloak and dagger crap. I'll explain myself, but first of all, have you eaten?'

Megan hadn't, so she let the American order steak sandwiches for them both. Despite not ever having met Frank Amonte before, Megan found herself liking the American, his expression open and friendly.

Megan watched Frank take a big bite from his sandwich before he spoke.

'You're a hell of a hard woman to find, Megan, I'll give you that.'

'Good,' Megan said with a brief smile. 'Who gave you my number?'

'A colleague of mine in Manhattan, someone you know – Michael Burnside.'

Megan nodded slowly, picking up her sandwich.

'I haven't heard from Mike in a long time. How's he doing?'

'He's great, just great. In fact, it was partly his high opinion of you that brought me out here.'

'And what did bring you out here, Frank?'

'I understand that you have a talent for finding people.'

Megan Mitchell paused with the sandwich at her lips, before setting it back on her plate. She took a sip of coke instead. 'Is that so? And why would that bring you all the way here?'

Frank's sighed heavily, shadows passing like clouds behind his eyes.

'Four weeks ago, an investigative reporter from one of our offices flew from the United States to Europe. She was following leads that I know nothing about. What I do know is that she stayed in contact via strict pre–arranged calls with me, same time every night. She never missed that call until eight days ago. Nothing has been heard from her since.'

Megan nodded, pushing her sandwich to one side. 'And?'

'I've tried every avenue that I can to locate this person but nobody knows a thing. In the end I decided that the only option was to broadcast her disappearance, get it on the news so that maybe something would come up or maybe she'd get in touch somehow and let us know that she was okay.'

Megan drained her coke and reached for her jacket.

'So publish the piece.'

'I couldn't,' Frank said urgently, sensing that Megan was already losing interest. 'They wouldn't let me.'

'Who wouldn't let you?'

'GNN, Global News Network. They've blocked all broadcasts from the region where the reporter disappeared.'

'That's unusual, but I can't help you,' Megan replied and stood from her chair.

Frank Amonte frowned.

'What do you mean? Can't help or won't help?'

'A bit of both, actually. I'm sorry, but right now the last thing I'm going to do is travel half–way around the world looking for lost souls.'

Megan opened her wallet and dropped a ten pound note on the table before turning away. Frank Amonte's slightly raised voice drew glances from the pub's customers and staff.

'I read about you. I know what you did. You spent years searching for lost people in Colombia. You found a girl in Thailand who'd been missing for three years. You're experienced in this kind of work.'

Megan smiled bleakly over her shoulder.

'In case you failed to finish your research, I never found many of the people in Colombia and I was lucky to escape from Thailand with my life. I hope you have better luck.'

As Megan walked, the American's voice followed her and rising in urgency the further away she got.

'There's an old retired couple who live in Oklahoma, one of those small towns surrounded by miles of nothing but wheat and barley fields. The old man's a former veteran, Vietnam, the old lady a faithful wife. They're good people, honest people, the kind of people we'd like to be some day. Their last wish in life is to see their daughter returned safely to them and I'm the person they came to. Right now they're worrying their way to an early cardiac arrest. They're willing to pay for your work, Megan. God knows they haven't got much, but it's yours if you'll help.'

Megan paused, glancing without interest over her shoulder.

'If it's so important to you Frank, then you go after her.'

Frank reached down and with an effort wheeled himself backward from under the table. He turned his wheelchair and rolled it toward Megan, who stood momentarily stricken in the middle of the pub – Frank's hefty jacket had hidden the wheelchair's handles. The American rolled to a halt in front of her.

'This is as far as I can go. I'm a desk jockey, no use in the field. I just can't do any more than I have – if I could I wouldn't be wasting my time having this conversation.'

Megan dropped a thin blanket of curiosity over her shame.

'Did the old folks know Mike Burnside?'

Frank Amonte's lips curled into a haunted, sad smile.

'No, but they knew who you were and that you could help.'

Megan dropped the act instantly.

'What? How would an old couple from the Mid–West know who I am?'

Frank reached down into a pocket on the side of his wheelchair and withdrew a slim folder, from which he retrieved a black and white photograph.

'Because their daughter told them all about you, the reporter who searched for lost souls, and about how she helped you.'

A hefty slab of anxiety landed in Megan's stomach as Frank handed her the photograph. The image was of a young girl in her late–twenties, her long, lustrous black hair framing a beautiful face, olive skin and a bright smile.

'Amy,' Megan whispered, 'Amy O'Hara. She's the missing reporter?'

'And we figured you owe her.'

'Where was she when she went missing?'

Frank's features hardened.

'The Republic of Mordania, southern Russia.'

***

4

Megan switched on the television when she returned to her apartment with Frank, the huge plasma screen recessed into the wall glowing into life. On her coffee table was scattered the contents of the folder that the American had passed to her, containing everything Frank had uncovered about Amy O'Hara's work in the Republic of Mordania.

'If there's any clue to what happened to Amy it will be amongst these papers, but I haven't been able to find much,' Amonte said, sitting in his wheelchair and watching the big screen.

The 24–hour news networks all flashed up sporadic broadcasts on Mordania, enough to glean that there had been a vicious civil war raging within the mountainous country ever since a spectacular attempted military coup by a deranged Air Force General, Mikhail Rameron. Megan noted various reports of incidences of 'ethnic–cleansing', along with military movements by Islamist insurgents against the beleaguered government forces centred around the Mordanian capital city, Thessalia. The Russians were watching the events with "extreme concern", rattling their sabres and threatening major troop movements in opposition to United Nations discussions over a proposed peace–keeping force.

'There's no clue as to what Amy was researching, and presumably she didn't tell anyone because she felt that she might have had a scoop,' Frank said. 'On the other hand, she might just have felt that the Mordanian situation was under–reported and wanted to take a chance.'

'It's possible,' Megan nodded, 'Amy can be quite an impulsive girl. What's been happening out there in Mordania?'

'Don't you watch the news?' Frank asked, gesturing to the plasma–screen. 'If I had a television that big I'd never leave my apartment.'

'Not if I can help it,' Megan muttered, focusing on the news clippings and story fragments on the table before her.

From the corner of her eye she saw Frank looking out of the windows of the apartment and then around the place itself, noting the tastefully expensive furniture and the general exclusivity of the abode. The American eyed a row of empty liquor bottles visible on the counter in the kitchen.

'Amy's folks told me that you spent literally every penny you had during a search in Mexico,' Frank observed quietly. 'You look like you bounced back real fast.'

'I worked hard,' Megan said without looking at the American.

'Jeez, well, if your papers pay as well as this I'm hot–tailing it over here right now.'

'I earned it all freelance.'

'Care to share?'

'It's a long story.'

'Thought so.'

Megan gestured to the news prints that Frank had gathered together.

'You say that she disappeared on the 14th?'

'There or thereabouts – her last contact was the day before.'

'Two days later, the ban on foreign journalists travelling in Mordania started.'

Frank nodded.

'That's what I thought – maybe she found something she shouldn't have, got busted, and they decided to clamp down on people nosing around in Mordanian affairs.'

Megan frowned, looking at the different cuttings on the coffee table.

'And you were prevented from broadcasting her disappearance?'

'GNN told me that they'd look into it, but I've heard nothing. It's unheard of for journalists to be abandoned in such a way by their employers – it's as if they don't want to know what's happened to her.'

Megan nodded, but did not reply. She turned off the television and walked across to the broad windows of her apartment, looking south across the city at the afternoon sun reflecting off the densely packed rooftops. In the distance she could see the London Eye rotating slowly, the windows of the carriages sparkling in the sunlight. Everything was peaceful and calm, so far away from the horrific slaughter that Megan knew was occurring right at that very moment in any number of countries around the world. Megan rarely watched the news or read the papers any more. The ceaseless barrage of pain, loss, hardship, misery and then more misery still had long since dulled her senses until she cared no more. There was nothing out there, nothing that Megan wanted to be a part of, nothing that she wanted to see and nobody that she wanted to meet. *Nothing and nobody out there, love.* Megan, by careful planning and determination, had vacuum–sealed herself in a bubble of solitude.

She did not want the peace that she had finally found, after so long, to end.

She turned back to the coffee table and picked up the photograph of Amy O'Hara. The monochrome image could not conceal the buoyant, vibrant colour of her personality nor the tenacity of her spirit. Megan owed her, that much she knew. Amy had unfailingly assisted her through the darkest years of her life as she had scoured the jungle wilderness of Mexico, hunted through the ramshackle, sweltering alleys of cities, climbed mountains, forged rivers, bribed corrupt policemen – and all of it for a person she had never found.

Megan closed her eyes, her fist clenching the photograph and creasing it. She inhaled deeply, fighting off the nausea that infected her whenever she thought of those years and of the indescribable torment she had endured. Still endured. She forced herself to relinquish the pain, and slowly it faded back into some deep neural tract where it would no longer bother her.

'Are you okay?' Frank asked.

Megan had briefly forgotten that the American was there. She let the breath go. 'Tell me everything that has happened in Mordania that might be of help. Amy must have travelled there for a reason.'

'The country's a former Soviet state that declared independence from Russia in 1996 after a peaceful "purple" revolution, as is the fashion these days. Although a quasi–Russian is the local dialect, the majority of the population are a mixture of ethnic Muslims and highland tribesmen, with complete allegiance to neither the Mother State nor Islam. The country has been governed by a democratically elected president since 1995, supported by a chamber of regional and ethnic representatives.'

'So far, so normal,' Megan observed.

'Until late last year. The government announced a series of deals with American oil companies which were to invest in Mordania's extensive fossil–fuel deposits and provide further access to the Caspian Sea, thus boosting the economy and creating more jobs as well as strengthening ties with the west. It was at that point that a senior military figure, General Mikhail Rameron, opposed the deals and suggested that the government had a corrupt agenda of some kind. Things went from bad to worse as the government tried to clamp down on the renegade general, who in response instigated an attempted military coup. Most of the army and air force came down on the general's side, dominating the north of the country where the majority of their airbases are located. The secret–police fell in with the government in the south around the capital city, Thessalia.'

'And that's the state of play so far?' Megan asked.

'Rameron has led his troops south against the government's forces and has bested them at every turn, occupying towns and advancing toward the capital with the usual stories of bloodlust and massacre following him. The government is in dire need of military assistance from the UN or America but right now nobody knows how to help, save for protecting Thessalia itself and several large refugee camps. After the debacles in Iraq and Afghanistan, nobody wants to intervene. It's Syria all over again.'

Megan nodded, absorbing the information. She closed her eyes.

'You can help me, from New York? Information, research, anything that I need?'

'You got it,' Frank promised. 'Anything, any time.'

Megan opened her eyes.

'You said that Amy's folks in Oklahoma wanted to pay? What's their account number?'

Frank Amonte frowned before fishing a contact card from his pocket, a bank name and account number written on the reverse side.

'They don't have much money,' he said quietly as he handed the card over.

'I don't want their money,' Megan assured the American before picking up her cell phone from the coffee table, selecting a number from the call list and letting the phone speed–dial.

'GNN UK, how may I help?'

'Harrison Forbes, please.'

'He's in a meeting right now, may I help?'

'Tell him that Megan Mitchell got his call and is coming in to see him.'

***

5

Global News Network (UK)

London

Megan had never much liked working in an office, having spent the better part of two decades plying her trade in the field. Things were much worse now, since everyone was staring at her with jaws agape, whispers flitting like live current around the operations room.

She walked between the ranks of desks, nodding in response to some of the guarded smiles offered and ignoring the more gormless expressions as she worked her way toward a row of offices that looked out over the operations room. A series of large plasma screens high on one wall showed live–news feeds from around the world.

'Hey Meg, how's it going?'

The voice belonged to Tom Abbot, a former soldier, capable investigative journalist and one of the few people in the office that Megan could talk to without feeling as though she were bleeding from the ears.

'Fine, thanks Tom. Is the boss in?'

'Go right ahead,' Tom pointed, and then added: 'Did you get my message? I called the other day.'

'I got your message,' she replied as she swept past him.

'You can't play hard–to–get forever. I won't stop calling,' Tom called after her.

'I won't start replying.'

Megan headed in the indicated direction and at once saw the stocky figure of Harrison Forbes in his office, staring down with a cold, piercing gaze at what looked like a junior member of staff who cowered with his back to the windows. Forbes finished his oratory and pointed abruptly at his own office door. The junior staffer whirled, yanked open the door and shot through it as though fired from a catapult.

Megan dodged neatly to one side as the teenager bolted past her, and then moved to stand in the editor's doorway.

'The anger management classes weren't a great hit then,' Megan said.

Harrison's icy glare locked onto Megan and then the merest hint of a thaw crept into his expression, concealed as quickly as it had emerged.

'Well, it's about time Mitchell. I wondered when you'd manage to haul your lazy backside up here from that opulent little pad you've nested in. Close the damn door.'

Megan shut the door behind her as Harrison moved around his desk. Megan was about six inches shorter than Harrison, who had receding grey hair and bright blue eyes but remained as sturdy as solid oak. Harrison was surrounded by an tangible aura of competence that intimidated younger members of staff at GNN. He stood before Megan in contemplative silence for a moment before shaking her hand firmly.

'Good to see you, how have you been?'

'I'm good. How's the family?'

'In order,' Forbes reported, and offered Megan a seat. The editor retook his own ancient swivel chair and regarded Megan curiously.

'So, you finally managed to respond to one of my calls, the seventeenth in fact.'

'I've been busy.'

'Really? What could you have been up to? Sitting? Standing? Sleeping? Eating?'

'All the above.'

'From what I hear you've done nothing but jog around the city, eat in cafes and generally let yourself degenerate into an inert bag of under–employed chemicals.'

'You've been watching me?' Megan raised an eyebrow.

'We're investigative reporters. Besides, it's not hard to keep track of a woman who doesn't go anywhere.'

'I've travelled enough, recently,' Megan replied quietly.

Harrison Forbes nodded, his features becoming slightly taut as though the skin were being stretched across his bones.

'Look, I want to say that I'm sorry for what happened.' He hesitated. 'You know.'

Megan kept her features impassive, and gave Forbes his escape. 'I know.'

The editor nodded briskly, grateful to let the moment pass. He stood up and walked across to a worn map of the globe tacked across one wall of the office, as it had been for the last ten years. Brightly coloured pins denoted 'areas of interest', as Forbes referred to them.

'I promised you any assignment you wanted. You're possibly the best investigative reporter whose life I've ever had the privilege of endangering, so this one's a freebie, a milk–run. Democratic elections in Prague? Gay marriage rights in California? The state of the waterways in Venice? Climate change in Bali?'

Harrison Forbes turned from the map and regarded Megan expectantly.

'I'll take Mordania.'

Harrison's carefully cultivated expression experienced a transient slippage. He looked as though he'd been slapped.

'Mordania?'

'There's a story in there somewhere and I want to cover it.'

'I give you an island in the South Pacific and you ask for an illiterate former–Soviet backwater in the grip of a civil war.'

'You said I could have any assignment I wanted.'

The editor's eyes flickered as a thousand calculations whipped past behind them in the time it took Megan to inhale a tentative breath.

'You don't return my calls for months, never visit the office and then suddenly you're here demanding coverage rights to a story about the boil on the arse of the world. What's going on?'

Megan took another breath, just to be sure, before speaking.

'I was approached today by a man from New York. He told me that one of his associates had vanished whilst working in Mordania and hasn't been heard from for over a week. The missing person is Amy O'Hara, a journalist from Chicago and a friend of mine. I'm going to go and find out what happened to her.'

The skin stretched once again on Forbes' features, and Megan could sense that he was choosing his words with care.

'Look, I know all about what happened in Mexico and afterward, but I can't let you go running around searching for lost souls on company time.'

'This isn't about lost souls, Harry. This is about someone I know being in danger.'

'And the last time it happened you spent five years and your entire life savings searching for them.' Harrison pointed out. 'You quit your job, you lost everything and half of this office thinks that you're a recovering alcoholic who went insane.'

Megan blinked, then remembered that everyone had been staring at her when she had walked through the operations room.

'I didn't go insane, Harry.'

'Maybe not, and I've got sympathy for your cause here Megan, but think about how this looks. Having apparently wrecked your life and gone off the rails you're now back here, bold as brass, living the high life in a place that the entire staff here couldn't afford if they pooled their salaries, and asking for help to do it all over again.' Harrison paused. 'I need some kind of assurance that you're not going to.., disappear.'

Megan stood up, walking across to the map and gesturing to the small country marked on the west coast of the Caspian Sea by a red pin.

'Of all the democratically governed countries on our planet, only a single one has proved resistant to access from the world's press. It is considered too dangerous for civilian reporters to engage with the populace. Nobody, anywhere on earth, is reporting from beyond the country's capital, Thessalia.' Megan turned to the editor. 'I'll change that for you, and give you the scoop you need to put GNN UK back on the map.'

Harrison shook his head.

'We've already got somebody on the ground in Thessalia.'

'Who?'

'Martin Sigby.'

'Oh, right,' Megan muttered, 'well I might just as well go home and give up right now then.'

'Martin Sigby is a rock–solid, reliable correspondent.'

'Yes he is,' Megan agreed, 'he's by the book, by the numbers and bypassed by the entire population as sinfully boring. He won't get you what I can.'

'And the small matter of *how*?'

'Leave that to me. Will you get me in under the GNN press corps? Once there, I'll be on my own.'

'I can't say that I will,' Harrison snapped.

'Fine, I'll go across to NCN, or the CCB, or maybe the Murich Corporation.'

'Pah!' Harrison Forbes raised his right hand as though taking the oath in a court of law. 'Here at Murich we do solemnly swear to report crap, all crap and nothing but crap!' He shot Megan a pitying look. 'Please.'

'It's your call,' Megan replied. 'But GNN UK isn't exactly getting the headlines right now, is it?'

The editor turned away for a moment, concealing his displeasure.

'All right, you're GNN cleared. That'll get you into Thessalia but beyond the city you're on your own. Who do you want for cameras?'

'I've got that covered but I'll need a second pass.'

'Surely not for that damned Scotsman?'

'The same,' Megan replied. 'Who's running the UN liaison office in Mordania?'

'Sir Thomas Wilkins, CBE, your friend from Kuwait. One of the old–boy network tied up with the Saudis during the first Gulf War.'

'Good, it'll be useful to have a someone on the inside.'

'I take it that you don't need a salary for this jaunt of yours?'

'I have the number of an account in Oklahoma, United States. Send any payment there.'

'Oklahoma,' Forbes echoed, and then shook his head. 'You're keeping me in the dark. I didn't like it before and I don't like it now.'

'It's probably for the best.'

'Still drinking, Megan?'

It was an old journalist's trick, an unexpected question thrown in on a whim to catch out an unsuspecting witness. Megan hesitated for just an instant too long.

'Not at all.'

Harrison's eyes narrowed but he didn't pursue the matter.

'Once you're in the country, I expect a call once every day at twenty–one hundred hours GMT, understood?'

Megan felt a tightening in her gullet at the demand, but she nodded and turned for the office door, hesitating as she reached for the handle.

'One more thing,' she said, 'make sure Martin Sigby understands that he answers to *me*. I don't need him dragging his feet or throwing a hissy–fit if I go in–country and he can't.'

'He won't like it,' Harrison warned, 'it'll put sand up his arse if you try to steal his show.'

'Like you said, he's a company man, by the book,' Megan said as she left the office. 'Convince him.'

***

6

Shere, Surrey

The house was nestled beneath the rolling hills of Newland's Corner, a quaint quarried–stone cottage that had been extended to cater for the family of five now living there. Megan Mitchell drove her Lotus Caterham Seven onto the gravel drive outside the cottage, parked beneath the shade of a large apple tree, and climbed out.

The front door opened and out strode Callum McGregor, a broad smile on his angular face, a hammer in one meaty hand and a chisel in the other.

'If you've just committed a grisly murder,' Megan called, 'you've been caught red–handed.'

'Not guilty y'honour,' Callum set his tools down and greeted Megan with a bear–hug that lifted her of the ground. 'Not yet, anyway.'

Callum released Megan, shook her hand vigorously and gestured for her to follow him. They walked inside and through to the living room, which Callum was extending into a conservatory at the back of the cottage. A beautiful garden spread away from the shell of the conservatory, centred around an elaborate rock–feature and surrounded by willow trees.

'Aunty Meg!'

A trio of voices rang out the moment Megan appeared in the lounge, and Callum's three young daughters came bustling in from the back garden, all of them jostling with each other and competing for Megan's attention. Vicky, Nina and Sam were all eight years old, triplets borne to Callum's wife, Maria, who followed them in and greeted Megan with a smile.

'Leave Meg alone girls, she only just got through the front door.'

Maria pecked Megan on the cheek and gathered the three giggling girls together.

'Haven't seen you for a while,' she said, a hint of concern in her expression.

'I've been away,' Megan said. 'Took the boat down to Spain for a few weeks over the summer.'

'Very nice,' Maria smiled, and looked at her daughters. 'And Aunty Megan didn't invite us?'

'Aunty Megan,' Callum interjected before the three girls could challenge him, 'has important business to discuss.'

'What's more important than taking us girls to Spain?' Maria smiled slyly.

'The next time,' Megan promised as Maria ushered her daughters out of the conservatory.

'Can I get you a…, beer?' Callum asked cautiously.

'Just a coke,' Megan said, shaking her car–keys and ignoring the furtive expression on Callum's features, 'but why don't you have one?'

'Don't mind if I do,' Callum agreed, and strolled across to a small refrigerator plugged into one of the wall sockets. He retrieved a beer and a can of coke, passing it to Megan. Callum opened his beer and took a long pull as he sat down on the edge of a make–shift workbench standing nearby.

'How's the life of the country gent?' Megan asked.

'Much like that of the city slicker I suspect,' Callum replied with a grin. 'Beats working for a living, doesn't it?'

'Sure does,' Megan replied, sitting on a deck–chair that had been abandoned in the middle of the conservatory. 'You got your share through, and all the paperwork cleared?'

'Every penny,' Callum nodded, his ever–cheerful eyes twinkling even brighter than they had used to. 'Everything went fine. I've been working on this place ever since and watching the interest quietly build up in every account Maria and I have.'

'Do you hear much from Pete?'

'Not so much now. He's all set up down in South Africa. Converted his share into SA Rand, ended up being worth five times its relative value in Sterling. I'm surprised he didn't just buy Botswana.'

Megan nodded in contemplative silence, looking around at the idyllic cottage and its garden.

'You got your yuppie pad in the city I take it,' Callum enquired.

'All done, and the marina there's just right for the boat. Everything's perfect.'

Callum chuckled, shaking his head.

'The three of us sure pulled off the coup of the century out there, didn't we?'

'Once in a lifetime opportunity,' Megan nodded.

'Do you ever wake up in the night fearing that it's all going to end, as though it's all been just a big dream?'

'Used to all the time,' Megan replied, 'less now though.'

'Me too. Which is why I suppose I'm a little worried that you're here. This isn't a social call, is it.'

'No, it's not.'

Callum looked around at the cottage and smiled to himself.

'I suppose you had to call it in one day or another, but I wasn't expecting it to be so soon.'

'Something came up.'

'Tell me.'

'Do you remember when I was working in Mexico?'

Callum's face fell as though he'd just recalled a particularly bad nightmare.

'I could hardly forget – you were gone for years.'

'An investigative reporter from Chicago got interested in my stories on abductions helped me out.'

'Amy something–or–other,' Callum nodded. 'Sure, how is she?'

'I don't know, that's the problem. She's disappeared.'

The Scotsman's features hardened like granite, thick fingers playing distractedly with his beer can. 'You're going after her.'

'I need your help on this one.'

Callum took a deep breath.

'Megan, I know you've got a thing about lost people, but maybe this isn't something you should be doing right now, after – after what happened, you know?'

'I know what I'm doing,' Megan replied evenly. 'This isn't a crusade and I'm not looking to become a martyr in the process. I owe her, Callum. She went the distance for me more times that I can remember. Without her I'd never have got as far as I did.'

'Where was she last seen?'

'The Republic of Mordania.'

Callum paused half–way through a mouthful of beer, peering at Megan over the edge of the can. He swallowed and wiped his mouth across the back of one thick forearm.

'Smashing.'

The Scotsman stood up, crushing the can in one giant fist before dropping it into an old tin bucket with a loud rattle. Megan stood up.

'I'm sorry,' she said. 'I'd never drag you into something like this unless I absolutely had to, but I've got nobody else that I can rely on.'

Callum nodded, smiling.

'I know, and without you I wouldn't have all of this, so I guess that I'd be doing the same if you went missing.' He shook his head. 'I'm just afraid to lose everything I've got here.'

Megan clasped the big man's shoulder.

'You're not going to lose anything. All I need is support. We go in, we find out where she is, we grab her and we get the hell out.'

'You think it'll be that easy? From what I can gather from the news, Mordania's in a mess. You can't leave the capital without risking being shot and Russia's on the border threatening an invasion of its own. And how are we getting out there? All commercial flights into the country have been banned.'

Megan smiled.

'We're going back into the journalism business. Have you still got your cameras?'

'We're going in as press? Don't tell me you went wandering back into Harrison's office?'

'Yes we are and yes I did,' Megan confirmed, finishing the last of her coke. 'We've got *carte blanche*, provided we get Harrison some good footage and something resembling a decent story.'

'Reporters have been banned from leaving the capital because the insurgents are tearing up the countryside and everyone in it. If we get collared shooting frames out there…,'

'We'll be discreet,' Megan promised, 'just like back in the Gulf.'

Callum smiled briefly at the memory, but wrung his hands as he spoke.

'That was when I was in the infantry and you were embedded with us. Desert Storm might have got you on the map as a war correspondent but all it got me was bullets, bombs and sand up my arse. It'll be good to work together again but that was for money, which I already have.'

Megan grabbed her keys.

'This trip's not about money. It's a rescue mission.'

'Straight in and straight out, right?' Callum asked again.

'That's right. Do you still know enough people to get us inside the country?'

Callum nodded, following as Megan hurried from the house.

'I still drink with loadmasters from Lyneham, good RAF guys.'

'Perfect. As soon as you can, Callum.' Megan stopped at the front door and gripped her friend's hand. 'This will be over quickly, I promise.'

***

7

Principality of Monaco,

Cote D'Azure

The broad harbour glittered a beautiful Indian blue beneath the Mediterranean sun, soaring mountains overlooking a city basking beneath trembling blankets of heat. Ranks of exclusive hotels and casinos rose high above the bay into the hard blue sky, towering over hundreds of yachts moored beside the restaurants that ringed the entire marina. In the centre of the harbour were anchored the largest vessels, those too big to moor.

Sherman G. Kruger sat upon the quarterdeck of one of those vessels, the pearlescent white hull of his personal yacht almost painful to look at in the bright sunlight. He adjusted his Gucci sunglasses, ignoring the smaller vessels scuttling past his yacht like insects around a swan and instead admiring the huge blue helicopter perched on the stern.

'Julia, wine.'

A young, white–suited girl walked out of the shade of the yacht's interior with a suitably expensive looking bottle in a chrome chiller. Julia opened the bottle before Kruger and poured sparkling Chardonnay into a crystal glass before handing it to him with a smile.

The old man took the glass with one hand, and with the other grabbed one of Julia's pert buttocks. 'Prepare the master bedroom, and yourself,' he said.

Julia's carefully cultivated smile slipped. Kruger waved her away with one wiry hand a crewman appeared in a nearby doorway.

'Seth Cain is here to see you, sir.'

A man walked out onto the deck, his inky black suit stark against the pure white deck like a crow cruising above ice. Kruger turned his head fractionally, acknowledged his guest with a barely perceptible nod and pointed to one of the chairs opposite. Seth Cain sat down.

'You're late,' Kruger said.

'You're clearly in no rush.'

Kruger coughed and then laughed. 'I should have you thrown overboard.'

'I'm not one of your puppets Sherman,' Cain replied. 'Why am I here?'

Kruger set his glass down and folded his skeletal hands under his chin.

'The Mordanian situation has not proceeded as we had expected. Our purpose remains the same, but we must be more careful now than ever before. The slightest slip in our timetable could prove devastating to our cause.'

Seth Cain leaned forward over the table, plucking a grape from a nearby bowl of fruits. He popped it into his mouth before speaking.

'Devestating to *your* cause, Sherman. I'm only here because you're paying me to be here. Your little war–games hold no interest for me.'

'They should hold an interest for you, Seth, as they should hold an interest for the entire Western world.' He pointed a gnarled finger at Cain. 'Kruger Petrochemicals controls virtually the entire network of oil pipelines from the Middle East and Russia to Europe and the United States. That flow has made me enviably wealthy. However, with Russia playing political games in the Ukraine by cutting off European gas and oil supplies whenever it suits them, and with Iran seemingly intent on destabilising the entire Middle East, we need to properly secure the flow before our countries are brought to their knees.'

Cain raised an eyebrow.

'Surely such moves are merely political posturing. Both Russia and Iran need the flow of revenue that results from the west's dependence on oil.'

'So you might think, and yet they flaunt their control of the fields before our very eyes. Our ability to make the most financially from every barrel is being diminished by their new and bold front. Think about it. The United States did not go to war in Iraq just to gain control of the oil fields. It went there to push up the *price* of oil. As long as there is instability in the Middle East, oil will remain expensive.'

'But it is also difficult to maintain a secure supply,' Cain said.

'Exactly. So we need a secondary supply line, something that bypasses Iran, Iraq, Russia – something that we can reply upon should we fall on political or diplomatic hard–times. Maintaining a prolonged war–footing in the Middle East may have worked before, but eventually that strategy will cease to serve a purpose and besides, it remains an impossible tactic against Russia. As long as the markets *think* that oil supplies are under threat, the price will remain suitably elevated. What we really need is a source of supply that remains permanently indebtded to our influences.'

Cain shook his head slowly in admiration.

'You've got it all worked out, haven't you?'

Kruger smiled but his eyes remained hard as ice.

'Mordania's location on the Caspian Sea, between Russia and Dagestan, is perfect. It has extensive reserves of coal and can receive oil across the Caspian from Kazakhstan and direct it through Georgia, a country that has already demonstrated a desire to join both NATO and the European Union. Russia's military actions in Georgia are a bluff – they don't want another situation like Chechnya. Georgia itself is on the Black Sea coast and from there oil can make its way through the Bosporus and out into the west. Our only competition will be from the Chinese, who are even now trying to secure the Kazakhstan fields for themselves. We must move quickly and ensure Mordanian compliance with our aims.'

'That all works, provided the Mordanian government can wrest control of the rebel insurgency,' Cain pointed out.

'Which is why you are here,' Kruger agreed. 'Our purpose, in the face of this unexpected and unwelcome rebellion, is to ensure that the United Nations will support the democratic government of Mordania. The financial support needed to bring Mordania into the twenty–first century can come only from the World Bank and the International Monetary Fund – once they're on board, Mordania is effectively ours. It will take them hundreds of years to repay the loans. The rebels must be crushed, and the contracts we have negotiated with the government signed into Mordanian law. Those pipelines will be worth over thirty billion dollars to Kruger Petrochemicals over the next ten years, and I don't intend to see either that profit or the investments I have already made compromised by a militia of illiterate *peasants*.'

Kruger spat the last word along with a spray of spittle. He pointed at Cain.

'Corporate America, along with various major banks, control the vast majority of the western world's news networks and broadcasting houses, my friend. You control what the world sees, Seth, and you can influence what they see too. Your role in this endeavour is quite simple. Use Global News Network to ensure public sympathy for intervention in Mordania, even an invasion and air–war if you like. The United Nations or United States – whoever – must wrest control of Mordania from the rebel factions and support the pro–Western government.'

Cain frowned.

'GNN doesn't have the power anymore, Sherman, you know that. We've lost influence over the last decade, offices have closed in over twelve countries. Staff are flocking to rival networks like rats off a sinking ship and my investors are damn close to following. I no longer have the controlling share in the company, let alone the influence to alter policy.'

'Then ensure that whatever you do in Mordania is spectacular enough to change public opinion of both the conflict and GNN. Do something extravagant, Seth. Get the people watching.'

'Easier said than done,' Cain murmured. 'The Board of Directors could easily buy me out should this little endeavour of yours fail. I just don't have the resources to keep those blood–sucking bastards at bay, not to mention that threats of hostile takeovers from other broadcasters.'

Kruger's leathery face creased into a thin fracture of a smile.

'Oh, Seth, calm yourself. The controlling share of GNN will become yours.'

Cain laughed. 'Even you don't have that kind of money.'

Kruger's smile withered, the rheumy old eyes turning hard as steel.

'I have more money than you could ever dream of, Seth, and don't you ever forget it. Your forty–six percent share of GNN will become fifty–one percent, rest assured.' The old man leaned forward. 'Make the world see something spectacular, and your company will save itself and you, board or no. Just ensure that whatever it is, it serves our purpose – the Mordanian governement's continued rule.'

'Collateral?'

'What will be, will be.'

Cain snorted.

'The president is highly opposed to using American military intervention in foreign affairs, especially after the mess previous administrations have made of foreign policy. Everybody remembers Iraq, and they didn't bother with Syria. Neither the White House nor the public will be easily swayed.'

Kruger regarded his wine glass for a moment, and then looked through the open doors to the master bedroom. In the shadowy interior he could see a young, naked body lying upon the huge bed.

'Ensure that the good, hard–working, law–abiding citizens of the west learn all about the democratic struggles of our valiant allies in the Mordanian Government,' he said finally, 'and that they fully understand just what a bunch of unholy shits the rebel Islamist forces represent. In due course the war will end in our favour and democracy, as you call it, will prevail to the endless joy of one and all.'

'There'll be blood,' Cain said, 'one way or the other.'

'There always is,' Kruger agreed as he levered himself up onto his aged legs, 'but at least there'll be profit, and nobody really cares about some pissy little backwater of a country where clean water is considered a luxury. To hell with them. They'll be better off with the revenue generated by the pipelines anyway – it'll bring some light into their miserable little lives.'

Cain stood and turned away. As he did so, Kruger saw him catch a glimpse of Julia lying inside the bedroom.

'Tempted, Seth?' Kruger murmured. 'She's very willing.'

Cain strode away as Kruger's voice rattled after him.

'You shouldn't deny yourself the chance to take something young and full of promise, and thoroughly shaft it Seth! It's what we'll be doing to Mordania!'

***

8

City of Thessalia,

Republic of Mordania

The massive C–130J C/4 Hercules transport aircraft from XXIV Squadron, Royal Air Force banked over into a steep turn, vibrating under the power of its four huge Allison turboprop engines. Megan sat strapped into a small folding seat against one wall of the cavernous fuselage, Callum McGregor next to her. The rest of the aircraft was filled with troops from the Prince of Wales Royal Regiment, all heavily burdened with weapons, webbing and Bergens.

The Loadmaster gave Megan and Callum a thumbs–up and shouted to be heard above the noise.

'We're on a glide–slope for a *Khe–San* tactical descent to avoid possible Surface to Air Missiles or RPG attacks from rebel forces, so hold on!'

The aircraft's undercarriage and flaps whined down, and then without further warning it plunged out of the sky. Megan felt her heart and stomach lift into her throat as the Hercules plummetted at what felt like a near vertical angle toward the ground, her knuckles turning white as she held on to the rim of her seat.

Suddenly the G–forces reversed, slamming her down into the seat as the Hercules crew pulled out of their suicidal descent and hauled the nose of the aircraft up into its landing flare. Megan caught a vertiginous glimpse of rushing grey rocks through the open cockpit doorway and then the runway appeared ahead as the nose came up and she felt a thump that reverberated through her spine as the Hercules settled onto the ground.

The pilot's voice spoke in clipped tones over the intercom.

'Ladies and gentlemen, thank you for flying Royal Air Force and welcome to hell. We hope you have a pleasant stay.'

Megan and Callum removed their headphones and unclipped their kit from the fuselage webbing as the Hercules taxied onto Thessalia Airport's dispersal pan, the aircraft under the watchful eye of armed United Nations troops distinctive in their disruptive–pattern camouflage kit and pale blue helmets.

The aircraft came to a stop and the rear ramp opened, letting in a blast of cold air. The Loadmaster approached Callum McGregor and shook his hand, shouting to be heard above the roar of the still turning engines.

'End of the line, Callum! Most of the journo's are camped out in the Thessalia Hilton, or at least that's what they're calling it. It's a former administrative block to the east of the city centre. This whole country is a shit–hole of misery mate, makes Bosnia look like the Algarve. Are you sure you wouldn't rather just stay on board?'

'Not my choice,' Callum replied, gesturing briefly to Megan. 'Thanks for the ride Alan, see you back home, right?'

'Sooner the better!'

Megan hefted a large rucksack onto her back and followed Callum down the ramp as the engines shut down, the infantry soldiers marching down alongside them and mustering beneath the aircraft's broad wings.

Megan looked around at their surroundings. The flat surface of the airfield was hemmed in on three sides by mountain ranges that vanished into heavy grey clouds tumbling overhead on a cold and blustery wind. Tiny flakes of snow whipped past Megan's eyes as she surveyed the airfield, its squat and ugly grey terminal surrounded by machine gun nests. Armed Mordanian police marched everywhere, and in the distance she could see the urban sprawl of Thessalia, rising slightly on an incline of hills that overlooked the airfield.

Callum moved to stand beside Megan with an expectant look on his face.

'So, here we are. What's the plan?'

Megan tightened the straps on her shoulders and gestured toward the city.

'We check into the Hilton, and start asking questions.'

*

'Welcome to the Thessalia Hilton, where soap is a thing of the past.'

Megan Mitchell dropped her heavy rucksack and shook Hillary Cook's hand.

'Been a while,' she said, grateful to see a familiar face. 'Yugoslavia.'

'Yeah, that was it. What a party,' Hillary murmured.

Hillary Cook looked younger than her forty–six years, but two decades of reporting on the worst that mankind had to offer had lined her skin and jaded the light in her eyes to a pale shadow of what it had once been.

Megan looked around at the crumbling walls and peeling plaster of Thessalia's finest, and indeed last, hotel.

'A bit better than Srebrenica.'

'Anything is better than Srebrenica,' Hillary replied, and glanced at Callum as he made his way through the hotel's entrance. 'So you're still hanging around together then?'

'Wouldn't have it any other way,' Callum replied, picking Hillary up in his customary bear hug. 'Still loitering in dangerous places?'

Hillary looked at them both seriously as Callum set her down.

'It's dangerous here all right. The government has forbidden any foreign journalists to travel beyond the UN controlled safe–haven of Thessalia. Apparently two journos found themselves on the wrong end of a rebel assault last week. What was left of them came back here in bags.'

Megan picked up her rucksack. 'Any idea on why they got hit?'

'None,' Hillary admitted, 'but probably they just stumbled on something that somebody didn't want them to see. Kind of puts the brakes on our line of work. Come on, I'll show you to your excuse of a room.'

Callum looked at Megan in surprise.

'We have rooms already?'

'I asked Harrison Forbes to call ahead,' Megan explained as they climbed what had once been a grand spiral staircase to the hotel's upper floors. 'Our old friend Sir Wilkins is running the UN show from the capital.'

'Is he going to help?'

'That's what we're going to find out next.'

The three of them were half way up the stairs when a journalist coming down in the opposite direction blocked their way.

'Well, now I've seen everything.'

Megan Mitchell looked up and caught sight of Martin Sigby descending toward her, followed by his cameraman, Robert. Sigby was a couple of inches shorter than Megan, slightly overweight and with one of those faces that looked as though it had been flattened by repeated blows from a shovel. Sigby extended his hand, which Megan shook reluctantly.

'I thought we'd seen the last of you in South America,' Sigby said.

'Good to see you again too, Martin.'

Sigby smiled with his lips only. 'What are you doing here in Thessalia?'

'Business.'

'What kind of business?'

Callum took a step closer to Sigby. 'None of yours.'

'Oh, but it is my business,' Sigby replied, regarding Megan with interest, 'after what happened.'

Megan did not reply, but Hillary looked at her questioningly.

'You didn't hear, Hillary?' Sigby enquired. 'Didn't Megan tell you, about the fiasco in Mexico and her subsequent disappearance? Or how she returned to London suspiciously wealthy despite having last been seen lugging nets on a fishing boat in Singapore? I think we'd all be interested to know how that happened.' Sigby's oily smile returned again. 'It must be a story all on its own, how Megan here avoided being committed to an asylum or spending the rest of her days swigging bottled cider in an alley in Manila.'

'We're working for GNN,' Callum said before Megan could reply, 'and we have work to do, so why don't you move your squat little backside out of our way?'

Sigby's carefully cultivated expression faltered, and then he chuckled.

'Still keeping the finest company, Megan. Please, don't let me keep you, there must be so much for you to do here in a country where there is nothing to report.'

Megan pushed past the correspondent, with Hillary following.

'There's always something to report,' Megan said.

'That's right,' Sigby said as they ascended the remainder of the staircase. 'And I am the man doing it, so there'll be scant work for you here my friend. There's just Thessalia and nothing beyond.'

Callum McGregor drew level with Martin Sigby and paused, looking down at him. Sigby craned his head to look up at the towering Scot.

'Murder on your mind, Callum? Wouldn't go down well on camera,' he said, gesturing to his following cameraman.

'That depends on who's watching,' Callum murmured coldly before moving on.

Sigby turned to call after them.

'One call to Harrison Forbes and I'll have you both on a plane out of here. I'm running the show in Thessalia.'

Megan turned at the top of the stairs, regarding Sigby for a moment.

'Well, you're not doing much of a job of it if there's nothing to report.'

Sigby's face screwed up into a ball of indignation, but he said nothing more.

Megan let a smile hang on her features for a moment before turning to follow Hillary away down an adjoining corridor. Hillary looked at her.

'Is that true, what he said?'

'Every word,' Megan replied, 'except twisted to make it sound far worse than it actually is.'

'So you're not off your rocker then?

Megan laughed out loud and shook her head.

'Sadly, I remain appallingly sane. I just took time out of life for my own reasons. Listen, Hillary, I need you to contact Sir Wilkins in the city for me, let him know that I'm here and that I need to speak with him.'

'Sure, no problem. He's staying at Government House on the main square.' Hillary led her to a doorway. 'Here's the room. Finest in all of what's left of Mordania.'

Megan and Callum walked inside the small, musty room. Callum looked around at the creeping damp, peeling walls and grubby windows.

'I like what they've done with the place.'

Megan tossed her rucksack down onto one of the two thin mattresses in the room and peered out of the window over the city.

'It's damp, cold and ugly,' Hillary said, 'a bit like Martin Sigby, but it's safe, at least for now.'

'For now?' Megan echoed her.

Hillary gestured out of the window, toward the north.

'The rebels are advancing, taking towns day by day. The UN Protection Force is a gesture only – they can't legally engage the rebels except in self–defence. You can hear the rebel artillery at night. Sooner or later, they're going to reach Thessalia.'

Megan nodded slowly.

'And like Srebrenica, they'll breach the city.'

Callum stared hard at Megan.

'And we don't want to be here when they do that.'

***

9

'In Mordanian, Thessalia means"The city with no name".'

Hillary Cook's voice carried on the cold air as she walked with Megan through the streets toward Government House.

'Why?' Megan asked.

'Take a look around you. This place was built by everybody and by nobody.'

The architecture of Thessalia was a curious mixture of squat, Soviet style concrete blocks, with the occasional picturesque minaret striking upward toward the slate grey sky. The Islamic monuments betrayed a population made up of almost entirely of Muslims, along with a smattering of Russians, Georgians and smaller ethnic groups living mostly in the highlands of the Greater Caucasus Mountains.

'It's one of the oldest of the Caucasian republics,' Hillary went on. 'The capital was established sometime over a thousand years ago, around 900AD, and spent most of its time as a key trading port for the flow of goods between the East and the West, especially when the overland routes like the Great Silk Road became too dangerous for travellers and traders alike.'

The street upon which they walked was cobbled – work done, Megan imagined, by the Romans millennia before. Old stone apartment blocks with small windows stood on either side of the street, their shutters closed to keep out the winter chill. A few bedraggled citizens struggled to and fro, wrapped up in blankets against the wind, casting wary glances at the heavily armed UN troops patrolling the streets on foot and in jeeps.

'What's the humanitarian situation?' Megan asked.

'At crisis level,' Hillary said. 'There's a major refugee encampment spread along the edge of the Ganibe River to the west of the city. The last reliable figures I heard suggested maybe a quarter of a million refugees there, most of them ethnic Muslims and Russians fleeing from the rebel advance. It's being handled by the UN in terms of supplies of grain and water, but it's mostly Red Cross, *Medicines Sans Frontiers* and all the other aid groups who are doing the leg–work on the ground.'

'Missing people?'

Hillary looked at Megan for a moment before replying.

'Hundreds at least, maybe thousands, mostly as a result of the breakdown in infrastructure. The Red Cross is handling that – they have a special department of some kind.'

'I know,' Megan replied. 'Is anyone getting out of the safe–haven and into the countryside?'

'Only the French, *Medicines Sans Frontiers*,' Hillary said. 'They're refusing to confine their activities to Thessalia. The government is tolerating their movements because they don't venture much more than ten miles beyond the city, and they never move north of the Tornikov River. That's bandit country.'

The end of the street opened up onto Pevestraka Square, a vast, Soviet style pedestrian area dominated by Government House on the opposite side. The huge and elaborate edifice of the building towered over the smaller administrative offices that ringed the square, and on the roof of one side of the building ranks of satellite dishes stared blankly up into the cold grey sky. On the opposite side of the square stood a tall, Gothic looking church, whilst the square itself had a large statue in its centre.

'Who's that?' Megan asked as they walked, pointing to the centre of the square.

The large iron statue of a rampant horse was surrounded by corroded water spouts whose fountains had fallen dormant long ago. Upon the horse was a man with a heavy beard on his face and an equally heavy sword in his hand pointing vigorously forward, his face stoic with the courage of ages gone by.

'Balthazar the Great, one of several legendary Mordanian heroes who stood against the Mongol invasions and Tamerlane's raids in 1389. Dagestan suffered heavily during the Mongol actions, but Balthazar held the Mordanian line to the north and with it his country's independence.'

Megan looked at the bitter, immoveable lines of the man's features as they walked beneath the statue and imagined that he had been as hard as iron in real life too. Hillary pointed to the church.

'That's the Thessalia clock tower,' she said, pointing to a large and simple white–faced clock atop the gothic church bell–tower. 'It's rumoured to have never stopped in over five hundred years and kept perfect time throughout. Mordanians say that you can set your heart by that clock.'

Hillary walked with Megan past the church to the gates of Government House, manned by two military policemen who spoke halting English. Hillary managed to convey who Megan was and that Sir Wilkins was expecting her.

'This is as far as I go,' Hillary said. 'I've got a live UK broadcast in two hours and sod–all to say.'

'I'll see you at the hotel,' Megan promised, as one of the policemen returned and opened the gates.

Megan walked inside the compound, the gate closing behind her as the policeman gestured for her to follow. They walked through the main door of the house and into the hush of the building itself.

The main reception hall was broad and flanked by opposing staircases carpeted in faded red fabric. Mock chandeliers hung from the high ceilings on long cables. Megan sensed the musty odour of age and aeons of dust as she followed her escort down a long corridor to the right of the reception hall.

Despite the winter chill outside there seemed to be no heating in the massive building. Iron–barred windows to her right looked out over the compound, whilst the walls to her left were adorned with large canvass paintings of what Megan assumed to be politicians or Mordanian Kings.

'Megan!'

Sir Thomas Wilkins strode toward Megan from one of the offices adjoining the corridor. The escort peeled away as Wilkins grasped Megan's hand firmly and kissed her on both her cheeks, his wild white hair as wavy as ever and his florid skin betraying decades of fine dining and late–night brandy drinking with the dignitaries of dozens of countries.

'So good to see you back in the field again, Megan!'

'And you Tom,' Megan replied. 'It's been a while.'

Sir Thomas Wilkins had been a servant of the United Nations for well over a decade, and before that had served the UK Foreign Office in Kuwait, presiding over Kuwaiti liaisons with the extraordinary multi–national coalition that had responded to Iraq's invasion of that country in 1991. It had been there that Megan had first met the animated, enthusiastic Wilkins, a man who had been a key asset to Megan's investigations into Iraqi atrocities against the Kurds both before and during the Gulf War.

'I'm only here for a temporary assignment,' Megan replied. 'I'm working for GNN.'

'Thought you might be,' Wilkins confided. 'Come, my offices are right around the corner.'

Megan followed Wilkins into a large room that had probably once served as a dining hall but was filled now with computer desks and filing cabinets. UN staff tapped busily away at computer terminals or talked with serious expressions on telephones.

'Totally mobile communications,' Wilkins explained, 'modern technological marvels. We supply New York with on–the–spot, up–to–date information on events here, so that they can determine the required responses immediately.'

'What about local broadcast resources?' Megan asked.

'That's based in the communications centre of Government House – you may have seen the satellite dishes on your way in. State–owned television is broadcast from there, and selectively censored broadcasts from the outside world allowed in. It's very carefully controlled here, Megan. The transmission dishes atop government house essentially control what the Mordanian people see on a day–to–day basis, all of it filtered through a communications centre beneath the building that's controlled by the secret police.'

Wilkins led her into an office and closed the door. A small fire crackled energetically in the corner of the room, filling it with light and blessed warmth.

'Sit, sit,' he insisted. 'Coffee? Tea? A dram?'

'Coffee's fine, Tom.'

'So,' Wilkins began as he poured. 'What brings you to Mordania? I wouldn't have thought that there was much for a journalist of your calibre to cover here right now.'

Megan decided not to beat about the bush.

'I'm not here for journalistic purposes, Tom. I'm looking for someone.'

'Ah,' Wilkins said, setting a mug in front of Megan and taking a seat opposite with his back to the broad windows. He regarded Megan for a moment. 'I had rather hoped that you were past all that, terrible business that it was.'

'I am,' Megan replied. 'This is somebody different.'

Megan pulled a copy of the picture of Amy O'Hara from her pocket and handed it to Wilkins. The old man looked at it for a moment before speaking.

'A beautiful girl, Megan, no doubt about it. Who is she?'

Megan filled the attachÃ© in on the details. Wilkins sipped his coffee, but shook his head.

'Well, there are plenty of journalists on the ground here in Thessalia and have been for some months now, but we don't intervene in individual cases for fear of accusations of favouritism. Besides, our main concern is displaced locals rather than journalists. I'd like to help, but in all honesty Megan I would have thought that the resident journalists at the Hilton would know more than I about this young girl's whereabouts. How long did you say she's been missing?'

'At least ten days,' Megan replied, her voice tense. 'It's important to me, Tom. I need to know what has happened to her, one way or the other.'

Wilkins studied the look on Megan's face for a moment and then smiled kindly.

10

'Please wait here,' a smartly dressed secretary said in an effortlessly gentle voice. 'The president will see you shortly.'

Megan felt slightly uncomfortable as she followed Sir Wilkins into a waiting room that adjoined the president's briefing room, where he held court with his administrative officers and party members. Wilkins gestured to the door of the briefing room and whispered softly.

'The Parliament of Mordania is a People's Assembly, very democratic and all that, consisting of just over a hundred deputees elected for four–year terms. The President is the highest executive member and has been elected by popular vote since Mordania's successful 'Purple Revolution' in 1996. This is Mukhari Akim's first term as president.' Wilkins shook his head. 'Such a shame that a military coup should be attempted during his tenure.'

The door to the briefing room opened and Wilkins and Megan watched as a procession of smartly suited men walked out of the room. Wilkins spoke softly out of the corner of his mouth.

'Parliamentary representatives for the various ethnicities of Mordania; Aguls, Avars, Chechens, Laks, Russians, Rutuls and Taskhurs. Quite a mix, don't you think?'

The secretary reappeared and beckoned for them to follow her. Feeling as though she were about to walk on hallowed ground of some kind, Megan followed Wilkins into the briefing room.

The room was dominated by a long, highly polished mahogany table, lined with gently flickering candles. Thick red folders had been discarded at each seat by the recently departed parliamentary representatives, along with jugs and glasses of water.

President Mukhuri Akim was older than Megan had imagined but tall and broad, his face weather–beaten and his hair salt–and–pepper grey. A heavy jaw and thick nose gave the impression of a retired boxer.

The president was standing with a dark skinned man who wore the camouflage and patches of the Mordanian Secret Police. His jaw was shadowed gun–metal grey against his deeply tanned skin. He turned to survey Wilkins and Megan with heavily browed obsidian eyes as they approached.

'Sir Wilkins,' the president greeted the attachÃ© in awkwardly pronounced English.

'May I present the President of Mordania, Mukhari Akim,' Wilkins announced grandly. 'Sir, this is Megan Mitchell.'

Megan shook the president's hand firmly. 'Thank you for agreeing to see us.'

'It is no problem at all,' Mukhari replied. 'This is my Chief of Police, Alexei Severov.'

Severov shook Megan's hand with a grip just a little tighter than was necessary, his dark eyes boring into Megan's.

'A pleasure.'

'What can we do for you?' the president asked.

Megan once again produced the photograph of Amy O'Hara and explained to the president the circumstances surrounding her disappearance. Mukhari studied the photograph with an expression of deep concern before passing it to Severov. The policeman looked at the photograph for several seconds before shaking his head, passing it back to Megan as Mukhari spoke.

'Miss Mitchell, there are believed to be some two hundred thousand or more displaced people, my people, living in regrettable conditions in the refugee camp outside the city. Our hands are full, even with the generous assistance of the European aid groups in organising and providing for these refugees.'

Megan nodded in understanding.

'I do not wish to impose upon your personnel for assistance in locating Amy O'Hara,' she said. 'Only that sufficient awareness of her disappearance is broadcast to those with the will and the means to locate her. It means a lot to me that she is found, sir.'

Mukhari watched Megan for a long moment.

'I will have copies of this photograph distributed to all of our guard posts around the city, throughout the refugee camp and at the food halls in Thessalia. If we cast our net wide it is likely that someone will recognise her, or may know of what has happened to her.'

'I appreciate that, sir,' Megan replied.

She was about to politely take her leave when Severov addressed her from one side. His dark eyes shone with curiosity as he spoke.

'You are here to search for this woman?'

Megan shrugged non–commitally.

'I promised that I would try to find her, but I am not unaware of the brutality of the rebel forces. Amy is the kind of girl to go looking in places that she should not.'

Severov seemed satisfied, nodding in agreement.

'As Chief of Police I consider myself responsible for the safety of all residents of Thessalia, especially in these difficult times. I understand your need to find your friend, but I have no desire to launch a search and rescue operation should you too go missing. We simply don't have the resources.'

Megan nodded.

'Have no concern. Our enquiries will be limited to the city itself. I don't want to share whatever fate has befallen Amy.'

Severov bowed slightly, his gaze never leaving Megan's, and he walked slowly away and out of the briefing chamber.

President Akim sighed heavily and rubbed a hand wearily across his forehead.

'Not since the time of the Mongols has our country faced such a threat to its existence,' he said forlornly. 'Even Russia's dominance over our people lacked the ferocity of this rebellion.'

'There has been no cessation of hostilities?' Sir Wilkins asked the president. 'The rebels continue to advance?'

'Every day,' Mukhuri replied solemnly, glancing toward the north through the office windows. 'Most of the villages and towns have only local militia, no defence against such a well trained army turned against them, the very people that the rebellious forces were supposed to protect. The advance is unstoppable, at least until they reach the city.'

Megan raised an eyebrow.

'You'll fight?'

President Mukhari Akim straightened slightly to his full height, tall and broad enough to become physically imposing.

'All Mordanians will fight to protect their right to a government of their choosing and their freedom. We will stand as Balthazar the Great stood, and lead the charge against the enemy.'

Megan nodded, raising a placatory hand.

'I don't question your courage sir, or that of your police. It's just that urban warfare will bring the battle into the heart of the city and to the doors of your citizens. When that happens, if that happens, then the safe–haven will no longer be safe for anyone.'

Mukhari held Megan's gaze for a moment and then sighed again, his powerful frame seeming to shrink with the burden of responsibility. He nodded.

'This we know, and if we do not get the assistance and security we need, from the United Nations – men, equipment, soldiers, it will be the fate of our people to die in their own homes, victims of their own countrymen, led by the rule of a madman. Yet, if we cannot be shown to protect our own without outside assistance, then the people will lose faith in our ability to lead and to govern. All rests on the assistance of the west, yet they will not commit without my signing of the loans and contracts necessary from the World Bank to rebuild our country. It would be like signing away the very soul of Mordania.' He turned to look at Megan. 'Would you sign your family away, for safety's sake, and perhaps in doing so lose their very identity?'

Megan performed a rapid calculation.

'I would do whatever I had to, to protect them.'

The president thought for a moment and then sagged further, and Sir Wilkins turned to Megan.

'Perhaps we should be getting along, Megan. Mister President, thank you for your time once again.'

Mukhari nodded vaguely with the most fleeting of smiles before turning away to stand silhouetted before the bright windows, his hands behind his back and the weight of two million lives upon his shoulders.

Megan breathed a sigh of relief when she and Sir Wilkins had left the chamber and closed the door.

'Intense,' Megan murmured.

'Poor man. He has the strength of an ox and a heart of gold. I cannot bear to see him suffer in this way.'

'With great power comes great responsibility,' Megan murmured. 'What do you make of that policeman, Severov?'

'A capable man, no doubt. He's an ethnic Mordanian, of his country's blood, and apparently was trained by former Spetsnaz mercenaries, Russian Special Forces. He was attached to Mukhari Akim about eighteen years ago, when Mukhari was a Parliamentary Representative for the Ethnic Mordanians.'

'That tells me *who* he is, not what you think of him. Come on Tom, stop playing the diplomat.'

Sir Wilkins looked at Megan as though surprised, before speaking.

'I don't like him. He's too secretive and seems prone toward aggressive behaviour. The locals seem to dislike him too, which probably says more than anything.'

Megan nodded, before Sir Wilkins spoke again. 'What will you do now?'

Megan zipped her coat back up as they walked, preparing for the chill outside.

'The refugee camp. It's the most likely place that we'll find people who've come in from the interior and may know what's happened to Amy. After that, it's in the hands of fate.'

'I'll do what I can for you, Megan, spread the word. Maybe we can salvage something from this terrible war and send this young girl home again.'

***

11

Megan had been to some rough places in her time, but always and without fail the most heartbreaking were the refugee camps, places where souls who had lost everything but the beating of their hearts came to grieve together in a vast and chaotic communion of pain and loss.

Thessalia's camp lay along the southern banks of the broad Ganibe River, its surface frosted with a thin sheet of fractured ice floating on dark, frigid waters. Makeshift tents were spread as far as the eye could see, punctuated by thousands of camp fires burning anything available to stave off the bitter cold.

'Hell on earth,' Callum said as he and Megan walked amidst the pitiful throng. 'I'd have brought the camera, if the world hadn't already seen this all before and forgotten how to care.'

'The people care,' Megan replied. 'It's the governments that fail to do anything.'

Families huddled around fires boiling rice and grain, the meagre flames whipping and snapping on the wind. Voices filled that wind, but the commingled chorus of two hundred and fifty thousand people was a background murmur – no children laughed, no adults joked. Dark, empty eyes devoid of any emotion she could recognise stared forlornly at Megan and Callum as they weaved their way toward rows of large canvass tents, each flying banners or flags on poles that rippled on the cold wind. They were the command centres of the aid charities and medical organisations, islands of sanctuary amidst a moaning sea of human suffering.

'That's the one,' Megan pointed. 'Medicines Sans Frontiers.'

'You sure you want to try this?' Callum cautioned as they veered torward the huge hospital tent.

'No,' Megan admitted, hurrying as snow began to fall in tiny myriad specks that spiralled around them on the wind. 'But right now it could be our only relatively safe means of access to the interior.'

A ragged queue of Mordanian refugees were standing in the cold waiting for access to the tent, the entrance to which was guarded by two UN Peacekeepers. Megan and Callum briefly flashed their GNN identity badges and slipped into the tent.

The interior was not a great deal warmer than the exterior, but it was sealed well enough to keep out the bitter wind. Megan advanced past rows of refugees standing in line with bowls and spoons as aid workers ladled hot soup from giant metal vats that belched clouds of steam onto the cold air.

Further on, beyond a wall of canvass with a transparent plastic door, was the hospital section of the MSF tent. Megan walked toward it, easing past ranks of emaciated children chewing on chunks of bread that they dipped into their soup. She pushed the transparent plastic flap aside and moved into the hospital.

A group of French MSF nurses were sitting beside tables stacked with syringes, inoculating children against whatever unspeakable contagions might threaten them in the camps. Other nurses were handing out blankets at the far end of the tent, where a large UN lorry had reversed up to another, larger transparent door. Soldiers handed the blankets down to the nurses, who diligently stacked them in neat piles nearby.

'Qui etes vous?'

Megan turned to see a young female nurse approaching her with a stern expression on her features. She had barely a moment to register her face, beautiful in a simple way, long brown hair tied in a pony tail, one wisp of it dangling down over sharp green eyes.

'Who are you?' the girl repeated in heavily accented English.

Megan, on an impulse, extended a hand.

'Megan Mitchell, pleased to meet you. And you are?'

The girl gave Megan's hand the briefest of shakes before releasing it as though it were poisonous.

'Sophie Vernoux,' she said in her softly lilting French accent. 'I am the head of this department. What do you think you're doing in here?'

'We were looking for someone.'

'Well now you've found someone, haven't you? You're press.'

Megan blinked, quite taken aback both by the Sophie's abruptness and by her apparently supernatural instinct.

'Well, yes, but..,'

'No buts,' Sophie cut her off sharply. 'There are no press allowed in the hospital tent, full stop, you see? I will not allow it.'

Megan stared at her in shock. 'Why on earth not?'

'Because all you're here for is your stories, and most of them are damned lies. You're not interested in helping the suffering, you're interested in helping yourselves and getting whatever silly little award it is that you're after. Get out.'

Megan was almost speechless for the first time in years. Sophie Vernoux looked at her as though she were retarded.

'What's the matter? Did I go too fast? No–press–in–here–get–out–now!'

Sohpie's green eyes blazed their challenge into Megan's, and for a moment Megan was about to turn around and leave. Instead, she gathered herself together and reached into her jacket. Sophie winced pitifully.

'I don't want your card because I'm not going to change my mind,' she snapped.

The anger finally hit Megan's nervous system, scalding through her synapses. She pulled out several copies of the photograph of Amy O'Hara and slapped them down on the table beside her. Her voice when she spoke sounded like a cobra's hiss.

'Missing, presumed dead, last seen in Thessalia around two weeks ago. Her name's Amy O'Hara. I'd like to find her if I can because she's important to me. Put these up where they can be seen. Sorry to have been such an irritation to your day. Have a nice life.'

Megan whirled, only just catching the look of surprise on the girl's face as she forged past Callum, who had watched the entire exchange in silence. Sophie Vernoux looked down at the photographs, and then at Callum.

'We've had a long day,' the Scotsman said, by way of an explanation.

'Haven't we all,' Sophie replied, rediscovering some of her haughtiness, but it was half–hearted and without passion. She called out. 'Wait!'

Megan halted near the hospital exit and turned, glowering at Sophie.

The nurse picked up one of the pictures. 'We will put them up.'

Megan took a few paces back toward her.

'We need to get access into the interior of the country.'

'Why?'

'We're journalists, but we are mainly here to find this girl and get her home. We believe that she may have been abducted by rebel forces or factions, perhaps as a bargaining tool or as a human shield. We have some leads but we can't follow them whilst we're stuck here in Thessalia. Let us help you, and in return we'll get the chance to find her.'

Sophie gripped the picture tighter, appalled by Megan's request.

'You're just chasing stories, not people.'

'No,' Megan snapped back. 'We're chasing the truth. If the truth leads us to this girl, then all the better. One way or another, we're going in–country, with or without your help. Medicines Sans Frontiers – that means *doctors without borders*, doesn't it? So do you have borders between nurses helping people and journalists doing the same? Do you want to help her, or hinder us?'

A thin, bleak smile cracked across Sophie's features.

'That is appalling emotional blackmail, even for a journalist.'

'That's all we've got, I'm afraid, and right now I don't care how we get her back.'

Megan watched as Sophie eyed her testily.

'What would you know of reporting the truth? The world doesn't want to know what happens in places like Mordania, or Bosnia, or Sierra Leone or Sudan. You'll not get close to the truth, because none of the reporters here have managed it.'

Megan stared into her clear green eyes.

'I will, whatever it takes.'

Sophie Vernoux snorted dismissively before looking one more time at the photograph. Then she spun away from Megan and Callum, snapping over her shoulder.

'The next aid column leaves at eight tomorrow morning.'

***

12

The first heavy snow fell during the night, spiralling down silently through the lights of the city as though a galaxy of stars were falling from the night sky. By the time the pale, cold light of dawn broke over the river, a blanket of pure white had smothered the entire city.

'Did you hear the guns?' Megan asked Callum.

They walked across Pevestraka Square, their boots crunching softly in the snow as they passed beneath Balthazar's statue.

'Eighty–eights,' Callum replied, 'heavy artillery. It's difficult to judge distance at night, but I'd say they were no more than forty miles away and probably less as the mountains shelter Thessalia from the noise.'

Megan had seen, against the distant clouds, brief flashes of light as mortar shells impacted the ancient earth. Pops and rumbles were just audible, a distant hymn of war echoing through the night as it had done for thousands of years.

'We're running out of time already. If the rebel forces take the city we'll have to leave too.'

Callum nodded, adjusting the heavy body–armour that he wore, modified from a standard NATO item.

'We're not done yet. They won't break the Thessalia line for a few days.'

They continued walking in silence, and had reached the edge of the refugee camp when Callum muttered from the corner of his mouth.

'There he is.'

Megan glanced across to their right in time to see Martin Sigby standing in front of his cameraman, who was filming against a backdrop of shivering human misery. Sigby saw them almost at the same moment and immediately curtailed his report, moving towards Megan.

'Where are you going?'

'None of your business,' Megan muttered back, but Sigby was already intercepting them before they could vanish into the throng of the camp.

'We've already got the best shots,' Sigby said. 'There's no sense in you shooting the same scene and making the same report.'

Megan stopped and turned to face Sigby.

'You're shooting everything that's been seen a hundred times before and nobody will take a blind bit of notice. You're not showing them anything new, ergo, they will not watch.'

'This is my show, Mitchell,' Sigby pressed. 'Mordania was my call at GNN.'

Megan refrained from mentioning the fact that Amy O'Hara had been in Mordania weeks before.

'I know,' she replied. 'What I also know is that nobody has reported anything new from within this country for weeks. Therefore, I intend to change that by finding things out.'

Sigby darted forward, blocking Megan's path.

'You're going in country?!'

Megan did not reply, simply standing in front of Sigby and wondering whether he would figure it out or not. Sigby looked at Callum and observed the heavy body–warmer style armour that he wore. He glanced across the camp before looking back at Megan.

'You're going in with the aid convoys,' he said. 'Callum's going to shoot frames!'

Megan allowed a tiny smile to curl from the corner of her lips. Callum tapped the thick chest guard of his body armour. The garment was equipped with a concealed colour pinhole–camera with audio fitted into the armour, perfect for undercover filming. In his back–pack he carried a 40GB hard drive recorder. The camera faced forward from Callum's chest, below his left shoulder and almost level with his elbow, its body tucked into a pocket there and the lens concealed as a button.

'We used the same kit in Bosnia, Rwanda, you name it,' Callum said quietly so as not to be overheard. 'Near broadcast quality images, provided I keep reasonably still when the camera's filming.'

Sigby shook his head. 'You're both insane. If you get caught out you'll come back here in small wet pieces.'

Megan shrugged her shoulders and turned away toward the camp. 'No gain without risk, Martin.'

'Mordania is my show,' Sigby repeated as he pursued Megan.

'It was.'

'If you were caught filming, you'd be expelled from Thessalia!'

'We'll be careful then,' Megan said.

'You'll have to be more than that,' Sigby muttered.

Megan glanced at Callum, who in turn looked at Sigby. Before Megan could react the Scotsman had taken two long paces and grabbed the correspondent by the throat, almost lifting him off the ground.

'You wouldn't dare,' Callum hissed as Sigby's puny arms wind–milled in futility against him.

'Callum, let him go!' Megan moved alongside, watching as Sigby's panicked face began to turn an unhealthy shade of purple.

'Why?' Callum demanded, still crushing Sigby's throat.

'I didn't mean that!' Sigby gasped, his eyes bulging.

Megan rested her hand gently on Callum's massive forearm. The Scotsman relaxed his grip, Sigby staggering backward and massaging his throat as he fought for air.

'What did you mean?' Megan demanded.

Sigby's voice rasped as he coughed a few meagre sentences.

'If you shoot frames inside the country…, then everyone will know that you've been there…., and you'll be expelled anyway, if not arrested.'

Megan hesitated, glancing again at Callum. The Scotsman shrugged.

'The footage could have been made by Medcines Sans Frontiers staff, or Red Cross,' he said.

Sigby shook his head, regaining his breath.

'Then they'd prevent them from entering the country too, you damned fool! You'd be denying people inside the country what little aid they get.'

Megan thought for a moment.

'If you want Mordania so bad, you can have it. You're the face on the television, Martin. You're the anchor here for GNN. Whatever we shoot, you can use.'

Sigby looked at her, struggling to make rapid calculations despite the lack of oxygen reaching his brain.

'What do you mean?'

'What I mean,' Megan replied, 'is that we'll shoot whatever is happening in Mordania's interior and you can use the footage as your own. You'll never have to leave the safety of the compound, you'll never be under suspicion and yet you'll get the story of the month, maybe even the year.'

'What's the catch?' Sigby uttered.

'You tell nobody who is doing the filming, and you use your connections to research anything that I deem appropriate, no questions asked. Got it?'

Sigby sucked on his cheeks for a moment. 'Understood.'

Megan jabbed a thumb in Callum's direction.

'If you let me down, I'll make sure there's nobody around to see what he does to you.'

With that, Megan walked away into the camp. Callum moved alongside her, glancing back in Sigby's direction as the squat little man watched them depart.

'Either you're a genius or insane, Callum said. 'He can't be trusted and this little ploy of yours might not work.'

'As long as he's gaining something, he'll help. He won't let us down as long as we can get shots inside the country and what's going on there. As soon as we find Amy, we're out of here and Sigby can go whistle for his stories.'

A large lorry emblazoned with a red cross was parked alongside the back of the *MSF* tent, nurses and volunteers loading heavy sacks of grain, bedding and medical supplies on board. Megan and Callum worked their way around the edge of the volunteers and found Sophie Vernoux checking manifests on an upturned box, trying to write whilst wearing thick gloves and with her face partly concealed behind a fur–lined hood.

'Bonjour, mademoiselle,' Megan intoned laconically. 'Ca va?'

Sophie looked up and gestured with a curt nod toward the trucks.

'Bonjour. Help them load the vehicles and try not to get in the way. We have a timetable to keep.'

'We're fine, thanks for asking, bonne passe le journee.'

Megan and Callum began helping the volunteers finish loading the sacks into the lorry. After perhaps half an hour's worth of labour the lorry was full.

Two UN jeeps pulled up alongside the lorry as they were finishing, each with a manned machine–gun attached to the rear. Following them was a larger troop carrier with a dozen British soldiers cradling SA–80 rifles and wearing light blue UN helmets.

Sophie spoke briefly with the commanding officer of the patrol assigned to escort the aid convoy, a stocky, competent looking man named Lieutenant Kelsey, and then called out to the assembled nurses, doctors and volunteers.

'Those of you assigned to the convoy, please board now. Well see the rest of you this afternoon. Merci beau coup.'

The volunteers began to disperse, and Megan looked questioningly at Sophie. Her voice crossed the fifteen meters between them as though it were a fraction of the distance.

'You two, Bonnie and Clyde. You are to ride with me in the cab, non?'

Megan and Callum looked at each other in bemusement before joining Sophie as she clambered into the sparse cabin of the truck and got behind the wheel. Sophie started the engine with a belch of diesel smoke as Callum slammed the door shut. The cabin vibrated noisily as they waited for the UN escorts to take up station in front and behind. Sophie crunched the lorry awkwardly into gear to the sound of grinding metal, and Megan winced.

'Can you play any other tunes?'

Sophie neither replied nor looked at her.

Megan tried again. 'You know that we drive on the left, right?'

'I offered you a ride,' Sophie replied tartly, 'not conversation.'

The UN jeep in front pulled away and Sophie drove into line behind it along a bumped and rutted track already filled with dirty brown slush. After a few minutes they cleared the camp and turned left onto a properly surfaced road, heading north toward the mountains that soared into the dense cloud overhead.

Megan and Callum sat in silence, watching as Sophie drove the truck with some degree of skill out through the suburbs of the city. Gradually, the narrow streets and blocky apartments gave way to smaller farmhouses and abandoned allotments and fields.

'Here we go,' Callum murmured under his breath as they approached a check–point surrounded by armed UN soldiers and Mordanian police.

Sophie wound down the window, and as if from nowhere Alexei Severov appeared, his dark eyes glowing as she peered into the truck.

'Miss Mitchell, I was under the impression that you were working as a correspondent in Thessalia, not with Medicines Sans Frontiers.'

'Just helping out Sophie here,' Megan replied calmly, 'and handing out pictures of my missing friend.'

Severov's gaze scanned the cab of the truck suspiciously.

'Cameras?' he demanded.

'They don't have any,' Sophie replied, 'and we're on a tight schedule. If there's nothing else, commander?'

Severov eyed them for a long moment before speaking.

'You will need a translator,' he said. 'It may smooth your passage into the towns.'

Before either Megan or Sophie could reply, Severov turned and waved toward a small, oily looking man standing nearby. The man sauntered over, regarding the trucks and the soldiers as a deer would regard a pack of wolves.

'This is Bolav,' Severov announced, 'my personal liason officer to the United Nations envoy. He will accompany you and provide you with any assistance that he can.'

Sophie nodded and gestured to the troop carrier behind them. Bolav, looking intensely cold and unhappy, wandered disconsolately toward the vehicle and was hauled aboard by two of the soldiers.

Severov stood for several long seconds before backing away from the Sophie's truck. He turned and waved for the guards to open the check–point barrier.

Sophie's column advanced through the check–point and suddenly they were driving away from Thessalia and into the no man's land of Mordania.

***

13

'So, where are we going?'

Sophie did not answer Megan's question for several seconds as she negotiated a series of deep pot–holes in the road, following the jeep ahead as it curved awkwardly around the obstacles and debris littering the highway.

'Anterik, a small village just near the edge of the Caucasus mountain range, about five miles north of Thessalia.'

'What's there?'

'People who need help,' Sophie replied unhelpfully.

Megan took a deep breath, trying not to let Sophie's combative nature rile her.

'*Why* do they need help?'

Sophie tutted as one of the truck's wheels juddered through a deep rut in the road. She wrestled the truck out of the crevice.

'Most of the electrical grid in the country has been destroyed due to shelling and acts of sabotage further inland as the rebels try to cut off supplies and power to the capital. The entire country's infrastructure has imploded in the last few weeks, creating the humanitarian crisis we now face. It's always the same in situations like this, ordinary people suffering as the fighting forces attempt to undermine or disrupt their opponent's chain of supply. More people die as a result of this than do the soldiers actually involved in the fighting.'

Megan nodded, looking out of the windows at the dull grey clouds cloaking the mountain ranges and the forlorn, run–down farms that they passed by on the road.

'I know, I've seen it all before in Bosnia, amongst other places.'

'Bosnia was similar,' Sophie agreed, 'but it involved multiple factions split along religious lines, differing bloodlines that had feuded for centuries and were unleashed when Tito passed away and the fight for control of the country began. Mordania is different. This is a people's choice versus the government's democracy, soldier against soldier, Muslim against Muslim. There is no right or wrong side, no good or evil to choose between.'

Callum looked across at Sophie with a surprised expression.

'This General Rameron is the embodiment of evil, and his troops perhaps more so. I'd take a democracy over a dictatorship any day of the week.'

Sophie shook her head without taking her eyes off the road.

'Only because you want one. Most people on earth don't live under democratic rule and have no idea what it means. Take Afghanistan – it's been built over millennia under tribal rule. The people have it deeply ingrained in their psyche that strength is required to lead. Votes are not necessarily of interest to them. They need strong leaders and will violently oppose foreign intervention as they have done for centuries against Russia, Britain and now America.'

'That doesn't justify genocide,' Megan pointed out. 'The killing of civilians immediately removes the right of the killer to rule, victorious or not. The people will always rise again.'

Sophie nodded but smiled.

'And if this *is* that rising?' she challenged. 'None of us are well enough versed in the history of this country to understand the motivations of those who choose to challenge the prevailing authorities and their leadership. They may seek power to control, to rule, but they may also seek justice.'

'You sound like you're defending this Rameron,' Callum snorted.

'No, not defending,' Sophie countered. 'I'm just saying that trying to impose our methods of governance on others, no matter how well intentioned, often causes as many problems as it seeks to solve.'

Megan gestured out of the windows to the desolate and abandoned homes scattered across the frozen countryside.

'Our countries have big enough problems of their own, without messing about here,' Megan pointed out.'

'That sounds like an excuse for doing nothing,' Sophie argued.

'Nobody can change the world on their own.'

'They can do more than someone who does nothing.'

The window beside Megan shattered with an ear–splitting crash and showered the interior of the cab with thousands of glass chips.

Sophie let out a shriek of alarm and jerked the truck's wheel to one side, the vehicle swerving violently as the jeep ahead of them skidded to a halt. Megan and Callum instinctively bent forward in their seats, dropping as low as possible as the truck slid to a halt on the slushy road, its rear now facing the way the bullet had entered the cabin, the cargo shielding Megan, Callum and Sophie from view. Frantic voices shouted from outside.

'Sniper! Two hundred metres!'

'Move! Now!'

Megan sat upright, looking across at Sophie with sudden admiration.

'Quick thinking. Are you okay?'

Sophie nodded as she checked herself over for injuries. Megan and Callum did the same, and then looked at the window. The bullet had passed low through the glass and had then travelled through the cab to exit through Sophie's door less than an inch above her right thigh.

Sophie opened her door a fraction, calling out to the soldiers now crouched behind their vehicles.

'The sniper's elevated!' she shouted. 'The bullet dropped two or three inches through the cab!'

From where he crouched behind a troop carrier, Lieutenant Kelsey scanned the buildings scattered across the landscape in the lee of the mountains, gauging the distances and the assumed angle of the shot. He spied an old village hall with a raised clock tower protruding from its roof.

'Try the tower,' he whispered to a sniper laying prone next to his feet, down beside the tyre of the troop carrier.

The sniper, breathing calmly, swung his rifle around slightly and focused on the clock–tower, watching patiently.

'Nobody move,' a nearby sergeant said calmly but loudly enough to be heard by the nervous troops huddling behind the vehicles. 'Easy now.'

In the truck, Megan strained to hear what was going on.

'Who's shooting?' Sophie whispered. 'The rebels haven't come this far yet, surely?'

'It's not rebels,' Callum said. 'When law and order break down, people tend to get carried away with themselves. It's probably a disgruntled local or a drugged–out youth. There's nobody around to arrest them now.'

A tense silence reigned for several minutes as the British soldiers tried to identify the sniper's location. Megan was about to suggest a careful egress from the area when the sniper at Lieutenant Kelsey's feet whispered in a harsh voice.

'*Enemy.*'

'Where?' the lieutenant asked.

'The tower.' The soldier's voice was a whisper. 'Movement inside, from the left to the right window.'

'Weapon?'

'Stand by.'

The sniper watched silently through the scope of his rifle, ignoring the tiny flakes of snow landing on his face. The silhouette of a body lay facing him in the window of the clock tower. He caught a glint of something in the pale light, a flash of metal or the glass of a telescopic–sight.

'*Weapon*,' he whispered, then, '*Incoming!*'

A tiny puff of smoke had burst from the clock–tower window. Almost instantly, a bullet ricocheted off the side of the troop carrier, causing the soldiers crouched there to flinch. An instant later the report reached them on the cold wind, its echo careering off the nearby mountains and into the wilderness.

'Take him down,' Lieutenant Kelsey ordered.

The sniper waited until the shadowy figure in the window stood to change position after his shot, and then held his breath for a single beat of his heart before pulling the trigger. The rifle in his grip shuddered as a terrific report crackled on the wind.

The sniper saw the shape of a body hurled backwards and out of sight from the distant window.

'Enemy down,' he whispered.

The lieutenant gave his sergeant a thumbs–up and the troops gave a brief cheer.

'Fun's over!' the sergeant snapped. 'Let's get moving.'

In the truck, Sophie started the engine and began reversing to put the vehicle straight on the road.

'Rough neighbourhood,' Megan remarked as they began moving again.

'You should see Anterik,' Sophie replied, then glanced across at Callum. 'Get any nice footage of people being shot?'

Callum had removed the camera lens from his pocket after the first shot had been fired, and had held it poking out of the window of the cab, roughly in the direction of the clock–tower.

'I'll find out when we get back. I can't download on the move.'

Sophie did not reply, and Megan got the distinct impression that she was regretting allowing them to come along with her.

'Have you always been this abrasive?' Megan asked as casually as she could manage.

Sophie remained silent, instead yanking the gear–lever with as much force as she could muster as they accelerated to keep up with the jeep in front.

Megan said no more for the next hour, until, after driving between the towering slopes of the mountains and seemingly endless debris strewn villages and abandoned houses, a larger village appeared ahead, straddling a narrow river that churned beneath a stone bridge.

'Anterik,' Sophie said softly.

The jeeps slowed ahead of the truck, and through the blustering snow Megan could see armed militia standing in the road that led to the village, waving the convoy down.

Sophie changed down a gear and took a deep breath.

'Let's hope they're in a good mood.'

***

14

The militia, far from being suspicious or aggressive toward the convoy, waved them through cheerily, clearly relieved to see the grain, medical supplies and well trained troops in their area. Their voices followed the truck as it passed them by.

'English, American, bravo niet?!'

Sophie nodded and waved to them as she drove the truck across a cattle–grid and on toward the main town.

'Jesus, it looks like the war's already been here,' Callum observed.

The houses and dull–grey apartment blocks that lined the streets were peppered with impact scars from mortars, shells and assorted small arms. Doors hung loosely from peeling frames, piles of rubble and shattered concrete lined the pavements and the skeletal steel shells of burnt out cars lay abandoned amongst the streets.

'Anterik and the surrounding areas have seen low–level guerrilla war since 2000, mostly spilling over from Chechnya,' Sophie explained. 'Most of the casualties have been federal servicemen and local police forces, which is why the town is guarded now by militia – they're just protecting their own homes and have no interest in Chechnya's war.'

'That explains why they were so pleased to see us,' Callum said.

'They have nothing,' Sophie went on, 'no water, no electricity, no effective sewage treatment, no hospital or doctors. Nothing. A UN convoy is like Christmas to these people.'

Megan looked at her in confusion.

'I thought that the Mordanian government was taking care of the humanitarian side of things within its own borders?'

'So did we,' Sophie replied.

As if on cue, from the rubble strew houses and apartments flocked small groups of children, running through the thick snow in sandals and torn shoes, their emaciated bodies wrapped in rugs and sheets of old canvass and anything else they could find to keep warm. They ignored the chill wind and swirling snow, their eyes bright and smiles broad as they jostled to keep up with the trucks.

Megan noticed that Sophie Vernoux came alive at the sight of the children, winding down her window and smiling as she reached into her pocket. Handfuls of colourful candy were thrown liberally out of the window, the children catching them in mid flight with cries of excitement.

The convoy drew into the town's main square, pulling around a crumbling monument to fallen World War One soldiers in the centre and stopping. The children were soon joined by small groups of elderly women and men all wrapped in threadbare clothes, their faces lined heavily with stress and fatigue.

Megan climbed down from the truck to stand beside Callum, and watched as Sophie began organising her volunteers to distribute the aid and medicines whilst Lieutenant Kelsey's troops set up a perimeter around the edge of the square.

'You think anyone here will recognise Amy from her picture?' Callum asked.

'I don't know, but she may well have passed through Anterik so it's worth a go. Try shooting some of this for the news tonight. We don't want to disappoint our new friend Martin Sigby.'

Callum strode off into the centre of the square as though nonchalantly looking at his surroundings, whilst Megan moved amongst the growing crowd of beleaguered Mordanians, searching for anyone who looked as though they might remember a girl from several weeks before.

'They're all elderly,' she remarked to Sophie as she moved alongside her.

'Most of the young men are either fighting the rebels or have joined them,' Sophie replied, hauling a sack of grain onto the bony shoulder of a child, whose other hand was clasped by what looked like his grandmother. The pair hobbled wearily away.

Megan shook her head, and then spotted a teenager amongst the throng, young but keen eyed. He looked to be at the sort of age where an attractive woman would not have gone unnoticed, but remained young enough not to have been called up to fight. Megan walked over to him as he hovered on the edge of the crowd, and held out the picture of Amy O'Hara to him.

The boy looked at her and then at the picture. He studied it for several long seconds and then put his fingers to his lips and let out a piercing whistle that rang in Megan's ears.

From nowhere a small knot of pubescent children bolted across to his side, and the boy gestured at the picture. Megan felt a lance of hope pierce her heart as the children exchanged rapid bursts of dialect with animated hand signals, several of them pointing north toward the ever looming mountains.

Megan tried to listen to them, to pick out words that she might recognise. Suddenly the boy gripped her arm and began talking, pointing north like the rest. Megan could understand the general idea, but didn't want to miss anything important.

'Callum?!'

The Scotsman heard her from the other side of the square, raising his head questioningly.

'Where's Bolav?'

Callum strolled across to Lieutenant Kelsey, spoke for a few moments and after a barked order from the officer, Bolav appeared and loped across, his hands shoved deeply in his jacket pockets and his head hunched down in his collar against the cold. Megan explained the situation, and Bolav turned to face the children.

'Problick ton junoilya?

The children immediately began gabbling back to him. Bolav glanced at the picture and understood, regarding Megan with a tired expression as he spoke.

'They say that she was here four weeks ago, maybe a little more. She was travelling alone and the locals told her it was dangerous to move further. She wouldn't listen. She was looking for someone.'

'Did she say who she was looking for?'

The children looked excitedly at Bolav.

'Ayoh den parletchi moisayt ech odysset?'

This time only one of the children spoke, the older boy. Bolav listened, responded with surprise, and then turned to Megan.

'Aslian here says she was looking for a friend, a family friend.'

Megan lowered the photograph and looked at the children. She moved across to the truck and grabbed a handful of candy bars from within before sharing them out amongst the pathetically grateful children. She noted that none of them pushed or shoved each other or fought over the candy. Aslian instantly gave his sweet to one of the smallest girls, presumably his sister, before speaking to Bolav. As the children drifted away like the snow on the wind, Bolav looked at Megan.

'He said that you should not follow her, because she did not come back.'

Megan handed Aslian two candy bars. 'I know.'

Callum appeared from nearby to stand alongside Megan.

'Any luck? he enquired, discreetly filming the troops and the aid trucks in the same shot.

Megan explained what she had learned, and Callum nodded.

'Good. If she's got connections here that we can identify then it could narrow down our search.'

'Or end it,' Megan pointed out. 'If she went too deep into the country, it could already be somewhere over–run by the rebels. We don't know how close their forces are or…,'

Callum was not looking at Megan and had frozen still. The Scotsman spoke in a voice as frigid as the winter winds.

'They're here.'

Megan turned to see a broad column of troops on the hill that rose over the town centre. Their ranks were silent, motionless, dark eyes watching the aid workers and civilians in the town square beneath them, and their aged Mordanian Army uniforms were ragged with the stains of war.

***

15

'Enemy rear!'

Lieutenant Kelsey spotted the ranks of rebels at almost the same moment that the Mordanian villagers did. In an instant, pandemonium broke out.

The villagers scattered in all directions, fleeing the central square and dragging screaming children and sacks of grain with them. Megan saw the British troops rearrange themselves with impressive speed to counter the unexpected appearance of rebel troops so close to Thessalia, covering their points and presenting the bulk of their firepower toward the hill.

Megan and Callum bolted for the cover of a collapsed wall of rubble on the western side of the square, whilst the aid workers variously ducked behind the trucks or hid in recessed doorways on the eastern side of the square.

The sound of the villager's fearful cries and the screams of children died out on the wind until it seemed as though Anterik was once again deserted and devoid of human presence.

Callum peered over the pile of rubble, trying to get a clear shot with his camera.

'There are too many, maybe eighty,' he whispered, watching the rebels. 'And they have the high ground. Our boys will be forced to fall back to the bridge.'

Megan nodded, glancing across at the British soldiers now watching the rebels through the sights of their SA–80's. Lieutenant Kelsey was watching the enemy also, but wisely had done nothing as yet to provoke the situation further.

'They're not moving,' Callum said, still eyeing the rebels.

'Maybe they won't attack an aid convoy,' Megan guessed.

'From what we've heard about these guys, they'll attack anything.'

Megan's eyes narrowed as she watched the rebels, still standing in plain view at the top of the hill. She checked again the position of the British, standing firm but not yet ready to offer truce.

Megan pulled her collar closer about her neck.

'Stay here and keep filming,' she said.

Before Callum could react, Megan stood up and strode into plain view in the centre of the square.

Megan heard a rush of shocked whispers on the cold wind as it whipped through the square, the gasps of the aid workers and the abrupt curses of the soldiers twenty yards behind her, but she did not move. Instead she waited until she was sure that every one of the rebels had seen her. She then moved to one side, grabbed a carton each of coffee and cigarettes from the aid pile, and began walking up the hill.

'Megan, what the hell are you doing?'

Callum had moved from cover slightly in order to film her, but Megan did not respond to the urgent whisper, instead climbing steadily toward the rebels. Her heart felt as though it was doing its best to batter its way out of her chest and bounce back down the hill to safety but she ignored it, trying to maintain a confident bearing.

Behind her, she heard Lieutenant Kelsey order his men's weapons to port arms, unwilling to risk Megan's life in a crossfire, and then she could hear nothing but an overwhelming silence as she climbed toward the enemy.

The rebels ahead were heavily armed, wearing dark blue belts around the waists of their camouflage. Kalashnikov AK–47's were held at port arms before them and grenades hung from their webbing. Some held RPG's, others heavy assault machine–guns. All wore pitiless expressions, their faces as hard and cold as the Mordanian winter. Megan noted their identical uniforms however, perhaps an indication of some kind of remnant discipline within their rebellious ranks.

As Megan came within ten metres of them, one of the rebels raised his weapon cautiously to point at her. Megan's heart changed tactics and tried to climb out of her throat as a hot flush of panic plunged in a nauseous ripple through her intestines.

Another, heavily bearded rebel reached out, gripped the barrel of the offending Kalashnikov and lowered it gently but firmly. Megan looked at the rebel and saw thin chevrons on his shoulders, perhaps denoting an officer or NCO. She changed direction slightly toward the man and stopped a few feet in front of him.

A silence enveloped the scene, time and space seeming to stand still for an endless procession of seconds, until Megan slowly and carefully reached into her pocket and produced a copy of Amy O'Hara's picture. She slowly held it out to the rebel NCO, who looked at it in momentary confusion.

Megan pointed to her own eyes, then to the picture, and then at the NCO and his accompanying troops in general. The NCO understood and took the photograph, looked at it and passed it on to the men behind him.

Megan handed over the cigarettes and coffee, which the NCO took, looking at Megan with a curious expression on his face. He opened both of the boxes before passing them back to his men, Megan assuming that he was making sure there were no explosives inside.

Megan waited for what felt like an hour but was in fact just a few minutes, before the picture of Amy was handed back to the NCO with a brief exchange of gruff dialect. The NCO handed Megan back his picture, then smiled a small, curious little smile that creased his thick, silvering beard.

'You are American, no?'

Megan felt a wave of relief sweep through her chest.

'British.'

'Ah, yes, British. Only an Englishman would be insane enough to confront us alone. Know this,' the NCO said, 'that we will not allow foreigners to govern the rule of our country and control our resources. We will not stand by and watch our country used as an economic experiment by the Americans.'

Megan blinked, not sure if she understood what the Mordanian meant.

'Have you seen her?' she asked instead.

The NCO smiled again, more warmly this time.

'This woman was seen by two of my men in a small town called Talyn, fifteen miles north of here.'

'Do they know when she was seen?' Megan pressed hopefully.

The NCO called out a question without taking his eyes off Megan, and from somewhere in the rear ranks a voice called back.

'A week ago, at the most,' the NCO said, and looked down the hill toward the square. 'You are an aid group?'

'Medicines Sans Frontiers,' Megan replied, 'the people down there are getting pretty desperate. You?'

The NCO regarded her with a guarded expression. 'Reconnaisance. Good luck in your search.'

With that he barked an order in an extremely loud voice that made Megan jump half out of her skin. With practised efficiency, the rebel troops wheeled about on their heels and marched back the way they had come.

Megan stood stock still for almost a minute, watching the rebels march away, before she turned and walked back down the hill. The British soldiers and the aid workers moved out of cover and congregated at the base of the hill as Megan reached them. Lieutenant Kelsey stormed across to stand rigidly before her and jabbed a finger at her chest.

'What the hell was that all about? What the devil did you think you were doing?'

'What I came here to do,' Megan replied. 'What do you know about a town called Talyn?'

The lieutenant blinked and performed a rapid calculation.

'Maybe twenty or so kilometres north of here. It's on the fringes of rebel occupied territory, not all that far from the nerve–centre of General Rameron's forces. Why?'

Megan looked at Callum, who had come to stand alongside the British officer.

'We need to go there.'

'I was afraid you'd say something like that,' Callum murmured bleakly.

Sophie Vernoux was standing next to the cab of her truck, watching the exchange and regarding Megan quietly. She spoke now to Megan, her voice no longer as abrasive as before.

'Talyn is beyond our reach. We cannot travel that far into the interior.'

'Not to mention the fact that we can't protect you,' Lieutenant Kelsey pointed out. 'Talyn is probably as dangerous a place as you're likely to find in Mordania.'

'That's right,' Megan replied, 'and my friend's somewhere out there in the middle of it. I appreciate your concern, sir, but I came here to find someone and that's what I'm going to do.'

Megan looked at the faces of the aid volunteers and the soldiers and she realised that she had inadvertently gained their complete attention.

'Let's get this stuff unloaded and get the hell out of here,' she said instinctively.

As though they were her own employees, the entire gathering split eagerly to complete their work. As Megan walked away with Callum, she saw Sophie watching her quietly from her vantage point by the truck.

Sophie turned quickly away from Megan's gaze and began calling orders out to her volunteers.

***

16

'Megan? Is that you?'

Megan struggled to hear the American accent over the distortion plaguing the telephone line.

'Yeah, it's me Frank. Listen, I need some information.'

Megan was sitting in Martin Sigby's room, using the correspondent's satellite phone in the flickering light of a dozen or so candles. It had taken several minutes of intense bargaining to persuade the defensive Sigby to let Megan use the damned device, including threats of withholding the footage that Callum had gathered during the day.

'Anything Megan, name it.'

'Find out if Amy had any friends in Mordania, specifically family accquaintances. I've uncovered evidence that she may have been looking for someone, and that she disappeared whilst doing so.'

Megan was acutely aware of Martin Sigby listening in as she spoke. The correspondent was preparing for his nightly live broadcast from the hotel roof, no doubt with the distant flashes of conflict glowing against the night sky behind him for maximum impact. Frank Amonte's voice reached Megan's ear from New York city.

'They didn't mention anything before, but I'll check it out and get back to you as soon as I know anything.'

'There's something else,' Megan added in a whisper. 'I need you to do a search for an employee of Medicines Sans Frontiers, a Sophie Vernoux.'

'What's her connection to Amy?'

'There isn't one Frank, it's just a hunch.'

'Will do, take care out there okay?'

Megan shut off the phone and looked thoughtfully out of the windows into the darkness of the night. The distant sound of an artillery shell pounding a hillside rolled through the blackness.

'You're looking for someone,' Martin Sigby said.

'And people say you're dense.'

'The footage,' the correspondent demanded, holding out a stubby hand.

Callum, sitting on the edge of the bed nearby, stood up and loomed over Sigby for a menacing moment before handing him a slim Flash–Ram drive. Sigby grabbed it and then rushed across to his laptop, plugged the drive in and accessed the video files.

Megan and Callum watched as Sigby viewed the twenty or so minutes of footage. The correspondent looked around at them only once, as Callum filmed Megan's ascent toward the rebels on the hill.

'Oh my God,' he murmured as he watched.

When the video reel ended, he turned to look at Megan.

'Incendiary,' he said, quite awestruck. 'This will cause a storm back home.'

Megan stood and turned for the door.

'Enjoy your fifteen minutes,' she said, opening the door to leave with Callum following.

'Wait.' Sigby shot up from his seat.

Megan turned cooly as Sigby glanced briefly at the laptop before speaking.

'Let me use your name,' he said. 'You did a hell of a thing there and you deserve the recognition.'

Megan replied without revealing her surprise at Sigby's gesture.

'Recognition's the last thing I want. Just say that it's an aid worker, and only use the shots where you can't see my face.'

With that, Megan turned and with Callum walked out of the hotel room, leaving Sigby to his broadcast. Callum appeared confused as they walked away down the chilly, dark corridor outside.

'I thought you'd still want the exposure,' he remarked. 'It might help us.'

Megan shook her head.

'I'm done with being on the news. Let Sigby get the credit – it'll make him more inclined to keep helping us.'

*

Global News Network UK Ltd,

London

'Twenty seconds! Let's run the feed and get ready to fit him in!'

Harrison Forbes' voice crackled from his office as the large plasma screens along one wall above the operations room showed news broadcasts in several languages, all part of the GNN chain of news networks in different countries.

Harrison focused on the British television broadcast as the night's anchor, a female presenter with a suitably sombre expression, spoke in a clear, cut–glass English accent.

'The situation in Mordania has been one of confusion over the past few weeks, with a dearth of accurate information coming from the country's interior. Despite two resolutions being passed within the United Nations, no clear path forward for either the humanitarian effort or the proposed military solution to the conflict have been put forward. However, in a ground–breaking exclusive report our correspondent in Mordania has successfully obtained footage from inside the country, giving a window into a secret world of suffering that nobody in the west has seen for months. Martin, can you hear me?'

'Roll feed and link!' Harrison snapped.

The screens split and an image of Martin Sigby appeared alongside that of the anchor, the city of Thessalia framing the night behind him, occasional forlorn street lights flickering weakly in the distance.

'Hello Charlotte, yes I can hear you.'

'What can you tell us about the extraordinary footage you have for us tonight?'

Martin Sigby cultivated a solemn expression.

'Well, Charlotte, as you know there have been no reliable and authentic, neutral news reports from within Mordania for more than four months now, despite an abundance of rumours of heavy fighting and a severe humanitarian crises. The government here in Mordania has claimed that it has provided suitable resources for the population that remains within its reach, but our footage throws doubt upon those claims.' Sigby's face became deeply serious. *'Some people may find the following images disturbing.'*

Harrison Forbes's eyes narrowed as he watched, and he became aware that the fifty or so people in the broadcast room had fallen silent.

An image of a grubby, rubble strewn village filled the screen, clearly shot from a moving vehicle. Martin Sigby's voice intoned over the scenes.

'The remains of what was once a beautiful town in rural Mordania, the jewel of a democratic state shattered by the hammer of civil war. The people here are starving despite living barely five miles from the government controlled capital city, Thessalia. The conflict has reached even here, the rage of a rebel force undiminished even this far from the centre of the conflict.'

A gunshot, and suddenly the vehicle is swerving off the road and screeching to a halt. Shouts, echoes, commands and heavy, nervous breathing.

'This is not an attack on a military brigade,' Sigby's voice intoned. *'This is an aid convoy en–route to a village in the mountains. No target is considered off–limits by the rebel forces.'*

Harrison Forbes raised an eyebrow.

'Well done, Mister Sigby.' He turned to an associate sitting behind a computer terminal. 'What are the viewing figures?'

The associate glanced at his screen.

'Undetermined, but climbing rapidly.'

Forbes thought for a moment. Sigby had either developed a previously unknown sense of initiative and made contact with someone who could travel freely in the country, or had taken the risk and gone himself. Neither seemed likely to Forbes, and he smiled quietly to himself.

'Megan.'

*

Principality of Monaco,

Cote D'azure

Sherman Kruger sat in a reclining chair in the main lounge of his yacht, a half eaten meal of lobster discarded before him on a glass–topped table rimmed with gold leaf. The lights from the city twinkled beautifully through the broad glass doors to one side of him, but he did not see them. All of his attention was focused upon the plasma screen before him and the correspondent speaking over the footage being beamed across the entire globe.

'The aid convoy had only been in the tiny village of Anterik for a few minutes, distributing aid, when the rebels appeared over a hill to the north of the town, heavily armed, merciless and defiant.'

Kruger squinted as he watched the slightly unsteady camera footage, of an aid volunteer advancing toward the rebels.

'It was only the quick thinking and courage of this unknown volunteer, who exchanged a handful of supply cartons for the safety of the aid convoy, that prevented a fire–fight between the rebels and the convoy's British escort, or worse.'

The footage vanished to be replaced by Martin Sigby's live feed and that of the presenter sitting in England, who adopted an expression of vague mirth.

'For the benefit of the viewers at home, and for that matter the United Nations, what is your assessment of the situation inside Mordania right now?'

One cue, Martin Sigby smiled the presenter's caustic wit before frowning as though considering a complex mathematical problem.

'It's my feeling, Charlotte, that the situation within Mordania is now beyond the control of the government in Thessalia. The sheer suffering of ordinary citizens so close to the capital suggests that they simply cannot maintain order, with the growing size of the refugee camps ample evidence of that. And let me just say that it is a fact that the rebel forces are advancing toward the capital day by day, as proven by recconaisance photographs recently taken by a Royal Air Force Tornado aircraft.'

'So you're saying that you think the capital is lost already?' the presenter asked.

'I'm saying only that without external assistance beyond the capital city, either in the form of bolstered UN defences or outright military action against the rebel forces ranged against them, the battle is over for the civilians and militia trying to guard their homes, and I have no confidence in the strength of the remaining government forces to effectively defend Thessalia. As you have seen from recent footage of the refugee camps and this footage of towns close to Thessalia, the government is not providing sufficiently for the remaining citizens under its protection, and the aid groups here can hardly be expected to support the population on their own.'

The presenter turned away from the image of the correspondent.

'Martin Sigby, in Mordania, thank you for that astonishing footage.'

Sigby offered the camera a brief, modest smile.

Kruger shut off his television and smiled, the heavy lines in his face creasing with self–satisfaction.

'It is time,' he murmured to himself, 'for Mordania to come in from the cold.'

***

17

'That was most impressive, Martin.'

Harrison's Forbes's voice lost none of its potency over the laptop computer's conference speaker in Martin Sigby's room.

'Thank you,' Sigby replied, removing his heavy winter coat. 'It will certainly spread awareness of the crisis here in Mordania.'

'The networks are alive. There have been follow–up reports already all across the United States and Europe. Networks are queuing up to buy the rights to the reels you shot. To say that they are sensational would be something of an understatement.'

'Just doing my job.'

'Tell me,' Harrison went on, *'how did you get that footage? Who shot it?'*

Sigby stiffened.

'I have an associate who is prepared to move behind enemy lines and obtain the footage I require,' he said.

'I see,' Harrison went on. *'Somebody we know, perhaps?'*

'We have an agreement,' Sigby muttered. 'Why is Megan here at all? What's her part in all this?'

'None of my business and none of yours,' Harrison said. *'Give her what she wants and no doubt she'll provide you with the footage that we need. Keep her sweet, Martin. Without her, there's no story.'*

'Thank you for the vote of confidence,' Sigby replied tartly as he shut the communication link down.

'Pardon monsieur?

Sigby turned from the computer to see a young girl standing in the doorway of his room.

'What is it?'

'I am sorry, I am searching for Megan Mitchell.'

'As is everybody, it would seem. She's three rooms down the hall, on the right.'

Sophie Vernoux smiled a brief "thank you" and walked down the hall. From various rooms she could hear conversations, some that sounded like people recording themselves. Reporters and correspondents, she reflected with disdain, revelling in the misery that they conveyed to the world.

*

Megan sat on the edge of a bed in her damp little room, rifling through piles of papers that Frank Amonte had given to her in London. She took a long sip from a glass of whisky as she worked, acutely aware of Callum quietly watching her from the other side of the room.

'You drink much more of that with all of these candles about,' the Scotsman observed, 'and you'll be in danger of spontaneously combusting.'

'Better to be warm than cold,' Megan muttered without looking up.

Callum looked ready to continue pressuring Megan, but was interrupted by a voice from outside the door.

'Miss Mitchell?'

Megan looked up. 'This is she.'

'J'voudrais parle moi, si'l vous plait?'

Callum's right eyebrow flickered in amusement. Megan ignored him.

'Pray, enter.'

Sophie opened the door and walked cautiously into the room. Callum smiled at her and took the door. 'I was just leaving,' he said cheerfully as he slipped out of the room and closed the door behind him.

Megan got to her feet.

'I'm honoured,' she said, bowing grandly. 'To what do I owe this pleasure, madamoiselle?'

'We don't really use that word. Madame is more usual.'

'I beg forgiveness,' Megan chanted.

'You mock me?' Sophie asked, a little of the indignance returning.

Megan dropped the act.

'No. Please, come in, sit down. Make yourself at home. Coffee?'

Sophie sat down on the bed opposite Megan as she poured her a mug of coffee from a flask on a desk nearby. The unheated hotel was bitterly cold, their breath fogging in the light of the flickering candles that were placed around the room. Megan refilled her own glass.

Sophie sipped her coffee gratefully and scanned the papers on Megan's bed as she sat back down.

'You are researching something?' she asked.

Megan nodded, rearranging the papers.

'I'm trying to understand what would have brought my friend here to Mordania, why she had taken such risks to enter a country at war.'

Sophie shrugged as though it were obvious.

'To find her story, that's what you people do, non?'

'Yes, but this is different. She wasn't just covering the conflict – she could have done that from Thessalia or the surrounding areas. It's as if she had a goal, a purpose here. She was chasing something.'

'As are you,' Sophie said quietly. 'You take risks in your search for your friend. Maybe she too was searching for someone.'

Megan smiled.

'You'd have made a good investigator. I think that she was too. I've got people looking into it, but until they get back to me there's nothing much to go on.'

'In Anterik,' Sophie said quietly, 'you were very brave and your bodyguard filmed it, but they did not mention your name on the reports.'

'Callum's not my bodyguard,' Megan laughed. 'He's my cameraman.'

'How do you know him so well?'

'Well, after leaving university I was a journalist, a rookie, and like so many I was despatched to Kuwait when Iraq invaded in 1990. When the Coalition gathered I got lucky and was embedded with a company of soldiers from the Royal Green Jackets regiment. Callum was a sergeant at that time.' Megan gathered her papers together and closed them inside the folder. 'When he left the army, we teamed up.'

Sophie seemed troubled.

'He does not want to be here or take risks like you do.'

'Callum has a family and a future in England. He's only here because he owed me a favour. He wants to go home and so do I.'

'And where is your home, Megan?'

'London, near Tower Bridge.'

'And you don't want to be here either.'

Megan's mind emptied briefly of thoughts at the direct nature of Sophie's comment.

'What makes you say that?'

Sophie sighed softly, but Megan saw her glance at the bottle beside Megan's table.

'I did not know that you came here to find someone, to rescue them. I thought that you were here to make your name on television. Now I think that you are an honest person.' She hesitated. 'The news broadcast that the other man made, Simby?'

Megan managed to refrain from smiling.

'Yes, Simby. Marvin Simby.'

'Oui, Simby. You were not mentioned, even though it was you who confronted an entire platoon of rebel soldiers.'

'I didn't confront them,' Megan said. 'I walked up to them to ask for help.'

'It was a very brave thing to do,' Sophie insisted. 'Why do you not want to be the one who tells the world what is happening here?'

Megan shrugged.

'I'm not interested in fame,' she said. 'I don't want to be recognised. I'm here to do my job and go home.'

Sophie nodded as though understanding completely.

'Me too,' she whispered softly. 'You are not a reporter any more, are you.'

'What makes you say that?'

'That watch you wear is expensive, and you live in an exclusive part of Central London. You should not be able to afford all of that. And you are in pain, I can tell. People always seem distant to others, when they are suffering.'

Megan throat suddenly felt constricted.

'I'm self employed,' she said, 'and I like to live alone.'

'Why?'

Megan stood up and carried her folder across the room to the desk, just for something to do.

'Because that's what I like to do.'

She could feel Sophie watching her, sensing her discomfort. Sophie finished her coffee and stood, approaching Megan until she was standing directly in front of her, her green eyes like pools of water shimmering in the candlelight.

'Tomorrow, there is something that I want to show you. You will need Callum to come with you, with his camera.'

'Where?'

'Outside Thessalia, maybe ten miles north–west of here, near the mountains.' Sophie's expression darkened slightly. 'It needs to be seen by the world.'

Megan nodded slowly.

'We'll be there.'

*

'How did this happen?'

President Mukhari Akim stood before the broad windows of his personal chambers in Government House, watching the snow falling like myriad stars through the sparsely twinkling lights of the city.

'I do not know, sir,' Severov said, standing just behind his president. 'The MSF aid column must have harboured a journalist, or perhaps someone with a simple camera. The volunteers know the rules and they have broken them.'

President Akim turned away from the blackened windows to face his chief of police.

'This Martin Sigby – he knows who supplied him with the footage?'

Severov's expression turned as dark and cold as the night outside. 'I can find out.'

The president dismissed Severov's insinuation with a wave of his hand.

'These are western reporters, Alexei, and they cannot be harmed in such ways. Besides, this is not the time of the Tsars or the Kremlin. I will not use coercion as a weapon as they did. Fear and oppression do not instill loyalty in people, only resentment and hatred.'

'His informant,' Severov suggested, 'may not possess the same immunity.'

President Akim's jaw hardened as he ground his teeth in his skull.

'Enough, Alexei, if you value your service to me.'

Severov stared silently past the president, who calmed himself with a visible force of will, rubbing his tempes wearily before speaking again.

'This man's work is exactly the kind of news that our enemies wish to hear. If they believe that we are unable to hold our position here it will embolden them further and the fall of the city will be hastened. I cannot allow that to happen. I *will* not allow that to happen.'

'What would you have me do, sir?'

'I want you to ensure that no further footage of Mordania reaches the national press. We must gain military support from NATO or the Americans before the rebels reach the walls of the city, or it is all over. *We* are all over. Is that understood?'

Severov bowed deeply.

'It will be so.'

The Chief of Police walked away to do his duty, leaving the president alone to mull over his rapidly shrinking country.

***

18

'Did she tell you what we're going to see?'

Callum's voice sounded hollow in the cold morning air as he walked with Megan toward the sprawling refugee camp.

'No, but she seemed convinced that it was important enough to take the risk.'

The refugee camp was never, ever entirely silent – a quarter of a million people made a lot of noise even when asleep, but now, at seven o'clock on a gloomy morning, it was almost quiet.

Megan and Callum picked their way through the camp toward the MSF tents, seeing Sophie waiting for them, wrapped in a thick coat. Her voice was a whisper as she spoke.

'We'll use our pick–up. It's parked on the edge of the camp.'

They followed Sophie to the northern edge of the sea of tents, where a small truck was being guarded by two bored–looking British soldiers cradling their rifles. They looked up as Sophie approached the vehicle with her keys.

'That's our escort?' Callum asked, looking at the two soldiers.

'Two men was all Lieutenant Kelsey was willing to spare,' Sophie explained. 'He's already got his hands full covering the perimeter of the camp.'

Megan tossed her rucksack into the back of the truck, and was about to walk around to the passenger side of the vehicle when the sudden clattering of an approaching diesel engine caused them all to turn.

Through the centre of the camp a large troop–carrier bumped and weaved its way toward them, headlights bright in the gloom, the smoky engine deafening in the relative quiet of dawn. Sophie grimaced as the vehicle drew level with the pick–up, its back filled with military police troopers looking down upon them.

The cab door opened and Alexei Severov dropped athletically to the ground, a cigarette smouldering between his teeth as he looked at Sophie's truck.

'What is happening here?' he demanded.

'Distributing supplies,' Sophie replied, not intimidated by the Mordanian's accusing glare.

Severov glanced at Megan and Callum. 'And why do you need these two with you?'

'They volunteered,' Sophie said. 'It's known as charity.'

Severov's eyes narrowed as he sensed the subtle insult, his heavy eyebrows knitting together thoughtfully. He looked at the two British troopers standing forlornly nearby.

'Then let me assist. Two soldiers are not sufficient to protect you in the interior of the country. My men and I shall accompany you.'

Sophie smiled non–commitally.

'That won't be necessary,' she said. 'We're not going far.'

'Then it will be no problem for us,' Severov replied. 'We are happy to help.'

'We don't need a large escort,' Megan said.

Severov's smile did not slip but his eyes darkened even further and his words grated in his throat.

'I am responsible for all civilian movements inside Thessalia and beyond its borders, right out to the front line. If you're going out there, I'm coming with you whether you like it or not.'

Before anybody else could protest, Severov launched himself back into the cab of the troop transporter, slammed the door and waited expectantly. Megan and Callum exchanged a glance before climbing into the pick–up, and the little convoy began its journey through the gloomy dawn.

*

It took almost an hour to cover the distance between Thessalia and Sophie's destination. Megan became uncomfortable when they deliberately left the road and began driving along an old track that wound between thick pine forests, the tips of the trees lost in the ghostly grey mist above.

'Are you sure you know where you're going?' Megan asked.

Sophie nodded, concentrating on driving along the rugged track as she spoke.

'We were called out here a month or more ago by some locals who turned up at the refugee camp. At that time there were only half as many people in the tents. These locals claimed that people had stumbled into their farms in the dead of night, badly injured and incoherent with terror.'

Callum looked at her, his expression concerned.

'They led you out here, didn't they,' he said.

Sophie nodded. 'They were survivors.'

'Survivors of what?'

Sophie did not reply, driving instead deeper into the dense forests, the trees packed together so tightly that they seemed to hem the truck in from each side, reducing the pale dawn light even further. Branches and twigs brushed and snapped against the truck's windows like skeletal limbs probing for the vehicle as it passed, and Megan could see in her wing–mirror the following troop transporter struggling to make its way through.

'This is a bad place to be,' Callum said anxiously. 'It's perfect for a small–arms ambush.'

Sophie shook her head.

'Nobody comes here any more, ever,' she said.

The forest ahead slowly gave way to a clearing several hundred meters long and almost as wide, ringed entirely by the dense forest and with the brooding white–capped mountains rising above it into the dull sky. Sophie drove a short distance into the clearing, the truck's tyres crunching on the thick snow, before she pulled up and switched off the engine.

Megan climbed out of the truck as the troop transporter arrived nearby and the driver also turned off its engine. The sudden silence of the wilderness was deep, like something alive in the air and yet without a soul. Callum stood motionless, surveying the clearing with an uncomfortable expression.

'Bad vibes,' Megan murmured, and Callum nodded in response.

Alexei Severov stormed across to them from his troop transporter, his voice stark in the otherwise silent forest.

'This is not where you said you were going!' he snapped.

'I lied,' Sophie replied laconically. 'What are you going to do about it? Shoot me?'

Severov fumed but had no suitable retort. Megan smiled as Sophie turned her back on the commander and began walking out into the clearing. Megan followed her, with Callum close behind.

'What are we looking for?' she asked Sophie as they walked across the thickly snow–carpeted earth.

'A building,' Sophie replied.

Megan felt a chill run down her spine as Sophie stopped at a slight mound beneath the snow. Megan would not have recognised it as anything unusual until Sophie began scraping at the snow with her hands, brushing thick chunks of ice aside to reveal dark soil, almost black. There, laying on the earth were layers of scorched timber, damp and crumbling now beneath the snow.

Megan knelt down beside Sophie and lifted a sodden lump of carbonised wood in her hands, flakes of blackened charcoal crumbling in her grasp.

'Burned to the ground,' she said. 'What was here?'

'I don't know,' Sophie admitted. 'There's more.'

As Callum followed them, watching and discreetly filming as he went, Megan scanned the ground again and began to see features that she had not noticed before: long, low humps beneath the snow, too regularly positioned to be natural formations. Buildings had once stood here, and all of them had been destroyed.

'There was one large central building,' Sophie said, 'or so we were told by the survivors before they died. There were also smaller adjacent buildings and living quarters.'

Sophie walked out to an area of flat earth, and from her pocket produced latex gloves that she pulled over her hands. Megan had a sudden premonition of what was coming, but still she watched as Sophie brushed the snow away from the earth once more, this time using a biro from her pocket to prod into the soft, black soil. After a few pokes the pen touched on something. Grimacing, Sophie fumbled slightly with her gloved hand and with an effort heaved something out of the soil.

It took a moment for Megan's brain to comprehend what she was looking at. Sophie had lifted what looked like a piece of dirty fabric from the soil, but the effort she expended was too great for such a small fragment of material. It was only a moment later that she realised that the fabric was part of a pair of trousers, and that the trousers still adorned the leg of a body buried beneath the soil, the flesh wrinkled, pale white and flecked with an ugly kaleidoscope of purple and yellow blotches.

'Oh no,' Megan murmured.

Sophie rested the partially exposed leg on the ground. 'The snow and the timbers cover most of the remains.'

'How many?' Callum asked.

'Not less than eighty, so they said, but there's no way to know for sure.'

'Why wasn't this reported before?' Megan asked.

'The media ban,' Sophie said in a whisper, glancing over her shoulder. 'The government insists it has everything under control and will not allow negative press on the situation.'

Sophie fell silent. The two British soldiers and the military police had followed them out into the clearing. At their head, Alexei Severov moved forward and went down on one knee beside the remains.

'The rebels must have advanced further than we had thought,' he said, scanning the surrounding forests before standing again. 'We must pull back from this place and let them lie in peace.'

Megan ignored Severov and moved forward, gripping the trouser and pulling hard. The sodden, heavy earth lurched and sucked as Megan heaved with all of her strength. Callum grabbed the fabric of a jacket poking from the snow nearby and with a grunt of effort the body was sucked from the mud to lay on the snow.

'What are you doing?!' Severov snapped. 'These people were my countrymen, Mordanians! They deserve better!'

Megan dropped the leg onto the snow and turned to face Severov.

'They deserved better than murder, too, and they deserve not to have died without their cause of death being known. If you care about your countrymen, surely you would want to know who did this to them?'

Severov looked down at the body, clearly torn between his duty as a soldier and a superstitious fear of the dead. A waft of putrid odours roiled on the cold air, causing several of the soldiers to turn away, their complexions paling. Severov did not move. Megan held her breath for a moment and moved closer to the body.

The man had been in his fifties, as far as Megan could tell through the dirt and the decomposition. Bearded and with receding grey hair, he wore a check shirt and brown slacks. It took no genius to determine the cause of death. The man's chest and abdomen were peppered with bullet holes that had ripped the fabric of his clothes. Megan did not bother to look at the man's back, knowing that it would have been shredded by the exit wounds.

'Kalashnikovs, most liklely,' Callum said, examining the wounds, 'from close range.'

Megan turned to Sophie. 'Eighty of them?'

'Something like that,' Sophie nodded.

Megan looked at Severov.

'Have your men help us uncover the bodies, and put a call back to the Red Cross Headquarters in Thessalia. They'll need teams to come down here.'

Severov's fists clenched by his sides.

'This is a grave,' he hissed.

'This is a murder scene,' Megan snapped back, 'evidence of genocide, war crimes. If you do not help to protect this evidence it will be considered during any trials at the Hague. Do you understand?'

Severov struggled with himself for a moment longer.

'We cannot move them. It is already obvious what has happened here. I do not want forensic teams tearing up the ground!'

Sophie spoke from one side. 'We know nothing about what happened here.'

'What do you mean? Is it not obvious?' Severov demanded, turning to face her.

'We don't know who did this, nor why,' Sophie replied. 'You're assuming too much without evidence. For all you know it could have been men from Thessalia who did this.'

Severov took a threatening pace toward her.

'My men could not have done such a thing as this. It is the work of General Rameron and his terrorists!'

'Then where are they?' Callum challenged. 'If they had advanced this far, they would not then abandon their gains. We're just a few miles from Thessalia, the city that they wish to conquer.'

'I don't know,' Severov admitted.

Sophie shrugged. 'Then you don't know it wasn't your own men who did this.'

Severov whirled and raised an accusing finger to point at Sophie, and in an instant Callum reacted, looping his right arm over Severov's elbow and then pushing his right hand through under the commander's armpit. Callum's left arm came across and his forearm pinned Severov under the throat. The commander was instantly pitched backwards and off balance. The Scot held him there and whispered into his ear.

'It's rude to point.'

The surprise in Severov's eyes mutated grotesquely into terrible fury, black holes radiating hate. The military police nearby watched eagerly, never having seen their commander bested in such a way.

'Let me go or I shall gut you like a fish,' the commander growled, his one free hand dropping to grip a knife in a sheath by his left ankle.

Callum smiled and complied instantly. The police commander plummeted onto his back in the snow. He scrambled back onto his feet, his teeth bared in fury and his dark skin flushed with humiliation. He turned to glare at Megan.

'How dare you let him attack me?!'

Megan was about to reply when everyone, Severov included, suddenly looked past her. She turned to see what looked like a peasant farmer, who had emerged from the tree–line with two goats and a small donkey on a rope leash.

The military police instantly aimed their Kalashnikovs at the old man.

The farmer stared at them in surprise and then turned to flee back toward the forest.

Severov, his pride damaged and his blood up, instantly lunged in pursuit.

'Alexei, wait!' Megan shouted.

***

19

The old man had barely reached the tree line when Severov caught him by the collar, lifting him almost bodily off the ground.

'Alexei!' Megan shouted. 'Let him go!'

Severov ignored Megan and dragged the old man back toward the military police. The farmer was weeping in terror, begging and pleading with his captor.

'I said let him go!' Megan repeated, moving to intercept the commander.

Severov pulled his service pistol from its holster and aimed it at Megan.

'This is police business and you will stay out of it!'

Megan hesitated, sensing the blind fury now contaminating Severov as he dragged the old man to where the dead body lay in the snow and dropped him down next to it. The commander aimed his pistol at the old man.

'What do you know of this?!' he demanded in Mordanian, pointing at the corpse.

The old man scrambled weakly to his knees as Megan watched, his gnarled old hands clasped before him as he begged for his life in juddering Mordanian.

'What do you know of this?!' Severov bellowed again.

The old man continued to plead, until Severov grabbed him by the collar with his free hand and brought the butt of the pistol crashing down across his temple with a sickening crunch.

'Stop that!' Sophie screamed, rushing forward.

Megan and Callum exchanged a silent glance.

Severov hit the old man again. Megan moved swiftly forward into Severov's right side, reaching out for the pistol. Severov aimed the weapon at her, and in that instant Callum moved in from behind the commander and grabbed the pistol, his hand curling over the barrel and twisting it awkwardly down and to the right. Severov's fingers parted under the pressure and the pistol slipped from his grasp.

The commander whirled to face Callum, his fist raised to hit the Scotsman. Megan reached up and grabbed Severov's arm from behind, belaying the blow. In the same instant Callum's own chunky fist slammed into Severov's jaw with a crack loud enough to echo off the treeline, sending the commander sprawling into the snow.

A rush of shocked gasps rippled through the military police gathered nearby, and a few of their weapons snapped up to point in Callum's general direction. The two British troopers instantly raised their own weapons in return, but mostly the Mordanians were transfixed by the sight of their disarmed commander, who had briefly lost consciousness but now rolled over, dragging himself unsteadily to his feet. Severov glared at Megan and Callum in turn, his expression twisted with incoherent hatred. After a few moments he wrenched his features into something approaching dignity and moved to stand silently in front of Callum

The commander held out his hand, palm–up, glaring silently at the Scotsman. Callum, unintimidated, handed the commander back his service pistol. Severov holstered the weapon, his dark eyes never leaving Callum's, before turning back to the old man.

Sophie was already tending to the farmer's head wound, and Megan moved slightly to one side, blocking Severov's path.

'Enough for one day, Alexei.'

'I came here to protect you,' Severov growled, 'and this is how you repay me?'

Megan gestured to the old man sitting in the snow behind her, who mumbled quietly to himself as Sophie patched her up.

'Protecting us?' Megan murmured. 'From such a bloodthirsty savage as him? What ever would we have done without you, Alexei?'

The two British troopers chuckled under their breath and lowered their weapons, and the Mordanian police, sensing the jibe, relaxed. Severov cast a final glare in their direction before stalking away toward the troop–carrier.

'He'll not forget this, Megan,' Sophie cautioned as she applied a medical pad to the old man's head. 'Mordanians never forget an insult.'

Megan shrugged.

'We'll be gone soon enough.'

Megan turned to the two British troopers.

'Can you guys give us a hand?'

Together, the soldiers, Megan and Callum hauled body after body out of the freezing snow and mud, partially exposing them to the elements. Megan then went over the bodies, searching without luck for identification documents.

'Stripped of posessions before they were shot,' Callum said as Megan wiped her hands in the snow.

Sophie, who had been watching them work as she finished tending to the old man, looked across the grisly, barren haul of bodies and broken earth.

'Somebody is responsible for this,' she said softly.

Megan sighed.

'Without papers or witnesses, there's nothing for us to go on.'

She cast her gaze across the bodies again, and then her eyes caught on something, a pattern visible through the grime, slush and decay. She knelt down again beside one of the bodies and examined it more closely.

'What is it?' Sophie asked, moving closer.

Megan moved to another body, and then another, checking their ankles each time.

'These are all male victims,' she said as she moved from one body to another, 'most of them middle aged or older.'

'So?' Sophie asked.

'It's the shoes,' Megan replied.

'The shoes?' Callum asked, following them both closely and filming as he went.

'They're all wearing the same kind of shoes,' Megan said, pointing to one of the corpses. 'These aren't the kind of shoes that people wear to travel in the snow. These are indoor shoes. These people either lived or were employed here. Look.'

Callum leaned close to the shoe that Megan held up for him demonstratively. It was a thin soled shoe, almost like a sports trainer but without laces. Instead it was tied with neat straps over the bridge of the foot.

'There wouldn't be any warmth in them,' Callum agreed.

'They all have the same logo on the bottom,' Megan said, pointing to the sole of the shoe.

'*Estrom*,' Callum read the label. 'Some kind of company, specialist footwear?'

Megan nodded, lowering the leg she held back into the slush.

'They were all employees of some kind,' Megan said, turning to Sophie and gesturing toward the old man. 'Does he know what they were doing here before the fire?'

Sophie turned to the old man and in faltering Mordanian relayed the question. A garbled response tumbled from his mouth, accompanied by wild and enthusiastic gesticulating. Sophie frowned as she concentrated, and then looked at Megan.

'I think he's saying that she doesn't really know, but there were lots of movements at night, vehicles delivering equipment and personnel from an airfield somewhere north of here. It was a busy place, but he did not return for a long time.' She listened as the old man gabbled on before translating further. 'This morning was the first time that he has come back here, when he heard vehicles while working on his fields on the other side of the valley.'

Megan turned and looked at the surrounding mountains, climbing high into the chill clouds. The valley in which they stood was surrounded by the soaring peaks, steep hillsides and plunging valleys leading out into the wilderness. She looked questioningly at Callum.

'Some kind of research facility?' the Scotsman hazarded. 'Maybe military, although there's no evidence of a defensive structure here, so perhaps industrial.'

'There's not much more we can do,' Megan said, 'except get the Red Cross down and let Sir Wilkins know what we've found. I don't want him to see it on the news first.'

'I've got plenty of footage,' Callum murmured discreetly, and patted his jacket.

Megan nodded. 'Good. Get a few establishing shots for Sigby and then let's get out of here.'

Sophie looked at the old man. 'What about him?'

Megan looked at the old farmer before glancing over her shoulder at Severov, who sat smoking in the cab of the troop–carrier whilst watching them with sullen eyes.

'Let the old man go and make sure our psychopathic escort doesn't follow him.'

At that moment, Callum's cell–phone rang. Mildly surprised, he retrieved and answered it. After listening for a few moments, his eyes widened in disbelief.

'You're kidding?' he said, looking across at Megan. 'Anterik? They moved in on the town and they did what?'

Both Megan and Sophie moved closer, mutually curious as to what was being said to Callum.

'They just went in and went out again, just like that? And it's on the news?'

Callum listened some more and then nodded, shutting the phone off and looking at Megan with a bemused smile on his face.

'You're not going to believe this,' he said, 'but your little endeavour of yesterday is having a bigger impact than I think any of us could have anticipated.'

*

Alexei Severov watched closely as Sophie Vernoux let the farmer go, the old man thanking her with pathetic gestures of gratitude before hobbling away into the tree line and disappearing.

The commander drew deeply on his cigarette, watching as Mitchell and her friend, the big man with the strange accent, began moving again amongst the bodies. Severov observed them for a few more moments, noting the strange path that they took, and then turned to the driver sitting beside him in the cab.

'Start the engine,' he snapped. 'The cab is cold.'

The driver blinked. 'You have your door open, Alexei.'

Severov's gaze swivelled toward the driver with murderous intent. The driver reached for the keys without another word and fired the engine. Severov continued to watch Megan Mitchell and smiled quietly to himself.

'Let's see what you're really doing here,' he whispered.

***

20

Principality of Monaco,

Cote D'azure

'Good evening, this is the GNN six o'clock news. I'm Mandie Carmen.'

'And I'm Jake Hennley.'

Mandie and Jake's perfectly proportioned features became mutually serious as a computer generated map of Mordania appeared magically on the screen behind them. Mandie's voice dropped a suitably ominous octave lower.

'Tonight's exclusive report comes from the break–away Russian state of Mordania. As the civil war intensifies, an extraordinary report from a British correspondent within the country exposes evidence of crimes against humanity within twenty miles of the capital itself, Thessalia.'

The camera zoomed in on Jake's thermo–nuclear tan.

'The British correspondent, Martin Sigby, has managed to obtain access to footage from within the country despite a complete ban on foreign journalists travelling outside of the capital city Thessalia. I should like to warn our viewers that this report contains scenes that they will find immensely disturbing.'

The image of Jake Hennley vanished to be replaced by one of the bitter landscape of Mordania, a snowy clearing ringed with dense forests of pine. Martin Sigby's voice droned over the images.

'Borack district, just ten miles north of Thessalia City. Here, during a routine aid mission by Medicines Sans Frontiers volunteers, the remains of what was once a thriving settlement is found beneath the ice and snow.'

The image changed to close–ups, shot as the hands of unseen individuals handled lumps of charred wood and then fragments of grubby clothing.

'An entire village razed to the ground by fire, and amidst the scorched shards of timber and glass, the remains of the people who had once lived here.'

A shot of a hand holding up a leg, the ankle and calf visible beneath the fabric of clothing, the skin pale and blotched by decay.

'They are believed to number in excess of eighty souls, all of whom show evidence of being executed where they stood. Given the state of the bodies and the putrefaction of tissues, they can have died little more than days ago.'

The screen changed to an image of Martin Sigby standing on the roof of the Thessalia Hilton, facing the camera with a microphone in his hand.

'Although the Red Cross has been notified of the discovery of the remains, and though it will be some time before forensic officers can obtain more accurate information about the terrible fate of these innocent victims of an increasingly brutal war, it remains clear that genocide is now a factor in this bitter conflict. The biggest question that hangs over this most distressing of discoveries is that fact that the murders have occurred so close to, and in fact within, government held territory. Despite the obvious efforts being made by the government of President Mukhari Akim to protect civilians here in Thessalia, the presence of such a massacre so close to the city once again throws doubt onto the government' s ability, and will, to defend the safe haven, and that of the UN to assist them in doing so. It would seem now that the United Nations may call the Mordanian government to task on this most terrible of atrocities, and demand that they do more to protect the people from the ferocity of the forces under the rebel leader Mikhail Rameron. Martin Sigby, Mordania.'

Sherman Kruger grimaced as he watched, sucking on his cheeks as he rested his chin on the uneven pillow of his gnarled, blotchy hands.

The screen flicked back to Mandie and Jake's perma–perfect features as Mandie continued speaking.

'Despite the shocking scenes depicted in that report, it is not the biggest news coming out of Mordania today. Jake?'

Jake's features brightened as though he'd been suddenly plugged into a wall–socket.

'That's right Mandie. An extraordinary event has occurred since Martin Sigby's first report was broadcast from within Mordania from the village of Anterik. It appears that the reports reaching viewers around the world are not just informing us of events that were until now concealed from the world. It actually appears that these exclusive reports are having an effect on the conflict itself!'

Sherman Kruger leaned forward in sudden consternation, staring hard at the screen as Jake introduced their live correspondent on the ground in Thessalia, Steven Ayres.

'The reports from Mordania by Martin Sigby have suddenly had an effect on the ground here in Thessalia and the surrounding areas. We've recently received reports that Anterik, a village suffering from extreme hardship and poverty during the course of the war to date, has received aid shipments not from the UN or the Red Cross or any other of the charity agencies working out here, but from the rebel forces themselves. It appears, Jake, believe it or not, that forces on the ground here are beginning to react to the reports that they know are reaching the outside world.'

Jake's expression became robotically surprised.

'That's incredible Steven, and you're saying that they're actively trying to improve the conditions for the citizens of the village, knowing that the fact will be broadcast live around the world?'

'That's exactly what I'm saying Jake,' Steven enthused, *'and I can tell you that since the first broadcast by the British correspondent Martin Sigby on the appalling discovery of human remains in a destroyed village outside of Thessalia, rebel forces have been observed advancing on the area and forming a loose ring around the forest. However, they have not acted aggressively toward any teams accessing the site.'*

Sherman Kruger's ageing features turned purple with fury and he slammed a wiry hand down on the side of his chair.

'You little shits,' he spat. 'You scheming, interfering little bastards.'

Jake Hennley thoughtfully furrowed his brow.

'You're saying that they're trying to protect the activities ongoing at the site?'

'That's exactly what I'm saying, Jake. They've effectively formed a perimeter around the area but have remained out of contact with the aid agencies and UN inspectors now on site at the remains of the village. It's as if they're trying to say "we're here to protect you while you work" without making direct contact.'

'Unbelievable,' Jake replied, shaking his head and looking at the camera.

The studio went dark and silent as Kruger turned off the television and gripped the remote in his hand.

'Unbelievable, Jake,' he agreed.

Kruger speed–dialled a number on his phone pad and it was picked up on the second ring by a female secretary.

'Seth Cain's office.'

'Put Seth on the line, and yes, it's urgent.'

There was a moment of shocked hesitation and then the line clicked as it was transferred.

'Seth Cain.'

'You've seen the news, I take it, Seth.'

'I don't know where the hell this guy's getting his reels from,' Cain replied. *'The whole world's watching this jerk, and now it would seem that the rebels are trying to polish their image through his reporting.'*

'It's got to stop, Seth,' Kruger hissed, 'and it's got to stop now! We had an agreement, remember? I said create something spectacular, not screw up our entire operation!'

'I remember,' Cain replied. *'I'm due to see the Vice President shortly. If I can convince him that the time to move on Mordania is now, he may be able to sway the president's opinion. There are still enough hawks in the administration to lobby for a military solution to the problem.'*

Kruger's grip on the television remote tightened.

'That pig–faced little squirt who's been getting these reels from Mordania, Sigby is it? It says on the reports that he works for GNN UK, correct?'

'He does,' Cain replied.

'Then make damned sure that his next report covers, in unflinching detail, the appalling atrocities of the rebel forces and the valiant defiance of the democratic government of Mordania. Then I want him out of that country, is that clear?'

'I'm not sure that I can simply pull him out, now that he's surrounded by such media attention. It'll do more harm to our cause than good.'

Kruger hurled the television remote at a wall nearby, the device shattering with a sharp crack.

'Then arrange a tragic accident for him and wrap this charade up with a terrifically sad epitaph for his courage and devotion to the noble cause! I don't care how you do it just get him off the damned television!'

There was a long pause on the line, and then Seth Cain spoke thoughtfully.

'There may be another way. Perhaps we can turn this to our advantage.'

'Whatever. If you let me down Seth, I'll buy GNN and fire you my goddamned self!'

Kruger cut the line off and fumed in impotent silence as Julia appeared from nowhere and quietly began picking up the plastic fragments of the television remote.

***

21

'Ella mon Giet, what has happened out there Alexei?'

President Mukhari Akim's voice was laden with displeasure as he stood behind his desk. Alexei Sevrov stood to attention before him, his dark eyes staring somewhere above the president.

'As I said before, sir, it is my suspicion that one of the aid volunteers has been carrying a concealed camera into the country and filming things that do not concern them, in direct deficance of your policies as president of..,'

'I don't care about the footage!' President Akim exploded, his barrel chest projecting his voice like cannon fire around the office. 'I'm talking about the massacre! Our people have died at the hands of butchers!'

Severov performed a rapid mental calculation.

'I do not know, sir. Their Red Cross are on the site right now. I have troops stationed to protect them from any interference from the rebel positions to their north.'

The president slowly moved from behind his desk, massaging his temple with one hand as he walked to stand beside the office windows, looking down onto the square and the statue of Balthazaar the Great far below.

'The murder of civilians, a cold–blooded massacre, will change the course of the conflict entirely. The United Nations will no longer wish to stand by as an exclusively neutral observer, but more importantly they may decide not to support *us*. How could they be seen to support a government they suspect may have murdered its own civilians!?' He turned to face his chief of police. 'We are witnessing the complete destruction of our independence as a nation.'

Severov, still at attention, cleared his throat.

'I can find out who is filming these broadcasts and bring an end to this. The people of the world have seen such images countless times, every year. They'll be more concerned with weather reports once we've closed this renegade cameraman down.'

President Akim shook his head and exhaled noisily, glancing out the windows again at the snow falling thickly from the ghost–grey sky before making a decision.

'We can no longer afford to be passive observers ourselves, Alexei. We must ensure that there are no longer any further obstacles created by foreigners in the land of our fathers. How long before you know who is responsible for the broadcast footage?'

Severov's teeth flashed in a wicked smile beneath his thick grey stubble.

'Perhaps a few seconds,' he said. 'You recorded the broadcast, as I suggested?'

The president nodded and activated an ancient VCR beneath a television in the corner of the office. Immediately, the broadcast detailing the discovery of the murder victims and the razed village played.

'Turn up the volume,' Severov said, moving close to the television and looking at the images of the bodies partly concealed beneath the snow.

President Akim raised the volume, listening with Severov. After a few moments, as a hand was lifting yet another decaying leg from the mud and slush, the sound of a large truck engine starting–up echoed across the barren clearing.

'There!' Severov said. 'This footage was not taken by the Red Cross when they arrived at the scene. This was taken by the MSF aid group volunteers when I was present. It was shot when I was there!'

'The engine in the background?' the president said.

'I told my driver to start the engine. I knew that if somebody was filming it would record the sound in the background and I'd know who was at the scene.'

The President looked at his chief of police seriously. 'Who was it?'

Severov's skin flushed with blood as the first possibility of revenge entered his mind.

'Megan Mitchell and her big friend. They are the ones doing the filming. I can arrest them right now sir.'

The president glanced again at the recording, now showing Martin Sigby presenting his report from the snowy roof of the Thessalia Hilton.

'No. There is another way.'

*

'Estrom? I don't know of them off–hand, dear girl.'

Sir Wilkins stood in the Government House UN offices, his eyes searching the ceiling as he tried to place the name.

'They were all wearing the same shoes,' Megan said. 'It's my guess that they were employed doing some kind of laboratory work. Whoever killed these people also stripped the buildings of any evidence of what was there before they torched the place.'

Sir Wilkins nodded thoughtfully.

'You've spoken to the Red Cross teams about this?' he asked.

'As soon as we got back. They're not able to find anything on the work that might have gone on here, but they feel certain that they will be able to identify at least some of the dead.'

'Good,' Sir Wilkins replied, punching one fist into the palm of his other hand. 'There will be families who will be spared the agony of not knowing what happened to their loved ones.' The attache looked at Megan and blanched slightly. 'Sorry, didn't mean to refer to, you know, all that business.'

'It's okay,' Megan said. 'Can you find out who makes these shoes and what they're for?'

'Of course,' Sir Wilkins said. 'We have the Internet here, along with most of the UN's files on Mordania. There's bound to be something. I'll have a word with one of the girls next door, if you'll give me a minute.'

'Thanks, Tom,' Megan said, turning to see Callum standing in the doorway with a satellite phone in his hand.

'It's your friend from the Big Apple.'

Megan took the phone and heard the bouyant drawl of Frank Amonte on the line.

'Hey Megan, sorry it took so long to get back to you. I managed to speak to Amy's folks again and they filled me in on this Mordanian mystery.'

'Go on,' Megan encouraged.

'Well, it turns out that her father's family line is of Mordanian stock, which is probably where Amy got her exotic looks from. Anyway, when I questioned them about their history in Mordania, it turns out that her father had several close friends in the country from his childhood, just after World War Two. He said that Amy mentioned one of them from time to time, a man whom her father remained in contact with after he emigrated to America.'

'Who, and how did she know him?'

'That's the thing. The Mordanian is a scientist who worked in the automotive industry during the post–war period. His name is Petra Milankovich. According to Amy's father, Petra had a great deal of contact recently with Amy, but her father doesn't know whether it has anything to do with her having travelled to Mordania or whether it's just a coincidence. Personally, I'd imagine it's relevant – Amy had never met this man before yet they've had considerable contact over the past twelve months. I couldn't find a permanent address for the guy, but I've found a place that she stayed at regularly while working out there – it's a farmstead near the town of Talyn. I'll forward it to you.'

'Good work Frank,' Megan replied. 'That makes sense, that she might have travelled here to meet him. I'll look into it. What about the other thing that I asked you about?'

'Ah, now that's really interesting. Sophie Vernoux, Medicines Sans Frontiers, right? Well, I checked every personnel file that I could lay my hands on going back almost twelve years, and I can tell you something for sure: MSF have never employed a Sophie Vernoux who matches the description of your friend over there.'

Megan felt her heart flutter in her chest as it missed a beat.

'You're sure, Frank?'

'One hundred percent sure. Whoever she is, it ain't who she's sayin' she is. Take it from me.'

'Okay Frank, good work. I'll be in touch.'

Frank Amonte rang off and Megan sat for a moment, picturing Sophie Vernoux in her mind. She looked over at Sir Wilkins, who was returning from his officers with a sheet of paper.

'Anything?' Megan asked.

Sir Wilkins handed Megan the sheet of paper with a triumphant flourish.

'Estrom Betrick Incorporated,' he said as Megan read the details on the sheet. 'Suppliers of high quality foot–wear to laboratories all over the Caspian region, specifically to industrial and manufacturing plants. They specialise in clothing designed to withstand abrasion with minimal flaking of material, to avoid contaminating laboratory conditions.'

Megan looked across at Callum.

'The guy that Amy knew here in Mordania, who she might have been searching for, was a scientist,' she said.

'One of the ones who was killed?' Callum said in surprise. 'The plot thickens.'

Megan turned to Sir Wilkins.

'The site of the massacre and the razed village: do you know what was being done there?'

Sir Wilkins shook his head.

'The Red Cross are already making enquiries about it but so far they've drawn a total blank. There's nothing to indicate any kind of official research development programs there. It's as if the place never existed, which means either the paperwork has been destroyed by the people who destroyed the village…,'

Megan nodded thoughtfully, finishing the sentence.

'Or there never was any paperwork and the entire endeavour, whatever it was, was being funded externally from elsewhere with only the physical work being done in the village.'

'That could mean anywhere,' Sir Wilkins pointed out. 'With this kind of sheer destructive will, we could be looking at a situation where neither the government nor the rebel factions are responsible. This could be the work of Islamic militants, or Russian mafia running a drug factory, or simply mercenaries run amok. As long as those kinds of people are paid sufficiently they'll do just about anything.'

'When I met the rebels at Anterik,' Megan said, 'one of them told me that his people would not allow the west to conduct their economic experiments here in Mordania. Do you know what he might have meant by that?'

Wilkins shook his head slowly.

'No, I don't. Who knows, though, what these people might have been told by their leader in order to have them fight as they do.'

Megan shook her head, frowning as she stood.

'There's something missing, something we're not seeing here. Whatever it is, it's the reason that Amy O'Hara travelled so far and the reason those people were murdered. Something tells me that there's something bigger at work.'

'How do you know?' the attache asked as Megan grabbed her jacket.

'Gut instinct,' Megan replied. 'Something stinks, and I'm going to find out what it is.'

***

22

Hart Senate Building,

Washington DC, USA

'Mister Vice President!'

Seth Cain strode across the vast multi–storey lobby of the Hart Senate building, intercepting Vice–President Richard Hobbs as he made his way in the opposite direction.

'Seth,' Hobbs greeted the media tycoon warmly. 'Been a while.'

'Too long,' Cain agreed, gesturing toward the exit. 'Lunch?

The Vice President shook his head as they walked together, flanked by secret–service agents in dark suits and obligatory sunglasses.

'I'm due at the White House. The Director of the CIA and the National Security Advisor have been trying to get the president to sit down for five minutes so they can discuss the deterioration in relations with Russia. It's not a briefing I can afford to miss.'

'That's fine Richard, really. Can I offer you a ride to Pennsylvania Avenue? There's something important we need to discuss.'

Hobbs turned with Cain and they walked outside and down a broad flight of steps toward a slender black car with tinted windows. Cain graciously opened the door for the vice–president, ignoring the sudden flurry of flashing cameras as a gaggle of press reporters dashed across from where the vice–president's official ride was parked to get a better shot of the two men. Cain ducked inside and slammed the door and the car pulled smoothly away from the reporters.

'So, what's on your mind, Seth?' Hobbs asked amiably.

'Mordania.'

'Mordania,' Hobbs echoed. 'Who'd have thought such a meagre scrap of real–estate would be on the lips of so many? I would have thought that the recent success of that British reporter of yours would be making you smile in your sleep. What's his name? Slingsby?'

'Sigby,' Cain replied. 'And yes, the reports from within Mordania have indeed been sensational. However they are not the greatest of concerns for us right now, Richard. The continuing destablisation of the Mordanian government is beginning to tip the balance of power in favour of General

Rameron's insurgency. The matter is growing more critical with every passing day. You've watched the news yourself, Richard. The government is going to collapse.'

The vice–president nodded in agreement but seemed unpreturbed.

'The United States can't be there to wipe the nose of every president who faces a leadership crisis, Seth. Mordania simply does not have the strategic importance to us to warrant a military solution to the conflict. You know this already. The president has repeatedly said that he will not interfere with the United Nation's decisions on these matters. He wants to repair US–UN relations, not wreck them.'

Seth Cain sighed heavily.

'Political niceities aside, Richard, Mordania has immense importance in the greater scheme of things. Its location as a conduit for oil supplies from the Middle East may become of greater value than you think. Both Russia and Iran continue to threaten western oil supplies by playing havoc with the flow of crude overland and by sea, using the supplies as a political weapon against us. Mordania is the perfect platform for ensuring a safe flow in the long term, bypassing less reliable suppliers.'

'I agree, absolutely,' the vice–president said, 'but we have an obligation to let these nations develop on their own. We can't keep doing what previous American administrations have done and simply invade other countries on our own agenda. We're damned whatever we do, Seth. If we do nothing we're abandoning innocent civilians to their doom, and if we do make a move then we're the Great Satan invading lesser countries for our own devious ends.'

Cain made a gesture of helplessness.

'Oh come on Richard, you're dodging too many issues trying to support this administration's pacifist approach. Russia is growing ever more powerful, spreading its influcence throughout the Urals and the Middle East, seeking to construct another empire founded on an anti–American consensus. It's the Cold War all over again. We need western–friendly governments around the Caspian. Chechnya, Georgia, Mordania – they've all shown a willingness and an interest in becoming members of NATO and the EU. You name it, they want it and we've got it. What better bulwark against Russian expansion into the Middle East could you want? Look at Europe, the spread of democracy by choice. It's worked there.'

'Maybe,' Hobbs said, 'but you said it yourself – democracy by *choice*. Besides, our country is already stretched to its military limit in other operations around the globe. We just don't have the manpower. Anyway, with the environmental issues at stake here it's as wise to invest money in alternative energy programs as it is to plough it into another invasion exercise, to which I might add there is no guarantee of success. We learned enough lessons in Iraq to give us pause for thought when deploying our forces for a prolonged foreign engagement.'

Seth Cain lowered his hands.

'Richard, you and I have known each other for how long?'

'About twenty years,' Hobbs replied. 'Good years, too.'

'Then you can understand how important it was for me, and for the president's other benefactors, that the policies upon which he built his campaign are upheld now that he is in office. The people of America are concerned about the security of their energy supplies and are all too aware of what's required to maintain that security. America must make efforts to control of all the world's energy resources, regardless of the obstacles.'

The vice–president looked at Cain seriously.

'What's this to you, Seth? Since when did you care about oil?' Hobb's eyes narrowed. 'Is the Board on your back again?'

'They have a stake,' Cain admitted, looking out of the window at the passing traffic and the pedestrians, all oblivious to the complexity of the greater world beyond their own. 'It's in our interest to protect our investments.'

'*Their* investments,' Hobbs corrected him. 'You should stay out of their political shennanigans Seth, before you get dragged down with them.'

Cain looked back at the vice–president once more.

'They want the president to ensure that their interests in the Caspian region are protected. They believe that the president promised that he would do that.'

'But we will not achieve that aim by force or arms, nor did we ever suggest that we should!'

Cain's hitherto amiable expression finally hardened.

'The means are not at question here, Richard, only the end result. I and more than a dozen other benefactors provided the funds for your party's campaign on the understanding that certain policies would become part of law and that certain concerns of ours would be addressed, and that's not happening.'

Richard Hobbs stared at Seth Cain with a shocked expression.

'What part, exactly, of the words *democratic government* have you failed to understand Seth?'

'Democracy?!' Cain laughed bitterly. 'You don't seriously expect me to believe that we still live in democracies do you Richard? Where leaders bow to the will of their people? That's crap and you know it. Administrations the world over are voted into power on the basis of grand promises of how wonderful life will be under their guidance, and one after the other, term after term, they fail to deliver.'

'That's a deeply cynical line of thought,' Hobbs observed.

'But it's the truth, isn't it? True rule of the people, by the people, *for* the people is not democracy. It's *isocracy*, a form of leadership not sufficient for the massive populations of our planet today. So we make do with democracy. People are raised to office by a popular vote, and then spend their years in power doing whatever they like. If you reduce the number of potential leaders to a handful of people who will all more or less do what their benefactors want once they're in power, you've gotten rid of democracy all together. That's modern politics Richard, and you know it. The White House does not control America – corporations control it. Oil controls it. Manufacturing controls it. The media controls it. Capitalism in all its glory, and we pull the strings.'

Richard Hobbs shot Cain an aggressive look.

'Get to your point, Seth.'

'We own America and its president. My media corporation only broadcasts news reports that are favourable to the administration, as we promised we would. We can change that in the blink of an eye, should we feel that our alliance is not being honoured by the president.'

'You do not own the White House, nor the president, nor the people of this country! I would sooner resign from office than be dictated to by a glorified office gossip!'

Cain's features collapsed into frustration as the car drew to a stop close to the White House.

'We need to go into Mordania. That is what we want.'

'That is what *you* want, Seth. I don't know what you're involved in but I'm damned sure it's not going to influence this administration's policies, and that's final!'

With that, Hobbs got out of the car, slamming the door behind him. Seth Cain dragged a hand down his face and reached out for the car–phone nestled in his arm rest. He dialled a number.

'Kruger.'

'It's Seth. He didn't go for it. I tried everything, absolutely everything, to the extent that I believe I may have lost a powerful ally within the administration. They're not going to interfere in the Mordania situation and that's final.'

There was the sound of a deep, rattling breath on the line

'On the contrary, Seth, they're about to learn that they have no choice.'

'What do you mean?'

'I'm implementing phase two.'

'Phase two?' Cain echoed. 'What's that?'

He heard a throaty chuckle on the line.

'Make sure that your people in London ensure that damned reporter in Mordania says what we want him to.'

'What are you going to do, Sherman?'

'Let's just say that if you really need something doing, you just have to do it yourself. If America won't go to war against Mordania's rebels, then the rebels will have to go to war against America.'

The line clicked off in Seth Cain's ear before he could respond, leaving him with an ominous feeling tingling down his spine.

***

23

GNN UK Ltd,

London

Harrison Forbes strode confidently through the GNN operations room, his eyes scanning the plasma screens showing news reports from around the globe.

'I'm willing to bet last years' salary that the next footage we see coming out of Mordania will make every other piece of news look about as interesting as the shipping forecast.'

'Martin Sigby is still at the top of the news ratings,' his aide, Shelley, said as she hurried to keep up with Harrison's marathon–winning strides. 'People are following this by the minute, on television, on line and on the radio. The coverage is immense.'

Harrison nodded, pausing to watch Martin Sigby's image as it was broadcast on a Japanese 24–hour news channel.

'I've never seen anything like it,' he admitted. 'I don't honestly believe that the news coverage of a conflict has ever before actually begun to affect the *course* of that conflict.'

'At least not as clearly as this,' Shelley said from his side, watching the broadcasts as she spoke. 'Sigby's last two reports have resulted in benign rebel movements further to the north–west of Thessalia, mostly occupying small villages. We have reliable reports from our other correspondents in the city that Royal Air Force reconnaisance flights have identified rebel convoys delivering aid within government controlled zones.'

'They're doing it for the beneficial coverage that they receive,' Harrison said.

'Pretty much, although whether anyone actually believes that these savages hold human rights in such high regard is questionable. Public opinion is still very much against their cause.'

'But it's also turning against the Mordanian government,' Harrison pointed out. 'Martin's reports have been on the front page of every major English speaking newspaper in the world, two days running.'

Another aide jogged up to Harrison Forbes's side.

'Boss, there's an urgent call for you from Seth Cain in Washington.'

Harrison felt a warm spot begin to glow within him. Finally, it seemed, Harrison Forbes had been put on the map of the high and mighty.

'I'll take it in my office,' he said and hurried across the newsroom, closing the door behind him and picking up the phone. 'Harrison Forbes.'

'Harry! You've been making some serious waves my friend.'

'It's all down to my man on the ground there, Seth. He's pulling off a remarkable job.'

'Figures are the highest I've ever seen for a UK reporter,' Seth confirmed. *'However, Harry, there's something of a problem here.'*

'Problem?'

'Yeah, Harry, I don't really know how to tell you this, but the word is that we really need to pull Martin Sigby from the story.'

'What?!!'

'Harry, I know how you feel, but this isn't a decision that's being made lightly here. There's a real fear that his success in covering this conflict could have repercussions beyond what we're seeing right now.'

Harrison Forbes's skin darkened beneath his beard, and he became aware of people outside watching him as he boomed into the phone.

'Beyond finding the truth? You consider the truth a repercussion? Against who exactly?'

'The people of Mordania, Harry,' Cain said, trying to sound reasonable. *'Nobody knows how far this thing's going to go now that it's running. There are a few big wheels in the senate and the administration who don't like what they're seeing here. It's new and it's unpredictable, and you know how these political types can get agitated when they feel they're not in control of things.'*

'You're damned right I do!' Harrison yelled. 'They usually start shitting themselves because they fear that someone's turned whistleblower on them, or that they've been photographed with a cheap hooker in a roadside hotel or been busted for tax evasion. Don't screw around with me Seth, tell me why this is happening.'

There was a long pause on the line.

'Let's just say that those to whom we answer don't want the boat rocked in Mordania any further than it has been already. They don't like seeing a democratic government being criticised whilst it's facing an non–democratic uprising, a rebellion. They fear that it undermines trust in what democratic rule can do, and that it could potentially damage the advance of democracy into the developing world.'

Harrison Forbes thought for a moment.

'Utter crap. These countries chose democracies because they wanted them, not because the rest of the world suggested it was a good idea. What you really mean is that someone, somewhere will probably stand to lose a lot of money, respect or credibility if Martin Sigby continues to tell the truth. They don't like the fact that he can't be controlled.'

'Your words, Harry, not mine. That's the deal and we're stuck with it.'

'We? You mean *me*!'

'That's the way it is Harry, and it's on you to ensure that Martin Sigby bows gracefully out of the Mordanian arena.'

Harrison stood for a long moment, holding the phone in a vice–like grip before speaking.

'No.'

There was a long pause.

'That is not an option, Forbes.'

'I'm not pulling Martin Sigby off Mordania because of political niceties. He's staying.'

'Don't make me come over there.'

'Up yours!'

Harrison slammed the phone down in utter disbelief. He ran a hand across his head and then looked out of his office windows to where his entire staff stood frozen in silence, watching him.

'Do I look like a sodding ornamental side–show?! Get back to bloody work!'

*

Government House, Thessalia

'The president will see you now, Mister Sigby.'

The secretary pointed toward the door of the president's personal suite. Martin Sigby crept forward, swallowed, and opened the door.

He had been caught entirely unawares by the request for a personal meeting with President Akim. His senses felt as though they were supernaturally attuned, hearing the touch of his shoes on the thick carpet, flames licking wood in an ornate grating, his own breathing in his ears.

The suite was, like most of the rooms in the building, expansive, and was also one of the few that was heated, the crackling fire glowing on the opposite side of the room. The president stood in front of the hearth with his hands behind his back, facing away from Martin as the reporter quietly closed the door behind him.

'Mister Sigby,' the president's voice rumbled.

'Yes, sir?' Martin said uncertainly, wondering briefly whether the man had eyes in the back of his head.

President Mukhari Akim turned away from the fire and regarded Martin Sigby's diminutive form with a curious expression.

'Please, sit,' he said.

Martin Sigby took a seat on one of the plush sofas and realised for the first time that the Chief of Police, Alexei Severov, stood nearby in the shadows, his arms folded across his chest and his expression stony. The president produced two tumblers from a cabinet in one corner of the room, along with a decanter of dark liquor. He poured two glasses, handing one to the correspondent before pacing slowly up and down the room as he spoke.

'You have enjoyed remarkable success here in Mordania, Mister Sigby. You must be eager to continue your work.'

Martin Sigby felt overwhelmed by the sense that he was in the presence of an intellect far greater than his own.

'I seek only to report the truth of what is happening here, to the people of the world.'

President Mukhari nodded, taking a long and thoughtful sip of his drink before turning and facing Martin Sigby directly.

'And yet you speculate, Mister Sigby. You make uneducated guesses about the state of this country, and those guesses put ideas into the minds of people. They ruminate and discuss and debate in their homes and their governments and in their rebel bases. They make judgements based upon your innaccurate assessments of the safety or otherwise of this country, and upon those judgements they do this government an ill service.'

The president moved to tower over Martin Sigby, who grasped his glass tightly as the president spoke.

'You are becoming famous for being the man who has changed the face of a country with his reports, who has perhaps begun to influence the course of a war with his broadcasts. But neither yourself nor your viewers have stopped to consider the possibility that the effect will worsen events, not improve them.'

Martin Sigby got up from the sofa, feeling uncomfortable being dominated by Mukhari's sheer presence. His voice sounded reedy and thin in the room compared to the president's deep and melodious tones.

'We report what we see. Our work is unbiased and shows only what is happening. It is hardly my fault if your government and its police are no longer able to provide security for the people living in Thessalia and the surrounding areas.'

President Akim's eyes seemed as deep as the universe as he looked down at Sigby, and the reporter began to feel as though the enormous pressures bearing down on this man's shoulders were somehow being transferred to his own. The president raised the thick index finger of one large hand to point at the correspondent's chest.

'You report to the world that we are unable to protect our own, Mister Sigby, and yet do not consider the consequences of such brazen and dangerous statements. Out there, beyond the mountains, lays a force of more than ten thousand men who will stop at nothing to destroy everything that I represent. They advance with neither fear nor mercy. They are well equipped and well trained, and have already proven themselves savage fighters with no desire to give quarter to those they conquer. They come closer by the day, moving even as we speak, to bring fire and sword to this city.'

The president was leaning toward Sigby, his powerful frame seeming to fill the room. Suddenly, he seemed to realise his proximity to the British correspondent and backed away.

'I am responsible,' the president went on, 'for the lives of the two million people who consider themselves Mordanians, people who are proud to call themselves so. Do you have any idea how incredibly frustrating it is to be made aware on a daily basis that I am failing them? That they become more disappointed with each passing day? That they may even now ridicule me under their breath, or hate me, perhaps even yearn for the rebel attack that must soon come to these walls?'

Sigby did not reply, unable to speak, as though some great pressure on his chest had trapped his thoughts and his voice. The president looked into the flames of the fire, his voice distant now.

'I fought in a war, in Afghanistan, when Russia invaded from the north. I saw my friends die, saw good men fall as the young so often do, in mud and horror and pain and confusion. I swore to myself that if I ever achieved an office of any kind of stature, that I would never commit men to such terrible actions except in an act of self defence.'

He turned back to Martin Sigby, his expression both proud and saddened, his voice raw with grief.

'I never have, until now, until there was no other choice. This last stand is that of a man who was voted into power by the people he wished to serve, and then saw his legitimate government defied by the very people who swore to defend it. I have nothing left, and this country has nothing left, if it cannot hold on to the principles of government that it chose for itself and that I swore to uphold. Your reports, describing the weakness and ineptitude of my staff, are hastening that downfall. You, sir, are destroying what's left of the country and constitution that I built for the benefit of all Mordanians.'

Martin Sigby stood his ground, shaking his head.

'My reports have uncovered the things that you refused the rest of the world the right to see. You banned foreign journalists from travelling through your country. You denied your own people the one thing that a democracy demands – a free press. By defying their own wishes, by going against the principles that you claim to uphold, you made it inevitable that somebody would eventually find a way to reveal what was happening here. You caused the problem by concealing your government's failures!'

'And you compounded the problem by blaming me for them,' the president replied. 'You have made me look weak, a laughing stock to my own people and to the international community. Did it not cross your mind, Mister Sigby, that I might have wanted to protect the lives of foreign journalists in Thessalia with the travel ban, because I knew that I would not be able to protect them outside of the city?'

Martin Sigby shook his head dismissively.

'Foreign journalists understand the risks they take, sir.'

'Did it not occur to you then, that by preventing journalism from exposing the weakened conditions of this city, I was also preventing a brutal and aggressive enemy from knowing the true state of affairs and thus delaying their decision to advance and attack?'

Martin Sigby hesitated uncertainly, and then swallowed.

'It did not,' he admitted.

The president shook his head slowly.

'There is more to this conflict than your stories, Mister Sigby. There is so much that you do not consider, fail to understand, lack the experience to translate into a meaningful interpretation of a country in crisis. Two million souls, Mister Sigby. Two million people rely now not upon what I say, as they should, but upon what *you* say.'

'That was not my intention,' Sigby said.

From the shadows, Severov spoke for the first time. 'Yet it is the result of your actions.'

The president set his glass down on a table, not looming over Sigby as before but addressing him frankly.

'Do you want to lead my people into the chaos and terror of conflict and possible conquest by a violent and implacable enemy? Or will you provide them with the spirit they need to defend themselves in this, their darkest of hours?'

Martin Sigby's eyes narrowed slightly.

'What do you mean?'

'What I mean is, will you report on the truth of the desire of my government to lead its people from this conflict and into the light of democracy and freedom? Or will you continue to undermine it with your reports on how the rebels bring aid to the needy while I stand by and ignore their suffering?'

Martin Sigby opened his mouth to speak, but no sound issued forth.

'You're being used of course,' Alexei Severov said from one side, moving out into the light. 'The rebels act only because they know that you will duly report their deeds to the outside world. Do you really think that such savages will continue to aid the needy once you have gone, once this war is over?'

'I must report what is true.'

'Yet how can you be sure of what is true?' the president challenged. 'Or what is false?'

Severov smiled slightly in the flickering light of the fire, moving closer.

'Perhaps we could help you, to find the truth.' Sigby saw President Akim shoot Severov a sharp look, but the Chief of Police went on. 'I could give you absolute and legal access to the interior, without barriers. You could literally become the only man actually allowed to traverse Mordania, and send your reports without fear of census or arrest. And I will ensure that you are rewarded well for your work, both professionally and financially.'

President Akim opened his mouth to protest, but Martin Sigby's eyes began to sparkle with barely restrained excitement.

'In exchange for what?' Sigby asked, unable to remove the image of Megan Mitchell from his mind. 'What would you want of me?'

Again, Severov smiled, glancing briefly at President Akim before speaking.

'Here is what you must do.'

***

24

'They were all scientists?'

Sophie Vernoux stood beside Megan Mitchell in the UN offices of Government House as a Red Cross officer relayed to them what the investigation team had managed to learn about the bodies found in the forest.

'All of them. We know that the Red Cross teams have found evidence of broken laboratory equipment amongst the debris of the main building. Taken with the attire of the dead men, it would seem likely that they were at the very least working in some kind of controlled laboratory conditions.'

Sophie shook her head in confusion.

'Why would these people be killed in this way? What on earth could they have been researching to get themselves murdered?'

The assistant shrugged his shoulders.

'There's no evidence to identify what they were working on,' he said dejectedly. 'This may simply have been an act of random violence. There's nothing to suggest a motive for anyone to attack this site or the people employed within it.'

'Has their been any formal identification of the victims?' Megan asked.

The assistant nodded and produced a sheet of paper.

'Seventeen of the victims were local men with either identifiable dental records or visually recognisable despite their condition.'

Megan took the sheet and scanned down the list before reaching the name she had desperately hoped not to see. *Petra Milankovich.* Sophie saw the look on her face.

'He's one of the victims, isn't he,' she said softly.

Megan nodded and handed the piece of paper back to the officer. She thought for a moment and then walked briskly out of the room. Sophie followed, hurrying to keep up with her.

'What are you going to do?' she asked, convinced by the purposeful nature of Megan's stride that she was up to something.

'We're going to have to get this out to the world, and quickly. There's nothing random about this: those people were killed for a reason. The perpetrators were seeking to destroy everything, not just the workers. There's something being covered up here.'

'What makes you so sure?' Sophie asked.

'The burning of an entire village would probably have been visible for miles around for hours, and yet nobody bothered to investigate at an official level. There were no phone calls, no emergency services requested, no nothing. That research facility, or whatever it was, wasn't so isolated that locals would not have realised it was under attack, much less on fire.'

Sophie thought for a moment as she kept pace with Megan.

'The country was at war by then. Local people might have been afraid, would not have wanted to get closer or to get involved. They might have just ignored the flames and the gunfire.'

Megan nodded, understanding that the people living in the foothills might have indeed wished to avoid the fighting.

'I'm running out of options here.'

'Why do you not ask Martin Sigby to help?' Sophie asked. 'He could broadcast the fact that Amy is missing, non? The more people that know about her, the more chance there is of someone coming forward who knows something.'

Megan winced.

'Sigby won't do a damn thing unless there's something in it for him.'

'Perhaps you could disguise your request.'

'What do you mean?' Megan asked, stopping in the corridor.

Sophie wrapped her coat around her more tightly and hugged herself against the cold.

'I don't know, maybe give her the name of the person that Amy was looking for. It is one of the dead men, so it is relevant to the story, non? A connection?'

Megan blinked, thinking for a moment.

'It may be a way to get this out in the open a little more,' she agreed as she walked out into the cold air outside Government House. 'But I still don't know if Sigby can be trusted and besides, if Amy is being held against her will or has been killed then the people responsible will know that we're searching for her. It could make it all much harder for us.'

'Or it could bring people forward,' Sophie replied. 'You have said it yourself, Megan. You are out of options.'

*

'I'm busy.'

Martin Sigby's tone was stiff and unfriendly, but Megan remained standing in the doorway to his room in the Thessalia Hilton, blocking his exit.

'It's important, Martin.'

'So is my next broadcast,' Sigby snapped back.

'Without me, you don't *have* a next broadcast.'

Martin Sigby smiled, his eyes squinting tightly as he did so.

'I'm getting a bit tired of this back–scratching game of yours, Mitchell. You've been shoving it up my arse for days now and I really need a break.'

'Fine,' Megan capitulated. 'We have some more footage from the Red Cross investigation and it's yours, okay? But I need you to do something for me.'

'What?' Sigby uttered.

Megan produced one of the photographs of Amy O'Hara.

'This girl, the person that we've been looking for. There's a strong possibility that she is connected to one of the murdered people from Borack.'

Martin Sigby raised an eyebrow. 'And how would you have come to that conclusion?'

'I have evidence that she was communcating for some months with an individual from Mordania, whom she eventually travelled here to meet. Bear in mind that she did so when the civil–war had already begun, so whatever it was that brought her here, it was important. She was last seen heading north for the town of Talyn.'

'You think that she's amongst the dead?'

'I did, but they haven't found any female bodies. I think that whatever happened in that village, she was not killed. However, that does not mean that she wasn't there.'

'What do you want me to do?'

Megan handed him a sheet of paper with a few notes scribbled upon it.

'This is a brief of everything we know so far, including the name of the person we believe Amy was searching for, Petra Milankovich. I want you to include it in your next broadcast. Callum and I are fast running out of ways to locate her, Martin, and with the fighting drawing closer we're less able to get out of Thessalia.' Megan looked at Sigby for a moment. 'We need this, Martin, if we're to get her back. If there's a name that can be connected to Amy, something tangible to follow, then we can move on it.'

'There's only so much time in our broadcast window,' Sigby said abruptly, looking at the sheet. 'I don't know how much I'll be able to get in.'

'As much as you can,' Megan said, handing over a Flash–Ram drive and a business card. 'The footage Callum got today. All of the victims were scientists, that's the verdict of the Red Cross team on site right now. This was an act of genocide. This business card belongs to Frank Amonte, who first approached me about Amy's disappearance. If you need anything else regarding the story, he'll back you up. Just say it's on my behalf.'

Martin Sigby looked at Megan in confusion.

'All this will do is draw attention to her fate and perhaps give those who are holding her or murdered her a headstart. They'll run.'

'I need to get access to the interior again, but further than the site of the massacre. There is an airfield, somewhere north of the village, that an old farmer we met at Borack mentioned as being connected to the site. We think that it was being used to supply the laboratory. I need access to it. There may be clues there both to Amy's whereabouts and to what was being done at the facility. If it can be linked to the events there, it may be considered important enough for an armed convoy to check it out.'

Martin's eyes narrowed thoughtfully. 'And you'll be on that convoy, correct?

Megan did not reply. Instead, she turned and walked away down the corridor outside.

***

25

Congress of the United States of America,

Washington DC

'So they've been bugging you again, Richard?'

President Matthew Baker spoke discreetly out of the corner of his mouth, looking around at the congress as its members settled into their chairs. Vice President Richard Hobbs sighed mightily.

'Every day. They're lobbying like never before for us to move into Mordania. I've told them in no uncertain terms that this administration will not involve our country in another military venture without absolute conditions being met, and that Mordania does not meet those criteria. I might as well be talking to myself.'

The president smiled.

'Let me guess – the petrochemicals industry, maybe some automotive, manufacturing, that sort of thing?'

'All of them,' Hobbs confirmed, but then added thoughtfully, 'although there's another one barking up my tree now, louder than the rest. Seth Cain.'

'The media magnate? What's his stake in the field?'

'Who knows? He's never tried to use leverage like he did when we last met. You'd have thought his financing of your campaign was a damned take–over bid. He was acting like he had the right to be sitting where you're sitting now.'

The President frowned thoughtfully.

'We've seen this before, Richard. Look at some previous administrations, infested with right–wing evangelicals demanding that abortion be criminalised, or that evolution not be taught in schools, and all of it based on nothing more than the bigotry of the believers and the greed for power of their heirachy. This is no different. The evangelicals thought that they had God on their side and thus were justified to do anything – these corporations hassling you are among the most powerful on earth and believe they are more valuable and more powerful than us, their government.'

Hobbs shook his head.

'It's not the same, Mister President. The God–Squad aren't followed by America because there are enough sane people left to point out the flaws in their ideaology. But these guys, their motivations are concealed and the voters don't see what they're up to, especially people like Seth Cain. His ilk control virtually the entire media output of the United States. If he wants us to look bad he can damn well make us look bad, and by six o'clock tonight too.'

President Baker nodded as the Speaker of the House introduced him.

'Then we shall have to make sure that we keep a close eye on all of them, so that they never come under the impression that they can influence this government, no matter how much money they may have. Agreed?'

The vice president nodded, but he looked uncertain as a brief but rapturous applause filled the House. The president took to the dais, aware of the ever–present cameras and the news feeds that were watching him as he spoke.

'Ladies and Gentlemen of the House, Madam Speaker, thank you. As you will of course be aware, the recent budget requests that were submitted to Congress included the military spending paper, and that certain demands were made by congress of the administration concerning the usage of those funds in our military operations worldwide. There were concerns, across all parties, regarding the intentions of this administration toward foreign partners in conflict zones around the globe.'

The president, as was his habit, did not look at his notes when speaking

'I think that it has become clear to all of us that our country's foreign policy has often lacked the subtlety and attention to cultural divide that seperates the United States of America from our foreign cousins overseas. We have in the past presented a belligerrent, dominionist, heavy–handed face to those without the military might to stand against us, and have gone backwards in our rescinding of important treaties in place since the end of the Cold War.

'I would like to make it clear now, to the House, to the Speaker and to the citizens of this country, that the foreign policies that I upheld in my campaign, the promises that I made regarding American military presence worldwide, will be upheld. I do not, and will not, send any more sons and daughters of America into conflict unless we ourselves have been attacked. Our fighting forces have operated on a policy for decades that has served them well. That policy is that we do not fire until we are fired upon. We have ignored that policy at our peril over the past few years.'

President Matthew Baker looked around the House for a moment before speaking again.

'No more.' A quiet ripple of applause sounded through the House as he went on. 'From this moment on, our military strategy will revert to one of defence, not offence, and we will once again try to build bridges with those countries that have suffered beneath the might of unwarranted military aggression, wherever it may have occurred. Thank you.'

The ripple of applause suddenly thundered into a standing ovation as President Baker re–took his seat beside Vice President Hobbs. Hobbs leaned in close as he clapped, keeping the smile on his face for the benefit of the cameras as he spoke.

'Now we'll see what Cain puts across the news tonight.'

'Let him,' President Baker replied. 'The people of this country want peace, as do the people of all countries. Nothing Cain can say or do will change that.'

*

Principality of Monaco,

Cote D'Azure

Sherman Kruger watched his television as the Speaker of the House re–took the dais from the president and began speaking to congress. As he watched, he dialled a number on his phone, waiting for a reply. When it came, he spoke in a determined voice.

'They have betrayed our faith and our trust, and we must act accordingly.'

The foreign voice on the other end of the line was crisp and clear.

'Our friends in the Middle East will be keen to see success, but they also fear retribution should our methods be discovered. Are you sure this will work without complications? I have a great deal to lose if this should fail.'

'All will go according to plan. Just be sure that you play your role accordingly, and everything else will be taken care of. You forget, my friend, that you also have much to gain should we succeed. I take it that your payment is…, adequate?'

'More than, Mister Kruger. More than.'

Sherman Kruger replaced the phone in its cradle and leaned back in his leather chair, watching the television as the camera focused on the president, on his expression of concentration as he listened to the speaker.

'America belongs to me, Mister President,' Kruger rasped to himself.

***

26

'Do we have a connection?'

Martin Sigby stamped his feet against the cold night air as he stood on the roof of the Thessalia Hilton and watched his cameraman, Robert, tweaking the controls on their satellite dish.

'It should link any second,' Robert replied, pressing a button on a laptop computer and sitting back on his haunches patiently.

Sigby looked at his watch. Two minutes to go–live. The sound of distant mortar rounds impacting ancient earth rumbled on the air, a faint flash of light flickering against the low clouds enveloping the mountains.

'Make sure the camera sees that action,' Sigby instructed, gesturing with a nod of his head toward the sounds of battle. 'Always looks good on film.'

Robert nodded, and took up his position behind the camera. He pressed a finger to his ear as he heard their connection link up. The screen of the laptop flickered and an image of the news appeared, streamed directly via digital–link from the broadcasting satellite. Sigby could see the GNN anchor for the night, Charlotte Dennis, adjusting her skirt and hair as the broadcast prepared to go live from the UK. He watched her with interest, and then heard the call to go live. Charlotte finishing tidying herself and looked directly at the camera as the countdown and introductory music sounded over the speakers.

'Good evening, welcome to the six o'clock news. I'm Charlotte Dennis.'

'Oh, I know you are,' Sigby whispered to himself as he prepared to go live.

'Our headline tonight; in the war–torn capital of Mordania, more disturbing images and extraordinary exclusive reports from our correspondent on the scene. We go live now to Thessalia, where Martin Sigby is ready to talk to us about today's develoments in the conflict. Martin, can you hear me?'

*

Megan and Callum sat alongside three old women with broken teeth, crouched in old rags, sipping their hot coffee and hugging UN supplied thermal blankets to keep out the cold.

They, like everyone else in the MSF tent, were watching the report from Mordania as it was broadcast from the capital.

'I can hear you, Charlotte,' Martin Sigby said as he appeared on the split screen with the anchor in London.

'Martin, I understand that there have been several new developments in the genocide investigation inside Mordania, is that correct?'

Megan looked at Callum.

'Here's where we find out whether we get our ticket in–country or not,' she whispered.

'That's right, Charlotte. There have been surprising advances in the understanding of what has occurred here in Mordania, sufficiently so for the president himself to make an official announcement to the world's press. I can tell you, Charlotte, that I have spoken personally with President Mukhari Akim and bring news of his plans for his country in this, its darkest of hours.'

Callum raised an eyebrow and looked at Megan.

'He's gotten himself friends in high places. How'd he manage that?'

'I don't know,' Megan said.

The image of Martin Sigby was suddenly replaced with that of President Mukhari Akim, standing in his personal chamber. He addressed the camera directly, his face impassioned, his gestures articulate.

'Citizens of the west, I speak to you now from the remnants of what was once a great and proud country, on behalf of a people who had embraced democracy and had hoped to embark upon a road to prosperity and inclusion within the international community. Sadly, due to the brutal and dangerous regime that now seeks to wrest power from the democratically elected government which I lead, those hopes are now the ashes of dreams.'

Megan watched as the president gestured out of the windows of the room in which he stood.

'Out there, advancing swiftly and without mercy, are ten thousand rebel soldiers who are intent on destroying everything that my government has sought to build. They are pitiless in their killing, slaying men, women and children without hesitation. They prefer anarchy to democracy, violence to dialogue, war to peace.' The president hesitated before finishing. *'And I cannot stop them.'*

'What's this?' Callum asked in surprise, as Sophie Vernoux came over to join them.

'I am appealing to the world, to the United Nations, to the United States, to anyone with a will, for help in repelling the imminent attack of the rebel force under the command of the traitor General Mikhail Rameron. I and my men cannot protect the city of Thessalia. Our forces are already depleted and retreating before the might of the rebel army.'

The president moved closer to the camera, his eyes blazing with both deference and desperation.

'I am aware that the United States is seeking a more pacifist approach to its foreign policy, and that the United Nations is reluctant to intefere directly in the affairs of sovereign nations, but what you are seeing here in Mordania is not the collapse of a regime or the fall of a dictator. This is the total destruction of a democracy, like yours, like the ones you so proudly hold up to be the model for good governance around the world. This is what you wanted from us. This is what you told us we should do, what our people would want. We did it. It is being destroyed. I implore you – help us, for we can no longer help ourselves.

The camera lingered on his face for a moment longer, and then snapped back to the silent faces of Charlotte Dennis in her studio and Martin Sigby in Thessalia.

'Extraordinary,' Charlotte said. *'Remarkable words there from President Mukhari Akim, and at a time when the west is trying to distance itself from engagement in foreign conflicts. Martin, you say that there have also been developments within Mordania itself? And how will President Akim's statement affect the situation in Mordania?'*

Megan leaned close, expectantly.

'Well, Charlotte, considering the announcement today by the President of the United States Matthew Baker, I suspect that Mukhari Akim's words may fall on agonised but none the less deaf ears in Europe. The United Nations is powerless to intervene in Mordania without agreement from its member nations and a program for moving forward, which of course cannot occur without the attendent resolution invoking a military solution to the conflict. However, the United States is not beholden to such resolutions and in light of the most recent discoveries here in Mordania, may decide on their own whether to intervene.'

'And what are those discoveries, Martin?'

'They are, Charlotte, that the individuals found murdered two days ago in a village in Mordania were actually combatants who may have been fighting here in Mordania, and not innocent scientists.'

Megan's blood ran cold as she stared at the screen.

'You're saying that they were not the victims of a genocide at all, but fighters themselves?' Charlotte asked in surprise.

'That's right, Charlotte. The Red Cross managed with the help of the Mordanian military police to identify one of the dead men as a Petra Milankovich. At about this time, the Mordanian police uncovered a cache of arms on the site of the massacre, most of which were stamped with the numbers of weapons that according to government records belonged to the Mordanian Air Force Regiment, whose men make up a considerable bulk of the rebel factions.'

Megan felt devoid of feeling, her own heartbeat a distant throbbing.

'That's not true,' she heard herself whisper.

'But if that's the case, then who killed them?' Charlotte enquired.

'The investigators do not know that at this time, Charlotte, but the feeling here on the ground is that they may have been an advance force of rebels who were fleeing General Mikhail Rameron's insurgency and trying to return home. They were caught hiding in this village by their former comrades, murdered, and the village burned to the ground as a warning to other potential deserters. It's a stark demonstration of the mercurial nature of the fighting forces here in Mordania.'

Charlotte Dennis waved her pencil in the air thoughtfully as she spoke.

'And there's nothing at all suggesting why they may have decided to occupy what appeared to be laboratories, or indeed what those laboratories were for?'

'Nothing, Charlotte. It was most likely just chance that they were caught where and when they were. The general feeling here is that no connection can be found because there is none. It would seem that the big story right now is President Mukhari's heart–felt plea to the world, and how the world reacts to it. Martin Sigby, Thessalia, Mordania.'

Megan stared into space for several long seconds with an expression drained of emotion, Callum and Sophie watching her.

Then she lurched to her feet and shot out of the tent at a run.

***

27

Megan raced into the Thessalia Hilton with Callum and Sophie in hot pursuit.

Megan stormed up the stairs to the first floor and turned toward Martin Sigby's room in time to see Sigby walking toward them with his cameraman just behind. She pointed one arm like a shotgun at him.

'Sigby!'

Martin Sigby looked up and saw Megan bearing down upon him. He halted in the corridor and his face blanched, but he stood his ground.

'You lied!' Megan shouted as advanced toward him. 'You lied about the scientists! It wasn't the truth!'

Sigby drew himself up to his full height, raised his chin and scoffed dismissively as Megan reached him.

'I reported only what I have been told by the police.'

'Bollocks!'

Megan swung for the correspondent's face, telegraphing her punch around with full power and maximum rage. Her fist smacked into Sigby's jaw with a dull crack that lifted the reporter off the floor and propelled him backward past Robert. Sigby ricocheted off a nearby wall and spun as he dropped onto the grubby carpet.

Megan was about to hit Sigby's stunned and cowering cameraman for good measure when she felt herself lifted bodily off the floor in a bear grip. Callum pulled her backwards and away from the innocent man.

'All right Rocky,' Callum said, 'that's enough.'

Callum released Megan but remained next to her as Sophie barged past them both. She knelt down next to Sigby, whose eyes were rolling loosely in their sockets, and pulled the journalist up into a sitting position as he gradually regained consciousness. Sigby shook his head, massaging his jaw as his brain re–booted itself. His memory returned at the same time as the pain hit him and he saw Megan glowering down at him.

'You're worth nothing,' Megan snapped. 'You're worse than scum, you're not worth the ground that scum walk upon.'

A bolt of latent fury snapped down Sigby's spine and he staggered to his feet.

'To hell with you, Mitchell! Who the hell do you think you are, coming in here and telling me what I should and shouldn't say? You've nothing to offer me now. You're old news!'

Megan struggled to prevent herself from striking out again.

'You lied! There were no guns in that village, those people were not soldiers and you know it. You've been paid off, haven't you!'

Sigby wiped his nose on his sleeve, avoiding Megan's penetrating glare. Sophie, who was still steadying the correspondent by the shoulder, released him as though he were diseased. Megan stalked closer.

'Somebody didn't want those bodies found and they got to you, didn't they?'

'There's more to it than that, Mitchell,' Sigby spat back. 'There's a country at stake here and there are people trying to save it. They need help and international intervention is how they can get it. I did it for them.'

'Bollocks!' Megan shot back. 'You've never done a damn thing for anyone else in your life without something in return. You're paid to learn the truth and convey it to the rest of the world. Instead you take money from liars and say what they tell you to, like a poodle to its master.'

Sigby sneered at Megan, pointing an accusing finger at her.

'Don't think that I don't know what you're up to, Mitchell! You've been up to something ever since you came here. It's probably the reason *why* you came here. You've smelt another opportunity, haven't you, another chance for Megan Mitchell to profit from the suffering of those around her.'

Sophie looked questioningly at Megan, but she ignored her.

'What the hell are you talking about? You're the one who's taking back–handers. Who was it? Severov? The president?!'

'Oh, and you're a fine one to talk about being paid off!' Sigby uttered. 'Megan Mitchell, investigative reporter extraordinaire, who frolicks around the globe with her fancy stories and her wonderful reports! But then, alas, it all falls apart and you end up wandering around the world on a wild goose–chase looking for yourself, ending up somewhere in the Malay with nothing but booze to keep you company and no money to buy even that!'

Sophie glanced from Martin Sigby to Megan, her eyes wide as she tried to digest the unexpected nature of what she was hearing.

Megan's features emptied of expression, her gaze cold and direct as Martin Sigby jabbed a finger in her direction, his face screwed up with contempt.

'And then, lo and behold, you make your oh–so glorious return from the depths of poverty to sudden grandeur, living in the finest of penthouses and with enough money in the bank to never work again, a boat in the marina and who knows what else!?'

Sigby was standing in front of Megan now, ablaze with righteous indignation.

'And you're telling me that you, the great and good Megan Mitchell, doesn't know about being paid off?! Tell me, Megan, how was it done? What did you do, eh? Who paid *you* off? Because if they hadn't you'd be locked up in a mental home with the rest of the fruit–loops, so don't talk to me about being paid off!!'

The corridor fell silent as Megan stood immobile before Martin Sigby. For several long seconds nobody moved. Sigby's rage withered in the silence as he stared uncertainly at Megan, who remained utterly motionless as though carved from granite. When she finally spoke, her voice sounded as though it came from another planet.

'If Amy O'Hara had a chance of survival in this country then you just ruined it with your broadcast, because you didn't tell the truth.'

Sigby's indignance vanished as a wave of self–loathing churned through his stomach. Megan turned away from Sigby and walked down the hall toward her own room.

Callum silently followed Megan away down the hall. Sophie watched them go, and then looked at Sigby with an expression of such utter disgust that the correspondent physically wilted beneath her gaze.

***

28

'She'll want to be left alone. I'm going to stay down the sergeant's mess tonight.'

Callum had put on his jacket and closed the door of the room he shared with Megan.

'She might want to talk,' Sophie protested.

Callum snorted a brief laugh and turned away down the corridor. 'Don't say I didn't warn you.'

Sophie hesitated for several moments before gingerly knocking on Megan's door. A feint voice sounded from within the room.

'Go away. Drinking.'

Sophie smiled faintly. 'I know, I want some too.'

There was a moment's silence and then the door opened, Megan standing before her. Sophie waited expectantly and Megan finally backed away and let her into the room, closing the door after her.

'You certainly have a way with people,' Sophie said as she stood in the centre of the room.

'Gentle touch,' Megan replied. 'From my mother's side.'

She moved across to a table, where a bottle of Single Malt stood with two tumblers. She gestured demonstratively to them.

'Care to share?'

'Merci, madame.'

Megan poured Sophie a glass and one for herself before sitting in the crooked chair at the table. Sophie, cradling her tumbler, sat on the edge of the bed looking at her.

'Bad day,' Sophie observed quietly.

'I've had better.'

'Would you like to talk about it?'

'I'd prefer to forget it.'

'Things go away more easily if you talk them over.'

'I find it prolongs the agony.'

'You might think differently if you..,'

'What do you want?'

Megan's tone had changed dramatically, becoming hard–edged and cold like a blade. Sophie hesitated before speaking.

'I just want to help.'

Megan focused on one of the candles flickering on a nearby shelf.

'Doesn't everybody.'

Sophie took another sip of her drink, watching Megan as she did so. Megan looked at her own drink for a moment before speaking.

'What's your real name, Sophie?'

A long silence hung in the room, during which Sophie did not move nor speak. When she finally did her voice was quiet, as though the spirit and verve within her had suddenly and unexpectedly been vanquished.

'Sophie D'Aoust. It's an old name, from the Picardie region of northern France, so I'm told. Vernoux was from my mother's side, her maiden name.'

Megan nodded slowly, as though that explained everything. She took a sip of whisky and gasped as the liquor hit her throat.

'So why do you use it, and why are you here?'

Sophie sighed softly.

'My father, Pierre–Paul D'Aoust, was a farmer. He passed away two years ago. Our family is relatively wealthy, due to the ownership of a lot of land. I used to be proud of it, until I found out how he continued to make money even though the majority of our land lay fallow.' She turned to look at Megan. 'Did you know that if all of the fields of France were allowed to grow and distribute grain freely, there would not be a single person on earth who would be hungry?'

Megan shook her head, and Sophie went on, her expression pained.

'The fields of France, or of any similarly sized European country, are easily capable of feeding every human being on this planet. Famines should not occur. Do you know why they do? Money. Farmers are actually paid *not* to grow things, to prevent grain mountains forming from excess growth. We don't need the food, so farmers are subsidised by the government to not grow the food that could save millions of lives every year.'

'You rebelled,' Megan said with a faint smile.

'More than that,' Sophie said softly. 'I had trained as a nurse after school, but I quit my job and joined activist movements. We did demonstration, protests, trying to get people to change their ways. It didn't work, so some of our people decided to go further. They set fields on fire in southern France. One blaze got out of control, three people died, one of the victims himself an activist. Somehow word got out that I was the daughter of a farmer, the media got hold of the story, and before I knew it I was the poster–child of radical anarchistic groups.'

'Ah,' Megan murmured. 'That's why you hate journalists and reporters so much.'

'They lied,' Sophie said, 'twisted everything. I just wanted to make a statement, but they made me out to be an accomplice to murder. It all got out of hand and before I knew it I'd left France for Italy.' Sophie sighed again, hanging her head.

'You can't go home?' Megan said.

'No,' Sophie replied. 'I'd most likely be tried for manslaughter. Two other members of the protest group are serving time in prison for what they did. I was not a part of it but now it's too late to defend myself. I've come to accept it.'

Megan nodded, shocked by what she had heard and yet somehow immune to stories of hardship and injustice. People suffered: that was a part of life, just like breathing.

'The aid groups took you in though? They must have known who you really were?'

'Maybe,' Sophie said. 'But they need all the help they can get. I applied under my assumed name, I had enough sympathetic friends to get the necessary references, and my desire to help others proved the rest. I worked in Uganda and Afghanistan before coming here.'

'You've been to all of the finest places,' Megan observed.

A silence fell in the room, each of them lost in their own memories until Sophie looked up at Megan.

'Is it true, what Martin Sigby said?' she asked.

Megan sighed heavily, and chuckled to herself at the absurdity of it all.

'Which bit?'

Sophie shrugged, but kept watching in silence until Megan finally answered her question, staring into her drink as she did so.

'All of it's true, but all of it's bullshit at the same time. People have a way of taking what they hear about others and twisting it to suit their own opinions. Martin Sigby dislikes me intensely, so he twists the stories to make them sound worse.'

'Tell me what happened,' Sophie said.

'It's not worth the telling.'

'It is to me.'

Megan shook her head, looking away from Sophie and out of the window even though there was nothing to see but the inky blackness of another freezing night. Sophie put her glass down on the bedside table before speaking.

'Since you came here I have taken risks for you, letting you ride with our convoys. I know that you do what you do for a good cause but I think you owe it to me to at least convince me that I am not aiding and abetting a psychopath.'

'You really believe that I'm a nut–case?' Megan asked.

'No,' Sophie replied. 'That's why I want to know the truth. Isn't that what you said to Martin Sigby, that the truth was more important? You are a woman who seems to have many contradictions, Madame Mitchell. I just want to know who you are.'

Megan exhaled whisky fumes onto the cold air. She looked at Sophie for a long moment before whispering a name as though she were speaking of a ghost.

'James.'

Sophie stared at her for a moment, not daring to move. 'Is who?'

'Was,' Megan said, one half of her face starkly lit by the candles on the window sill and the other in deep shadow. 'James Mitchell was my father, also a journalist who worked for GNN. He was the one who got me into all of this, told me stories when I was growing up about the world around me, made me feel like so much was happening all the time, that it was all so exciting. We worked freelance, travelling together to wherever the news was, with Callum as cameraman and Pete Beke, a South African, as our technician. You name it, we were there. Europe, America, the Clinton trial, Bosnia, Mogadishu, Somalia. We covered everything, got some of the best footage ever broadcast. Networks would queue up to buy our material.'

Sophie watched Megan as she spoke, not looking at her but staring into the moving shadows sprawled like slumbering demons around the walls.

'We covered September 2001 in New York, took some of the major aftermath footage. It wasn't pretty. We both recognised that the terror attacks were something new, that a change was coming, that a new war had begun. It wasn't about terrorism but about control of a government over its people, about using the threat of terrorism to keep people afraid, which let governments surveil them more closely, pass laws giving the police unwarranted and unprecedented access to our lives.' Megan sighed. 'We decided to go to countries where corruption was worst, to show how things could become.'

'Where did you go? Sophie asked in a whisper.

'Mexico,' Megan replied. 'We'd uncovered a lot of reports from there of abductions, criminal syndicates that owned the police forces, a hostage–ransom industry, not to mention the trade in drugs coming from the forests of South America. We decided that it was worth investigating, and flew there to learn more.'

Megan took a deep breath, downing the rest of her glass before continuing.

'We wrote several articles that made the international press, but I guess that somehow we dug too deep or pissed off too many people who were making too much money to see their dirty little industries exposed and shut down. My father disappeared from Mexico City.'

Sophie stopped watching Megan, her own mind imagining that hot, violent city and its dangerous streets as Megan went on.

'I spent the next year searching for him. I used up all of our savings, sold everything we possessed, spent months scouring the jungles and the backstreets and hostels and villages for him. I printed thousands upon thousands of pictures of him and put them up all over the city.' She shook her head. 'I never heard a word, from anyone.'

Megan reached out for the bottle of whisky and poured herself another glass. Sophie waited patiently until she had swallowed another sip and went on.

'Then, a year to the day after he had vanished, I woke up in my hotel room to find a parcel at my door. In it was my father's head and hands.'

Sophie's throat clenched shut and she squeezed her eyes tight as she tried to prevent the horrific images and emotions that Megan must have experienced from penetrating her thoughts.

'When the money ran out I thought I'd just curl up and die, that there was no point in going on because there was nothing worth going on for. It was Amy O'Hara, the person we're searching for now, who had helped me all along from Chicago. She told me that there was nothing more that I could do, nothing that I could offer or provide that would bring my father back. That if I didn't leave Mexico I'd just destroy myself, if the drug cartels didn't decide to murder me first.'

'So I did. I worked a passage across the Pacific on a freighter out of Sau Paulo, wound my way across southern Australia and then up through the Malay Archipelago. I got as far as Singapore before the drinking cost more than I earned, and about there I hit rock–bottom. The thing about it was, I didn't care, didn't give a damn. I might just as well have been dead already.'

Megan fell silent as though caught in the web of her own traumatised memories, of months and years lost in a paralysis of grief. Sophie spoke softly in the half light.

'What happened next?'

Megan roused herself, perhaps from being hypnotised by the simultaneously warming and numbing effect of the alcohol, perhaps because she actually wanted to stay in a state of torpor, away from the world outside.

'Callum,' she said, with a faint smile. 'We'd stayed in touch until I'd reached Australia, where I lost my cell phone after a particularly heavy session in Melbourne. He knew that I was in the Malay because Pete Beke, the clever sod, was able to track some of my movements from expenses I'd put on my debit card, until it got blocked. Callum found me in Singapore.'

'And he brought you back home,' Sophie hazarded.

'Far from it. He brought me the news that somebody was looking for me. It turned out that a wealthy landowner in Sumatra, one of these property billionaires, had lost his daughter to Malay pirates, of all things. They're still pretty common out there. Ransoms had been demanded but nobody could find where she was being hidden. He'd heard about me after reading one of Amy O'Hara's reports on Mexico in the New York Journal.'

'He wanted you to search for his daughter?' Sophie asked, intrigued.

Megan nodded.

'I had nothing to lose and I had experience, so to speak, so Callum, Pete and I worked for the next three months to find her. It took a hell of a job and it was dangerous, really dangerous. Those pirates are savages, no doubt about it. But we found her and got her out.' She shook her head again. 'The stink of it was that the property magnate, her father, had been in league with these pirates all along, paying them to terrorise the local communities into moving out so that the magnate could buy the land cheap and build his resorts on it. When he failed to pay them one time, they took his daughter in revenge. In return, he refused to pay the ransom.'

Sophie shook her head in silence, and then she began to think about what Sigby had said about Megan's money and looked up at her.

'You blackmailed him,' she whispered. 'You sold out.'

'I had nothing left and no faith in life any more,' Megan replied. 'I didn't care. If we'd revealed what we knew about what this magnate had been up to, we could have brought him down completely. Under the law he would have been sent to jail for life, and no amount of money or connections would have saved him. We had his daughter and we could tell the police everything, so we gave him a choice. Pay us a healthy tax–free sum to make us happy and we'd forget it had happened, or else she could take his chances in the courts.'

Sophie watched Megan in the candlelight. 'How much?'

Megan smiled, a mercenary, ghostly little smile without warmth.

'Fifteen million, Sterling,' she said softly. 'Nothing to a man like him, everything to people like Callum, Pete and I. We split it evenly between us and then went our separate ways. Pete returned to South Africa, Callum to England to build his dream home, and I bought a boat and sailed it from Singapore to London. It's moored outside my apartment near Tower

Bridge. I named her *Icarus,* after the Greek story of a boy who flew too close to the sun and fell to his death, to remind me of what happened to my father. I take her out alone onto the ocean whenever I feel like I've had enough of people.'

Sophie smiled. 'So you like to disappear too, sometimes.'

Megan felt Sophie's penetrating gaze on her, but went on talking quietly.

'He was a great person, my father. You'd have liked him. He loved life. Always full of energy, always quick with a joke. One of those kind of people that you can't help but like.'

Megan voice started to become strained as though her vocal chords were being twisted.

'You can't begin to imagine what it's like to lose your own father like that, to see that he was beaten to a pulp even before they severed his hands and head. He was blind in both eyes long before he died, and most of his teeth were missing.'

Megan glanced around the cold room, not seeing Sophie any longer through her blurred and glistening eyes as she spoke.

'I've still got his wrist watch in my bag, can't travel without it, it's all I've got left of him…'

Megan's still–full glass dropped from her hand and shattered on the floor as she slid off the chair. Sophie launched herself off the edge of the bed and knelt down beside her, wrapping her arms around Megan as tightly as she could and holding her shaking body, not really sure what she should do next, sure only that she should not leave.

Megan calmed after a few minutes and rubbed the back of her hand across her eyes.

'Sorry,' she uttered, not looking at her.

'So am I.'

Without another word, Sophie helped Megan to her feet and walked her across to the bed, pulled back the sheets and directed her to lay down. Megan complied silently, and Sophie tucked Megan in before picking up the bottle and glasses and silently leaving the room.

Megan fell asleep within moments.

***

29

44th Parallel 'No Fly Zone'

Black Sea, 250km West of the Georgian coast

'Voodoo flight this is strike; contact, single target track bearing zero–eight–five at sixty five miles, heading two–four–zero degrees, inbound.'

Lieutenant Heather *'Miller'* Millard heard the call over the RT earpiece in her helmet and glanced at her Horizontal Situation Display. Her voice sounded distorted in her own ears over the intercom as she spoke.

'Copy strike, zero–eight–five, IFF transponder activated. Let's see who's coming out to play.'

The sky at thirty thousand feet was a perfect powder blue, the sun a flaring white orb. Heather adjusted the course of her F–18E Super Hornet with a deft flick of the control column, the agile jet responding instantly. She glanced out of her cockpit canopy to where a tiny sliver of grey metal seemed to hover against the pale blue void a mile away.

'You copy that, voodoo two?'

The answer from Lieutenant Mike *'Boomer'* Mitchell came back instantly.

'Roger that, maintaining battle flight, waiting for tactical. How d'you wanna play this?'

'Let's keep our cool and see who they are. It's probably just another wayward airliner.'

The two Super Hornets streaked through the ethereal high–altitude dawn, Heather maintaining her course and waiting for the tactical display to pick up the incoming target. Her own radar remained on stand–by to prevent the signal from betraying her location. Instead, one of the three Multi–Function–Display screens in the Hornet's cockpit displayed a radar image transmitted by a Grumman E2–C Hawkeye surveillance aircraft almost a hundred miles to the west of her position. With the Hawkeye doing the scanning, Heather could see the enemy and close on them without being detected until the last moment.

'Voodoo flight this is strike; take angels right, one–one–zero.'

USS Theodore Roosevelt (CVN–71)

US Navy Carrier Battle Group, Black Sea

'What's the trade?'

Admiral James Fry stood behind a teenage operative whose gaze was affixed to a complex radar screen. The operations room looked like a scene from *Star Wars* with its multiple displays and low lighting. An observer might never have deduced that they were standing on the bridge of the largest nuclear–powered aircraft carrier on earth.

'Single target,' the operative replied, 'coming in from the east, zero–eight–zero, flight level three–zero–zero. Identification Friend or Foe recorded as a negative response sir. No radio contact.'

Admiral Fry nodded, thinking for a moment as he turned to his Executive Officer.

'Flight path would have taken then clear over Georgia, assuming they've maintained the same trajectory.'

'Georgian air–space remains clear,' the XO replied. 'Nothing from them reporting any over–flights that shouldn't be there, but their radar coverage isn't the best.'

'Tactical approach?' Admiral Fry pressed.

'It's possible an aircraft could slip through the Georgian mountains undetected and then climb for height over the sea without anyone successfully tracking it.'

Admiral Fry nodded and made his decision.

'General Alert. Order Miller and Boomer onto a direct intercept course. Have the alert aircraft on deck to back them up.'

'Aye aye, sir.'

Without another word from the captain the huge aircraft carrier turned into the wind as half a squadron of F–18E's scrambled to flight readiness upon its flight deck. The radar operator spoke into his mic', watching the closing blips on his radar screen.

'Voodoo flight, you are a go for intercept.'

*

'Roger that, strike.'

Heather and Boomer's aircraft manoeuvered into position, one mile apart and with Boomer's F–18 two thousand feet higher than Heather's. The tactical separation enabled them to commit to aggressive turns against incoming aircraft without getting in each other's way and giving them options in the vertical to win the onrushing confrontation.

Heather keyed her microphone transmit button.

'Voodoo two, IFF negative, repeat IFF negative. Broadcast on all channels.'

Heather listened as Boomer's voice sounded on an all–frequency channel.

'Unidentified aircraft flight level three–zero–zero, heading two–five–zero, you are entering the controlled airspace of a United States Carrier Battle Group. Please identify.'

A hiss of empty static filled Heather's helmet earphones, an ominous silence that unnerved her. She listened as Boomer tried three more times on an open channel before finally calling the carrier and reporting no–joy.

Heather looked at her tactical display. The incoming aircraft was now within twenty nautical miles.

'Eight hundred knots closure, heading steady,' Boomer observed. *'It's coming right at us.'*

Heather was about to reply when she heard the crew of the Hawkeye over the RT.

'Voodoo flight, Lincoln One, be advised that the bogey is a pair, repeat one–pair, two aircraft in close formation.'

Heather felt a lance of anxiety bolt down her spine as she responded.

'Roger that Lincoln One. Boomer, fangs out!'

Instantly both pilots activated their Hornet's fire–control radar and set their weapons to 'active'. In a split second they had converted their aircraft from neutral interceptors to active aggressors.

'Ten miles,' Boomer called.

Heather could hear the slight tension in his voice.

'Easy, Boomer, here we go. No traumas.'

Heather's cockpit suddenly lit up like a Christmas tree and a warbling siren sounded in her ears. Boomer's voice was sharp over the sudden noise.

'Holy shit, we're being painted! Fire–control radar, they've got lock!!'

For several fractions of a second Heather's mind registered the flashing warning lights and the signals on her Heads–Up–Display, and then the words that she had thought she would never, ever hear slammed through the field of her awareness like a bullet through glass.

'Fox Two! Missile in the air!!'

The Hawkeye pilot's voice followed a second later. *'Missiles fired, Voodoo flight evasive now!!'*

Heather snapped out of her trance a split–second later.

'Defensive break!'

Heather slammed her control column over to the right and then hauled back on it, the Hornet rolling onto its side and loading up into an six–G hard–right break. Terrific centrifugal force slammed her into her ejection seat, her flight suit constricting her stomach and legs to prevent her blood from draining from her head and upper torso.

'Missile tracking voodoo one!'

Heather rolled her wings level and glimpsed the two enemy fighters in the distance and the fine trail of missile exhaust rocketing toward her aircraft. Heather's gloved hand changed position slightly on her throttle. She had put the incoming missile on her 'three–nine–line', travelling perpendicular to its line of flight. As it zoomed in at immense speed, all at once Heather dumped chaff and flare to distract the missile's sensors and hauled the Hornet into a parabolic dive, spiralling on all three axis at once in order to spoil the missile's chances of hitting her.

Heather saw nearly eight–G on her instruments as the Hornet gyrated violently through the sky, and suddenly the sirens in her cockpit went silent.

'Missile overshoot!' Boomer called. *'I'm engaging!'*

In the passing of a heartbeat, Heather Millard went from pure terror to cold fury, reversing her fighter's roll and breaking into a turn back in the direction the enemy aircraft had passed.

'Strike this is Voodoo One, do we have permission to fire?'

The response came through immediately.

'Voodoo one, Foxtrot Alpha Whisky; repeat, Fire At Will!'

Heather hauled her Hornet around its turn, her throttles in full–afterburner and she fought against the G–forces and searched the skies.

'Boomer, snap–visual!'

Boomer's voice came back, bursting with restrained tension.

'Bandits heading two–seven–zero, breaking left through twenty–eight thousand.'

Heather reacted without thought, pulling through her turn to head almost directly west and looking up a couple of thousand feet above her. Instantly she saw the two fighters, arcing left in a moderately hard turn, Boomer's F–18 curving into an attacking position behind them.

'They're Mig–23's,' Heather identified them. 'NATO call–sign Flogger.'

Closer to the aggressor aircraft, Boomer's call identified the enemy planes.

'They're Mordanian fighters. I can see the markings!'

Heather was closing in fast, watching as the two enemy aircraft continued their left turn. A strange sense of caution crept into her thoughts as she watched the enemy aircraft turning.

'They're not evading,' she said over the RT.

'Who cares?!' Boomer replied. *'I've got tone. Missile lock!'*

Instantly, the two Mordanian fighters split, one pulling hard right, the other rocketing upward into a vertical climb.

Boomer's F–18 went vertical in pursuit of the climbing Mig–23, and Heather followed him up, watching as Boomer fired.

'Fox Two!'

The short–range Sidewinder missile rocketed away off the Hornet's wing, and Heather watched as it tracked the Mig–23 pulling over the top of a loop. The hot jet exhaust silhouetted against the freezing blue sky made it an easy target. Seconds later, the heat–seeking missile slammed into the Mordanian fighter in a bright orange fireball, blowing half of the tail clean off and sending the forward section of the jet spiralling lazily down toward the distant clouds below, trailing a plume of oily black smoke.

'Splash one!' Boomer called jubilantly. *'Snap–visual on second bandit?'*

'I've got him,' Heather replied, 'eight o'clock low.'

As soon as Boomer's missile had struck home, Heather had pulled hard over the top of her own loop, diving back down toward the second Mig, which appeared to be trying to make a run for it toward the cloud layer fifteen thousand feet below.

'No way buddy,' Heather murmured to herself with cold determination.

The Sidewinder missile she had selected began to growl in her ear–phones as it signalled a firm lock on the fleeing fighter. Heather eased her fighter to point directly at the enemy Mig, and then fired.

'Voodoo One, Fox Two!'

The Sidewinder leapt off the wing–rail and shot away into the distance ahead of her Hornet, leaving behind it a distinctive weaving trail of smoke. She watched the weapon track for several seconds and then saw a bright plume of flame and smoke.

'Splash two!'

The Mordanian jet ahead of her spiralled down toward the clouds in a shallow flat–spin. Heather slowed her jet, watching the stricken Mig falling from the sky.

'Come on,' she urged the nameless pilot within the stricken aircraft, 'your game's up. Eject.'

She watched, her eyes fixed to the Mordanian fighter as it spiralled down. No parachutes emerged from the aircraft and it finally vanished from sight into the clouds far below.

'Voodoo Two, Boomer? You see any 'chutes?'

'Negative, no parachutes from bandit one.'

Heather felt a deep melancholia envelope her as she spoke into her RT.

'Strike, this is Voodoo Flight, all bandits down, skies are clear. No parachutes, but scramble Search and Rescue just in case, over.'

As she listened to the reply, Heather found herself thinking furiously about the dogfight that had just occurred.

*

Admiral James Fry turned to his Executive Officer with a serious expression.

'Order Miller and Boomer to land immediately. Pull the fleet an extra hundred miles off the Georgian coast and get all available fighters into the air. I want a tight defensive screen at two hundred miles – if so much as an angy wasp gets through I'll crack some heads!'

'Yes sir!'

The Admiral rubbed his temples with one hand as he spoke.

'Then put a Priority–One call through to the Admiralty and the Secretary of Defence. Inform them that we have been attacked, that the Republic of Mordania has committed an act of war against the United States of America.'

***

30

Megan awoke slowly, not really aware of where she was, lost somewhere in an oblivion of unconnected dreams conjured from within her slumbering mind.

She felt warm and strangely calm, suffused with something that she had not experienced in what felt like several centuries, as though an internal abscess of pain that she had not realised she harboured had been suddenly lanced, the pressure released, the poison drained.

'Something's happened.'

The voice reached Megan from afar, pulling her out of her comfortable doze and into the present. She felt the cold air on her face, stark compared to the warmth of the bed. She recognised the accent in the voice and opened her eyes.

Sophie was standing near the bed, a mug of steaming coffee in her hands.

'What time is it?' Megan asked, confused now and slightly disorientated.

'Eleven o'clock,' Sophie replied, handing her the mug as she sat up in bed, 'and everything's changed.'

Megan took a sip of the coffee. 'What do you mean?'

Sophie walked across the room to Megan's laptop computer and moved the mouse cursor. The screen came out of its dormant mode and revealed a direct link to a news channel, the laptop picking up the feed via its wireless connection. Sophie turned the screen to face Megan and removed the head–phones she had evidently been using to listen to the news. The words of the news anchor on the screen sounded through the room.

'… coming in with this exclusive and shocking news, that the Mordanian Air Force under the command of the infamous General Mikail Rameron has launched an aerial attack against the United States Battle Group in the Black Sea. The reports that we have are sketchy at the moment, but seem to indicate that the Mordanian fighters were destroyed by American interceptors before they could strike the fleet.'

Megan stared at the screen, her eyes wide.

'The commander of the United States Atlantic Fleet and the Secretary of Defence are said to be at this moment briefing the President and advising the best course of action. It's already being speculated that this extraordinary move by the renegade Mordanian General may be the result of the American president's recent decision to refuse assistance to the beleaguered President of Mordania, a tactic which many critics said would

embolden the rebel forces. Our political correspondent feels that we may be in for the biggest reversal of presidental policy in American history. We go now to our…,'

'Oh shit.'

Megan leapt out of the bed and moved for the door.

*

'What the hell did he want to go and do that for?'

Callum met Megan at the entrance to the Thessalia Hilton.

'I have absolutely no idea,' Megan replied, zipping up her jacket and walking with Callum through the steadily falling snow.

'All hell's going to break loose now,' Callum said. 'Anybody who lives within fity miles of the capital is going to make a bee–line for it. Nobody's going to want to be hiding in the hills if our American cousins decide to carpet–bomb the countryside.'

Megan nodded in agreement.

'Thessalia will be the only safe place to be. But I still can't understand why Rameron would do this. American intervention will ruin his campaign – he can't stand up to that kind of firepower.'

'That may not have been his plan,' Callum said. 'His forces are stretched protecting the ground that they've covered as they've moved south. His supply lines are at their longest. He may have decided that rather than fight all the way to Thessalia, he'll provoke fear of an American air strike and get everyone to run *into* Thessalia.'

Megan looked at Callum in surprise.

'You think it's a bluff? That he's done it on purpose?'

'It's one hell of a gutsy move, I'll admit that, but if he times it right and makes a rapid advance upon Thessalia before the Americans can deploy from the Black Sea, he can take the airport, the roads and harbours and then totally dominate Thessalia with artillery from the mountains over there.'

Megan looked in the indicated direction and understood.

'The Americans won't be able to bomb anything for fear of hitting the civilian population and won't be able to deploy in time to secure a foot–hold without storming an occupied and heavily defended coast.' Megan shook her head. 'Brillant. Utterly insane, but brilliant. Whatever happens, everyone's going to fall back on Thessalia and Rameron will follow.'

'Which makes a balls–up of our plans,' Callum pointed out. 'The city will be under siege.'

Megan punched a gloved fist into her other hand.

'Not if we're as clever as Rameron. We need a transport.'

'I was afraid you might say that,' Callum uttered.

'With everyone else running in the opposite direction we might just be able to push far enough north to reach Talyn before the rebels do,' Megan said. 'At least we'll be able to make enquiries there. If nothing comes up we'll head back, I promise.'

Callum shook his head.

'This is not good, Megan. We'll be running straight into the teeth of the enemy. Once they do start moving they'll stop at nothing to beseige Thessalia. Their own lives will depend upon it.'

'Then we'll have to be quick.'

Callum moved off in another direction to search for a suitable vehicle to hire, whilst Megan continued in the direction of Government House. Sophie Vernoux caught up with her as she walked.

'Where are you going?' Sophie asked.

'To see Sir Wilkins. I'm going to need help.'

'You can't go into the country now, it's too dangerous.'

'All the more reason why I have to go,' Megan replied without breaking step.

Sophie grabbed the arm of her jacket to stop her.

'You have to let her go,' she said softly. 'You can't keep doing this, Madame Mitchell. You cannot save everybody. She may not even want to be found, for all you know.'

Megan gently removed Sophie's hand from her arm.

'My name is Megan, okay, and everyone wants to be found.'

Sophie smiled faintly.

'But not everyone wants to be located, Megan. She may even be gone already, in another country, or perhaps she is dead. I'm sorry, but it's true – she may already be dead.'

Megan frowned.

'I can't leave her here without trying.'

Sophie sighed and took a step back.

'There is only so much that you can do before you begin to destroy yourself again,' she said. 'You should know that by now.'

'I know,' Megan replied quietly.

Something shifted in Sophie's eyes and a little smile touched her lips.

'You are a different woman now, Megan Mitchell,' she said. 'I can see it. You have a true purpose again.'

With that, she turned and walked slowly away in the snow through the crowds of panicked Mordanians.

***

31

The Gold Room, Pentagon,

Virginia, USA

'The Commander in Chief of Atlantic Operations has put the fleet on high alert, Mister President. He wants you to know that they're ready for anything.'

President Baker nodded toward the image on a television screen of the Chairman of the Senate Select Committee on Intelligence.

'Thank you, Jack.'

Vice President Hobbs sat next to the president, with Secretary of Defence Margaret Stone sitting opposite them both. Three of the eight screens in the room were illuminated for the conference briefing; one connecting to the Select Committee in the Hart Senate Building in Washington DC, another to Admiral James Fry aboard the USS Theodore Roosevelt in the Black Sea, and the last to the Chiefs of Staff, the president's military advisors.

'Ladies and gentlemen, talk to me,' the president said. 'Admiral?'

Admiral James Fry spoke with the frank and honest tones of an experienced naval aviator and commander.

'I've debriefed both of my pilots individually and I consider their testimonies to be accurate and without flaws. The aircraft that attacked them were Mig–23 Floggers of the Mordanian Air Force. No warnings were given by the enemy aircraft and no communications were made with the fleet or ground sources. My pilots were attacked in the process of intercepting the Mordanian jets, which they identified by their markings, and then defended themselves and the fleet accordingly. Both enemy aircraft were shot down and sank in the Black Sea. We found little wreckage.'

'The enemy pilots?' the president hazarded.

'There were no survivors sir, I'm afraid,' Admiral Fry replied. 'Both of my pilots looked for parachutes but none were spotted. Search and Rescue also drew a blank.'

The president nodded and looked at Margaret Stone, SECDEF.

'The situation has changed radically,' she said, 'and badly affects our foreign policy commitments, but we have to consider the possibility that this is a deliberate attempt to cause panic on the ground in Mordania, which would be of great advantage to General Rameron. He can use the opportunity to advance on Thessalia and secure his positions before we can deploy men and equipment. That would mean air–strikes to break up his lines of communication and support, followed by a difficult and protracted ground deployment, in all likelihood against a determined guerilla movement.'

'Iraq all over again, in other words,' the president noted bitterly.

Hobbs spoke up from the president's side.

'We must also consider the possibility that this is a direct challenge to US military authority in the region. General Rameron is being watched closely by Russia, not to mention Iran and China. They could easily be encouraged to back his movement as a fight for freedom from American influence. Nobody in the region is blind to the importance of oil supplies from the Caspian Sea – the area has been part of the great game of east and west over oil for decades.'

The president looked to his Chief of Staff, for all of whom spoke their Chairman, Four–Star General Tom Solomon, a broad shouldered, heavy jawed man with fiercely cropped steel–grey hair and piercing ice blue eyes. He sat so upright in his chair it seemed as though he might topple backwards over it.

'General Solomon?'

The general suddenly shot bolt–upright from his chair as though a live current had been discharged directly through his buttocks.

'The Mordanian military machine is fundamentally weak,' he announced promptly as though addressing a parade ground. 'It's capacity to withstand prolonged aerial bombardment in any theatre of operations is severely limited. Its air force consists of no more than twenty five second–generation Soviet–class fighters and assorted training aircraft, significant for the region but both obsolete and irrelevant compared to even a single US Battle Group. The Army is reasonably well trained but numbers just a few thousand men, some artillery units and a scattering of militia drawn from the local populace.'

The president thought for a moment.

'If pressured into a military solution, how would you proceed?'

'Mister President, I would initiate an aerial bombardment of all major supply lines and choke points such as highways and bridges, and ensure the complete destruction of any aircraft and airfields available to the rebel forces in the north. This I would follow with an aggressive deployment into

Thessalia and Khobal Airfield to its east, with airborne units dropped somewhere behind the main thrust of the rebel advance on Thessalia, should it occur. Our thinking is that if we separate General Rameron's forces from each other and break the chain of command and supply, morale and equipment will degenerate sufficiently to force surrender or a rout. The presence of US troops both before and behind the enemy, and military police units within Thessalia, may be enough to deflect the imminent attack and thus protect the civilian populace.'

The president nodded. 'Thank you, general.'

'Thank you, Mister President!'

The general dropped like a stone, resuming his rigid seated posture. The president looked around the room for a long moment before speaking.

'We have to do something, whatever it is. The United Nations has already begun an emergency session regarding their response, but most wars are over before they're ready to commit troops on the ground.'

'Mister President,' Hobbs said from his side, 'I hardly need to remind you of the political ramifications of deploying troops into Mordania. Our forces are stretched thin as it is and your entire administrative campaign was based on a policy of reduced intervention in foreign affairs. If you commit to a military solution in the Mordanian crisis, your popularity in the polls will be severely affected.'

Matthew Baker nodded in agreement.

'That is quite true,' he said simply, 'but I did not take this office in order to become popular. I took it in order to do the right thing. I can't let us just sit by whilst a rebel army storms a democratically governed city, especially after the commander of that army has just attacked one of our carrier groups!'

Margaret Stone agreed.

'We should go in and hit them hard. Once the government is back on its feet and its troops able to control the city, we pull out again.'

Hobbs smiled bleakly. 'That's what they said about Iraq.'

'Iraq was an entirely different situation,' Margaret Stone shot back. 'This is not a major power with a large army. This is a pop–gun state with no coherent policy for…'

'This is a country struggling for its identity,' Hobbs cut across her, 'with human beings living within who will be severely affected by a military campaign.'

'They already are!' the secretary of defence snapped. 'We need to end that campaign and restore order!'

President Baker slammed a hand on the table. 'Enough!'

Hobbs and Stone fell silent. The president looked at the television screens.

'General Solomon, do we know of the location of General Rameron's base of operations?'

'No sir, Mister President. Current intelligence places him north of Thessalia, near the mountain town of Talyn, but we can't pin him down closer than that.'

The Vice President looked at the president for a long beat.

'Are you going to do what I think you're going to do?'

The president closed his eyes for a moment before speaking.

'The people of Mordania aren't to blame for this war, and even the rebels under General Rameron are only Mordanians themselves. The impetus for confict has come from one man, Rameron himself. That is where our war should be.'

The president stood from his chair, resting his hands on the table and lowering his head in thought for a long few seconds. When he finally looked up again, he had made up his mind.

'Admiral Fry?'

'Yes sir, Mister President?'

'Prepare your marines for a shock assault, to deploy once I have spoken to congress and obtained authority for military action. I want a plan for air–superiority to be secured around a one–hundred nautical mile perimeter of Thessalia, with all access and supply routes north of that perimeter destroyed, ready to go on my word.'

'Yes sir!'

Admiral Fry saluted crisply and the screen went blank. The president turned to General Solomon.

'General, organise what you can from our troops in Afghanistan. Pull a few strings if you have to, but I need a reserve force ready to back up Admiral Fry's marines en route to Thessalia within twenty–four hours.'

Another bolt of live current shot up through the general's nether regions and he jerked upright out of his chair and saluted.

'They'll be there, Mister President sir!'

The screen went blank, and the Chairman of the Select Committee spoke.

'I'll talk to the committee and ensure cross–party support, Mister President.'

His screen too went blank, and President Baker leaned back in his chair and ran his hands down his face.

'This isn't just about our role in world affairs,' Hobbs said. 'You're playing directly into the hands of the media, of Seth Cain. This is what they wanted. They're controlling *us*!'

'You'd better organise a press announcement,' the president said, shaking his head. 'They're gonna love this about as much as the public are going to hate it.'

***

32

The refugee camp was a frightening place.

He had never seen so many people in one place before, camped out in the freezing snow and mud in endless rows of tents that seemed to stretch forever. He too was cold, wrapped up against the bitter wind and the snow that tumbled thickly from the pale clouds above to drift in dense whorls on the wind.

He hobbled on through the slush, looking for a familiar face amongst the hordes of miserable strangers, their dark eyes framed with hoods and scarves and watching him as he passed. His legs were weary with fatigue and his body ached from the cold but he travelled on determinedly, for his mission was an urgent one.

Pausing, he retrieved from his coat pocket a scrap of paper with a hastily scribbled drawing upon it and a single word beneath the sketch. He looked at the large tents dominating the camp, at the flags fluttering in the wind above them, and found the one he sought.

The tent was cavernous as he walked inside, past huge metal vats boiling soups and cooking grain, clouds of steam enveloping the queues waiting to eat. He passed them by, heading toward the plastic sheets dangling beneath a large red–cross sign at the rear of the tent, and pushed through them to stand in the hospital.

Two queues of people, young and old, were being administered to by young volunteer nurses, who variously gave them injections or patched wounds and dabbed at cuts. He advanced, moving past the queues, until his eyes fixed upon someone he knew.

Weakly he moved forward to where the young girl, dressed in a heavy coat to keep out the cold, was stacking boxes and ticking them off a roster at the rear of the hospital. He was almost next to her before she noticed him.

'Bonjour monsieur, ca va?' she asked, looking down at his frail form.

The old man smiled up at her from beneath his hood.

'Mowpheen,' he pronounced awkwardly.

'Morphine?' Sophie Vernoux repeated with a slight smile.

'Ya, ya,' the old man grinned in delight. 'Mawfeen!'

Sophie chuckled and pointed to the queues.

'You need to queue, over there.'

The old man looked at the queue, still smiling, and then back at Sophie, offering her a shake of his head.

'Niet, mawfeen,' he said and pointed toward the exit.

'We can't just hand out morphine,' Sophie replied, feeling sorry for the old man. 'You need to bring the patient here.'

The old man's face creased with confusion as he tried to understand what Sophie was trying to tell him.

'Mawfeen?' he repeated.

Sophie gave up and called out across the hospital tent.

'Do we have a translator here?'

Sophie brushed past the old man as she tried to hear the various calls and shouts that came in reply to her question. The old man let her pass and looked idly around the boxes and crates and sacks stacked around the tent, obviously the place where goods were brought in. He wondered briefly whether he might find the mysterious mawfeen amongst the boxes, and was moving to have a look when he saw a picture tacked to one of the wooden posts supporting the framework of the tent.

A young girl, a black and white photograph, the face smiling out at him. His breath caught in his throat as he stared mesmerised at the picture.

'What are you doing?!'

The old man whirled to see the young girl standing behind him with her hands on her hips, watching him with a stern expression. Quickly, the man pointed at the picture.

'Mawfeen,' he said, jabbing at the picture. 'Mawfeen.'

Sophie looked at the picture for a moment and was about to berate the old man when she suddenly caught on. Her eyes widened as she looked again at the old man. On an impulse she pointed at him, then at her own eyes, and then at the picture.

'You have seen her?' she said slowly.

The man nodded eagerly, mirroring her gestures and pointing at the picture.

'Mawfeen!'

The old man lifted his hood to reveal a large medical patch over his left temple, and Sophie suddenly realised that he was the farmer she had treated, the old man that Severov had beaten days before.

The old man produced a piece of paper with a crude picture of the MSF logo, and beneath it a single word. Morphine. Sophie looked at it, and then the old man pointed at Amy O'Hara's picture again.

'Oh merde,' Sophie said as she whirled and dashed away.

*

'You're absolutely sure?'

Megan looked uncertainly at the old man, who returned her gaze with a broad toothy grin and nodded repeatedly despite not having the slightest clue as to what she was saying.

'His name is Sergei and he's seen her,' Sophie insisted, 'and I think that he came here on behalf of someone else who needs morphine, perhaps for your missing girl, Amy. I was wrong Megan. She's not dead, she's still out there.'

Megan frowned, folding her arms over her chest.

'He might just want it for himself, to cure the headaches he's probably still getting,' Megan suggested. The old man grinned, nodded and drooled. 'We need a translator,' Megan added.

'I've looked everywhere, but the damned news crews have grabbed them all. They can pay money that we can't afford.'

'Bloody journalists,' Megan smiled at Sophie.

The grinding, clattering sound of an engine outside caused Megan to get up and move out of the tent and into the softly falling snow.

Callum sat at the wheel of a battered white jeep with an engine that sounded as though it were on the verge of seizing. Megan walked up to the vehicle as the Scotsman jumped out.

'It doesn't look like much,' Callum said cheerily, 'and that's because it isn't.'

'The engine sounds like it's shot,' Megan frowned.

'Lack of decent oil,' Callum replied. 'I've already changed that and managed to scrounge a new filter off the REME guys in the Thessalia depot. She'll sound better once she's had a chance to warm up a bit.'

Megan didn't see much point in debating with him, and instead opened the creaking rear door and tossed her rucksack inside.

'Do we have an escort?' Callum asked seriously.

'Leave that to me,' Megan said and hurried away.

*

'I must say that I strongly disapprove of what you're intending, Megan.'

Sir Wilkins was clearly up to his neck, his staff running back and forth between offices and Wilkins himself striding rapidly with thick wads of official–looking papers in his hands.

'This guy says that he's seen Amy O'Hara.'

'That doesn't mean that she's alive!' Sir Wilkins retorted. 'It's probably a ruse that this old man's using to get his hands on morphine for his damned head. You said it yourself, he can barely string a sentence together!'

'It's all I've got left,' Megan insisted, walking alongside him. 'This is probably the last chance we'll ever get to reach Talyn. Rameron's forces will be moving rapidly south as soon as the populace flees for the city. We can dodge the bulk of his army if they pass us before we reach Talyn and locate Amy, or find out where she might have gone.'

Sir Wilkins stopped and waved his papers at Megan.

'And if they identify you? Or if the Americans decide to launch pre–emptive attacks against rebel strongholds, which they will no doubt do if Congress decides to respond with military strikes? If you reach Talyn you may end up trapped there, and if America does attack then Talyn will end up a lot flatter than it is right now.'

'That's *my* problem,' Megan snapped. 'I need just a few men and a translator, that's all. Forty–eight hours maximum.'

Sir Wilkins snorted in disbelief and continued on his way.

'A few men? Of course, but we're a bit short on bloody champagne for when you get back.'

'Four men,' Megan repeated. 'No more.'

'I can't just appropriate resources to what my superiors will consider to be a wild goose–chase Megan! I need justification, the promise of a result!'

Sir Wilkins paused in the corridor, driving the ends of his fingers into his closed eyes. Megan saw him wavering, and pushed her advantage.

'I've come this far, Tom. If she's not in Talyn I'll give it up, but if she is we'll have saved her life. Her life, Tom.'

'Fine!' Wilkins said abruptly, and then laughed. 'You know how to push a man, Megan. I'll have them meet you on the edge of the refugee camps.'

Megan was already walking away from the attache. 'I owe you,' she said over her shoulder.

Sir Wilkins watched Megan vanish around a corner at a near run, then shook his head and chuckled to himself as he continued on his way.

*

Megan arrived back at the refugee camp within a few minutes of speaking to Sir Wilkins.

'The escort should be here shortly,' she reported to Callum.

'How the hell do you pull things like this off?' the Scotsman asked, mystified.

Sophie Vernoux appeared genie–like from nearby, watching Megan and Callum as they loaded the jeep with water and rations, plus a few blankets and boxes of survival equipment.

'Talyn is a dangerous place Megan,' she said gloomily. 'You know that.'

Megan hefted a five–gallon tank of water onto the back seat of the jeep. She smiled and gestured at Sergei, who had hobbled outside to watch them.

'We've got our guide and escort now. He'll protect us. Right now I'm more worried about you. You need to rest.'

Sophie's features were lined with fatigue and worry.

'I have too much to do,' she replied.

'You can't save everybody,' Megan said.

'Any more than you can?'

There was a moment of awkward silence, Megan momentarily lost for words. She opened her mouth to speak when the sound of an approaching truck drowned her out. They both turned to see a military truck pull up, with half a dozen policemen cradling AK–47 rifles sitting in the rear.

Megan moved forward as the cab door opened, then stopped as Alexei Severov stepped down from the cab, a cigarette gripped between his teeth and his eyes glowing with malevolent pleasure.

'We're already cleared to leave,' Callum snapped from nearby. 'If you've got a problem with that, then take it up with Sir Wilkins at government house.'

Severov looked at Callum, still smiling, and then advanced to stand before Megan, his voice clear for all to hear.

'I know,' he said cheerfully. 'I'm your escort and you need a translator. Bolav is with me.'

Megan stared at Severov for several seconds. 'You?'

'Me,' Severov confirmed. 'Considering the nature of where you are going, Sir Wilkins felt that you needed truly professional assistance.'

'Then why did he send you?' Megan asked.

The carefully cultivated smile on Severov's face slipped. At that moment he caught sight of Sergei, who watched Severov with a fearful gaze. Megan shifted position to block Severov's view.

'Get back in your truck and piss off. I'll talk to Sir Wilkins and get somebody else.'

'There is nobody else,' Severov hissed. 'All of my units are preparing for the inevitable rebel attack. These men are hand–picked, the best of my troops. They will not fail to ensure your safety. Or perhaps your mission is not as important as you claimed it was, in which case none of us will be going anywhere.' Severov grinned around his cigarette. 'How do you say? Your call?'

Megan shook his head, then turned and called out to Callum.

'Let's go.'

Megan cast a last glance at Sophie and saw the deep concern etched into her features. A quick wave at old Sergei to follow and she leapt into the rear of the truck with a spritely gait, eager to escape the probing glare of the chief of police.

***

33

'Good evening, I'm Charlotte Dennis. Tonight's main headlines; chaos in Mordania as the populace flees for the capital city Thessalia amidst fears that the United States is mobilising its forces for an aerial bombardment of rebel forces north of the city. In America, President Baker has put the case to congress for military intervention in the crisis in a spectacular reversal of policy.'

Harrison Forbes stood in the control room of GNN UK Ltd, watching as the anchor read the day's main stories off the auto–cue. Martin Sigby's main report was due as the lead story but far from being excited, Harrison felt a growing sense of unease about the situation. Sigby's most recent reports had lacked the sheer impact of his earlier work and Harrison suspected he knew why. Megan Mitchell had ceased to make contact with GNN, which meant that she had either succeeded in her goal of finding the missing woman, or she had vanished into the interior of the country in order to locate her.

Martin Sigby had earned the ear of the Mordanian President, Mukhari Akim, in itself an extraordinary achievement for a foreign correspondent. But inevitably that had exposed him to accusations of bias in favour of broadcasts supporting the president.

'Sigby's on in fifteen seconds,' an assistant whispered to Harrison.

'Link him up.'

The image of Martin Sigby appeared on one of the main screens, slightly fuzzy due to the heavy snowfall in Mordania disrupting even digital signals. Harrison watched the little man adjust his jacket and stamp his feet to keep warm as he waited to go live on television.

Charlotte Dennis's voice became a little louder.

'And now we go live to our correspondent in Thessalia, Martin Sigby. Martin, what's the feeling in the city at the moment at this time in the face of an impending invasion? Can you convey something of what it's like for the ordinary people in the city?'

Martin's expression came alive as he spoke.

'Well, Charlotte, as you can imagine, fear and concern are the words that would describe the mood here in Thessalia. Behind me, in the refugee camp that you can see in the distance, literally tens of thousands of people have flooded into the city from the surrounding areas, from the few places that are not yet under rebel control. These people are running from the fear that the United States may attempt to intervene in events here with a military solution, and engage the rebel forces on their very doorsteps.'

'And do you think that the government can cope with this sudden influx of people?'

'In a word Charlotte? No. Put simply, even with the aid groups and the United Nations operations going on here, Thessalia is in a state of crisis in terms of water supply, electricity, grain and oil. The manpower to support the growing populace both within and around the city does not exist and the government of President Mukhari Akim knows it.'

Harrison Forbes moved closer to the screens as Charlotte went on.

'I'd like to talk about the government there for a moment, Martin. What was the response on the ground to President Mukhari's impassioned plea of the other night for international intervention in the crisis?'

'It was as expected, Charlotte. There has been a sense that the government has lost control of the situation and is admitting that it cannot protect its citizens from the insurgency. The people here seek strong leaders and have the greatest respect for dominant rule, even if the decisions made are not naturally in the favour of the people. It's all about pride and strength, and President Mukhari's announcement frankly appeared to signal weakness and not resolve. It has only added to the chaos and fear here, and may even have contributed to a greater sense of respect for the rebel leader, General Rameron, whose leadership could only be described as uncompromising.'

'Then why make such an announcement, do you think?'

'Well, Charlotte, I had the chance to ask the president that question myself this morning, and here is what he had to say.'

Harrison Forbes started in surprise as President Mukari Akim's image, seated in his personal chamber, replaced that of Martin Sigby's snowy roof–top domain. The president was clearly answering Martin's questions at a time earlier in the day.

'What I want to do Martin,' the president said, *'is to finalise and secure permanent ties with the west. I firmly believe that this country needs to involve the United States in this conflict not just to defeat the insurgency of Mikhail Rameron but to affirm our determination to move away from a Communist agenda and begin a new era of democratic cooperation with the west.'*

Martin's voice was heard over the president's image.

'You're saying, sir, that this crisis, this most desperate hour, is something that you believe is necessary for your country in order for it to develop in the future, to become part of the west?'

Harrison Forbes almost laughed out loud in delight and surprise.

'Oh my God, how the hell did he come up with that?! That's genius!'

President Akim gripped one of his chunky fists in the palm of his other hand, his features radiant with determination.

'Communism, and with it Russian dominance of the Urals, ended long ago. Their method of governance did not work. Our future must be based upon democracy, a method of governance that does work. But I alone cannot convince my people that such a dramatic change can achieve the prosperity and economic advantages that we hope it will. We may have had our democratic revolution, but ten years on ours is still a poor country. No, alone I am nothing, as all leaders are. A leader only possesses influence when he has people to follow him. I need to know, and the people of this country need to know, that our choice of governance, our allegiance to democracy, our hopes of friendship and collaboration with the west will be honoured with the support that we need in this darkest of hours.'

The president took a moment to think, and Harrison Forbes smiled as he listened.

'This is our moment of truth. This is our first and our last stand. If the democratic west will not lend its support to our government, will not protect us from those that countries like America claim to despise, then why should we have a democratic government at all? We will remain as isolated as we always were, abandoned at the hour of our greatest need by those who claimed to support us. My message is simple. If you do not help us, then you are by choice abandoning the very principles that you have preached to the world, and our efforts will vanish amidst the carnage of anarchy and despotism that you stand by and watch overcome us.'

The image of the president vanished to be replaced by Martin Sigby's snowy countenance as he spoke to the camera.

'It's extraordinary, Charlotte, but President Akim has made a strong case for western intervention in Mordania. If the west claims to promote democracy and see its advance across the globe, then it's got to respond to and assist those who are trying to defend it. Martin Sigby, Thessalia.'

Harrison Forbes slammed a fist down on the edge of a table. 'Brilliant!'

An aide rushed up to Harrison's side, his face flushed with excitement.

'It's Seth Cain!' he gabbled, his eyes wide.

'What about him?' Harrison Forbes snapped. 'Which line is he on?'

'He's not!' the aide replied quickly. 'He's here!'

Harrison looked up to the entrance to the operations room. The entire staff were sitting at their desks and staring at the door as Seth Cain swept through it, his long dark coat billowing like a cape, ice–blue mirrored sunglasses reflecting the colourful banks of television screens. The line of his jaw was hard with restrained displeasure.

Cain did not approach Forbes, instead cutting across the operations room and striding into Forbes's office, leaving the door open.

Harrison Forbes walked across and followed Cain into the office, shutting the door behind him.

'Mister Cain,' he said. 'This is an unexpected pleasure.'

Cain stared at the map on the wall of the office before turning to look at Forbes from behind his mirrored lenses.

'What's pleasurable about it, Harry?'

The editor gave up the act. 'What do you want?'

Cain perched on the edge of Forbes's desk, regarding the office outside of the windows.

'I want to know, right now, how your man in Mordania is getting his reels.'

'Talent, I think it's known as.'

'How is he doing it?' Cain repeated.

Forbes leaned against the wall behind him and folded his arms.

'What's your beef with Martin Sigby anyway? He's just doing his job, remarkably well if I say so myself.'

'I don't give the smallest shit what you think,' Cain sneered. 'I want Sigby on the line, in here, right now, and I want to know how he's getting what he's getting.'

'He'll just tell you what the rest of the world already knows, Seth. He's getting his reels from the President himself. And if you think that I'm pulling him out of Mordania, you've got another *think* coming.'

'Far from it,' Cain smiled. 'The population of our planet has become attached to your gallant little correspondent. I wouldn't want to harm the viewing numbers by pulling him off the air now. But you know, as well as I do, that he could not have gotten the footage that he did without assistance and I want names.'

Harrison's eyes narrowed. 'Client confidentiality, Seth.'

Cain glowered with fury, his body trembling as he raised a finger and jabbed it toward Forbes's chest.

'You know who it is, don't you? Believe me, Harry, you're going to tell me, because if you don't I'll have you out of this office in thirty minutes and your entire career history erased from the GNN databank. I'll make damned sure that you never, ever work again.'

Harrison Forbes took a deep breath, considering Cain's point for a long moment before speaking.

'Okay, okay. If you want it that badly, I'll tell you,' he said resignedly. 'It was the tooth fairy. Every night she comes into Martin Sigby's bed and whispers sweet–nothings in his ear about what the nasty people in Mordania have been up to.'

Cain shot bolt upright but Harrison Forbes cut off his tirade.

'Go to hell, Seth. I'll have cleared my desk long before your goons get the chance to ransack it for me. There's no way I'd give the name of an informant to you. Whatever it is in that country that you're trying to hide, Sigby will find it sooner or later. You are trying to hide something, aren't you Seth?'

Cain stood fuming on the spot in silence for a moment before looking out of the office windows at the hundred or so staff, most of whom were casting curious glances in his direction. Cain grinned.

'I hope that your staff feel the same loyalty as you do,' he uttered.

'What do you mean?'

'I'll ensure that they are all replaced by the morning. Every, single, last one of them will be jobless by tonight, and all because the good and the great Harrison Forbes refused to cooperate with his superiors.'

'There's nothing superior about you.'

'Sticks and stones, Harrison,' Cain tutted in mock disappointment. 'I thought that such would be beneath you. Now, tell me, what will it be? A name, for the sake of your staff and their livelihoods?'

Harrison Forbes looked out of his office windows, sighed, and made his decision.

***

34

'How much farther?'

Callum's jeep had survived admirably well and they had passed Anterik an hour previously, Commander Severov's troop carrier following them along the slushy roads and through ghostly, abandoned villages that seemed to Megan to be haunted by loneliness and despair.

'Maybe another five or six miles,' Callum said, glancing at the map he had tacked to the dashboard. 'Talyn's on the other side of the Tornikov River.'

Megan looked at the map, frowning.

'There's a bridge there. Do you think it will be occupied?'

Callum shrugged.

'If I were in command, then yes, but Rameron's troops may simply be relying on their dominance to hold onto strategic choke–points for now.'

Megan peered in the mirror at the troop carrier following them.

'I don't trust Severov either,' Callum said as he drove, guessing Megan's thoughts, 'but we need the extra firepower and support. He got us through that check–point didn't he?'

The convoy had recently encountered a platoon of Mordanian troops, some of the handful of loyalists who had not joined Rameron's "glorious" revolution. They had been manning a makeshift artillery post and had halted the convoy on sight. Megan had recognised at once the dull glow of battle–fatigue burning in their eyes, a weary and yet merciless intolerance for all foreigners. Only Alexei Severov's presence had allowed them to pass through.

'That's what bothers me,' Megan murmured in reply. 'His eagerness to help. He hates us both.'

'He's got his orders,' Callum said, guiding the jeep around a large ice–filled crater in the road. 'For a soldier, sometimes doing things that you dislike is just part and parcel of the job.'

Megan was about to reply when she saw faint tendrils of grey smoke drifting in the air to the left of the road, stark against the forested mountain ranges in the distance. She leaned forward, trying to peer through the trees.

'Could be trouble,' Callum said, eyeing the smoke.

As Callum drove the jeep clear of the crater, Megan saw a gap in the thick forest lining the road, and through it the stark white tail of an aircraft, pointing up into the air at an awkward angle.

'That's it, the airfield that Sergei talked about, shipping supplies to Petra Milankovich and his colleagues.'

At the mention of his name, the old farmer nodded from his seat in the rear and offered them a toothless grin, pointing at the aeroplane and mumbling quietly to himself.

'Let's pull over and take a look,' Megan suggested.

'It could be occupied by Rameron's men.'

'Well, they haven't harmed us yet.'

Callum reluctantly pulled the jeep into a left turn toward a wide track that led between the trees and out onto the abandoned airfield. Megan could see that it had once been a significant base, equipped with crumbling aircraft shelters, huge hangars and a full runway. A tattered orange windsock hung limp on the cold air in the distance, and a control tower with shattered windows stood forlornly on the opposite side of the strip.

'Looks deserted,' Callum said as he slowly drove out onto the airfield. 'The government forces must have abandoned it, and Rameron's men obviously haven't advanced close enough to occupy it.'

'Maybe they don't want to,' Megan murmured. 'The Americans will surely either occupy or bomb it if they decide to intervene here.'

Callum drove past a line of broken airframes, private light–aircraft variously burned or shattered with incendiary devices. Further ahead, a hanger was charred and broken by flame and age, faint wisps of smoke still drifting from its shattered embers.

'Over there,' Megan said, pointing at the hangar. 'It's still smouldering. Let's check that out.'

Callum pulled up beside the hangar and climbed out with Megan as Severov's vehicle pulled up behind and the police commander jumped out of his cab.

'We should not stop here. This is restricted area!'

Megan ignored him and walked up to the huge building where a door hung from one remaining hinge, the blackened interior of the hangar beckoning her inside. She strode in and looked up at the cavernous innards of the almost empty hangar. Smoke still tainted the air about her, debris and dark fluids staining the hangar floor.

'Done fairly recently, I'd say,' Callum said as he followed Megan through the hangar. 'But there hasn't been any recent fighting in this area that I'm aware of.'

'Someone was here,' Megan nodded in agreement.

Drips of moisture splattered about them in muted chorus, echoing through the cold and empty hangar. Megan saw a large bank of what looked like old burned fridges and approached them, kneeling down in front of the blackened metal boxes, each of which had heavy looking power cables snaking from their rears. The plastic sheaths of the cables had melted in the heat of the fire into puddles of congealed black plastic.

'Look at this,' Callum said, gesturing to one side of the machines.

Megan walked around to where Callum was standing over a large satellite receiver dish, its once perfect shape now warped with heat, scorched and partially melted.

'Some kind of transmission equipment?' Megan hazarded, moving around to the rear of the machines.

Megan stepped over the melted cables carefully, searching the backs of the machines until she found what she was searching for. Kneeling down, she fished her satellite phone from her pocket and dialled.

'Megan?'

'Frank, how's it going?'

'Not so bad. What can I do for ya?'

Megan scraped some carbon deposits off a series of labels adorning the rear of the computers.

'I need you to trace a set of serial numbers for me, if you can. Some are partials.'

'Read 'em on out to me, Megan.'

Megan read the numbers that she could make out in full and then the partials, before picking up the satellite dish and examining it. For good measure, she read what she could of the identifying marks.

'You any closer to Amy?' Frank asked.

'We're getting somewhere, I'm sure of that much Frank. Speak soon.'

As Megan rang off, Severov stamped one booted foot impatiently.

'We're very exposed here. Is this really necessary?'

Megan cast the commander a brief glance and then looked at Callum.

'He's right, Megan. We should get away from here as soon as we can.'

'Fine,' Megan replied.

Megan led the way back to the vehicles and Callum resumed their long drive north and away from the airfield. Megan did not speak as they travelled, her thoughts with the eerie abandoned airfield. She barely noticed that the intermittent canvass of forest and snowy fields was breaking up into another scattering of granite–grey buildings, a town a little larger than those that they had encountered up to now. Callum glanced at the map and then out of the windshield.

'There's the Tornikov River,' he said and pointed ahead.

Megan saw through a distant gap in the buildings a dark, cold looking strip of black water, its surface flecked with chunks of ice drifting downstream.

'Where's the bridge?' Megan asked, leaning forward.

'Somewhere at the end of the main street, there, just ahead.'

As Megan was looking, the truck behind them flashed its lights twice. Callum slowed and stopped on the outskirts of the deserted town as Severov jumped from his cab and jogged to the jeep's driver's window.

'Drive slowly into the town,' Severov urged. 'My men will walk either side of our vehicles. The enemy could be anywhere in there, so be ready.'

Callum nodded, and Severov jogged back to the troop–carrier and barked a series of orders. Megan looked at Callum, who reached down and pulled the corner of his jacket back. A 9mm pistol nestled in its holster under his arm.

'If he pulls anything,' Callum said, 'he'll get a shock.'

Megan watched as Severov's men deployed around the two vehicles, hugging the edges of the road and positioning themselves under whatever cover they could find, ready to move forward. At a command from Severov they began advancing ahead of the vehicles, shifting fluidly from cover to cover, their Kalashnikovs pointing unwaveringly ahead of them.

The truck behind flashed its lights once again and Callum pulled slowly away.

The road ahead continued between rows of two–storey buildings that had clearly once been shops and apartments. Megan could read faded signs advertising bakeries and tailors, salons and restaurants in Arabic, Russian and English. For a brief moment she had a vision of the village, alive and bustling in the summer, locals sitting in what had once been a small park, children playing on brightly painted swings that glistened in the sunlight. Young girls walked and giggled, young men watching them as they cruised through the streets in their cars. A man walking his dog, distant music from a sandwich bar, birds flitting across the blue sky above.

The jeep jolted as it crunched awkwardly through a mortar crater that had punctured the road, and Megan's vision was shattered. The broken shells of the apartment buildings stared vacantly back at her, the shattered fronts of shops scorched with flame and grime. The swings were broken and twisted, the park churned with mounds of earth blasted by artillery shells, and every wall was peppered with small–arms fire. Megan watched Severov's men advancing through the wreckage and felt herself enveloped by a deep sense of loss, of pity and remorse for what man was capable of doing to mankind, all in the name of power, of a dominance that was only ever temporary. She wondered how many previously happy lives had been lost or irrepairably damaged in Mordania by this war.

'There's the bridge,' Callum pointed.

The road curved gently, and as they followed it so it straightened and led to a causeway bridge that spanned the bitter blackness of the Tornikov River.

And all at once, everybody stopped. Callum braked as the troop carrier behind them slid to a halt on the slushy road. The policemen all froze or dove for cover in doorways and alleys either side of the main street.

'Bugger,' Callum muttered.

The bridge was blocked by a Soviet T–72 tank and surrounded by Mordanian troops and vehicles.

*

Megan stared through the windscreen as the rebel soldiers, perhaps as many as one hundred in number, all turned to stare at the little convoy. They were around one hundred metres away, smoking and talking amongst themselves. None of them made for cover, instead they simply watched the convoy through the falling snow.

'They're smarter than I thought,' Callum said.

Megan saw Severov climb from his truck and run forward in a low crouch, coming up alongside Megan's window. Megan wound it down.

'End of the road,' Severov said in a harsh whisper. 'We're outnumbered.'

Megan watched the rebels through the windscreen and then turned to Callum.

'Where are our binoculars?'

Callum reached behind her to one of their rucksacks, rummaging around and pulling out a pair of 10x50's. Megan took them and levelled them through the windscreen, scanning the rebel troops. It took her a few seconds to identify the NCO with the huge beard she had met in Anterik, watching them as a subordinate whispered in his ear.

'I'll take care of this,' Megan said.

She climbed out of the vehicle, as did Callum. Severov stared at them both in surprise.

'You cannot go there,' he protested in a harsh whisper. 'They will skin you alive for pleasure!'

'Not these ones,' Megan said. 'Do you have any cigarettes?'

Severov stared at Megan as though she had gone mad, but none the less he reached into his pocket and produced half a packet of what were probably Mordanian produced cigarettes, taking one for himself before handing the packet to Megan.

'Whatever you do,' Megan cautioned the commander, 'don't shoot, no matter what.'

Callum hurried around the front of the jeep and whispered in Megan's ear.

'You pulled this off once, but trying again is asking far too much.'

Megan began walking toward the tank.

'It's much harder to kill someone that you have met,' she replied, 'even as little as that man knows me. He won't do anything.'

'This time I stay close, just in case,' Callum insisted.

Behind them, Commander Severov watched them walk completely exposed down the centre of the main street toward the ranks of the enemy. His dark eyes scanned the tank and soldiers, the machine guns and rocket–propelled–grenades they were brandishing, and the length of the main street. A tiny smile curled from one corner of his lips and he turned, walking back to the truck to where a couple of his men were standing awaiting orders.

'Send the word,' Severov whispered to one of them, 'pull back, quietly.'

The soldier hurried off as Severov walked to the rear of his truck, hauled himself up and clambered inside. Amongst the kit of his men, several canvass–wrapped bundles were strapped to the rear of the cab. Severov loosened the straps on one of them and removed a camouflaged cylinder concealed within, before re–securing the bundle and hurrying out of the back of the vehicle.

As he moved back to see the street he could see his men falling back towards him, moving discreetly from cover to cover as they did so. Further toward the rebels, Megan Mitchell and her big friend continued walking.

Severov lit the cigarette he had taken from his packet and lifted the cylinder in his hands.

'Goodbye, Megan Mitchell.'

*

Callum was watching the rebels, trying to gauge their strength and morale as he walked alongside Megan. They showed no signs of aggression toward the approaching strangers, but then neither did they show any signs of greeting.

'I don't like this,' he muttered under his breath to Megan.

'Not exactly a riot for me either,' Megan whispered back. 'Just stay calm.'

The NCO with whom Megan had spoken before in Anterik recognised her and moved out in front of his men, a brief smile flickering beneath his beard. His men seemed to relax around him, sensing their commander's lack of concern.

Megan nodded at the NCO in recognition, then glanced to one side at the shattered hulk of what was once a mini–market, its shelves now collapsed behind broken windows. As she looked, she saw one of Severov's men dropping back and away from them.

Beside her, Callum looked over his shoulder and saw others doing the same. Instantly, he checked the other side of the street.

'Severov's pulling out,' Callum said quickly.

'We don't need him,' Megan replied. 'We can do the rest alone from here.'

'Are you sure?'

Megan was about to reply when a sudden commotion ahead caused a spark of fear to lance her spine. The rebels let out a sudden howl of protest as their NCO shouted a command and dove down into the cold slush.

Callum whirled and ploughed into Megan and sent them sprawling through the snow even as Commander Severov levelled the bazooka he carried on one shoulder and pulled the trigger.

The projectile blasted from the muzzle of the weapon amidst a cloud of smoke and with a whistling howl accelerated with frightening speed toward the rebel position. A trail of smoke followed it as it screeched straight down the centre of the street and struck the tank on its forward quarter with a terrible rending of tortured metal.

The explosion ripped through the ranks of the rebels, hurling shrapnel into the air amidst an expanding black and orange fireball that lifted both Callum and Megan off the ground and propelled them away from the blast.

Megan hit the ground hard, rolling as fragments of debris and shards of shrapnel blasted past her. Her ears rang violently, her vision blurring and her sense of direction and balance completely lost. She peered through the cloud of smoke and devastation at the rebel tank, its forward tracks now hanging from their wheels, the vehicle immobilised and the blood of fallen rebels splattered across its flanks. Rebel troops were variously lying motionless on the ground or crawling and screaming in agony, trailing shattered body parts across the crimson–stained snow.

It was then, at that critical moment of shock and confusion, that Severov's men attacked.

35

'Stay down!'

Callum's command reached Megan's ringing ears just as she heard Severov's muffled voice in the distance, shouting something in Mordanian at the top of his lungs.

The crack and cackle of machine gun fire ripped the air above Megan's head, bullets whipping and thudding as they cut into the rebel soldiers still alive and huddling around their tank and support vehicles.

Megan turned to see Callum roll over on the ground, his pistol in his hand as he scrambled to his feet and dashed in a crouch to Megan's side.

'Time to go!' he bellowed.

Megan scrambled to her feet and with Callum ran to one side of the street, pinning herself flat against a recessed wall as Severov's men began advancing back down the street toward them, firing as they went.

'That bastard's going to pay!' Callum shouted above the din of gunfire.

Megan winced and flicked her head aside as a bullet gouged out a nearby chunk of wall and spat chips of mortar and brick over them both.

'He wants us dead!' Megan shouted. 'So will those rebels if they survive. We need to leave!'

Callum tried to ignore the gunfire and peeked around the corner of the wall at the advancing troops, Severov waving his men to advance and shouting as he did so.

'We need the jeep,' Callum shouted.

Megan was about to reply when a new wave of gunfire burst out from the rebel positions. Megan turned and saw that they had recovered from the initial shock of Severov's attack, had regrouped and were beginning to return fire. At their front the bearded NCO was leading them, blood smeared across his face, firing an AK–47 at the advancing government troops.

Chunks of masonry burst from the wall to Megan's left as rifle fire ripped across it. Clouds of fine dust clogged her nose and stung her eyes as she tried to flatten herself into the recess as much as possible.

'Follow me!' Callum said and dashed to Megan's left.

Megan followed, running low as they rushed along the pavement and ducked into a side alley, high velocity rounds zipping through the air around them. Callum turned, checked his pistol and watched the battle rage on the street.

'We need to get past Severov's position and fall back. His men aren't going to last long against those rebels once they're back on their feet.'

Megan nodded.

'If we can get to the jeep, maybe we can find another way across the river.'

Callum shook his head.

'This is the only crossing for twenty miles in either direction. It's over. We'll just have to take our chances with Severov and get back to Thessalia.'

Megan winced and peered out into the street from her vantage position. Severov's men were drawing close to their position, but the rebels were recovering fast and beginning to lay down an increasingly heavy field of fire against the government forces. Their blood would be up now and Megan knew that if caught, both Callum and herself would likely be considered as complicit in the attack on the rebels. There was no choice.

'All right, let's go.'

The alley behind them ended in a sheer wall against which had once been attached an iron ladder, but that had corroded and collapsed years before. Megan knew that they would have to go back into the street.

Callum leaned against the wall on the edge of the pavement, watching the advancing rebels before looking at Severov's men as they began slowly falling back under the weight of fire. Callum saw one of them try to pull back from his concealed position behind the edge of a low wall. He sprinted quickly, but not quickly enough. Machine–gun fire raked the earth around the soldier and he twisted in mid–stride, a fine mist of innards spraying out behind him as a round pierced his side and exited his back with explosive force. The young soldier hit the ground and lay there writhing in agony.

Callum checked the street ahead again and then dashed out.

Megan followed, trying to keep her head down and run at the same time as bullets and chunks of debris were sprayed through the air around her.

*

Severov saw them the moment they broke cover.

He took aim at a rebel soldier advancing upon his position, squeezing the trigger of his AK–47 three times in quick succession, firing single rounds each time. The second round hit the rebel through the side of his chest and he tumbled into the snow to lie motionless, his eyes staring wide and empty toward Severov.

The commander set his rifle down while simultaneously drawing his service pistol from its holster in one fluid movement, bringing it up and firing four rounds at the big Scotsman as he ran. All four rounds missed as his target ducked down behind an abandoned vehicle, Megan Mitchell close behind him.

Severov cursed, picking up his AK–47 again and firing off a few rounds before shouting into the headset he now wore to communicate with his men.

'Fall back, prepare to retreat!'

Severov watched as his men began falling back rapidly, covering each other as they drew away from the fight whilst trying to keep the rebel force pinned down. Ahead, he could see the jeep that Megan Mitchell had used, and through the misted windows he realised that he could just make out the form of the old man huddled in terror on the back seat.

*

'They're leaving!' Callum shouted.

He could see past the wreck of the vehicle they were hiding behind, to where Severov's men were conducting a very efficient withdrawal under fire. Their own position was shielded from both Severov and that of the rebels, in the latter case by another abandoned vehicle, but not for long.

'That's been his plan all along,' Megan shouted in reply, crouched alongside Callum. 'If he goes, we're finished!'

Callum searched for a solution to their problem and knew that there was only one way to go. The jeep sat on its own, with Severov's men now withdrawing past it toward their own vehicle.

'We go for the jeep!' Callum shouted, readying himself.

Megan crouched lower in preparation, and then the pair of them launched themselves from cover and sprinted for the jeep.

*

Severov saw Callum and Megan break cover and instantly he raised his pistol, aiming carefully this time before pulling the trigger once.

He saw the big Scotsman spin violently as the bullet hit him and he tumbled into the snow amidst the gunfire, his pistol flying from his grip. Severov let out a howl of delight, firing this time at the more distant rebels flitting from cover to cover as they advanced, before shouting into his headset.

'Full retreat!'

Instantly, those of his men still firing upon the enemy abandoned their positions and fled toward the truck, which reversed rapidly back down the street, the troops jumping onto its sides and onto the cab as they fled.

Ahead, Severov saw Megan Mitchell dash to her friend's side, at about the same time as the rebels finally managed to get their tank working again. The commander checked that all of his surviving soldiers were on board and then turned to the translator, Bolav, who was sitting beside him.

'Let me know what happens to them,' Severov snarled.

Bolav stared at him in confusion, before Severov opened the cab door and grabbed him. The translator let out a scream of terror as he was hauled with brutal force from the moving vehicle, his flailing body hitting the ground in a cloud of snow. Severov watched as the little man scrambled to his feet, tears streaming down his face as he screamed in terror at the swiftly retreating vehicle, staggering through the snow in pursuit.

Severov slammed the door shut as the driver reversed the truck around a bend in the street and out of the line of fire. Instantly he turned the vehicle around and drove as fast as he dared away from the village.

*

'Callum!'

Megan dashed forward and slid down onto the snow beside her friend's inert form.

Deep scarlet blood stained the snow around the Scotsman, and Megan saw the wound from the bullet that had struck Callum deep in his left shoulder. The fact that the entry wound was on Callum's front left her in no doubt as to who had fired the shot. Severov had aimed for the chest, for the heart. He had missed the fatal shot but Callum was in trouble.

'Callum! Get up!'

The Scotsman did not respond, and Megan struggled with his body as the bullets whizzed and cracked the air around her. There was no way that she could lift Callum from the ground, so instead she grabbed his ankles and began dragging his body toward the jeep.

She turned to see Severov's truck reverse rapidly away from the village and vanish around the bend with the translator, Bolav, running after it. Megan looked at the jeep in desperation over her shoulder as she heaved Callum's heavy body through the snow.

'Sergei!'

The old man in the jeep did not respond, and Megan was about to call for his help again when a sudden boom made her look around.

The tank's gun–barrel was lost in a cloud of smoke. The tank itself may have been immobilised, but its turret was still operational. An instant later the jeep vanished amidst a blast that lifted it off the ground and sent it spinning fifteen metres through the air to land on its roof in flames on the opposite side of the street.

'Sergei!!'

Megan dropped to her knees in exhaustion, looking at Callum's body and the trail of blood through the snow. In the deafening silence of the aftermath of the tank's gun she realised that the shooting had stopped and that the snow was still falling softly around her, gently blanketing the dead bodies that lay scattered across the confined battlefield.

From the distance, stark against the sudden silence, the keening cries of men torn limb from limb haunted the abandoned town, drifting softly on the wind like ghosts with the snow.

As Megan looked up from Callum's unconscious form, she saw ranks of rebels advancing on her position in the road, their Kalashnikov's pointed at her and vengeance burning in their dark eyes.

***

36

Megan knelt in silence as the rebel soldiers closed in around her.

Beside her, Callum groaned. Megan looked down and tried to stem the bleeding from Callum's shoulder with one hand. The rebels closed in further, saying nothing, staring down the barrels of their rifles with pitiless expressions.

Megan tried to fathom what the rebels might do next, what they might say. For an interminably long time they simply stared at her where she knelt, flecks of snow building up on her jacket and hair.

Callum groaned again.

One of the rebel soldiers advanced and grabbed Megan by the hair, then yanked her away from Callum. Megan staggered to her feet, but the pain of the soldier's grasp angered her and she knocked the man's grip away.

The barrel of the soldier's rifle swung around hard, catching Megan's left temple and sending her reeling back down into the snow as primal fear pulsed like poison through her veins. A sudden burst of malevolent shouts of encouragement erupted from the rest of the troops. Another soldier raised his boot and kicked Megan in the side. Megan gagged as pain ripped through her ribcage, only to be dragged to her feet by two more men. They held her as a third leapt forward and windmilled his right fist down into Megan's stomach.

Megan felt the wind blast from her lungs. She collapsed to her knees as her captors released her, and sensed rather than saw the boot that curled toward her head, felt the cold snow and the scratch of dirt from the heavy sole as it smacked dully across the side of her face. Megan slammed down onto the unforgiving earth, and saw through blurred vision a burly soldier with a blood–splattered poncho and a bandana around his head stand over her and raise the butt of his rifle into the air, ready to bring it crashing down on Megan's head.

Megan closed her eyes.

The sound of a commotion made her open them again as the rebels all turned to look at something else. Megan rolled her head painfully to one side, and through the legs and boots of the soldiers she saw two rebels dragging a captive through the snow who was crying openly and begging his captors for mercy.

The man was dumped unceremoniously next to Megan and Callum. Megan recognised Severov's translator, Bolav, his face cut and muddied and his clothes torn. He looked at Megan with pleading eyes, clasped his hands together as though praying for divine intervention.

One of the rebel soldiers turned Bolav around and hit him full in the face to the laughter and encouragement of his fellow troops. Megan winced as the rebel's knuckles cracked across Bolav's nose and sent the translator face down into the snow. The little man, crying with terror, began trying to crawl away. The troops parted for him, laughing, as the rebel who had hit her followed the pathetic, writhing figure, grabbing him by the back of his collar and lifting him off the ground.

Bolav tried to get back onto his knees in the snow, his hands still clasped together as a stream of Mordanian dialect fell from his bloodied lips. The rebel soldier turned slightly away from Bolav and then spun back, sweeping his boot around to thud into the translator's skull. Bolev let out a cry of pain and whirled away, holding his head in his hands and sobbing into the dirt and the slush.

'Leave him alone!'

Megan's voice sounded weak, as though it had been spoken by somebody else, coming as it did from an impulse of empathy for the battered translator, and the rebels turned back to face her. The soldier who had been beating Bolav suddenly screamed in fury and rushed at Megan head on as she staggered to her feet.

Megan ducked to one side as the rebel soldier swung a punch for her, thrust her left fist out to knock the blow aside, and turned as the rebel stumbled off–balance past her. Megan lifted her right foot and stamped it down on the inside of the soldier's left knee, snapping the tendons within like dry twigs. The rebel screamed and collapsed into a heap in the snow, bellowing expletives.

Megan felt the butt of a rifle smash between her shoulder blades with so much force that she thought it might have burst out of her chest. Her vision starred and she sank to her knees in time for a second rebel to punch her full in the face. Megan twisted painfully onto her back in the snow once more. The rebel with the bloody poncho and bandana appeared above her again, glowering with malice as he stamped one boot down onto Megan's chest and raised his rifle above Megan's skull.

The gunshot sounded as though it had come from within Megan's own throbbing head. Megan watched the towering rebel spin backwards and away to fall to the earth. She turned her head to see Callum still lying on his back in the snow alongside her, holding his smoking pistol in his right hand.

The rebels began screaming and shouting, raising their rifles and backing away, Callum pointing the pistol threateningly at them.

'Belaye! Belaye!'

The roaring voice drowned out the shouts of the rebels, and Megan turned as the bearded NCO appeared from nearby, limping slightly from a leg wound but still standing. He fought his way across the street, one hand stemming the flow of blood from his thigh, and came to stand over Megan and Callum.

Megan looked into the man's eyes for a long beat, trying to ignore the pounding in her skull and the taste of blood on her lips, and then spoke softly to Callum.

'Give him your gun.' Callum did not respond, and Megan shot him an urgent look. 'Do it!'

Callum gritted his teeth before finally flipping the pistol in his hand and offering it to the NCO. The bearded Mordanian looked at the weapon for a moment and then reached out and snatched it from Callum's grasp.

He then turned to his men and barked a stern order to them. They responded instantly but sullenly, lifting Megan and Bolav to their feet and binding their wrists. Callum was eased upright into a sitting position, and a medic advanced to squat beside him with a small box of bandages.

The bearded NCO approached Megan and stood directly in front of her.

'You killed twelve of my men,' he hissed.

'We were betrayed,' Megan replied, every word sending pain across her cut lips. 'We had no reason to attack you. We are not part of this war.'

'You are now.'

'What are you going to do with us?'

'Your fate is not for us to decide,' the NCO snapped. 'Our general will decide that for you.'

Megan did not realise what the NCO meant until she thought about it.

They were going to be taken to General Mikhail Rameron.

***

37

Sophie knew that something was wrong the instant she saw the troop carrier driving slowly past the refugee camp, Megan Mitchell's jeep nowhere in sight. A phalanx of UN troops standing guard beside a checkpoint nearby raised their hands to halt the vehicle, which slowed obediently.

Sophie began walking toward the truck, and saw Martin Sigby and his cameraman filming as the chief of police jumped from the cab and began talking to the officer in command of the checkpoint.

Sophie walked straight past Martin Sigby and stormed across to Severov.

'Where is Megan Mitchell?' she demanded.

Commander Severov looked at her with eyes devoid of any emotion that she could recognise.

'There was an ambush,' Severov replied. 'We were heavily outnumbered by the enemy, who attacked us near a bridge in Talyn with a tank.'

Sophie took a pace closer to him.

'Answer the question,' she muttered.

Severov glanced at the British officer with a pained expression before speaking.

'They were trapped between us and the enemy as we fell back under heavy fire. We could not get to them. There was nowhere for them to run. I'm afraid that in all likelihood they were captured and are now likely to be dead.'

A wave of panic flickered across Sophie Vernoux's expression as she stared at the commander.

'You were supposed to protect them! You insisted that you should go with them, to protect them!'

The commander cultivated an apologetic expression.

'Madam, my men are capable but they are no match for a tank platoon, much less one that outnumbered us five to one. I lost six of my men and those of us left are lucky to have survived the encounter at all.'

Sophie stared blankly at Severov, her eyes wobbling in their sockets.

'How did they end up trapped so far from your men?'

Severov held his hands out palm upwards.

'The woman, Mitchell, she insisted on walking out to talk with the rebels. They were half way across the distance between us when the rebels opened fire. We could do nothing but try and cover the retreat of your friends and try to disable the tank, which we did. But we only destroyed its tracks, not its gun. That was why we had to withdraw.'

Sophie was mid–way between flying into a rage and crying.

'She did that in Anterik and the rebels did not attack her,' she protested.

'Different soldiers, different day,' Severov replied, looking at the British officer this time. 'There was little that we could do, and we did try to prevent Mitchell from going out there at all. It is just too dangerous now.'

Sophie looked desperately at the British lieutenant.

'Sir, please, surely you could send a column to search for them?'

Lieutenant Kelsey instantly shook his head.

'I'm sorry, ma'am, but there's no chance that a British column will get anywhere near Talyn now, let alone find your friends. I hate to hear that one of our own is stranded out there, but I'm afraid that Commander Severov here is right – they're on their own and too far away for us to help now.'

Sophie looked away from the lieutenant in dismay.

'Really, ma'am,' Lieutenant Kelsey said, 'if there was any chance of us locating them and bringing them back we would, but there isn't.'

Commander Severov reached out to her and placed his hand on her shoulder. Sophie whirled and her open palm cracked across the Mordanian's face like a gunshot.

'Don't you touch me,' she hissed.

Severov's hand moved instinctively for his service pistol.

'Commander,' the British Lieutenant said calmly but coldly, 'I think that you should be on your way. You are cleared to pass.'

Severov regained his composure, straightened his back even as his face reddened as he bowed to Sophie before climbing back into his cab. The vehicle pulled away into the camp, winding between the endless rows of snow covered tents.

Lieutenant Kelsey resumed his post with his men, leaving her standing alone to look out to the north, past the brooding mountains.

Martin Sigby moved alongside her. 'What happened to them?' he asked.

Sophie cast Sigby a poisonous glare and walked away without answering.

*

'Oh damn and blast it all to hell!'

Sir Wilkins slapped a thick wad of papers across the edge of his desk, causing Sophie to flinch at the noise. Wilkins put both of his hands to his head for a moment as he spoke.

'When did you learn of this?'

'Thirty minutes ago. Commander Severov's vehicle returned alone. He said that they had been ambushed by a tank in Talyn.'

'Quite likely,' Sir Wilkins nodded. 'The reconnaisance flights being made by the Royal Air Force indicate massive troop movements to the north near Talyn. They're probably moving their armoured columns ahead of the main body of infantry, to secure the remaining towns between Talyn and Thessalia and clear a path for the troops.'

Wilkins looked down at his maps and intelligence documents. Sophie's voice was furtive as she spoke.

'Is there any chance that someone could go out and look for them?'

Sir Wilkins shook his head, still pouring over the maps and placing his finger over an aerial photograph of Talyn.

'Not in the slightest, I'm afraid. If we knew their precise location I might be able to organise an extraction via helicopter, but as we cannot know even if they are alive or dead, much less their whereabouts, I'm afraid that we're powerless to assist them.'

'But if they're being held captive and the Americans attack Rameron's position, they'll be killed.'

Wilkins stood up from the maps and regarded Sophie with a gentle gaze.

'I really am sorry, my dear. If anything else is heard that might give us their location, I shall inform you immediately.'

Sophie nodded wearily and walked from the office. She had been gone only a few moments when Martin Sigby walked in silently, having waited for her departure. Sir Wilkins looked at him.

'The great and grand Mister Sigby, what might I do for you?'

'The president wishes to speak with you, at your convenience.'

Sir Wilkins smiled broadly, but his eyes seemed touched with discontent.

'My word, now you are not only his confidant but also his spokesperson and assistant. Such lofty heights, sir, in such little time.'

Sigby managed to retain his composure. 'We all have our jobs to do.'

'Don't we indeed,' Wilkins uttered. 'And your job will be that much harder now that the source of your footage is in the grasp of the enemy.'

'Mitchell's capture was nothing to do with me,' Sigby shot back. 'It was her choice to go to Talyn despite everyone advising against it.'

'Perhaps, Martin, she would not have had to go at all, had you done that which she had asked and reported on Amy O'Hara's disappearance.'

Sigby's expression soured further. 'You're an arsehole, Thomas.'

'Charming,' Sir Wilkins smiled, his eyes scanning the ceiling as though searching for his next words. 'Perhaps, Martin, we could discuss the several thousand Euros a day that Mukhari Akim's government is now shoving up yours?'

Martin Sigby's expression flared with alarm.

'Oh yes, Martin,' Wilkins said, 'we get to see all of the dirty little deals that go on here in Government House. There's not a single penny going in or out of this country that escapes my personal scrutiny. I have no doubt that your work is of the highest ethical order, no?'

'It's none of your business,' Sigby shot back, jabbing a finger at Wilkin's chest, 'so stay out of it.'

Wilkins picked up his thick sheaf of papers and pushed past Sigby.

'On the contrary, Martin, I wouldn't want any part of it.' He paused in the doorway and glanced back at Sigby. 'I wonder, Martin, how quickly your glorious campaign on the international stage will crumble if word should slip out about your ill–gotten gains?'

As he swept from the room Wilkins let the question hang in the air to torment Sigby.

***

38

The sack over Megan Mitchell's head prevented her from seeing anything and filled her nostrils with the musty smell of old canvass and dust. The rebels had also tied the sack tight enough around her neck to constrict her throat, making breathing difficult.

She and Callum, along with the translator Bolav, had been bundled into the rear of a truck and driven for perhaps thirty minutes along what Megan had judged to be a reasonably well maintained road. She knew that they had passed over the Tornikov River because she had heard its turbulent waters churning below the bridge. Thereafter, she had been unable to track their progress but assumed that they were travelling north.

Eventually they had reached a complex of some kind where the sound of many vehicles and marching troops suggested a military base. There, they had been dragged to a building and pushed inside, the door closed and locked after them. Megan knew that Bolav sat nearby in the darkness of their prison because she could hear him mumbling incoherently to himself, but she was sure that Callum had been taken elsewhere. She could only hope that he was being treated well.

A loud crack pierced the silence and Bolav let out a yelp of terror and began trying to squirm away from the opening door. Megan sensed an increase in the light and was dragged roughly to her feet. Something heavy slammed into her stomach, churning her guts and buckling her legs.

The unseen hands hauled her back onto her feet and dragged her, stumbling, out of the darkness. The door slammed shut behind her. Megan smelled fresh air filtering through the sack over her head, and heard the sounds of troops and engines once again. The hands that held her guided her over a step and into another building.

Megan let the men direct her up three flights of steps, heard them bark commands and sensed rather than saw other people being moved abruptly out of the way. She was pulled up to a halt and heard the sound of someone knocking on a door. The door was opened and Megan was propelled inside, falling forwards to slam painfully onto her knees on what felt like a thinly carpeted floor.

The hands hauled her upright again, shoved her into position and forced her into a seat. Megan felt her bonds being released, only to be tied again through the backrest of the chair with unnecessary force, the coarse ropes biting painfully into her wrists.

A long moment passed, until she felt the cord around her neck being mercifully untied, and without ceremony the bag was yanked from her head, bright light from rows of broad windows blinding her. Megan blinked as her eyes struggled to focus, the room in which she sat slowly taking shape around her.

A large office, stripped mostly bare by war but now with maps and charts pinned to the dull grey walls. Fluorescent strip lights above, tables with charts spread across them, a couple of telephones. An operations room of some kind, she realised.

And then she saw the man standing ten yards away, his arms folded, dressed in camouflaged fatigues, piercing eyes glaring malevolently into hers. Megan sat transfixed by that glowering expression, as she had been when she had first seen it on television days before, at home in London.

General Mikhail Rameron strode slowly toward her, his gaze never once leaving Megan's. He was a big man, Megan could tell, powerfully built despite his age and radiating both the professional pride of a soldier and the irrepressible determination of the true fanatic. Rameron stopped a metre away from Megan, regarding her silently for a moment before speaking.

'Welcome,' he rumbled ominously. 'You do not look like a soldier.'

Megan was surprised to hear Rameron speak English so well.

'You don't look like one of the good guys.'

Rameron's features remained as flat and immovable as granite.

'You attacked my men at Talyn,' Rameron said. 'A unit of my troops lost almost twenty men as a result.'

Megan struggled not to show any emotion that could be used against her. 'We did not attack anyone.'

'My men stated that you opened fire upon them with a rocket propelled grenade launcher or similar. You tell me that they are lying?'

Megan shook her head.

'They're not lying. The soldiers escorting us opened fire. We're press.'

General Rameron eyed Megan seriously for a moment.

'Press? For whom? Your belongings were searched by my men. They found no identity cards.'

'We're not carrying them. It's complicated.'

'It is now,' Rameron said, leaning close to Megan. 'I think that you're lying.'

Megan kept her expression neutral as best she could. 'I don't care.'

'You will.'

There was no malice in Rameron's tone, no vindictive pleasure in his eyes like Severov, and that scared Megan more than anything. General Rameron would do whatever it took to identify her and to learn whatever he could from her.

Rameron stood away from Megan again and nodded to someone standing behind her chair. A burly looking rebel soldier moved to stand beside Megan, one of the men who had been with the tank platoon at Talyn.

'Chekov here saw half of his friends die this morning in Talyn, after your attack,' Rameron said. 'He is not a happy man.'

Megan rolled her eyes.

'We did not attack anything. We..,'

The side of Megan's head exploded in pain as the soldier hit her with a full roundhouse punch, snapping her neck painfully away from the blow. Megan's vision went white and then swam with colours as a bolt of nausea churned in her guts. Rameron's voice drifted across the periphery of her awareness.

'You were there and you were part of their force. Either identify yourself or face the consequences.'

'I am Megan Mitchell and I work for GNN Ltd in London. I am not a Mordanian soldier, I'm bloody English for god's sake.'

'Which could make you a mercenary,' Rameron pointed out, 'a soldier for hire.'

'I am not a soldier nor a..,'

Another blow, this time from the left, sent a blade of white pain searing across Megan's retina. The nausea returned and Megan jerked awkwardly as she splattered a bolus of vomit onto the carpet between her boots. She coughed and wretched, spat the burning mucus from her mouth as she tried to regain her vision, listening to Rameron's voice.

'Outside, I have seventy–four men who were not injured by your attack who will smile and sing songs as they rip you limb from limb, Megan, so we are going to need some answers right now.'

Megan's fury vented itself from somewhere beneath her fear.

'I just told you who we are and what we're doing! We're press working out of Thessalia for GNN Ltd and we're..,'

The third punch slammed like a sledgehammer across Megan's face, snapping her head back and spilling blood into her mouth. The front of her face went numb as pain shot back and forth through her head like a live current. This time she cried out, releasing her fear in sobs of pain as she hung her head, feeling the blood dripping from her lips in scarlet globules and strings. She barely heard her own tortured whisper.

'We were looking for someone.'

General Rameron waved at the rebel soldier, who backed away from Megan.

'Who?' he demanded quietly.

Megan fought both for breath and to remain conscious.

'Amy O'Hara,' she whispered. 'She was press too, an American. She disappeared from somewhere around Talyn several weeks ago. We were looking for her.'

Rameron regarded without mercy Megan's crumpled, bloodied form.

'Why would you come into a war–zone to look for her?'

From somewhere, Megan found the strength to unsteadily lift her head, her vision wavering as she tried to focus on Rameron. She thought of Amy and what this man might have put her through, and her anger stirred again within her.

'Because I owe it to her,' she spat, 'something that you wouldn't understand, you twisted fucking lunatic.'

Chekov raised his fist, but Rameron belayed him with a tiny gesture.

'If you are press,' the general said, 'then you can do something for me and end this all right now. Tell me exactly where Martin Sigby is. I want to know where he is staying and how I can find him. Tell me, and I will release you and your friends.'

Megan looked up at the general in confusion for a moment, and then the penny dropped.

'So that you can force him to report in your favour, general?' she asked. 'So that you can threaten him with torture until he does what you want?' Megan took a breath and spat blood at Rameron. 'Not a chance. I'll not trade places with anyone so that you can do this to them.'

Rameron nodded slowly, thoughtfully, before looking at Chekov.

'Take her downstairs and bring me the other one, the translator. He'll be much easier to break.'

Megan glared at Rameron as she was suddenly hauled out of her chair.

'Leave him alone! He doesn't know anything about Martin Sigby!'

General Rameron ignored Megan's shouts, turning his back on her and walking away through his operations room.

***

39

Martin Sigby sat in his hotel room and watched the dull grey Mordanian sky grow darker as somewhere in the west the sun set behind the towering mountains. His laptop chortled with live–feeds from several news networks being streamed through the satellite dish on the roof of the Thessalia Hilton.

The snow had stopped outside, a minor mercy in this freezing and God–forsaken land. He knew that people were dying in the refugee camps from hypothermia, from exposure and from the first grotesque stirrings of dysentery that was breaking out in isolated pockets across the camps despite the best efforts of the humanitarian groups.

Martin looked at his watch. In ten minutes he had to be broadcasting live from the rooftop with more tales of woe. A small, tight ball of self loathing writhed deep in his stomach. He turned, looking again at the page that he had printed from his internet connection after accessing his personal bank account. A sizeable deposit had been made via international wire–transfer in Euros, with all deductions properly made, everything legal and above board.

Martin sighed, unable to loosen the ball in his stomach.

'We're on in ten.'

Martin's cameraman, Robert, poked his head around the door. His expression was one of concern. 'Are you okay?'

Martin looked again at the darkening clouds outside and shivered.

'Why are we here?' he asked distantly.

Robert stood in silence for a moment before replying. 'Because people need us to be here.'

'Who?' Sigby asked.

Robert walked into the room and stood beside the window, looked out into the bitter darkness at the few remaining street lights still glowing in Thessalia's snow filled streets.

'Them,' he said quietly. 'The people of this city, of this country, and the people of a hundred other countries suffering injustice beneath dictatorships. There are seven billion people on this planet, and every one of them relies upon people like us to let them know what's going on in their world.' Richard turned from the window. 'That's why we're here.'

'Free press,' Sigby whispered, and shook his head. 'What's free about it?'

'Your right to exercise it,' Robert replied adamantly, jabbing a thumb out of the window. 'And their right to receive it. Without it, our way of life is hopeless. We'd be going backwards.'

'Maybe we are.'

'What's this about?' Robert demanded.

Sigby sighed, and smiled bleakly up at his cameraman.

'Let's just say there's a conflict of interests between myself,' he said, gesturing to the window, 'and them.'

Robert did not reply for a long beat, glancing at the sheet of paper in Sigby's hand before speaking softly as he turned and walked from the room.

'It sounds like the only conflict you have is with yourself. We're on in five.'

Martin Sigby watched his cameraman vanish from the room and sat in silence. He looked at the satellite phone beside his laptop computer, thinking deeply. Quietly, and without ceremony, he closed his eyes and crushed the bank statement in his hand into a small ball, tossed it into a waste paper basket in one corner of the room.

The painful, acidic knot in his stomach eased slightly.

He stood up, walked across to the phone and picked it up, dialling a number from memory and waiting for the other line to pick up.

'UN attache's office, how may I help?'

'Martin Sigby, GNN UK Ltd. I need a line out to the Chandler and Morris Bank, London.'

'Do you have the number sir?'

Sigby passed on the number and the girl connected her to a cheerful sounding assistant more than a thousand miles away in London. Martin Sigby's voice was somewhat strained as he spoke.

'Hello, yes. I believe that there has been an error. Monies have been paid into my account that do not belong to me and I would like to see the transaction reversed.'

Martin waited until the girl had completed his request to his satisfaction, then he rang off and dialled another international number. Moments later a familiar voice answered.

'Harrison Forbes, GNN Ltd.'

'Harry, it's Martin.'

'Ah, the boy wonder!' Harrison said delightedly, making Martin smile. *'And what may I do for you?'*

'I need some details from you, that may need some digging.'

'That may be difficult,' Forbes said quietly. *'GNN's onto your case and I nearly lost my damned job over everything that' been happening.'*

'Why?' Sigby asked in surprise.

'I don't know, but there's been something going on ever since Megan Mitchell began filtering reels out of Mordania. Watch your back, Martin. What do you need exactly?'

'I need absolutely everything that you can get on a supply company named Elstrom, a man named Petra Milankovich and a woman named Amy O'Hara.'

'Milankovich? You have your doubts about the official line on the massacre story?'

'Let's just say that I'm not quite ready to let it go yet. There's something behind all of this and it's worth following.'

'Consider it done,' Harrison said, and rang off.

Martin Sigby set the phone down and wondered briefly if what he was doing was noble or just sheer madness. He pressed the Menu button on his phone and read back through the calls list until he found the one he was looking for, one that Megan had dialled days before. He dialled, waiting patiently until the line picked up.

'Frank Amonte.'

'Mister Amonte, Martin Sigby, GNN. Sir, I am calling on behalf of Megan Mitchell and I need your help.'

*

1600 Pennsylvania Avenue,

Washington DC, USA

'You're live in sixty seconds, Mister President.'

President Baker sat down behind the broad, highly polished desk in front of the American Eagle and its flanking Stars and Stripes flags. He adjusted his tie, more for something to do than because it was loose.

'You're absolutely sure about this?' Vice President Hobbs asked.

President Baker nodded once, curtly, his expression slightly strained.

'I don't see any choice. Do you?'

Hobbs shook his head, stepping out of shot as an aide began counting down from ten, and the Oval office went silent as President Baker put on his most serious expression, an air of quiet determination enveloping him as he began to speak.

'Fellow Americans, I speak to you this evening after a series of unexpected events that have overtaken our country almost, it seems, before we could react. I have little doubt that few of you are unaware that, yesterday afternoon, American forces in the Black Sea were subjected to an unprovoked act of war. They defended themselves with the vigour and spirit we expect of them, shooting down two warplanes of the Mordanian Air Force commandeered by the rebel general Mikhail Rameron.'

President Baker hesitated for a moment.

'It will come as no surprise that this act of war against the United States of America must take precedent over the policies with which I came to be sitting here today. An act of aggression against the American people cannot be seen to go unpunished, for we know and have always known that our enemies will only be emboldened by such irresolution. We did not begin this conflict. We were not a part of this conflict. But we have been brought into this conflict by the actions of a man who would rather see a world in flames than a world at peace. It is both our right as a country and our place as a world leader to ensure that such aggression cannot be allowed to spread. Tonight, in the name of freedom and in the protection of a democracy under threat, I will commit the armed forces of our country to theatre in the defence of the oppressed. As of now, my fellow Americans, our country is once again at war. Thank you and good night.'

***

40

USS Theodore Roosevelt (CVN–71)

Black Sea

'Cap'n on the deck!'

Admiral James Fry walked onto the bridge of the huge aircraft carrier, moved to the port windows and looked down over the flight deck. Two Hornets were waiting on the forward catapults as a third sailed down onto the runway, wings quivering and undercarriage straining as the fighter was brought to an abrupt halt by the arrestor cables.

'Ex–O, status report.'

The Executive Officer glanced briefly at the flight–board.

'All CAP's airborne, everything quiet at the moment. The alert flight's on the *cats* ready to go if we need them. Personally, I was about to recommend that they stand down for now.'

The admiral nodded thoughtfully before responding.

'Agreed. Any word from Washington?'

'Not yet sir. The president's still debating with the Chiefs of Staff over the precise course of action, but at least it's official now – we're at war.'

'This'll be over by the time the pen–pushers and bean–counters have wrangled their way to an agreement about who stands to make the most money out of another conflict.'

The XO smiled but did not respond. A junior officer came up onto the bridge and approached the admiral.

'Sir, Lieutenant Millard to see you, sir!'

The admiral nodded as Heather '*Miller*' Milllard walked onto the bridge. She was dressed in her flight suit but without the regalia of G–suit, hoses and cables used to plug the pilots into their fighters. She was young, just twenty six, her blonde hair pulled back in a pony–tail, sharp blue eyes noticing everything. Most of the kids on the ship were less than twenty which made her an "old hand".

'Lieutenant.'

'Admiral,' Heather replied with a salute. 'Sir, regarding the debrief on the engagement.'

'I know it's on your mind, Miller, just relax. You did everything by the book. The navy's not going to take a bat to your ass for anything while I have a say.'

'Thank you sir,' Miller said with an awkward smile. 'But I was here for something else regarding the engagement.'

Admiral Fry looked at the young fighter pilot for a moment. 'Go on.'

'Sir, there was something odd about the way the planes were flying.'

'Odd?' Admiral Fry echoed her.

'Yes sir. I can't put my finger on it sir, but the way they attempted evasion just doesn't jive with their earlier aggression in opening fire.'

Admiral Fry glanced around the bridge, noting the attentive gazes of personnel who had no purpose being attentive to anything but their jobs. The admiral guided Heather across to a quieter corner of the bridge and whispered to her sternly.

'Lieutenant, your engagement with the Mordanian fighters was an international incident, an act of war against our country that will result in a major mobilisation of our forces. Are you telling me that you have doubts about your debrief?'

Miller shook her head.

'No, sir. Everything I reported was correct. After the debrief, Boomer and I went over everything in case we had ommitted any details. We both felt sure that we had everything down as it happened.'

'Then what's the issue?' Admiral Fry pushed her.

'Sir, think about what happened. Those aircraft snuck right across Georgia without being detected by radar from either ground or aerial sources. The Mig–23 has a limited range at sea level. That means some hot flying, at low level and high speed, for four hundred kilometres through mountainous terrain, in winter, in low visibility.'

The admiral's expression told Miller that she had his attention.

'Go on,' the old man encouraged.

'Sir, the aircraft then performed a rapid climb to altitude and exposed themselves to our radars, identified our patrol, intercepted at high speed and engaged us aggressively with short–range missiles. My problem is that having achieved all of that, the pilots then proceeded to fly like a pair of assholes, sir.'

'Assholes,' the admiral echoed her flatly.

'Yes, sir. It was as if they suddenly lost interest in flying and living. We shot them both down within sixty seconds of the first missile alert warning.

They had a complete advantage over us with a missile in the air and yet they squandered it with some pretty damn awful manoeuvering.'

'They don't have your levels of training in air to air combat, lieutenant.'

'They were smart enough to fly hard and shoot straight, sir. It doesn't add up.'

The admiral sighed heavily, looking out across the flight deck again.

'What's your analysis, lieutenant?'

'I don't have one sir.'

The old commander shot Miller a fearsome gaze.

'You don't come up here pissing on America's grand parade, lieutenant, without a damn good reason to do so. If you've got something to say then say it.'

Miller sighed.

'My guess sir, is that those jets were not Mordanian Mig–23's.'

Admiral Fry ground his jaw for a moment before speaking. 'If so, then who the hell were they?'

'I don't know sir, and that's what's bothering me.'

*

'Has there been any word?'

Sophie Vernoux's voice was brittle with anxiety, but Lieutenant Kelsey was forced to shake his head and speak over the noise of the hospital tent around them.

'Nothing, and with these conditions closing in there's little chance that we'll find anything. Believe me, ma'am, I've got all channels open listening for communications between rebel posts. If Megan Mitchell broadcasts anything, including her position, we'll know about it.'

The lieutenant turned away and strode off through the hospital. Sophie stared at the ground, lost in thought for several seconds, before sensing that she was being watched. She looked up to see Martin Sigby standing a few metres away.

'Nothing?' he asked simply.

Sophie searched for a suitable hostile retort to this pathetic excuse for a man, but nothing came to her. She shook her head and turned away.

'Wait,' Sigby said.

'Go away, I don't have the time.'

'I don't want your time, I need your help.'

Sophie blurted out an abrupt laugh. 'Really?'

'I can find Megan Mitchell.'

'Because you have a crystal ball, or the ability to transcend space and time?' Sophie enquired. 'The entire British Army cannot find him.'

She turned away as Martin spoke from behind her.

'That's because they can't do what I can do.'

Sophie rolled her eyes as she continued walking. 'And what's that?'

'Tell the entire world that she's missing.'

Sophie stopped walking and turned to look back at him. 'Why would you do that?'

Martin seemed to take a deep breath.

'Because I felt that it might be worthwhile going over some of the things that Megan was looking into before she disappeared and though I'm loathe to admit it, I learned that she may have been onto something big.'

'Big?'

'Big,' Martin affirmed, 'and I need your help to break the story, and in doing so, find Megan.'

***

41

'Good evening, I'm Harriet Holloway.'

'And I'm Jared Thornton, and you're watching GNN International News.'

Harrison Forbes watched as colourful graphic swashes of royal–blue and gold swirled across the giant plasma screens over the terminal pool, the logo of GNN dominating the screen amid animated searchlights, the music building to a suitably dramatic orchestral crescendo before fading out as the cameras focused on Jared Thornton's neatly chiselled features.

'Tonight's headline; the United States of America has formally declared war on the rebel forces of war criminal General Mikhail Rameron in Mordania. As we speak, the first major American task force to be deployed since the conflicts in Afghanistan and Iraq is making its way across the Black Sea to begin landing troops and conduct an air–war against the enemies of democracy. The governments of the United Kingdom, Germany and Italy have all pledged military support for the venture, and both Georgia and Turkey have offered the use of airbases for aerial strikes in the north of the country. Only Iran has condemned the decision for military action as another attempt by America to gain influence in the region.'

An uneasy silence had descended over the newsroom as Harrison Forbes spoke.

'Here we go again. Any news from Martin Sigby?'

'Nothing sir,' an aide said from one side. 'He refuses to brief us on his next report.'

Harrison winced. 'I don't like surprises, especially now.'

'It's his call, sir.'

Harrison did not reply as he waited for the anchors on the screen to finish their rhetoric and pass the feed over to Martin Sigby's live position in Thessalia's Government House.

'Viewing figures?' Harrison demanded.

Another aide glanced at a nearby monitor.

'Through the roof sir, domestically and abroad. Eight million plus for Europe, about the same for the US.'

Harrison nodded. It was still afternoon across most of America, with less viewers glued to their screens. That would change later in the evening.

'Here we go!' a floor assistant called, pointing to the technicians governing the live feed inputs. 'Sigby's feed live in – eight, seven, six...'

Harrison saw the two anchors introducing Martin Sigby, as if half the world did not already know the man, and then the feed went live in the studio. Harrison could see Martin Sigby standing in the darkness, the ever diminishing lights of Thessalia twinkling on the skyline behind him.

'Five, four...,' and then the assistant silently mouthed *three, two, one* and then pointed at the live camera feed. A button was pressed, and Martin Sigby's image was broadcast live to countless millions of viewers in the western hemisphere.

'Martin,' Harriet Holloway greeted him, a little louder than necessary, *'can you tell us how it feels to be in the city of Thessalia on the verge of a full–scale war?'*

Like a street party, you silly bloody cow, Harrison Forbes thought. Martin Sigby dealt with the question with his customary professional seriousness.

'Thank you Harriet. The situation here in Thessalia is more tense now, more charged, than in any city I have ever reported from. There is a real expectation here that this nation, bealeaguered as it is, is about to be crushed beneath the might of the American military machine. Behind me, right now, literally thousands of people are gathering their belongings ready for a long march tomorrow toward the borders of Georgia, Dagestan and Armenia. Despite the terrible cold here and the dangers of such a forced march, few people are willing to take the chance of coming under attack either from General Rameron's rapidly advancing forces or from the Americans moving toward Thessalia even as we speak. It is, in effect, a modern day exodus.'

'Martin, what about the government itself and President Akim?' asked Jared Thornton. *'How do they feel about the imminent arrival of Western forces?'*

'Well Jared, naturally they are relieved that they are receiving the support that they feel they deserve from the international community. I spoke with the president earlier today and he said that if order and democracy could be restored to his country by the combined efforts of allied nations supporting his government, then he would be willing to hold snap elections to give the people their choice of a new government, whether his or that of another. He feels sincerely that he has failed his people in not putting down this insurrection before it turned bloody, and thus must hear the will of his people before continuing to govern from Thessalia.'

'But couldn't that possibly create a power vacuum and replace one national crisis with another?' Harriet asked with a transient flash of initiative.

'Yes it could Harriet, but not just for the obvious reasons of political advancement and tribal discord that you and the viewers at home may be thinking of. Earlier today I was approached by a volunteer within Medicines Sans Frontiers, one of the foremost aid organisations currently working here in the city, and what she had to say about the reasons for going to war in this country may make for disturbing viewing.'

Harrison Forbes took an involuntary step forward.

'What's this?'

Martin's image on the screen was replaced with that of one of the sprawling refugee camps outside Thessalia. Martin's voice spoke solemnly over the images of suffering and neglect.

'Camp Bravo, the second of five major refugee camps now spread around Thessalia and home to almost forty thousand Mordanians, all of whom have lost everything they own. Amongst these casualties of war work people like Sophie Vernoux, a twenty–five year old volunteer who administers medicine, blankets, food and comfort as best she can to those in her care, despite the awful conditions in which she is forced to work.'

Harrison looked at the image of Sophie Vernoux spoon–feeding a young infant as what looked like the child's weary grandmother looked on. The mother, tellingly, was nowhere to be seen. Martin's voice went on over the harrowing images.

'Eighteen month old Nyla, orphaned by artillery fire during fighting in the north of the country just weeks ago. She lost her entire family but for her grandmother, who managed to reach Thessalia before the winter set in. Sophie cares for hundreds of such children, all of whom are victims of the supposed atrocities commited against the Mordanian people by the rebel forces of General Mikhal Rameron. But the story she has to tell is not the one that we have all been hearing up to now.'

The footage closed up on Sophie, sitting on a snow–covered wall and being interviewed by Martin. Harrison Forbes, his heart suddenly thumping in his chest, watched open–mouthed as the aid volunteer spoke.

'There have been no massacres in the south of the country by rebel forces,' Sophie said in exasperation, her French accent giving a gentle lilt to her voice. *'There were no rebel forces this far south when that village was attacked, and everybody here knows it.'*

'Holy shit!' Harrison shouted loud enough to bring utter silence to the operations room. 'Give that girl a medal – she'll make us all rich!'

Sophie Vernoux's voice rang out as clear as a claxon in the silent ops room and across the world.

'Every single Mordanian knows that the people in that village were scientists, working on projects being funded by an unknown benefactor. None of the people employed there were combatants, and none of them posessed weapons in the manner described by the government here.'

Martin leaned a little closer to her, his expression etched with seriousness as though he were considering a complex mathematical equation.

'You're saying, Sophie, that the people killed were not killed by rebels, and were not combatants at all?'

'Oui. I mean, yes, that's exactly what I mean. We were among the first people to find the bodies out there in the forest. We'd known for some time that something terrible had happened out there, because we heard rumours of survivors amongst the refugees from the

moment we arrived. It was by chance that a convoy of ours moving through the area stumbled upon the remains of the engineering buildings and then the bodies. I can tell you, without any shadow of a doubt, that there were no weapons with those bodies.'

'You mean to tell me, Sophie, that the weapons were planted afterwards?'

'Yes, after the bodies were found, after the Mordanian Secret Police became involved but before the International Red Cross arrived. Those people were killed long before the rebel forces of General Mikhail Rameron had moved this far south.'

Martin Sigby frowned thoughtfully.

'But I thought that the bodies found had been dead for only a few days, and that rebel forces had been seen in the area, tying them in with the massacre.'

Sophie smiled almost pityingly.

'It is a deception. The lack of decomposition of the bodies was not due to a recent death. It was the result of the bodies lying on or in near perma–frost conditions and covered with snow – the cold effectively preserved their bodies, slowing the rate of tissue decay. They had been dead for at least a month, of that we have absolutely no doubt. The government here has failed to release that essential information to the general public or the press in its case for western intervention in the conflict.'

'I'll be damned,' Harrison Forbes whispered as the screen flicked back to Martin, standing on top of the Thessalia Hilton.

'It can only be called incendiary, the charge that the crimes against humanity in this country may not have actually been caused by the rebel forces, but by agencies within the government itself. This in itself could be considered explosive enough, were it not for the initial source of the information.'

'Oh dear mother of God, there's more,' Harrison murmured.

Martin Sigby seemed to take a breath on–screen before speaking.

'The initial discovery of the bodies was made by a former investigative reporter by the name of Megan Mitchell, who was herself in Mordania searching for a missing American journalist, Amy O'Hara. Miss Mitchell, having discovered the true identity of those massacred as scientists, had continued her search for the missing American journalist only to have vanished herself somewhere in the bleak interior of this war–torn country.'

Harrison Forbes's delighted expression slowly folded in upon itself as he listened to Martin's voice, and saw upon the screens the images of Amy O'Hara and Megan Mitchell.

'What might have happened to Megan Mitchell and Amy O'Hara remains unthinkable. With the United States preparing for war in Mordania, and with President Akim's pleas for assistance against an enemy perhaps less brutal than his government's own troops now seeming somewhat hollow, the case for military assistance in Mordania has hit a crisis point; whom should we assist? There can be little doubt that in this land ravaged by civil–war and mass murder, nothing remains quite as it seems. Martin Sigby, GNN News, Mordania.'

Martin Sigby's image vanished and was replaced with Jared Thornton and Harriet Holloway, who seemed frozen in time until Jared snapped out of it and continued with the news.

Harrison Forbes sat down and stared blankly at the screens.

'When was the last time we heard from Megan Mitchell?' he asked quietly.

An assistant flicked through a few sheets of paper. 'About forty–eight hours ago.'

Harrison rubbed his temples and whispered to himself.

'Megan, what have you gotten yourself into?'

***

42

'Come with me.'

Chekov's voice was stern as a sack was once again placed over Megan's aching head and tight bonds wrapped around her wrists as she was led from the storage room and out into the bitter dusk. The base around her remained alive with activity, much of it now illuminated by large flood–lights.

The rebel soldier led Megan back to General Rameron's operations room, but this time they walked through it toward a large office at the back. Chekov led Megan inside and closed the door behind them before lifting the sack from Megan's head and sitting her forcefully on a chair. Megan swallowed thickly as the soldier then produced from his pocket a thick, metal knuckle–guard and slowly, demonstratively, fitted it over his right fist.

The office was spartan but for a large metal desk and a map of the Caspian Sea on one wall. A small television played in one corner of the room, its volume muted.

General Rameron sat behind the desk beneath the fluorescent light on the ceiling, engrossed in various papers and documents. The steel rimmed spectacles that he wore made him appear oddly sophisticated. He looked up with those pale eyes at Megan as though only vaguely interested, and then at the rebel standing beside him.

'You may begin, Chekov,' he said quietly.

Megan watched as the rebel moved to stand in front of her, and a wave of impotent outrage flooding her nervous system.

'I told you, we are not spies nor soldiers.'

The general did not look up from his paperwork as he replied. 'I heard you. I did not believe you.'

'What have you done with Bolav? Where is my cameraman, Callum?'

General Rameron stood slowly from behind his desk and moved around it to face Megan, standing no more than three feet away.

'They are none of your concern right now, Megan Mitchell. Your only concern is your survival, which is becoming increasingly unlikely.'

The general nodded to his soldier, who raised his right fist and swung the solid metal toward Megan's battered face. Megan shrieked with fear and closed her eyes as she tried to turn away from the blow.

It did not come. Megan opened one eye a fraction, to see the general holding his soldier's arm back whilst looking at the television in the corner.

Rameron released the soldier and walked across to the television, turning the sound up. Megan saw Martin Sigby speaking, heard him as the volume rose, and then started in surprise as she saw Sophie Vernoux talking earnestly to Martin.

A wave of incomparable relief washed over Megan as Sophie's words filled her ears, of her own disappearance, of the search for Amy O'Hara and of her own past as a war correspondent. Her brief joy was tinged with sudden concern as she remembered Sophie's own past. She was on television, being seen by millions of people. There was no way she would not be identified.

'Oh Sophie, what have you done?' Megan whispered.

Mikhail Rameron looked across at Megan. The general gestured to Megan's bonds.

'Chekov, release her please.'

Chekov, apparently disappointed, removed his knuckle–guard and placed it on a table nearby before moving across to Megan's chair. Megan felt the bonds being loosened from her wrists as she was released from the chair.

Megan moved like lightning, two hours of imprisoned rage bursting from within. She turned, grabbed Chekov by his smock and heard her own scream of rage as she stamped forward and head–butted him savagely, felt the cartilage in the man's nose crunching inward as he collapsed onto his knees. Megan turned, grabbed the knuckle–guard and smashed it across the rebel's face, knocking him unconscious before turning back toward Rameron. Megan flicked her right boot toward the general's stomach with maximum force, only to see Rameron spin aside from the blow.

Megan recovered her balance instantly, driven by furious instinct, dropping her right foot down and pivoting on it whilst delivering a powerful reverse chop with her elbow. Rameron caught it easily, pulled Megan off balance and slammed her onto her back upon the metal desk. Before Megan could move, one cold, dry hand was wrapped around her throat and a pistol was pressed to her face.

General Rameron regarded Megan as one might regard a winged–insect caught between finger and thumb. His voice was calm and unconcerned.

'If you wish to die then I will comply willingly, but I have no desire to harm you.'

Before Megan could concoct a suitably furious response, Rameron released her and stood back, re–holstering his pistol. Megan slowly sat upright on the desk, massaging her throat as Rameron spoke to her quickly, presumably to prevent Megan from launching another suicidal attack.

'I was a Mordanian Air Force fighter pilot for twenty–two years. In that time much of our training was against the obvious threat from the west, but also from renegade dictatorships in Kazakhstan and Iran. My men and I were well trained to defend ourselves if shot down in these countries, for they have little mercy in time of war.'

Megan blinked.

'Lack of mercy being something else you clearly learned in your career,' she muttered.

Rameron appeared unpreturbed by Megan's unveiled hatred.

'You are alive, are you not?' he challenged, and when Megan did not respond he gestured out of a window toward the storage room where she had been incarcerated. 'Your translator, Bolav, was unharmed. Your cameraman is being treated for his wounds, but will not be able to travel for a short while and we cannot adequately provide for him here. He needs some rest before you leave.'

Megan stopped massaging her throat.

'Where are we going?'

Rameron appeared vaguely bemused.

'I have no use for you and no stomach for prisoners, especially wounded ones. You will be transported to Thessalia in a prisoner exchange.'

Megan's tired and battered mind tried to calculate Rameron's reasoning, but failed.

'So you believe me now, then?' she said, glancing at the television.

'I just had to be sure you were not the enemy, sent here to try to return information to the government forces in Thessalia. My apologies for the apparent brutality of myself and my men, but they were genuinely angry and believed you responsible for the deaths of their comrades, as did I.'

Megan winced, rubbing her neck.

'So you're letting us go, just like that.'

'You are of no use to me.'

'Your cause is pointless. Your time is over. Once the Americans deploy here your forces will be driven back to the north.'

Rameron nodded, smiling what seemed to be a melancholy smile to himself.

'That is true,' he replied.

Megan waited for more but nothing came. The general resumed his seat at his desk and began rearranging the papers that had been scattered from their orderly piles. Megan stared at the general for a moment, her mind briefly off balance and confused.

'And you're going to go right ahead and attack Thessalia?'

General Rameron simply nodded, frowning at a small map of Georgia. Megan shook her head.

'Why?' she asked.

General Rameron sighed. 'Has your country ever been invaded, Megan?'

'People have tried,' Megan replied, 'but have not succeeded for centuries.'

'If it were to happen again, that your lands were threatened, the army helpless, the air force obsolete and a navy non–existent. If your people were under threat of extinction, would you not stand and fight?'

Megan leaned on the desk.

'Of course I would, but this isn't the same. You are the one who held the coup and started the war!'

General Rameron nodded slowly.

'So say all of the news networks that you work for, all of your people who come here to Mordania and tell the world what a monster I am and how that world should support President Akim and his supposedly democratic government.'

Megan's eyes narrowed slightly as her brain forced itself to consider what Rameron was saying.

'So that's it,' she said finally, 'you let us go and we run back to Thessalia and report that General Rameron isn't a baby–eating psychopath after all and happens to be quite a nice chap.' She pointed to her bruised and bloodied face. 'You think they'll believe that when they see me?'

The general put down the piece of paper he was holding and rubbed his temples before looking at Megan with the pitying gaze of a father for a wayward child.

'It wouldn't make any difference what you reported, now, in the past, or tomorrow. It is too late for that.'

'Is that before the military coup, the genocide, the human shield and the attacks on the American carrier fleet, or after?' Megan asked sarcastically.

General Rameron slammed an iron–hard fist onto his table with a deafening clang and shot upright out of his seat again to loom over Megan.

'How many fighter aircraft did the UN general briefing you received in Thessalia say that we posessed when you arrived?'

Megan performed an unexpected and rapid search of her memory.

'Twenty four – twenty fighters and four twin–seat trainers. Mig–23's.'

'That's correct,' Rameron growled. 'They are still here. Perhaps you would like to go and count them?'

Megan stood for a moment, unsure of how to respond. The general moved around his table once again, his powerful frame radiating pure, undiluted rage.

'Perhaps you might like to research more closely who deployed their troops first before the military coup, myself or President Akim. Perhaps you should go outside and ask the local people whether they are part of any supposed human shield or here because they fear to be alone in the hills. And the only genocide that I know of occurred near Thessalia, not here!'

Rameron turned away from Megan for a moment, attempting to master his fury. He turned slowly back to face Megan again, his expression troubled.

'This woman that you were searching for. Why did she come here?'

'She was searching for a family friend of her father's,' Megan said. 'An engineer, a man called Petra Milankovich.'

The general's eye twitched slightly at the mention of the name. He stared at the ground thoughtfully.

'The name is familiar to me. He died in the massacre near Thessalia, correct?'

'How do you know that?' Megan asked.

'Because they all died that day, the day this war really began.'

'What were they doing in that laboratory?' she asked, sensing the source of the undisclosed mystery.

General Rameron, however, was already turning away.

'I have said enough. I have work to do.'

Megan shook her head.

'Don't walk away from this. I need to know what they were doing in that laboratory!'

General Rameron looked at her for a long moment as two rebel guards appeared in the office, one taking hold of one of Megan's arms and the other kneeling down beside their still unconscious comrade. Megan realised that Rameron appeared tired now, devoid of energy or hope.

'If I were to tell you what they had been doing in there, you would never believe it. It will take Martin Sigby, now, to get the world to believe.'

Megan strained against the rebel soldier as she was manhandled toward the office door, shouting as Rameron turned his back.

'He won't come here! They won't let him leave the city now!'

General Rameron did not look back as she spoke. 'Then the war is already over.'

Megan managed to grab the edge of the door frame, shouting in desperation.

'There is a farmstead near here, something to do with Amy O'Hara and Petra Milankovich! Tell me where to find it! I can pass what I find to Martin Sigby! You may not like it, but right now I'm all you've got!'

General Rameron paused, thinking for a moment, and then looked at Megan over his shoulder.

'My men will take you there tonight, on your way to Thessalia. And you will have the chance to speak to Martin Sigby – because it is he for whom you will be exchanged.'

***

43

The Gold Room,

Pentagon

'Say that again?'

Vice President Hobb's voice had raised an octave or two, as though some unseen hand had thrust something painfully sharp into hidden parts of his anatomy.

President Baker sat listening to an open speaker as it relayed the message from Admiral Fry's carrier group on the Black Sea.

'There's nothing at all concrete to go on Mister Vice President, and that's what makes this such a dilemma. My pilot is adamant that there was something not right about the engagement and is willing to go on the record to voice her doubts.'

Hobbs cast a glance across the table at the President, who was rubbing his temples with his fingers and vaguely shaking his head.

'Can you tell us what you *do* know, admiral?' Hobbs asked.

'What we can say for sure is that the two aircraft in question made a very long and challenging flight, remaining undetected at low level for a long time, before engaging our fighters standing Combat Air Patrol two hundred miles out from the carrier group. The problem is that having reached their objective, they then allowed themselves to be destroyed almost without a fight.'

President Baker spoke without looking out from behind his hands.

'Make your point, admiral.'

'My point, Mister President, and the opinion of my pilots is that the aircraft involved in the engagement may not have been Mordanian fighters.'

'Jesus,' Hobbs said softly. 'Thank you, admiral. We will be in touch.'

Hobbs cut off the transmission and leaned back in his chair as the president let out a long sigh of despair.

'If these aircraft were not Mordanian then who the hell did they belong to?'

Hobbs exhaled with a dramatic sweep of his hands.

'The Mig–23 has been sold to dozens of countries over several decades – they could belong to anyone in the region; Iran, Kazakhstan, Georgia, even Chechnya might have been able to get their hands on a couple of airframes.'

President Baker stood for a moment with his hands on his hips.

'But why would they want us to invade Mordania? Bringing our forces there would put us on both sides of Iran, not something that would please them, and the same goes for Kazakhstan. Georgia might welcome the presence, as would Chechnya because it would counter Russian influence in the region, but neither could achieve much through dragging us into conflict there by cooercion or deception.'

Hobbs stroked his chin.

'I can see no reason as to why they would use jets to impersonate Mordanian fighters, Matthew. Admiral Fry may be reporting these suspicions to cover himself and his pilots in case something comes to light later. We can't afford to base a political decision on someone's wild hunch.'

President Baker smiled wryly.

'And how many decisions have we made based on hunches that turned out to be correct?'

Hobbs returned the rueful smile, but shook his head.

'Not many where wars are concerned.'

'How did this happen?' Baker asked.

'I don't know, Mister President,' Hobbs said.

'Jesus Christ.' The president shook his head and stood from his desk, pacing for a moment as he spoke, a habit that he had brought into the presidency from his senate days. 'You know, Richard, I came into this with such a clear picture of what I wanted to do. I wanted to do it right. I wanted to lead, and have the people of this country realise that for the first time in decades they could have a president whose actions and motivations they understood. What the hell happened to destroy that so quickly?'

The Vice President sighed and gestured helplessly with open palms.

'That's politics, Matthew. You knew it before you came here.'

'I knew what it was before I came here, and it's that which I wanted to change.'

'You couldn't have predicted any of this, least of all that President Akim's men might have conducted the genocide.'

'They're making a fool of me,' Baker snapped. 'I pledged my support for Akim's democratic government, and then learn that they may well be responsible for genocide. I commit to a war, then find out that there may be no case for war. What the hell am I going to say to congress? How the hell do I explain this to the American people?!'

President Baker rubbed his temples. Hobbs was about to speak when the president's desk–top speaker beeped softly. Baker pressed a button on the speaker.

'What is it Louise?'

'There's a Seth Cain here to see the vice–president, sir.'

The president and Hobbs exchanged a glance.

'Hold one moment,' Baker said, and took his finger off the button. 'Who the hell does he think he is, coming here?'

Hobbs stared vacantly out of the office window for a moment.

'They wanted this war, you know that.'

'They hoped for it,' the president said, suddenly cautious.

'What are you thinking?' Hobbs frowned seriously.

'The unthinkable. Let's see what he has to say for himself.'

The president cleared Cain to enter the Gold Room. The media tycoon arrived a couple of minutes later, sweeping into the office and extending his hand to the president.

'Mr President, thank you so much for seeing me at such short notice, sir.'

'At no notice,' Baker replied, mastering his displeasure and shaking the proffered hand. 'We have a great deal to do, so if I might ask you to be brief?'

'Of course,' Cain said, shaking Hobb's reluctant hand. 'Mr President, it would appear that your office, and as a result our country, has suffered something of a reversal of fortune. I'm speaking about the situation in Mordania of course.'

Baker and Hobbs again exchanged a glance but neither spoke, waiting instead for Cain to continue.

'I have a way of bringing these difficulties to an end,' the tycoon said.

'Is that so?' Hobbs uttered. 'What do you intend to do? Invade Mordania yourself with a bandolier and grenades?'

Cain smiled grimly.

'Many of our mutual issues are being caused by the media coverage distorting events on the ground in Mordania. False news, gentlemen, pre–arranged stories, fabricated interviews, falsified information. Much of what is being said about Mordania is not at all true, and I know who is causing it.'

'Who?' President Baker snapped.

'A woman named Megan Mitchell.'

'The one who's been captured by Rameron's troops?' Hobbs hazarded. 'She's not going to be much of a threat now.'

'You don't think?' Cain replied. 'It was she who got the footage from behind enemy lines for Martin Sigby's reports. She's the one who's trying to show the uprising of General Rameron in a favourable light. She knows that such explosive reports can make her fortune. Do you really think that the rebels aren't going to take full advantage of that? Before you know it, Mikhail Rameron will be the saviour of his people, the gallant freedom fighter, the rebel with a cause. It'll be Nelson Mandela all over again. By the time Mitchell's finished Rameron will have been knighted by the English Queen, interviewed by Oprah and blessed by the frigging pope.'

Hobbs looked uncertainly at the president, who in turn eyed Cain suspiciously.

'I'm not sure where you're coming from with this, Seth.'

The tycoon stood before Baker and Hobbs and raised a clenched fist demonstratively.

'Pull Mitchell out of Mordania, before she can do any more damage. Without her there the rebels will no longer have a means to put their twisted ideaology out to the world and President Akim's government can maintain some dignity in the face of their crisis. Hell, it would even look good for us: American Special Forces rescue a British reporter from the clutches of the evil tyrant Mikhail Rameron.'

Hobbs frowned.

'When you say *us,* who are you referring to?'

'America,' Cain replied neatly. 'Each and every one of us. If Rameron's men have the chance to use Mitchell as a weapon of propaganda the American position will continue to be weakened. Without her there you'll be able to crush the rebellion, reinstate the government of President Akim and bring peace to Mordania.'

Neither Hobbs nor Baker could think of anything to say. Cain watched them for a moment before pushing his case further.

'It's worth it gentlemen. Extract Megan Mitchell, and these difficulties will all come to an end. There are Special Forces units attached to the nearest carrier group, correct? They could be on the ground in two hours from now.'

'There are already SF units on the ground near Talyn,' Hobbs said speculatively, 'watching rebel movements to the north. They could be tasked very easily.'

The president was thinking furiously when his speaker–phone beeped again.

'What is it Louise?' he asked, trying to keep his voice calm.

'The French Embassy in New York, Mr President,' the aide said promptly. *'They have some issues regarding the recent televised report from Mordania by the GNN crew.'*

Hobbs raised an eyebrow and glanced at Cain.

'Go ahead,' the president said.

'They say that the woman in the interview is a fugitive sir, and has been on the run from the French authorities for several years. Something to do with an outlawed activist movement. They're demanding that President Akim's government apprehend her and repatriate her to France.'

President Baker nodded slowly. 'Thank you, Louise.'

He clicked the speaker–phone off and looked at Cain, whose face was creased with a sly grin as he reached into his pocket and retrieved an envelope. He opened it, and handed the contents to the president.

'Sophie D'Aoust is her real name, a former member of an anarchist movement in France responsible for several deaths. She has been on the run for years.'

Hobbs stepped forward from one side, looking at the picture of Sophie held by the president.

'Neat, Seth, I'll give you that,' Hobbs said.

The president nodded, also looking at Cain.

'I want you to release a report on all of your stations within two hours, containing every single precise detail of what that French girl did and of how utterly appalling it was. That will discredit everything that's been reported in Mikhail Rameron's favour.'

'Done,' Cain said without hesitation. 'By the time we're finished, she won't be able to settle into a civilised country anywhere on earth.'

Baker looked at Hobbs. 'I want you to call Mukhari Akim and suggest that he do exactly as the French have demanded.'

'I'm sure he will not have an issue with that,' Hobbs agreed. 'It'll clear the way for our forces too. Nobody's going to believe Martin Sigby's reports once this gets out. He'll be totally compromised.

The president regarded Cain for a long moment.

'What's in it for you, Seth?' Baker asked.

Cain smiled at the President.

'We get to film the war, exclusive rights to the coverage of the liberation of Thessalia. Give me that and I'll make sure that neither Megan Mitchell or Martin Sigby ever work again.'

***

44

It was both dark and bitterly cold outside as Megan was led across a large parade ground toward a hospital near the centre of Rameron's field headquarters. Her accompanying guards no longer restrained her, simply marching in step either side of her as she was led inside the hospital.

Rows of beds lined each of the walls, some with intravenous bags hanging from improvised leather hoops tacked to the ceiling. Wounded men lay everywhere, some with limbs missing, others suffering from burns or shrapnel lesions. The whole hospital was filled with the odours of burnt and decaying flesh, iodine and disinfectant.

Megan found Callum laying in a bed half way down the ward, his arm in a sling and a weary, lethargic expression on his face. He saw Megan coming and smiled weakly.

'You look bloody awful,' he said.

Megan had forgotten about her own battered features. She smiled broadly and pain creased her features as her lips split again.

'They're sending us back to Thessalia.'

Callum raised an eyebrow.

'That's jolly nice of them. What's the catch?'

'Prisoner exchange –for Martin Sigby.'

'No way,' Callum said as Megan helped him to his feet. 'They'll swallow him up and toss him to the dogs.'

'I don't think so,' Megan whispered. 'And there's something that they want to show us.'

Megan helped Callum walk to the front door where Bolav, the translator, stood waiting for them. He looked sheepishly at Megan's bruised and bloodied features.

'I am sorry, I am so sorry,' he pleaded emphatically. 'I told them everything about the man, Sigby.'

'Forget it,' Megan said, waving the pathetically apologetic Mordanian aside. 'We've got bigger problems right now, and Martin Sigby's safe enough in Thessalia.'

Bolav followed them meekly out into the night air. The sky above was clear for the first time in weeks, stars twinkling in the black velvet vacuum of space, but the bitter drop in temperature was turning the snow into ice, the white earth sparkling with crystalline stars of its own under the harsh lights of the compound.

A large truck was idling nearby, its exhaust puffing clouds of smoke that glowed blue–white in the compound's lights. Twelve rebel soldiers surrounded it, their weapons held at port arms. Megan helped Callum across to the vehicle, with Bolav miserably bringing up the rear.

As Megan climbed aboard after Callum she turned to look across the camp. At the top of the steps leading up to the command centre she could see General Mikhail Rameron watching them, his hands behind his back and his eyes piercing Megan's even from across the hundred yard compound.

'My cameras are here,' Callum said in surprise as he sat on a bench in the rear of the vehicle.

'I know,' Megan said quietly, still watching Rameron in the distance.

Bolav clambered aboard the truck and a soldier slammed the rear panel closed, bolting it into place. Surrounded by heavily armed Mordanian rebels huddling together against the bitter night chill, Megan watched out of the back of the truck as it drove through the compound and out of the gates into the dense forest. Within minutes, the brightly lit rebel base had vanished into the impenetrable blackness.

The truck carried them through the dense, pitch–black forests for more than half an hour, rolling them from side to side as the vehicle's broad and heavy wheels forged ahead through the pitted roads. None of the rebel troopers spoke, each alone with their thoughts, staring at their heavy, muddied boots and trying to ignore the biting cold.

Megan looked across to where Callum was propped against the canvass side of the truck, wrapped snugly in blankets and sleeping. Bolav sat next to him, hugging his knees to his chin and mumbling to himself in the darkness.

The road along which they travelled was only wide enough for one vehicle and was entirely enclosed by towering walls of pine forest, vaguely illuminated by the weakly probing tail lights glowing red against snows unmarked by the passage of men or vehicles, only by the feint tracks of wild animals. Even with a portable gas–heater blowing at maximum in the rear of the truck it was cold, Megan's breath wisping on the air. The forests to either side seemed as deep as those in old fairy tales, dark and full of secrets.

'How much farther?' Megan asked Bolav, who spoke to one of the senior NCO's accompanying them.

'Not far,' Bolav translated the soldier's mumbled reply.

'That's what you said last time.'

'That's what he said last time,' the Mordanian replied.

Megan looked back to the towering peaks of the pine forest. She could see against the inky blackness of the night sky the vague outline of soaring valleys, could discerne their outlined ridges where the stars no longer shone. A pale moon hovering somewhere in the bitterly cold night sky made their towering snow–covered heights glow a soft blue. For a moment Megan found herself transfixed, hypnotised by the sheer ethereal beauty of the rugged, spellbound land.

'It's beautiful,' Bolav said, seeing Megan's gaze. 'A beautiful land spoilt only by the stain of human conflict.'

Megan blinked at the Mordanian's poignant observation.

'Men could not spoil this place,' she replied.

The explosion hit the frozen night air and shattered it like a hammer through crystal. Megan was hurled across the back of the truck as a sudden clamour of shouts and screams filled her ears, bodies flailing, weapons spilling from the rear of the vehicle as it slid broadside across the road. Megan struggled across to Callum and wrapped her arms protectively around the Scotsman as the truck slid to a halt.

The Mordanian troops flooded from the rear of the truck, running and shouting and firing into the forests. Megan could see the muzzle flashes lighting up the trees, illuminating the faces of the enraged and yet terrified soldiers. In the confusion and noise she saw a Mordanian soldier stagger backwards as a single round hit him squarely in the chest with a dull thump. A split–second later a second round hit him full in the face, whipping his head aside as his lifeless body spun and slapped down into the snow.

'What's going on?!' Bolav screamed, his hands over his ears. '*Nouv alerittz eno saviant!* Mercy of God help us!!'

Megan helped Callum to his feet and staggered to the back of the truck, listening to the crackle and snap of weapons and trying to see into the darkness. Most of the soldiers seemed to be around the front of the truck, firing forwards. Megan jumped down from the rear of the truck, carefully avoiding the dead Mordanian lying nearby, and helped Callum down as Bolav skittered alongside him.

'Where are we going?!' the Mordanian screeched.

'Anywhere but here!' Megan shouted back. 'Grab his arm!'

Bolav gripped Callum's left arm and together they made for the nearby tree line, Megan trying to keep the truck between them and their unknown assailants. As they neared the ominous, inky blackness of the forest, Megan risked a glance back.

The remaining Mordanians were crouched around the cab of the truck, laying down heavy fire into the forest on the other side of the road, the bright flares of tracer fire streaming like laser beams into the darkness. As

Megan watched, one by one, the Mordanians were picked off with precise, accurate shots that came not from the forest nearby but from further away, up the road.

Megan hurried with Bolav and Callum into the darkness of the forest and squatted down amidst the frozen foliage, watching as the sound of gunfire was reduced to the single, forlorn Kalashnikov of the final remaining Mordanian soldier. The man fired a couple of random rounds into the forest and then shouted out into the darkness.

'Foriz tan specterk, monik implore aventick!'

The words seemed to hang on the icy air, haunting it. Megan listened, but no response came from the darkness.

'What did he say?' she asked Bolav in a whisper.

'He asked the ghosts of the forest to leave him be.'

Megan watched as the lone Mordanian stepped out from behind the truck, his AK–47 held high above his head, the puffs of his breath illuminated by the truck's headlights.

A long silence enveloped the forest as the man stood, his head turning as he searched the endless shadows between the trees.

A single shot rang out and the lone soldier quivered slightly. Megan started in shock, watching. The Mordanian stood for a few moments longer and then suddenly his legs buckled and his knees hit the cold earth with a dull crack. The weapon in his hands dropped beside him as he slowly toppled face down into the snow.

Megan, Bolav and Callum sat absolutely still for almost five minutes, watching, waiting, too afraid to move. Megan wondered how many men must have been in the forest to have killed over twenty Mordanian rebels so quickly. As she watched, so she got her answer.

Three men emerged from the tree line, all wearing Artic–combat suits and carrying assault weapons at the ready. They swept the carnage of the scene before them with practiced efficiency, alert like wild animals, legs crouched like coiled springs, faces hidden behind balaclavas.

From beside Megan, Callum whispered in a taut voice.

'Special Forces, probably British SAS.'

Megan nodded, but was not prepared for the harshly whispered voice that came from behind her.

'American, actually.'

The three of them whirled and Megan felt an almost supernatural wave of fear overcome her as part of the forest seemed to come alive. Two more of the elite troops rose up from the frozen forest floor, their weapons trained upon Megan and her companions. Megan tried uselessly to shield

Callum with her body. The American gestured with a movement of his weapon as he spoke.

'Into the road.'

Megan, Callum and Bolav moved out of the tree line and into the road, the American soldiers backing off to give them space. The man who had appeared behind them lifted his balaclava to reveal a surprisingly young face, a shaven head and keen, quick eyes.

'That her?' asked one of the other soldiers in a rough Chicago accent.

'That's her,' their young leader said knowingly. 'Megan Mitchell, correct?'

Megan blinked in surprise. 'You know me?'

'You're to come with us, ma'am,' the soldier said with abrupt, military efficiency. 'My name is Lieutenant Lincoln Cole, United States Navy Seals.'

Before Megan could reply another American soldier appeared, moving from further down the road to join them. He held a high–velocity sniper rifle in his grip.

'Road's clear, all hostiles down.'

Lieutenant Cole nodded, looking quickly at Callum, who was clearly favouring his injury.

'Let's go,' Cole decided promptly.

Megan did not move and looked down at the dead Mordanian who had surrendered.

'Why did you kill him?' she asked Cole quietly. 'He gave himself up.'

Cole's expression bore no trace of regret or remorse as he replied.

'He was an obstacle to our mission. We are charged to extract you from this country without anyone knowing of our being here. We have no contigency for hostages or prisoners of war. If he had been released, he would have reported what happened here. As it is, the shots will have been heard for miles around. We need to move now, and quickly.'

Megan shook her head.

'They were taking us somewhere safe. They were just an escort.'

'We'll be taking you somewhere safer,' Cole replied sharply but without raising his voice. 'Unless you'd rather remain here?'

Megan tried searching for a suitable retort, but before she could speak Callum gestured to one of the soldier's back–packs.

'Radio?'

'Not in this terrain,' Cole replied with a shake of his head. 'We'll need to clear the mountains by dawn to make it to our extraction point.'

'How far is that?' Megan asked.

'Twelve clicks, give or take.'

Megan shook her head. 'Callum's not going to make it that far in his condition.'

Lieutenant Cole glanced appraisingly at the towering Scotsman.

'He'll survive.'

Megan took a pace toward the American.

'These men were taking us to a farm out here, where we might find help. We could rest up there. It can't be far.'

'Our orders are not to make contact with any inhabitants of this area.'

'A bit late for that,' Callum said, jabbing a thumb in Bolav's direction. 'Besides, none of us are in suitable condition for a night out beneath the stars and we won't make the lowlands by dawn. We need shelter and we need food.'

Lieutenant Cole glanced at his men.

'Was there anything on this road to the south?'

'There was a farmstead,' the sniper replied from memory. 'Nothing else substantial until Anterik. I'd say they were taking them there.'

Lieutenant Cole glanced at Megan and her battered companions for a few moments more, and then turned away.

'Fine. Let's move!'

***

45

'Any sign of movement?' Lieutenant Cole whispered.

Megan crouched in the freezing darkness as the SEALS silently observed the way ahead. As Megan peered through the dense trees she thought she saw the faintest glimmer of light, a flicker barely noticeable beyond the trees.

The forest ended ahead of them, opening into a broad plain perhaps a kilometre square. In the moonlight Megan could just make out a cluster of buildings; a mill, houses, a small church and what looked like barns surrounded by ploughed fields thick with blankets of snow.

'Doesn't look like much,' she observed in a hushed whisper.

All of the windows of the buildings were closed with what appeared to be shutters, only the tiniest slivers of light visible. Callum surveyed the scene.

'No defences, no gates or walls or observation posts.'

Lieutenant Cole nodded.

'The village looks unharmed,' he said. 'Intelligence told us that this territory had been overrun by Rameron's forces.'

Bolav spoke from the impenetrable darkness that enveloped them.

'It was, weeks ago. Maybe they did not put up a big fight, no? Maybe they change sides?'

Cole did not respond, one finger pressing into his ear as he listened to one of his men. He turned to look over his shoulder at Megan.

'You all stay here and out of sight until we come for you.'

'What are you going to do?' Megan asked urgently.

'We're going to enter the buildings and ensure they're not being used as a barracks by rebel forces. We'll go in hard and shock them.'

The lieutenant made to move but Megan grabbed his arm insistently.

'If you go blazing in there just a moment too slowly, anyone with a radio will bring the rest of Rameron's forces down on us like a ton of bricks. Let *us* go inside instead.'

'You?' Cole muttered in contempt.

'I can knock on the door. Callum's injured, Bolav can interpret. We're on the run. If anyone in there has a shred of human decency, they'll let us in. If you don't hear from us in five minutes, then it's a rebel stronghold and you can come in with all the bloody force you want.'

Lieutenant Cole frowned in concern, scanning the tiny hamlet with his hawk–like gaze before looking back at Megan.

'Our mission is to extract you from Mordania *alive*.'

'I'm glad to hear it,' Megan replied. 'I'll wager that anyone living in there won't have any love for the conflict that's raging around them. They'll help. If they're pro–rebellion, then you'll know soon enough and we'll have lost nothing. You said it yourself, the enemy will have heard the gunfight in the forest.'

Cole hesitated for a moment longer and then nodded, speaking into his microphone to his men before turning to Megan.

'Five minutes from when the door opens. We'll surround the building. If you don't come out, we'll come in.'

The night air was bitter, piercing even Megan's thick coat as she led Bolav and Callum toward the buildings. Their feet crunched through the thick snow as they walked, and ahead the door of the nearest house suddenly opened, a bright rectangle of light spilling out across the snowy ground. A figure appeared, a man who must have heard their approach through the snow. His voice cut through the night.

'Alenk passe plezten?!'

The voice was deep, almost threatening, but Megan could hear the anxiety in the man's tones. Bolav called out in reply.

'Ally! Ally. Tun assistev!'

Bolav hurried through the door as Megan supported Callum. The interpreter exchanged a few words with the man before waving them to follow, and with a weighty sense of caution Megan guided Callum through the door as it was closed behind them by another, unseen person.

The house was filled with warmth and light, and Megan blinked at the contrast in temperature as she helped Callum into a seat, turning to see who had let them in.

The man was probably in his late fifties, with greying hair and a squat, stocky build. With his big brown eyes and his sleeves rolled up to his elbows, he looked like a cross between a clockmaker and a lumberjack. Megan took off her coat as Bolav spoke rapidly to the man, gesticulating as he explained the events of the past few days.

The man turned, looking at Megan and Callum.

'You have come far, you must be hungry,' he said in heavily accented English. 'And you must both hurt.'

'We've had better days,' Megan replied.

Megan turned again to see who had closed the door behind them. A slender, modestly dressed woman with long silver and black hair tied in a pony–tail smiled nervously at her.

'I am Alexandre Humek,' the farmer said to Megan, 'and this is my wife, Marin.' He gestured to a kitchen table dominated by a simple but welcome spread of breads, cheeses, hot coffee and tea, jam and both ham and pork.

'We were eating dinner. Please,' Alexandre said, 'help yourselves. I will return in a moment with medicine for your friend's injuries.'

Megan watched as Alexandre and Marin left the room and Bolav and Callum dove toward the food on the table. Megan did not move, glancing instead around the kitchen.

The house was large by Mordanian standards, well kept and with a comfortable air about it, a curious cross between modern materials and rustic styling. A fireplace dominated one wall of the room, but the heating was modern, radiators lining the opposite wall. The kettle and cooking implements were clean but old, perhaps turn of the century. Yet despite this, a fairly modern looking computer was visible in a study off the main hallway leading toward the kitchen.

'What are you thinking?' Callum asked from around a mouthful of bread.

Megan shook her head vaguely, looking around further.

'I'm not sure,' she said curiously. 'Where do you think they're getting their power from?'

'Diesel generator, most likely,' Callum guessed. 'It's a farm, after all.'

'I didn't hear one when we arrived,' Megan murmured.

'Alexandre's one of the good guys,' Callum said, taking another bite of bread. 'I can tell.'

'That so?' Megan enquired.

'It is so,' Callum confirmed cheerfully. 'It's a gift.'

Megan was about to reply when she heard Alexandre coming back down the hall. The farmer walked into the kitchen and looked at his guests.

'You are eating well?' he asked earnestly.

'Like kings,' Callum replied.

Alexandre nodded and looked at Megan.

'I am wondering, why are you here, in Mordania?' he asked.

'Bad luck,' Megan replied. 'We were working in Thessalia but had to travel into the country. We were caught by General Rameron, who extended his own personal courtesy to me.'

Megan gestured to the bruises and cuts on her face. Alexandre nodded vaguely, the edge of his bottom lip pursed in his teeth. Megan looked at his strange expression.

'What is it?'

The farmer seemed cautious suddenly, guarded.

'Why were you not in Thessalia, where it is safe?'

'We had to come out here,' Megan replied. 'We were looking for someone.'

The farmer nodded again, and looked briefly down at his feet.

Megan looked down at Alexandre's hands. In his right hand he held a chunky looking satellite phone. Megan saw that the farmer's hands were marked around the nails with the dirt of years' of honest work, the palms calloused and the skin tough. Yet it did not look like the work of a farmer, more the work of an engineer, the dirt not soil but oils or greases and lubricants.

Alexandre handed the satellite phone to Megan.

'You might be able to use this,' he said. 'It will help you to return to Thessalia. I think that you should leave as soon as possible.'

Megan took the phone from the farmer.

'You have a lot of modern equipment here,' Megan said, gesturing to the computer and the phone.

'We are isolated,' Alexandre replied. 'Sometimes these expensive toys can save lives, especially in the winter.'

Megan nodded, looking at the phone and catching Callum watching her with a raised eyebrow as she did so.

'How much power does it have?' Megan asked Alexandre.

'None,' the farmer confessed quickly, then more slowly. 'It has not been used for some time and we no longer possess the charger. I have been trying to find a way to charge it. Perhaps you might have an idea of how to do that.'

Megan looked at it curiously, turning it over in her hand. She was about to press the *'on'* button when her heart froze in her chest. She stared at the phone for a long moment before walking casually away from the table, putting some distance between himself and Alexandre.

'You have an expensive satellite phone that can save lives, but you have lost the charger?'

Alexandre looked at Megan blankly, then at Callum before replying.

'My country is at war. I have had other things on my mind.'

Megan saw Callum watching her strangely, suddenly alert and on guard. Bolav was watching the exchange uncertainly, his cheeks puffed out with unchewed food.

Megan looked again at the satellite phone in her hand.

'I used to have one of these,' she said quietly. 'This is more advanced than the one that I had, newer and more powerful. They're typically owned by reporters, especially war reporters.'

Callum was tensed now, ready to move. Alexandre looked suddenly concerned.

'I did not know that,' he said.

'It's true,' Megan said, walking slowly back toward the farmer. 'We use funny little vibrating pens to put our names on the backs of the phones, you see. The pens raise little bumps on the plastic surface of the phone so that it cannot be erased. I'm surprised that you did not notice it.'

Megan held the back of the phone out toward Callum, who could see the name written there. He shot the farmer a serious look. Megan came to within two feet of where Alexandre stood and held the phone out to him.

'This phone belonged to Amy O'Hara,' she said softly, looking down at the name etched indelibly into the rear of the satellite phone. 'How did you happen to come by it?'

Alexandre looked at Megan, and then suddenly he saw Callum get to his feet and come lumbering toward them both. He swallowed thickly, but he held his ground.

'I did not look at the phone much,' he said quietly.

Megan leaned closer to him.

'Where is she?' she demanded in a voice heavy with threat. 'Tell me, now.'

***

46

Alexandre stood still in the silence of the kitchen, watching Megan for what felt like a long time before speaking with a tone now devoid of welcome.

'Your friend here, Bolav, says that you have come from the rebel camp. He says that you have escaped from an escort of General Rameron's men.'

'That's right,' Megan said. 'There was an accident. Our escorts were unconscious or killed and we were able to flee into the forest.'

'Not very quickly,' Alexandre pointed out, looking at Callum. 'He cannot run in his condition.'

'We did the best we could,' Megan defended herself. 'There wasn't much choice.'

Alexandre remained unconvinced, looking at the three of them.

'I heard gunfire, an hour ago, to the north of here.'

'We heard it too,' Megan said honestly.

'Do you bring the war to my doorstep?' Alexandre challenged. 'I want no part of this conflict, no part of the fighting.'

'We are not bringing the war to you,' Megan insisted.

'Yet you escaped from the rebels no more than a mile or two from here, and in your haste must have left a trail to follow in the snow, that will lead to us.'

'We had no choice,' Megan repeated.

'The fighting that we heard, it was nothing to do with you?'

Megan hesitated only a fraction of a second before replying.

'The fighting was nothing to do with us.'

Alexandre suddenly shoved one heavy hand into the centre of Megan's chest. The stocky farmer was quick for his age and the blow sent Megan reeling backward into Callum, who staggered off balance.

Alexandre's apparent fear had vanished in an instant. The door slammed behind the farmer as he vanished down the hallway toward the kitchen. Megan leapt forward, yanking open the door and taking a single pace before stopping in the hall.

Silhouetted in the kitchen doorway, Alexandre stood with a double–barelled shotgun aimed directly at Megan's chest. Megan stared down the muzzle of the weapon, the farmer regarding her without fear from behind the sights.

'Get out of my house. You are no longer welcome here.'

Two more men appeared behind Alexandre in the hall, both armed and bearing grim and uncompromising expressions. Megan realised that Alexandre had gone with his wife not to fetch medicines, but reinforcements.

'We need your help,' Megan said quickly. 'Please put down your weapons.'

'You can either walk out of this building,' Alexandre hissed, 'or I can spend the night wiping you off the walls with a cloth.'

'You don't understand,' Megan pleaded. 'If you don't put...'

'Get out now!!' Alexandre bellowed loudly enough to make Megan flinch.

'No. I'm not leaving without Amy.'

'There is nobody here by that name.'

'I don't believe you,' Megan snapped harshly. 'Where is she? We've been looking for her!'

'You'll not find her here!'

'We're reporters, Amy is a friend of mine,' Megan tried to reason with Alexandre.

'I don't believe you.'

'It's the truth, ask Amy.'

'Get out of my house.'

Megan heard the farmer flick the shotgun's safety–catch off.

'I'm not leaving without her.'

A crash of shattered glass and wood from somewhere in the rear of the house broke the stand–off. Megan felt a bolt of panic slither inside her guts as Alexandre turned to see his two companions shouting in the hall as sleek, shadowy figures moved rapidly through the house toward them.

'Cole! Don't shoot!' Megan shouted.

The kitchen door burst open as Lieutenant Cole rushed through, his M–16 pointing at Alexandre's shocked face.

'Don't shoot!' Megan yelled. 'Don't shoot!'

Lieutenant Cole's men hesitated, their weapons trained unwaveringly on the Mordanians. Cole's voice was remarkably calm as she spoke.

'Hold your fire.' Cole shot Bolav a brief glance. 'Tell these men to drop their weapons.'

'I can hear you,' Alexandre growled furiously.

'Then do as you're told,' Cole snapped.

'Go to hell,' Alexandre snarled back.

Megan rushed forward and put herself between the Navy SEAL and Alexandre, raising placatory hands and trying to defuse the stand–off.

'Everyone back off.'

'You lied,' Alexandre muttered. 'Why should I trust these people?'

'Because they didn't want to be here either,' Megan replied. 'We're passing through and soon we'll be gone.'

'Get out of my way, Mitchell,' Cole said angrily, still aiming at what he could see of Alexandre.

Megan ignored the American, keeping her hands up. Alexandre glanced at the soldier's steely, dispassionate gaze and Megan knew that the Mordanian was preparing to face certain death. He and his fellow farmers could not hope to defeat the elite American team.

'You can't win,' Megan pressed, 'but you can live.'

Alexandre was about to speak when a sudden, desperate and shrill voice sounded through the house. Before anyone could react an old man hobbled down the corridor toward them, waving his arms frantically and shouting in Mordanian.

Megan stared in disbelief as Sergei burst into the kitchen.

'I don't believe it,' Callum said from one side. 'He's bloody immortal.'

'Who the hell is this?' Lieutenant Cole snapped.

Megan ignored her as Sergei began gesticulating wildly, pointing at Megan and Callum and mentioning 'mawpheen' several times. With each sentence, Alexandre's shotgun lowered a fraction and he looked at Megan in surprise.

'You know my uncle?'

'We've met,' Megan said, and despite the tension still filling the room she managed a smile in Sergei's direction. 'He came to us in Thessalia. For medicine, for an injured girl. Amy O'Hara.'

'Who the hell is Amy O'Hara?' Cole demanded in exasperation.

Alexandre ignored Cole and glanced back down the corridor to nod at his companions, who lowered their weapons, their wary expressions locked on the soldiers. Alexandre turned back to Megan.

'He says you saved his life.'

'I'd say that Sergei already has a remarkable capacity for survival. We thought that he was killed in Talyn.'

Alexandre eyed Megan testily, not willing to surrender yet. 'You are spies, servants of that corrupt despot.'

'We're bloody reporters,' Megan replied flatly, seeing no point now in pleading further. 'We came here looking for Amy.'

'You were released unharmed by that tyrranical monster, to continue your search for Amy,' Alexandre muttered in disgust, 'and yet you expect me to believe that you wish her no harm? I should shoot you anyway.'

'Go ahead,' Megan snapped. 'Just do it, if it's such a big deal to you.' She saw Alexandre's expression change slightly to one of surprise. 'But before you do, you take us to Amy and let her identify us. She knows me. Let *her* tell you who we are.'

Alexandre frowned.

'I cannot. She is dead.'

Megan gestured to Sergei. 'Then why send your uncle so far for morphine?'

'We have others here who are sick,' Alexandre mumbled.

'I don't doubt it,' Megan conceded, 'but if Amy is here and she is dead, then you have nothing to lose by letting me see her body. If she's dead, I can hardly harm her.'

Alexandre's voice stammered slightly as she spoke.

'What difference does it make? What do you care if you see her body or not?'

Megan shook his head.

'To me, nothing – if she is truly dead then there is nothing that I can do about it. But her parents live in Oklahoma in America, and they have heard nothing from her for weeks now. They need to know what happened to her. That is why we are here.'

Megan watched as the farmer hesitated. His two burly friends watched too, waiting to see what he would decide to do. Alexandre regarded Callum and Megan for a moment.

'She is in the church.'

Megan felt her throat constrict painfully.

'Tell me you're not lying Alexandre, please.'

'I am not lying,' the farmer replied.

Megan turned and waved at Cole to lower his weapon.

'If someone doesn't tell me what the hell is going on here,' Cole complained as he lowered his M–16, 'I swear I'll shoot the damned lot of you!'

'This is why we came here,' Megan said softly to the American, suddenly feeling at peace for the first time in years. 'We were looking for someone.'

47

Megan Mitchell walked through the thick snow with Callum beside her and Bolav bringing up the rear. Behind the Mordanian translator, Alexandre trudged with his shotgun at the ready for any sign of betrayal. Behind them, Lieutenant Cole followed, having left his men to guard the farmhouse. Above them the stars sparkled with a silent, unnatural lucidity in the darkened dome of the heavens.

Megan walked to the steps of the church, stopping there as Alexandre rapped on the heavy oaken doors. Megan could see a slim sliver of light glowing between the doors as she stamped her feet and clapped her hands to keep warm.

The thick doors opened a crack, and then wider as the pastor within recognised the face of Alexandre. The farmer gestured with the barrel of his shotgun at Megan, and she obligingly stepped into the church.

The interior was sparsely decorated, bare wooden pews and tall stone walls devoid of the excessive opulence normally associated with such buildings. A simple lecturn stood on a plinth at the far end of the church, which was lit with a galaxy of flickering candles suspended from simple chandeliers hanging from the cavernous ceiling.

The pastor of the church regarded the newcomers warily. Alexandre spoke a few soothing words to him as Cole closed the church doors behind them. The farmer then moved to Megan's side and prodded her with the shotgun.

'To the spare room,' he gestured with a tilt of his head toward the front of the church.

Megan walked down between the rows of ancient pews and saw a door leading off to one side of the pulpit. She walked through it and, with Alexandre following, climbed a set of stone steps that turned as they ascended to a narrow corridor with three widely seperated doors set into the left wall.

'The last one,' Alexandre prompted.

Megan walked down to the last door and reached out for the handle, gripping it and taking a deep breath. The farmer watched as Megan turned the handle and walked inside.

The room was small but warm, with lighting coming from a couple of candles set into small alcoves in the wall to the right, either side of a mirror.

To the left, a small dresser held a porcelain bowl of water and fresh cloths. In front of Megan, laying along the far wall beneath a tightly shuttered window, was a bed. Megan swallowed as she discerned in the low light the shape of a body beneath the thick covers, silent and unmoving.

She took a pace across the room and saw thick black hair spilling from the head of the bed over the covers, the face turned away from her. The candle threw flickering shadows across the walls as she advanced another pace. Beside the bowl on the dresser, Megan saw a small pile of used cloths, stained red. She swallowed, suddenly afraid.

When she spoke, her voice was dry and raspy.

'Amy?'

The body moved slightly, a barely perceptible tension in the shoulders beneath the covers, and then slowly it rolled over. The thick black hair spilled away and Megan gasped, her eyes flying wide.

Amy O'Hara was clearly sedated, probably by recently administered morphine that Alexandre and the pastor had used. Her eyes were limpid pools of darkness, her eyelids drooping slightly as she tried to focus. But that was not what caused Megan's heart to ache nor the tears that stung the corners of her eyes.

Amy O'Hara's chest had been lacerated by an exit wound the size of Megan's clenched fist. The bandages that sealed the wound were edged with dark, blood–encrusted shadows. Deeply bruised sclera circled her eyes, her lips dry and cracked.

All at once Megan forgot the shotgun hovering at the base of her spine and lurched forward, dropping to her knees beside Amy's battered face.

'Amy,' she whispered, barely able to speak at all.

Alexandre lunged forward, pressing the shotgun into Megan's back.

Megan looked into Amy's eyes, and Amy stared back with an expression of confusion, as though she were coming awake from a dream. Slowly, Megan reached out and took one of Amy's hands and held it for a few moments. From the depths of misery and suffering that Megan could only guess at, Amy's distinctive, gravelly Chicago accent drifted weakly into the room.

'Megan?'

Megan nodded, smiling now, briefly happy despite the terrible injuries she was witness to.

'I've come to take you home,' she said, holding Amy's hand firmly. 'You're going to be okay.'

Megan felt the gun pressing against her back vanish, and turned to see Alexandre step back from them, stricken with guilt now. Megan turned back as Amy reached out with a wavering hand and touched her cheek, whispering as her vision cleared slightly.

'What happened to your face? You look like shit.'

Megan laughed out loud, felt hot tears suddenly rolling down her cheeks.

'I had a bad day,' she replied.

Amy smiled and then her eyes closed gently. Megan put her hand back down on the bed, stood, and slowly backed out of the room, closing the door quietly behind her.

*

'I want to know everything. What happened to her?'

Alexandre sat on the edge of the kitchen table with a thick slab of bread and cheese in his hands. His wife, Marin, ate at the table with Callum and Bolav, while Alexandre's friends had presumably returned to their own houses on the farm. Lieutenant Cole sat impatiently nearby, unable to contain his curiosity as he listened to the conversation.

'We were working the fields in the early morning,' the farmer said, sipping hot coffee from a large, chipped mug. 'Myself, Olgin, Dimitri and Petrov, when we heard the sound of Volkodavs up in the valley.'

'Volkodavs?' Megan asked.

'Dogs,' Alexandre explained. 'Large Caucasian Mastiffs, hunting dogs used to protect rangers against mountain bears. We used to have some of our own here, but now we just borrow old Sergei's dogs. They're good, trusty and loyal animals if reared correctly, but if they're abused they become dangerous, aggressive. Lethal, even.'

'What did you do?'

Alexandre chewed mightily as he spoke.

'We decided to go and have a look. We thought maybe that Sergei's dogs had gotten loose, or that someone was in trouble and their animals were trying to raise the alarm. We could hear that the dogs were up on the ridge above the village, so we set off right away. We'd only gone a hundred paces when we heard the gunshots.'

Megan felt a chill ripple through her.

'Gunshots?'

'Yes. We went back and got our own weapons before climbing up into the valley.'

'You went up there *after* hearing shots?' Callum asked.

Alexandre looked at the Scotsman with a serious expression.

'This is my home. I will not have it attacked by anyone.'

'What did you find there?' Megan asked.

'Two bodies, a man and a woman's. The man was probably a soldier. He'd been shot in the chest with a pistol that we found in the woman's hand. Your friend Amy was the woman, and she'd been shot in the back at fairly close range, probably by the weapon the soldier was carrying. He'd hit her from an awkward angle with his shot: the bullet missed her heart and major organs. She was very lucky. There was a lot of blood, very messy wounds.'

Megan closed her eyes momentarily, mastering her revulsion before opening them again.

'So the soldier attacked her, she fought back, he shot her and she returned fire?'

'That's what we thought at first,' the farmer nodded. 'But when we arrived there was just the two bodies.'

'The dogs,' Megan realised. 'The dead soldier was not alone.'

'Exactly,' Alexandre smiled. 'Someone else did this to her. We got to her just in time. She had a pulse, but very weak. We got her back down to the village and Marin took her in straight away. She exhausted our supplies of morphine, so we sent Sergei to Thessalia to get more.'

'She owes you her life, Alexandre.'

'She owes me nothing, except an explanation. We still don't know who did this to her, but she will not speak to us. Perhaps, she will speak to you.'

Megan nodded.

'She's sleeping right now, but as soon as she comes around, I'll try to find out what I can.' She looked at Callum. 'Whatever Amy found out, it was big enough for someone to hunt her down with dogs and then shoot her.' Her voice turned cold. 'I want to know who that person was.'

***

48

Principality of Monaco

Cote D'Azure

'What news from the great and noble leaders of our free world, Seth?'

Sherman Kruger was lying on a sun–lounger on the deck of his yacht, his spindly legs absorbing the rays of the sun as a young, bikini–clad personal masseuse worked oil into his pale, purple–veined skin. His cell–phone lay open next to him, on speaker.

'President Baker has been pushed into an intractable position by the events in the Black Sea and Mordanian President Akim's televised plea for assistance in the region. The word on the hill is that the Americans will move on Thessalia imminently.'

Kruger smiled, watching the girl as she slowly rubbed lotion over his thigh.

'Then our position is as planned. After the military solution is put into action, an interim government with western allegiance and loyalty will be installed. There will be the usual obligatory democratic voting and all of the rest of the politically correct bullshit that accompanies any well–planned occupation of a foreign country. Once all of that is accomplished, foreign investment will be encouraged and Kruger oil will be there to ensure the future security and financial success of the Mordanian peoples.'

'At the right price,' Seth Cain said.

'At an extorionate price,' Kruger corrected him. 'Becoming a western democratic nation is not a cheap business these days, Seth. I take it that your man in Thessalia is now in compliance with our aims?'

'He is, and President Baker has seen the light. Those responsible for the reports coming out of Mordania will soon be removed from the field or so thoroughly discredited as to be irrelevant.'

'You threatened the president?' Kruger asked, somewhat surprised.

'I convinced him to act in the interests of democracy and liberty, as well as to save his own ratings in the polls. The Mordanian situation was making a fool of him .'

'Seth, your initiative surprises me.'

'Whilst we are speaking of initiative, don't forget why I am doing this Sherman. I have yet to see any evidence of the incentives that I was promised.'

'Seth, your work will not go unrewarded I assure you, but we cannot make such transactions without the IRS or perhaps even the media making too many connections and perhaps realising what we are doing.'

'I am the media,' Cain snorted down the line.

'Yes, but you are not the reporter. You cannot maintain a tight leash over your entire network, but at least I can assume that following your successes the board of directors is off your back? One slip, even now my friend, and everything that I have worked to achieve could be unravelled overnight. Once the deal is done, once the Mordanian government are in our pockets, then we shall both reap our rewards.'

'And if this little scheme of yours should fail?'

Kruger's voice crackled like forked lightning.

'I have already completed my work, Seth. It is now down to you to make sure that the rest of the world sees everything as we would wish them to. Failure, my friend, will rest only upon your shoulders.'

'Convenient,' Cain muttered disconsolately.

'Continue to show the world how desperately the Mordanian peoples are suffering, how much they *need* an American presence and assistance. It shouldn't be too hard, with all of those peasants shivering what's left of their pathetic lives away in the refugee camps. Keep showing plenty of footage of the aftermath of American air–strikes in Iraq, and of past genocides in Bosnia and let the public think it's from Mordania. Hell, half of America wouldn't know Mordania from goddamned Montana anyway. As long as they feel empathy for the Mordanians, that's all we need. *Justify the war* Seth, and you'll justify everything that goes with it.'

*

Government House,

Thessalia

President Mukhari Akim stood in his private quarters and watched as the cold grey dawn slowly illuminated the mountainous terrain of his homeland, as though it were reluctant to reveal the horrors therein. The snow was no longer falling, but low clouds had draped themselves in wreaths across the ethereal heights of the mountains.

The striking, beautiful scenery brought a temporary surcease to the pain that he felt as his country dissolved into chaos around him. The ceaseless, day–by–day grind of anxiety, stress, grief and crushing helplessness in the face of the fate of a land for which he had dreamed so much had filled his heart with a corrosive cocktail that flowed like poison through his veins.

He turned away from the window as Sir Wilkins knocked politely and entered his quarters, followed closely by Severov.

'What news?' Akim asked the attache wearily.

'There have been developments in the rebel camp. It would appear that they are asking for an exchange of prisoners.'

'For whom?' the president asked in mild surprise.

'They wish to return a number of unnamed captives in exchange for the reporter Martin Sigby. I have turned down the request, naturally.'

President Akim's eyes narrowed. 'You turned them down upon whose authority?'

'Sir,' Wilkins smiled politely, 'it is surely clear that they seek to use Sigby to further their cause in the eyes of the outside world. They will place him under duress and have him report what they wish to be heard – at this juncture, such propaganda could be highly detrimental to our cause.'

'Our cause?' Akim murmured.

Sir Wilkins shifted his feet.

'The fate of your country is fast becoming a benchmark for all fledgling democracies, a test–case of American loyalty to the mode of government that it preaches.' The attache handed the president a sheet of paper. 'In addition, we have found that Martin Sigby's *modus operandi* may leave much to be desired. The Medicines Sans Frontiers worker whom Sigby interviewed for his recent report is in fact not who she says she is.'

President Akim looked at the image on the paper as the attache continued speaking.

'She is a fugitive, wanted for a manslaughter case in her native France. Put simply, sir, she is an imposter and a liar.'

President Akim read the brief report sent from the French government, detailing the nature of Sophie D'Aoust's crimes and an immediate request for her repatriation to stand trial for them.

'How do you intend to break this news to the public?' the president asked.

'We have another correspondent who has completed a report in Martin Sigby's place.'

'Why does Sigby not do the report himself? And what of Megan Mitchell?'

'Martin Sigby refuses to retract his story. He's insisting that Miss Vernoux's – D'Aoust's, word is true. As for Megan Mitchell, we have heard nothing.'

'What do you suggest we do with Miss D'Aoust?'

'She should be arrested and returned to her native France with all possible haste. Sir.'

The president looked again at the image, and then at Severov.

'And Sigby? Should we let him travel to General Rameron's camp?'

'Absolutely not,' Severov muttered. 'He is a liability to our cause and has proven himself both contemptuous of the truth and lacking in his judgement. He may himself be open to bribery from the rebel forces. We cannot predict what propaganda he may report to the world at large and we can't afford further bad press at his hands. It would be better to keep him here, under our control.'

The president nodded slowly and gestured to the commander.

'Thank you, Alexei, you may leave now.'

Severov saluted crisply and marched from the room to leave Akim and Wilkins alone.

President Akim turned away from the attache and looked again out of his windows to the distant, mighty mountains. They had stood resolute for the countless procession of the ages, had not withered even before the power of nature herself. Akim felt new strength surge through him as he looked at them, as he thought of all of the great heroes of Mordania's past, of Balthazaar and of Verlin and of the countless thousands who had stood against the Tsars with guns, or against the Mongols in the freezing mountains with swords in their hands. Compared to their trials Mukhari's concerns were petty, trivial. There was new conviction and confidence in his voice when he finally spoke.

'You say that this woman, Sophie D'Aoust, is a fugitive who faces prison if she returns to France, and a liar in her claims.'

'It is clear, sir, that she has fabricated the whole thing,' Wilkins replied.

'Then why? If she is lying, why would she expose herself on television? She has doomed herself to jail in France for nothing.'

Wilkins hesitated before giving a non–commital shrug.

'I have no idea, sir. There's simply no telling with these kinds of people. Some are so vain that they'll do anything for their miniscule moment of fame and…'

'I think not,' President Akim murmured. 'The only logical conclusion is that she is in fact telling the truth, and in doing so has made a great sacrifice. In which case, not only were our own people responsible for the massacre but they deliberately misled investigators and tampered with the evidence to cover their crimes.'

Wilkins stood in silence before the president, who suddenly turned and loomed before him, one huge fist crushing the sheet of paper into a ball and his face turning stormy with rage.

'And we intend this country to become a true *democracy*!!?'

The president's voice boomed through the building, seeming almost to echo away into the distance. Sir Wilkins shook his head in apparent pity but his eyes wobbled with restrained panic.

'What your country becomes, sir, is what you make of it.'

Wilkins turned on his heel and walked out of the room. Akim followed him out onto the balcony that overlooked the entrance hall of government house. Below him, dozens of diplomats mingled and talked, United Nations soldiers and Mordanian police guarded the corridors, whilst American businessmen chattered to each other in animated ways. As he watched, President Akim realised that all of the Mordanians had worried, concerned expressions as they carried out their duties. Only the American businessmen were smiling.

As he watched, he saw Alexei Severov talking with a small group of those businessmen. The president caught the commander's eye for a long moment, and the feeling that the country was slipping from his grasp returned to ache in the president's chest.

***

49

Bolav sat on an old wooden crate beside the fire in the kitchen, fiddling with the battery of the satellite phone as he rewired it internally. It hadn't taken a great deal of expertise to adapt the charger unit from Megan Mitchell's cell phone to provide power to the satellite phone's battery. Left for several hours on a trickle–charge from the mains, Bolav had disconnected it from the socket and plugged it back into the phone.

'I didn't know you were an electrician,' Callum said from one side of the room, where he sat cradling his arm and drinking coffee.

'What do you think I did before the war?' Bolav asked as he snapped the back of the phone in place. 'There were no foreigners here before the war to translate, and when the fighting started the first thing that Rameron's rebels did was to destroy or otherwise cut off much of the electricity supply to the south.'

Megan Mitchell, sitting on a chair nearby, looked up at the light above the table.

'Where does Alexandre get his power from do you think, Bolav?'

The Mordanian looked up and around the room.

'I don't know,' he admitted, 'but it's a very steady supply, little variation in current. Best I've ever seen. And with this cold he must be running the heating day and night, so the question is really where is he getting his *fuel* from?'

'He didn't pick any up from Thessalia when Sergei went there,' Callum pointed out.

'And the power's out throughout the rest of this region,' Megan added.

'Ah–ha!' Bolav said.

The satellite phone beeped triumphantly, and Bolav grinned as he showed the brightly glowing display to Megan.

'Well done,' Megan said, and was about to take the phone from the Mordanian when Alexandre walked into the kitchen and looked at her.

'Amy is awake,' he said. 'She wants to talk to you.'

Megan stood from the table, the phone forgotten, and followed Alexandre hurriedly out of the room. Bolav watched them go and then glanced at Callum.

'I'm going outside to see if I can get a signal,' he said.

Callum nodded without any real interest, and Bolav put on a thick coat before stepping outside into the bitter night air. He walked a few paces away from the house, searching for the American soldiers guarding the property. He spotted them and moved away to a quite spot to dial a number from his memory.

There was a long pause, during which Bolav feared that the signal might not be strong enough to connect, but suddenly the line began to ring in his ear. He smiled to himself, proud of his work, and then the line picked up.

'Severov.'

'It is Bolav.'

'Bolav?!' Surprise was evident in the commander's tone. *'You are alive! I am overjoyed my friend.'*

'You threw me out of that truck to die,' Bolav hissed.

'I threw you out of the truck to do your job,' Severov replied. *'And you have succeeded. Tell me what you have found.'*

'I could have been killed. You betrayed me!'

'Bolav, my friend, why would I do such a thing? I gave you only the chance to excel, and you have valiantly survived even the most dangerous assignment. I am nothing but proud of you.'

'Is that so?' Bolav said through gritted teeth. 'Well, commander, I have news for you from the front lines, news that will displease you greatly.'

Severov's tone changed completely. *'What have you found?'*

Bolav grinned devilishly, enjoying Severov's discomfort.

'It might just be the end of you.'

'Bolav, tell me what you have found or I swear I shall find you, gut you and carve my name in your entrails.'

'Really? And I thought you had my safety at heart?'

'Tell me, you stinking, rabid, dog–mothered cretin!'

'Alexei,' Bolav taunted in a whisper, 'the girl, she is alive.'

*

'You're lucky to be alive.'

Amy O'Hara smiled faintly. 'Luck isn't something that I've had a great deal of lately.'

Amy was still lying in bed, clearly fatigued and slightly hazy due to the morphine that Alexandre had administered, but her spirits seemed higher than before.

'Why did you come for me?' she asked Megan.

'Surely you don't need to ask me that?'

Amy smiled, and squeezed Megan's hand in her own.

'That was a long time ago, and I helped you in your search from the comfort of my Chicago office. I didn't travel half way around the world and risk my life in the middle of a war zone.'

'I guess I'm just a hero, then,' Megan said with a shrug.

'You are,' Amy said, 'to me.'

Megan smiled but did not respond for a few moments.

'What brought you here Amy?' she asked finally. 'What the hell is all this about?'

Amy sighed to herself, shadows passing behind her eyes.

'Petra,' she said softly. 'My uncle.'

'Tell me.'

'Petra worked as a mechanical engineer for the Mordanian government,' Amy began. 'His work involved managing a team who were investigating the properties of heat–exchange engines. The work they were doing was entirely conventional and involved devising ways of extracting energy from geo–thermic sources with high degrees of efficiency.'

Megan blinked. 'You can say all of that on top of morphine?'

'It's just what Petra told me,' Amy smiled, 'spoken from memory. Anyway, a few weeks ago Petra contacted me urgently at my Chicago office. He said that he needed me, that I should come to Mordania as quickly as I could, that it was important and that I should tell nobody about it.'

'So far, so mysterious,' Megan said in the candlelight. 'So you came here.'

'Petra was a really nice guy,' Amy said softly. 'But his animosity toward my father's emigration meant that he had little contact with my family. That, as it turned out, became the problem.'

'Problem?'

'Yes. Petra's team had managed to do something extraordinary with these engines, and it seemed as though somebody did not want anybody else to find out. What Petra wanted me to do was document the engines and what they were doing with them, and then get out of the country. Petra told me that he was afraid that if someone did not tell the world about what they had achieved, nobody would ever know. Megan, Petra feared for his life even then, and he felt that he had nobody in the west he could contact except me.'

'What happened?'

'We documented the work and it was amazing, really earth–shattering stuff. But before we could get everything organised and before I could leave the country, all hell broke loose. The senior commander of the Mordanian

Army and Air Force broke with the government in an attempted military coup. Suddenly everyone was fighting. It happened almost overnight.'

'Rameron,' Megan murmured.

'Yes,' Amy said. 'The Mordanian Secret Police moved out of Thessalia headed north, and General Rameron's men headed south from the major bases they controlled. They met and fought several times. During the fighting, my uncle and his team were arrested one morning at dawn in their laboratory. Petra had tried to get me away into the forest, disguised as a peasant girl, before the troops came.'

Amy's voice wavered slightly.

'I managed to find somewhere to hide, and watched as Petra and his people were led outside the laboratory and lined up against a wall. There was no trial.' She shuddered beneath her covers. 'They were all executed. The soldiers burned the buildings to the ground, smashed up the machines and instruments with explosives, and buried the bodies of my uncle and his colleagues in the ground.'

Megan closed her eyes.

'We found their remains, Amy,' she said. 'The world knows what happened, or at least some of it. General Rameron and his men will pay for their crimes – I'll make sure of that.'

Amy shook her head.

'But Megan, it was not General Rameron's men who executed those scientists. It was the Mordanian Secret Police.'

***

50

'What?'

Megan sat stock still, a sudden dread filling her chest like icy water flooding a doomed ship.

'It was the secret police who killed my uncle,' Amy repeated.

'It can't be,' Megan said. 'General Rameron's men have committed crimes against humanity across the region.'

Amy shook her head sadly.

'No, Megan. That's not the way it has been. I know what you've heard but it's all a lie. And I have it all on video.'

Megan stared at her in amazement. 'You filmed it?!'

Amy nodded slowly.

'When Petra got me out of the laboratories, before the police arrived, I grabbed my camera and the files that I had shot of everything. I ran with them until I could go no further. I thought my hiding place was far away enough to be safe.'

'But it wasn't.'

'Not for long. I was on higher ground, and used the zoom on my camera to see what was happening. I recorded everything. They singled Petra out, you see, because he had family in the United States. They must have known that I was here, because they were showing him a photograph. It was too small to see from where I was, but I knew that it must have been of me. They were still searching the buildings, even though all of the scientists were standing in the yard.'

'And then they shot them?' Megan pressed.

'Yes, all of them. When the gunfire had passed away, I kept filming. All of it. When it was over, and the buildings were burning and the bodies were being buried, I decided that the best place to run was here. Alexandre and Petra were good friends, although they had little formal contact. They went to school together in Thessalia. I felt that the authorities would not connect the two men.'

'How did they find you?'

'Bad luck,' Amy said. 'I was walking uphill and away from the fires when one of their men must have spotted me. It was stupid of me, really stupid to let myself be seen so easily, but I was in tears and shock. I just wanted to get away. They came after me then, chased me for almost two hours with dogs, those big Mastiff things. I might have made it here, but I realised that it was no use. They would catch me eventually, and if I was here they would kill Alexandre and his wife and family too. I couldn't let that happen.'

Megan nodded, but her expression was hard now, her jaw clenched as she spoke.

'You said that you filmed everything. Where is the camera?'

'I hid it, before they captured me, on top of the hill at the edge of a clearing. There was a fallen tree. I wrapped it up and hid it inside. It was still running when I put it there.'

Megan nodded, her fists clenched by her side. 'Who was it? Who did this to you?'

Megan saw the revulsion in Amy's expression as she spoke a name.

'The commander of the military police. His name is Alexei Severov.'

*

'We need to get back to Thessalia, right now.'

Megan strode back into the kitchen with a face like thunder. Callum stood up, as did Bolav. Megan walked toward the translator, who took a step back, his face blanching. He flinched as Megan's hand flicked out and grabbed the satellite phone from him.

Megan turned away and walked across to the kitchen door, opening it and walking outside into the cold night air. She dialled a number, listening to the ring tone and looking at her watch. Even at this hour, she doubted that the call would be in vain.

'Sir Wilkin's office, UK attache,' came the prompt and polite voice of Wilkin's personal assistant.

'Is Sir Wilkins there?'

'One moment, may I ask who is calling?'

'Megan Mitchell.'

There was a click and a pause and then Sir Wilkin's voice blasted down the line into her ear.

'Good God above, Megan! You're alive!'

'And kicking,' Megan replied, a grim smile curling from one corner of her mouth. 'Tom, I need to get the hell out of here.'

'Don't we all dear girl, don't we all. But may I ask just where on earth "there" might be?'

'We're at a small farmstead somewhere south of Talyn, maybe ten miles at the most. We need an urgent evacuation. Callum's injured and needs medical assistance.'

There was a long pause.

'Megan, I'll see what I can do, but you obviously have not heard.'

'Heard what?'

'Congress in the United States formally authorised military intervention in Thessalia. A carrier–group task force is already making its way here.'

Megan grasped her forehead with one hand.

'All hell's going to break loose,' she said in exasperation.

'General Rameron's men will have to advance with maximum speed and force if they're to secure the capital before the bulk of the American military machine gets here. Megan, they'll strike by air first.'

'Is there nothing that you can send here to get us out? General Rameron wanted to initiate a prisoner exchange, ourselves for Martin Sigby.'

There was a long pause on the other end of the line.

'I know. Why does he want Martin Sigby specifically?'

'I don't know, we just need to get out of here as soon as we can. And listen to me, Tom: Commander Severov is the man who tried to kill Amy, and the man behind the genocide of the scientists.'

There was another long pause. *'You're sure?'*

'One hundred per cent,' Megan replied. 'She has video footage of the massacre. We've recovered it. Sophie D'Aoust could be in real danger from Severov, Tom. She exposed herself on live television to try to protect me. You need to get her into the US Embassy or out of the country before she's arrested.'

'The US Embassy can't help her,' Wilkins said. *'It's the US that's hunting for her the most.'*

'What?'

'They want her silenced, Megan. They've got everybody looking for her, along with you.'

'She must have gone into hiding. Can you find her Tom, and protect her?' Megan asked, her fists clenched with anxiety. 'If Severov gets his hands on her before the French or the Americans…'

'If there's any way at all Megan, I'll do it, I promise. You'll have to wait until daylight for your rescue though.'

'I understand Tom. Thanks.'

'I'll get you out, don't worry. Just sit tight and keep this line active. It'll give the rescue teams a signal to locate you.'

'People can track this signal?' Megan asked in surprise.

'I'll have GCHQ sort it out, they're our signals intelligence chaps. It all passes through the NSA in Maryland of course, but don't worry. It's all part of the surveillance game.'

'Can they listen too?'

'Sometimes, perhaps, depending on the equipment they use. Why?'

Megan gripped the handset tighter. 'Tom, I know where General Rameron is.'

'*You know where he is*?' Wilkins echoed down the line. *'How?'*

'We were captured outside of Talyn by his troops. They took us to him.'

'Where is he, Megan?'

'I can work it out on a map as soon as I get back.'

'I'll get someone there Megan, I promise.'

Megan rang off and walked back into the kitchen, closing the door behind her and looking at Alexandre, who was watching her expectantly.

'The Americans are coming and they mean business.'

'God damn!' Lieutenant Cole jubilantly smacked one clenched fist into his palm. 'Time to bring this charade to a close.'

Alexandre closed his eyes briefly. 'When?'

'I don't know, but imminently. I would expect military action within twenty four hours at the most, presumably opening with an aerial bombardment of General Rameron's forces. How far are they from here?'

'Talyn – twelve miles at the most, as the crow flies.'

Megan nodded and glanced at the clock hanging above the fireplace.

'We need to go out at first light and search the hills above the farm, the place where you found Amy.'

Alexandre nodded. 'I will be ready. What are we looking for?'

'Evidence of crimes against humanity,' Megan replied, and glanced at Callum, 'by Alexei Severov.'

Callum's face darkened. 'That bastard? You mean in the village we found?'

'The same,' Megan replied, and then looked again at Alexandre. 'Amy told me that you and Petra Milosovich were close, that you studied together, drank together.'

'This is true. Petra was a good friend.'

'Then you know something of what he was working on?'

Alexandre shifted his feet uncertainly.

'I wouldn't really know, it was all such complicated engineering. I am just a farmer.'

Megan smiled and gestured to the lights glowing in the building around them.

'A smart enough farmer to be generating the only electricity for miles around without a working national grid or a fuel–generator.'

Alexandre sighed softly.

'I know enough to explain what Petra explained to me.'

'That's all I need,' Megan encouraged. 'Amy filmed everything and hid the camera on top of the hills before she was captured. Between what you know and what that film will tell us, I think we might just have enough to understand everything else.'

Lieutenant Cole stepped up to them from one side.

'You appear to have forgotten about *us*,' he snapped. 'We are tasked with getting your ass the hell out of this country just as fast as we can, and nothing else matters. Especially not impromptu physics lessons.'

Megan shook her head vehemently.

'This whole war, lieutenant, is about more than you think and we're on the cusp of finding out what that something is and bringing it all to an end. Your fellow Americans, soldiers like you, are rushing headlong into another Iraq, another Vietnam. Would you really pass up the chance to let them go home alive to their families?'

Cole regarded her uncertainly. 'You think you can stop a war?'

Megan smiled.

'We already found a way to influence one. Stopping it is the next logical step.'

***

51

'We found her just up there.'

Alexandre's voice was only lightly touched with fatigue as he climbed the hillside. In contrast Megan wheezed and felt her face turning purple in the pale dawn light now glowing in the sky above as she laboured along behind the farmer. The hillside seemed to climb almost vertically above the village below.

Alexandre led Megan between clumps of crystalline foliage frozen overnight and past towering pine trees coated with sparkling ice. Megan glanced back down the hill, her chest heaving, and could barely see the village through the mist, a mile away and perhaps five hundred feet below them.

'Nearly there,' Alexandre gestured ahead.

Megan followed the farmer until they cleared the brow of the hill and stepped into a broad clearing surrounded by the dense forests. High above them, through the mist, the merest hint of eggshell–blue sky glimmered.

'The weather is improving,' Alexandre noted with a practiced eye. 'Not good news for us if the Americans decide to attack.'

'Right,' Megan agreed, then looked about the clearing. 'Where did you find Amy?'

'Just here,' Alexandre pointed to a dense cluster of bushes and ferns. 'She was lying on the edge of those ferns.'

Megan looked from that position on a trajectory toward the centre of the clearing.

'In what direction is the village where Petra was working, roughly?'

Alexandre looked around for a moment, getting his bearings, and then pointed confidently toward the south–west.

'Out there, perhaps five miles away near the river and Anterik.'

Megan nodded, trying to guess where Amy would have climbed the other side of the valley with Severov's men in pursuit, and where she would have emerged into the clearing. As she cast her eyes across the edge of the forest she saw what she was looking for.

A large fallen tree, the trunk half buried in snow and rotting at the edges. Megan quickly strode across the clearing and moved around the edge of the trunk, searching for cavities within. After a few moments she found what she was looking for and reached inside.

A large, stiff piece of fabric brushed her hand. Reaching in with both hands, Megan gently lifted the tightly wrapped package out, unfolding the layers of frozen canvass to reveal a modern and expensive looking digital video camera within. The black casing of the camera sparkled with frozen condensation.

'The cold will have destroyed the camera lens,' Alexandre pointed out.

'Maybe,' Megan agreed, 'but the wrapping and the camera case might have been enough to protect the flash memory inside, and that's all we need. Let's go.'

The descent back down the valley was equally arduous, and by the time they had reached the farmstead the morning sun was glowing above the misty horizon, a pale ball of light suspended in ethereal veils. Megan might have considered the serene dawn, the isolated farmstead and the winter–wonderland surroundings beautiful were it not for the dread gnawing at her insides.

The farmstead kitchen was warm as Megan followed Alexandre inside. Bolav stood up as they entered and Callum looked at Megan expectantly.

'Did you find it?' he asked.

Megan nodded, unwrapping the camera and looking at Bolav.

'Do you think that you can get this to work?'

The Mordanian looked at the camera for a moment, and then nodded before looking at Alexandre. 'May I use your computer?'

'If you think it will help,' the farmer replied.

'It will. If I can wire the camera to the computer, I might be able to download whatever is in the camera's memory direct to the computer, provided they can talk to each other. I'll need Callum's camera equipment – the USB cables might be helpful.'

'I'll get them for you,' Callum said.

Megan turned to Alexandre. 'I need to know what Petra Milosovich was doing to get himself executed by Alexei Severov and his secret police.'

Alexandre reluctantly waved for Megan to follow him.

'You will need to see this to believe it.'

*

GNN (UK) Ltd, London

Harrison Forbes watched the live feeds coming in from other television stations, as images of Sophie D'Aoust were beamed across the globe, and her story about the massacre in Mordania thoroughly discredited.

'What the hell is going on out there?' Harrison uttered to himself.

An aide peeked around the door to his office. 'Seth Cain's on the line for you.'

'Great,' Harrison grumbled. 'Any word from Sigby?'

'Radio silence,' the aide said. 'He's missed his last scheduled report slot since the word got out about that French woman being a fugitive.'

Harrison scowled as he punched a button on his desk phone. 'Seth?'

'Harrison. Where is Martin Sigby?!'

Seth Cain's voice blasted down the line into Harrison's ear loudly enough for even people outside his office to hear. Forbes kicked the office door shut with one heel.

'How the hell should I know? He's in another country, remember?'

'He shold have been on air an hour ago,' Cain hissed down the line. *'Martin Sigby was to refrain from reporting negatively regarding the Mordanian government, and cover the lies of that French woman. And what the hell was all that crap about an Amy O'Hara?'*

'There has never been any such agreement – you merely asked me who was getting Martin's reels. If what Martin has discovered since is not in line with your hopes then that's just tough shit because what he has reported happens to be the truth.'

'To hell with the truth! This is not about truth, this is about the news!'

Harrison Forbes searched the ceiling with his eyes for a moment. 'And you think that *I'm* missing something?'

'GNN has commitments of far greater importance than you could possibly conceive. Your remit is to ensure that Martin Sigby toes the company line. His sloppy reporting has caused incalculable damage to our reputation and his deviation from GNN's purpose has caused me extreme difficulties at a very sensitive time.'

'GNN's purpose?' Harrison echoed. 'And what precisely is our purpose, Seth?'

'To do as you're damned well told,' Seth raged. *'Where is Sigby?'*

'Missing,' Harrison finally snapped. 'In a war zone, so forgive me if I have greater concerns that your shareholder's profits!'

There was a long pause on the line.

'I am immensely displeased with your performance, Harry.'

Harrison Forbes ground his teeth in his jaw for a moment.

'Oh me, oh my, oh what must I do? To hell with you, Cain. I'm not your damned whipping boy.'

'You're done Forbes. I want you out of that office immediately!'

Harrison Forbes slammed the receiver down and stood with his hands on his hips for several long moments as he forced himself to calm down. He looked out of the office windows at his staff, and was about to move around his desk to announce his imminent retirement when he saw on his desk a small business card. He looked down and read the name upon it.

Frank Amonte.

Harrison Forbes picked the card up and looked at it for a long moment, trying to remember who had put it there. A line from his memory offered itself.

'I have the number of an account in Oklahoma, United States…'

Harrison turned the card over to see the account details written on the reverse side of the card.

Harrison thought to himself for a moment longer and then picked up his phone.

***

52

Alexandre led Megan across a barren field, the earth rock–hard beneath their feet and flecked with snow that sparkled in the light of the morning sun. Megan could see her own breath billowing in golden clouds in the otherwise silent air. She realised that she could in fact hear nothing else, as though she and the farmer were the only remaining human beings on the planet.

They walked toward a large, dilapidated old barn that stood on the edge of the fields. Megan could see light between the aged boards cladding the frame of the barn as they approached the doors, which stood slightly open. Clearly Alexandre had no concern for thieves in this lonely corner of the mountains.

'No lock,' Megan noted as they reached the doors.

Alexandre smiled.

'If I put a lock on it, someone might suspect that there was something of value inside. There is, of course, but why give the game away?'

The farmer pulled on the heavy door, which bowed slightly under the pressure before creaking open. Alexandre walked inside and Megan followed, detecting the odours of dust and hay, of mud and the faeces of farm animals. The darkness within the barn was deep, sliced through only by shafts of light streaming through the gaps in the cladding.

'My father built this barn,' Alexandre said as they walked between towering stacks of hay bales, 'fifty years ago or more now. He was a skillful man.'

They walked to the rear of the barn to where a pair of ancient tractors stood, one of them half–covered with old tarpaulins, the other with dust. Opposite stood a third tractor, a newer and glossier one that Alexandre gestured toward.

'That is what you are looking for,' he said.

Megan stared at the vehicle for a moment.

'A tractor? Petra Milosovich was working on a tractor?'

'Not the tractor,' the farmer smiled. 'He was working on what's inside it.'

Megan looked at the vehicle for a moment, and then suddenly she became aware of a faint hum emanating from somewhere beneath the hood of the vehicle. She took a pace closer as Alexandre strolled up to the tractor and removed the safety pins from the hood before opening it.

There, inside, was a large cylindrical device that resembled an engine, but not one that Megan had ever seen before. She could identify two large–bore pistons well enough, and the fact that the engine appeared to be operating. Cables snaked discreetly from one end of the engine, down into the ground. Alexandre saw the direction of Megan's gaze.

'My father built a shallow water–feed pipe between the barn and the farmstead's main water supply, to make watering the animals he kept here easier. We adapted it and ran a power cable from here back to the farm.'

Megan stared at the tractor's engine for a moment.

'You get all that power from this? It's so quiet.'

'Very. We'd have put it next to the house, but Petra felt that would be too dangerous.'

'Dangerous? Why? What fuel does it use?'

'Oh, it's not the fuel that's dangerous. Technically, it could run on vegetable oil if you really want it to. No. Petra realised that people would kill to prevent this from ever reaching the rest of the world, which was why we hid it like this, or at least this version of it.'

Megan shook her head in confusion.

'Why? What's the big deal?'

Alexandre gestured to a small cylinder, lying long and low across the top of the tractor engine.

'That cylinder contains a modest amount of helium. I think the last time that I replaced it would have been in the spring, maybe nine months ago.'

Megan was about to speak, but her jaw hung open. Her mind performed a few rapid calculations and she stared at the farmer in amazement. Alexandre smiled as he saw Megan begin to understand, and he spoke softly.

'The device is called a Sterling Engine. They've been around for a couple of hundred years, as it happens, although this is a very modern example. It's simply a closed–cycle, piston driven heat–exchange engine, much like the engine in your car, except that in a closed–cycle engine like this the working gas remains within the cylinders, whereas in your car it is vented into the atmosphere as an exhaust.'

Megan raised a hand.

'I didn't do motor mechanics at school I'm afraid.'

'Neither did I,' Alexandre admitted, 'but Petra told me all that I needed to know to understand what this is and why it is so important. It is all to do with efficiency, and how the methods we use to produce electrical energy to heat our homes and the engines we use to drive our cars are hugely *inefficient.*'

'And this, Sterling Engine, does it better?' Megan surmised.

'Much better,' Alexandre nodded. 'Petra was so excited about it. He told me that the average vehicle on the road, powered by the internal combustion engine, can produce a maximum efficiency of just fifteen per cent. That means that of all the power produced, eighty five per cent goes into overcoming friction within the engine or is lost as heat. A Sterling Engine like this, on the other hand, can produce energy with an efficiency of as much as sixty per cent.'

Megan looked at the engine before her, turning quietly over as they spoke like the cogs of her own mind as she considered what Alexandre was telling him.

'So if you put one of these in a car, it would only need a fraction of the fuel?'

'Precisely, although the mechanics of it are a bit more complicated. Essentially, the Sterling Engine has fewer moving parts, has no exhaust pollution, needs little maintenance and has a far greater operating life than the conventional internal combustion engine.'

Megan thought again for a moment, glancing around her at the barn.

'If this got onto the street, it would rapidly reduce the need for oil,' she said.

'Cars would not need to use as much fuel,' Alexandre agreed. 'They could probably run entirely on bio–fuels, hydrogen cells or even solar power in many countries. Industry, which uses more oil than transport, could follow suit.'

'I'm starting to get a nasty feeling that I understand what's been happening here,' Megan said. 'What I don't understand is, if these engines have been around for hundreds of years, how come they're not already on the market?'

Alexandre moved closer to the engine, pointing out various components as she spoke.

'These devices are heat–exchange engines. They work because they shift the working fluid or gas within between two different temperature states. They're classified as an external combustion engine, despite the fact that heat can be supplied by non–combusting sources such as solar and nuclear energy. This one operates through the use of an external heat source and an external heat sink, each maintained within a limited temperature range, and having a sufficiently large temperature difference between them.

'The problem for years has been that they are not able to produce sufficient power without becoming too large. It's fine if you want something with a continuous power–output that can be built on a grand scale, like marine engines for instance – ships use these all the time. But a Sterling Engine small enough to fit in a vehicle would not produce sufficient energy to move the vehicle forward. The pressures and temperature differentials would need to be too high, and the materials did not exist to contain them safely.'

'And that's where Petra Milosovich came in.'

Alexandre nodded.

'Petra worked for years in an engineering department within the government, both before and after the democratic revolution. Petra despised the polluting of the world by industry, and spent years pursuing ways in which the Sterling Engine could be improved and made accessible as a means of powering our world without the need for excessive pollution of the environment. Two years ago, he had a breakthrough.'

Alexandre moved away from the tractor and sat on the edge of a hay bale.

'He came to me when he discovered it. He had developed a ceramic material that had sufficient tensile strength along with a high enough density to efficiently contain a fuel source of helium.'

'The gas, helium?' Megan said.

'Hydrogen is the gas of choice for most of these devices,' Alexandre explained, 'but unfortunately the lightest of the gases is also the most combustible and can bleed through solid metal via osmosis, and thus is not considered safe for commercial use. Helium, however, is both abundant, cheap and highly unreactive. Petra realised that if he could contain helium then he was on his way, because if he could condense the gas to sufficient pressure within the engine, then the entire device could itself be made small enough to become viable for general commercial use. He eventually worked out not just how to fit them into cars but into aero–engines as well.'

Megan shook her head in wonder.

'That would mean that he could probably build them to power houses, like this one,' she observed. 'There would be no need for a national grid.'

Alexandre opened his arms in a broad gesture, his features alive with delight.

'Petra had gone even further than that. He envisaged a time when the temperature difference between the molten rock of the earth's upper crust, and the cold waters of the oceans could be used as potentially limitless sources of fuel for national energy generation via large banks of industrial scale Sterling Engines, true geo–engineering.'

The farmer's arms slowly fell again to his sides and his expression fell with them.

'He went directly to the Mordanian government and applied for world–wide patents; Europe, America, Australia. Everywhere.'

'What happened?'

'He was denied the patents repeatedly. He could not understand it. Nobody wanted to hear about his work. It shocked him, left him in dismay. Megan, if only you could have seen how that man's endless joy at making the discovery of a lifetime was crushed into depression and the collapse of his faith in humanity's spirit. It destroyed Petra Milosovich long before the secret police got hold of him.'

'And yet he was working on something near Anterik,' Megan said. 'The laboratories that were destroyed.'

'Yes,' Alexandre said. 'Petra would not give in to the government. He resigned his post and began working on a new project with a small team of like–minded scientists who believed that they could produce something highly commercial. They built four of these engines, and all of them were running in vehicles just before the war began.'

Megan guessed the rest.

'General Rameron must have found out. It must be he who holds connections to the oil businesses around the Caspian Sea. That's why they were murdered.'

Alexandre stood from his hay bale and shook his head.

'No, Megan. It was General Rameron who funded Petra's studies, in defiance of orders from the government.'

Megan stared at Alexandre for what felt like an age as the farmer continued.

'General Rameron was responsible for letting Petra Milosovich continue working on his Sterling Engines. When the government found out they threatened General Rameron with court–martial. The general refused an order to report to Thessalia. The government sent an armoured force to arrest Rameron and bring him to the city. The Air Force personnel defended their general, and the uprising began.'

Megan swallowed thickly, looking from the concealed tractor engine to the farmer and back again.

'You're telling me that General Rameron did not start this war,' she said, her voice trembling. 'You're telling me that it could be someone in the government that is working with the oil companies?'

Alexandre shook his head.

'I'm not telling you anything. All I'm saying is that Petra made a discovery that could have made oil obsolete, General Rameron defended him, and then the country disintegrated into civil war. If you ask me, this war is what the oil companies wanted – access to Mordania's oil, which meant huge investment in the country, and therefore neither the government nor the oil companies could not afford Petra's device becoming public knowledge.'

'So they killed him,' Megan said in sudden, overwhelming despair. She turned for the barn doors.

'Where are you going?' Alexandre asked, getting up to follow her.

'Sophie and Martin,' Megan gasped as she broke into a run. 'They're in danger.'

***

53

Martin Sigby watched the television in his room at the Thessalia Hilton, the glow from the screen contrasting with the flickering candles. An image from a United States aircraft carrier in the Black Sea showed waves of American F–18s launching from the ship's catapults, engines in full afterburner as they climbed into the glowing dawn sky.

'Is this live feed?' Robert, Sigby's cameraman, asked.

Sigby nodded, gesturing to the skies above the carrier. 'Looks to be,'

'You should have made your report an hour ago.'

'To hell with them,' Sigby muttered as he watched.

The television reporter's voice carried over the deafening roar of fighter engines as she explained what was happening.

'The word from Congress arrived here aboard the USS Theodore Roosevelt just forty minutes ago, and within ten minutes the Carrier Air Group began preperations for military action against Mordania. These fighters blasting off the deck behind me are setting up Combat Air Patrols over the Georgian coast, securing American air superiority over the entire region before the air assault against the rebel forces of General Mikhail Rameron begins.'

Robert shook his head.

'The shit's about to hit the fan Martin, and we're in the line of fire.'

Martin was about to reply when a junior staffer poked his head into the room.

'Mister Sigby, there's a message from government house for you. The president has requested that you meet him there.'

Martin stood slowly, and looked down at his cameraman. 'Robert, would you mind?'

The cameraman stood and grabbed his equipment.

'Let's go.'

There was a government jeep waiting for them as they left the Thessalia Hilton, driven by a pair of stone–faced corporals who spoke not a word to their passengers as they drove toward the towering edifice of government house. Around the jeep, hundreds of people moved to and fro, many of them carrying their life's belongings with them over their shoulders, on their backs or on makeshift trolleys. The dawn was breaking lethargically and a light and wispy snow was beginning to fall once more.

Martin and his cameraman were dropped outside Government House and walked into the cavernous foyeur. Sir Wilkins met them at the foot of the main stairs, his features flushed with concern.

'The Americans are preparing for their assault,' he said, 'and half of the population is in chaos. I could use you right now – Brussels needs footage to determine what's happening here.'

'I saw the report on Sophie D'Aoust. You've made her out to be a liar when it was plain that she was telling the truth.'

Sir Wilkins hesitated for a moment, apparently caught off guard.

'International media only reported what we knew to be true, Martin. Sophie D'Aoust is a wanted fugitive and there's no way that can be denied!'

'She was also telling the truth. They've unfairly discredited her.'

'She discredited herself,' Wilkins snapped back.

'Where is she?'

'Commander Severov and his men have her in custody.'

Sigby pushed past the attache in disgust. 'I have a meeting with the president.'

'I didn't know,' Wilkins said, suddenly defensive. 'Did he say what it was in reference to?'

Martin did not reply as he ascended the broad staircase toward the president's private chambers, Robert hefting their equipment up behind him. They had almost reached the president's offices when two police guards appeared in the hall ahead of them, both armed. One of them raised a hand at Robert.

'No cameras today,' he said in stern, accented English. 'You must wait here.'

Sigby looked at the two guards. 'Why?'

'Orders of the chief of police,' the other guard said. 'You may not proceed further.'

Sigby turned to leave and gave a start of surprise as he found himself staring into Alexei Severov's eyes, the police chief standing almost immediately behind him.

'I didn't hear you behind me,' Sigby said.

'The president will see you now,' Severov said with a smile, and then turned to look at Sigby's cameraman. 'You may wait in the foyeur.'

Robert looked at Sigby, who nodded once. The cameraman walked away and the guards parted as Sigby walked between them with Severov following in ghostly silence. Sigby saw the the president's private chamber door was open, and he walked inside to see the president standing beside a window with his hands behind his back, watching the falling snow.

'Mister President,' Sigby said formally.

Mukhari Akim turned slowly from the window and regarded Sigby for a long moment before glancing over the correspondent's shoulder.

'You may leave us,' he said to Severov.

The police commander hesitated for a moment before bowing slightly at the waist and turning, giving Sigby a last glance as he closed the door behind him.

The president looked again out of the window before speaking.

'It is snowing now, but clear skies are coming, perfect for the American airplanes. There will be chaos,' he said in his deep voice. 'The people are afraid. They do not know what will happen here. Will this become another Iraq? Another Afghanistan? Will they be liberated? Abandoned? Robbed?'

Sigby found himself choosing his words with care.

'At least they will no longer be alone.'

President Akim's eyes narrowed thoughtfully as he considered Sigby's response.

'You returned the money that you were paid,' he said finally.

'Yes, I did.'

'Why?'

Sigby hesitated before speaking.

'Because my job is to tell the truth, sir, whether it be palatable or not. I could not bring myself to abandon the principles that the rest of the world rely upon, to know that I and reporters like me will tell them what is really happening, and not what others would have them believe.'

President Akim nodded slowly.

'Your report on the possibility that the massacre near Talyn could have been conducted by my own people was deeply disturbing, Martin. It has further led to the chaos that we see outside.'

'That is not my responsibility, sir,' Martin replied. 'It's yours.'

President Akim stared silently at Martin Sigby for an intolerably long time, until finally he broke the silence as he walked slowly toward Sigby.

'I remember when I first spoke with you,' he rumbled darkly. 'I saw you for what you were then: a spineless vulture, scavenging on the rotting carcass of this country for the carrion of human suffering. You were just like all of the rest and I despised you for your weakness, your greed and your moral cowardice.'

Martin Sigby swallowed thickly and tried not to let his eyes water. 'What has changed, sir?'

President Akim glowered down at Sigby.

'Nothing.'

For a moment Sigby did not understand, but then the president smiled faintly, the hard gaze melting and the eyes twinkling with humour. Sigby felt a rush of air expelled from his lungs in relief as he felt a smile creep onto his own features. The president nodded.

'I thought all of that was true, until the money reappeared in the accounts,' he said. 'Then I knew that you were one of the good men after all.'

Sigby blinked as an unfamiliar sensation of pride welled up within him and overflowed into the surrounding room, filling it with a warmth he had not previously suspected was there.

'I'm relieved to hear that, sir.'

'No more than I,' the president said, and then his features became serious again. 'However, your report changed things immensely. There will be investigations, recriminations, fear and doubt amongst the populace. The enemy is almost upon us on one border, and a superior liberation force whose motives I cannot be sure of mounts upon another. Martin, I need you to remain straight and true, to work here with me to ensure that, whatever the outcome, the people of this world know what really happened, that they know who we really are and of what we had hoped for this nation. Can you do that for me?'

Martin Sigby had to physically prevent himself from saluting.

'I'll do all that I can, sir.'

President Akim nodded.

'I know that you will. I do not believe that the intentions of the American diplomats in this country are entirely honourable and I believe that they may have infiltrated my own staff, turning them against me. In addition, I have heard that General Mikhail Rameron is requesting the exchange of prisoners of war before the proposed aerial attack by American warplanes and has freed those reportedly held by him as a human shield. Clearly he does not wish anyone but those loyal to him to be in the firing line.'

'That seems uncharacteristically honourable of him,' Sigby pointed out.

'There is much, here, that I believe we have been led to misunderstand. He has asked for you, by name, to accompany the prisoner exchange and travel to meet him.'

'Me?' Sigby uttered in surprise. 'Why?'

'I do not know, Martin, but I believe that it needs to be done, and that you can do your job more effectively once you have all of the information.' One thick hand gripped Sigby's shoulder briefly and then the president turned away, walking back toward his desk. 'Go and attend to your work. Tell the truth; nothing but the truth, whatever shape that truth may take.'

Sigby turned, his chest filled with righteous determination and his mind blazing with pride in what he might accomplish. He opened the door and stepped outside into the corridor, closing the door behind him. He turned and walked straight into the cold barrel of a pistol that touched his forehead. Sigby's heart stopped in his chest for a moment as he stared into the hard and unforgiving eyes of Alexei Severov.

Before he could utter even a single word or cry of help or warning a hand clamped over his mouth and strong arms dragged him backwards and away from the president's door. Thick tape was plastered across his mouth and Sigby was literally lifted into the air.

The police commander did not speak. Instead he simply pushed his finger over his own lips in a gesture for his men to remain silent, and then pointed down the corridor. The guards carried Sigby swiftly toward the rear of the building, to places that Sigby had never seen before.

***

54

The guards descended the steps with their squirming, writhing burden, the temperature falling as they moved into the bowels of Government House.

Sigby smelled the odours of damp, rotting canvass and oil–burning candles. They were carrying him down into what seemed like a basement, the walls made of old stone, cold and featureless. As he was carried, Sigby looked to one side out of a row of windows to where tall chain–link fences seperated a military parade ground from what looked like large kennels. The reporter's eyes widened as he saw huge dogs padding around within the compound.

Suddenly, the guards carrying him reached a door, kicked it open and carried Sigby inside before dropping him unceremoniously onto the cold stone floor. The guards closed the door behind them, unslinging their weapons from their shoulders and standing guard either side of the door, behind Severov.

The room was large, stretching away into the darkness behind Sigby. Stone pillars supported a wooden ceiling above, while the sides of the room were taken up with racks holding laundry, steel tins and food stocks.

Sigby struggled to his feet and ripped the duct–tape from his mouth as Alexei Severov stood watching. Sigby glared at the police chief.

'What the hell do you think you're doing?!'

Severov took a single pace toward Sigby, span on his heel and directed a straight side–kick into the centre of Sigby's chest. The reporter was lifted off the ground as his breath burst from his lungs and his vision starred. His body rotated in mid air and slammed into a stone pillar. Sigby crashed to the ground, gasping for air.

'You will learn respect,' Severov stated matter–of–factly, 'for your life now depends upon it.'

Sigby crawled onto his hands and knees, coughing as his chest heaved and beads of sweat broke out on his brow. 'Go to hell,' he wheezed.

Severov laughed, glancing at the two guards, who were smiling also.

'You have accquired a new sense of courage,' Severov observed, approaching the kneeling reporter. The police chief's face twisted with pathological fury. 'I find it most disappointing.'

The police commander grabbed Sigby by the hair and yanked him up onto his knees and then span on one heel, driving the point of his knee into Sigby's left kidney. Sigby felt white pain rip through his body and gagged reflexively as he spun onto his back, his skull smacking against the stone floor.

'A pity,' Severov said as he looked down at Sigby's writhing form. 'I much preferred the selfish little bastard that you were before. Still, there is the chance for redemption, should you wish to take it.'

Sigby was crying now, hugging his own body as though it were that of a new–born. He rolled onto his side, struggling through his pain, trying to regain his breath and his senses. He peered up at Severov through bleary eyes, his teeth gritted as he spoke.

'They'll look for me,' he whispered in impotent fury. 'You'll not get away with this. They are expecting me, in Talyn.'

Severov smiled in mock pity, tilting his head to one side as he looked down at the reporter.

'Who, Martin? Who is expecting you? Who will come looking? Your cameraman is on his way back to the hotel, safe and sound in the knowledge that you are in audience with the president right now. The rebel forces cannot contact the UN nor the Americans. Nobody will miss you, Martin. Nobody at all.'

Sigby's senses finally straightened enough for him to think.

'You,' he said finally. 'It was you who killed those scientists.'

Severov shrugged, speaking as he examined the tips of his fingernails.

'They were traitors, enemies of the state.Their actions could have caused the collapse of our future economy, and that would have had unthinkable consequences.'

'The oil connection,' Sigby rasped. 'You're on someone else's payroll.'

'Money makes the world go round,' Severov said with a smile that conveyed no humour, only pure evil, the evil of mankind's propensity for greed.

'The president trusted you,' Sigby said in horror.

'Mukhari Akim is a fool, a man who thinks that noble leadership is a replacement for strength, democracy a suitable alternative to true power. He will be gone before this war is done because he stands in the way of progress. Politics, as you know Martin, is just a way of making money out of the masses whilst convincing them that they cannot live without you. Why do you think that there are never any *good* men in power? Because it is not beneficial to have *good* men in power, doing *good* things for the people. There's too much money to be made for politics to be left in the hands of the good few, or in the hands of the masses who would stand to gain the most from an *isocracy*, the true rule of the people. If that were the case, Martin, then there would no longer be the corruption, the sleaze and the indictments of elected officials.'

Sigby struggled to his knees, still holding his side.

'You're insane,' he said. 'You'll be arrested for your crimes eventually.'

'Ahhh,' Severov said, 'justice will always prevail. Those who commit their crimes shall be punished. That's what happens to criminals, isn't it Martin, in your western democratic world? Oh, unless of course, the person in question is themselves a politician, in which case it is all – how do you say? – *swept under the carpet.*'

Sigby staggered to his feet and somehow managed a choked laugh.

'You? A politician? You'd never make it through the door.'

Severov whirled and swung his clenched fist down into Sigby's belly, folding the reporter up with a strained gasp of agony as he collapsed back onto his knees.

'Self service, Martin, is what politics is all about. And as for my chances, I should imagine that President Akim should be delighted that I take his place as leader of this country. Even if he isn't, I'm sure that America would be only too happy to place someone in power who is more inclined to lead in a way that they deem suitable.'

'They'll find out,' Sigby gasped. 'Sooner or later, and you'll fall.'

Severov crouched down alongside the correspondent.

'No, they won't, Mister Sigby, because you are going to make sure that they love me. You are going to make the world cheer my name as the saviour of Mordania. And you're going to tell me where I can find Megan Mitchell and Amy O'Hara.'

Sigby, despite his pain and his fear, shook his head.

'Not a chance. If you're going to kill me, then kill me, but I'll not say a word to support you or tell you where Megan is.'

'Kill you?' Severov whispered into Sigby's ear, and then tutted mockingly. 'I'm not going to kill you, Martin. Far from it. You are going to live a long and healthy life my friend. But if you do not do exactly as I say, I will kill her.'

Sigby didn't understand for a moment, then turned his head to see Severov jabbing a thumb over his own shoulder. Sigby looked, and his heart missed a beat.

Sophie D'Aoust was on her knees, bound by her wrists and her ankles, lying on the floor perhaps six metres from where Martin himself lay. Her eyes were swollen and bruised, dried blood caked on her lips, her hair dishevelled.

'Such a shame,' Severov said, 'such beauty wasted. She will live only as long as you serve both myself and my future cabinet. Should you fail, well, a traitorous woman who has vanished from her country will not be missed, by her people or by her government. She'll make good sport for my dogs.'

Sigby lunged toward Severov and lashed out with his teeth, sinking them into the police commander's cheek and biting with inhuman savagery. He felt the commander's flesh crunch and rip in his bite, tasted thick and coppery blood as it spilled down his chin onto the bare stone, heard Severov's deafening, anguished scream in his ear.

A chunk of flesh parted with a sickening, sucking sound as Severov hurled himself away. Sigby spat out the bloody mass of tissue as the commander whirled and swung his boot into Sigby's belly. Sigby doubled over as the contents of his stomach splattered across the stones at his feet.

Severov ploughed into him like a freight train, his boots and fists flying.

The sound of the reporter's agonised cries were not loud enough to escape past the heavy basement door and its guards.

***

55

'Pick up damn it!'

Megan listened to Martin Sigby's answerphone for the eighth time and then angrily shut the satellite phone off.

'Maybe he's doing a broadcast,' Callum said.

Megan ran a hand through her hair in exasperation and turned to look at Bolav, who was working at the kitchen table on the camera.

'How's that coming?'

'Almost there,' she said. 'Most of the camera is broken now from the cold and damp, but the memory cartridge is fine. Here we go.'

Bolav plugged a USB cable into the camera and then ran it to the computer in the corner of the room. Alexandre, standing to one side, watched as the Mordanian plugged the USB cable into the computer and then tapped a few key commands.

'Donwloading,' he said, as Megan and Callum gathered beside him.

'I don't know if I want to watch this,' Alexandre said.

As Megan watched, the computer's video player began running film. For a few seconds the screen was blank, and then the screen showed the village in the forest, the scientists being lined up by what looked like rebel soldiers but could have been the secret police wearing fake uniforms. Megan saw Petra Milosovich being shown photographs, shaking his head, then being lined up by the soldiers against a wall before being gunned down in cold blood. The screen went blank.

'Ella mon Giet,' Bolav murmured, and touched his index finger to his forehead and shoulders.

'There's more,' Callum said, pointing to the screen.

Moments later, they could see Amy O'Hara running away from the camera, across a forest clearing. She halted abruptly in the distance, her hands in the air as a soldier appeared nearby, his weapon aimed unwaveringly at her.

They watched as the rest of the soldiers arrived in the clearing, accompanied by the huge Mastiffs that bayed and growled and strained at their leashes. An officer walked out from their ranks, and Megan's complexion darkened.

'Severov.'

It took no more than three or four minutes for the rest of the film to play out, and for the soldier's gunshot to end Amy O'Hara's suffering. They watched as Severov killed the soldier responsible and arranged the two bodies, then the small force began abandoning the lonely clearing.

Lieutenant Cole's expression was murderous as he looked across at Megan.

'I want that man's head in my hands, Mitchell. I want to look into his eyes before I kill him.'

Megan watched the screen as Severov and his men left the scene. Callum gestured to the timer–bar at the bottom of the screen.

'The camera stayed on for another couple of hours,' she said.

Megan nodded.

'Speed it forward.'

Bolav complied, and within an hour new figures emerged into the clearing from a different direction.

'Alexandre,' Megan said, and the farmer crossed the room to look at the screen, surprise etched into his features.

'Yes, that is Dimitri and myself.'

Megan watched as they located Amy's near–dead body, and carefully carried her and the dead soldier away from the clearing, descending the opposite side of the valley and out of shot. Megan straightened.

'That's it, all we need to finish the Mordanian secret police. We get all of this back to the city and to the United Nations offices as soon as our ride arrives.'

'You might have to be quicker than that,' Alexandre said.

Megan turned to look at him, about to ask why, when she saw the direction of the farmer's gaze. He was looking out of the kitchen windows with a concerned look upon his face.

Megan strode across to the window and peered outside.

'What is it?' Bolav asked.

'Trouble,' Megan replied. 'The rebels are coming.'

Outside on the distant horizon, a train of troop transports, artillery pieces and hundreds of troops were advancing toward them across the snowy wilderness.

Lieutenant Cole picked up his M–16.

'It's time to leave.' He looked at Megan. '*All* of us.'

*

USS Theodore Roosevelt (CVN–71)

Black Sea

'All elements away, wave complete sir.'

Admiral Fry nodded without looking at the lieutenant who had spoken, turning instead to his Executive Officer.

'Sit–rep?'

'All clear,' the XO said with a touch of caution in his voice. 'The Hawkeyes report no aerial activity either over Georgia, as expected, or over Mordania. If there's going to be an air war, this Rameron man needs to get his jets up or they'll be smashed to pieces on the ground.'

Admiral Fry thought for a moment.

'I want the forward fighters to maintain standard Combat Air Patrols over Mordanian airspace. Tell the Forward Air Controller to direct the strike packages to attack SAM sites and artillery defences only.'

The XO glanced at his Admiral for a moment.

'You're still bothered about what Miller reported to you?'

'Not bothered, just curious.'

'She's just over–hyped by the combat, looking for ways to justify the fact that she's killed someone. Happened in Vietnam all the time, you know that.'

Admiral Fry nodded vacantly.

'Maybe, but if they're not even putting up defensive CAPs with their fighters, it begs the question of their commander's intentions, does it not? It's no secret that we're coming – with all the damned media coverage I'd be surprised if anyone *didn't* know we were coming. He's not defending himself.'

'Another ploy, to earn media sympathy. We can't stand around here wringing our hands or putting our heads up our asses worrying about consequences.' The XO straightened apologetically. 'Sir.'

'Eloquently put,' Admiral Fry noted. 'None the less, hold the strike packages back from attacking any infrastructure other than offensive anti–aircraft emplacements and troop concentrations inside Talyn.'

The XO hesitated only for a moment longer before relaying the order.

Admiral Fry looked at the radar tracks of his fighter wings and strike packages soaring away toward Mordania.

'Let's see what's really on your mind, General Rameron,' he whispered to himself.

*

'Move, damn it!'

Lieutenant Cole's voice sounded stark in the crisp morning air as he hurried across a rutted track toward the tree line. Callum struggled along behind with the SEAL team following, placing themselves between the advancing rebel forces and Megan's beleaguered little group. Alexandre waited for them beside the tree line of the enclosing forests. Megan's arms ached already from the strain of carrying Amy on her hastily constructed stretcher, and Bolav's diminutive form seemed positively crushed beneath the burden.

'You'll never make it in time, Thessalia's too far,' Alexandre said worriedly as Megan reached his side.

'No choice,' Megan replied. 'The rebels will have found their dead companions and tracked us here, and we've got to get this film back to the UN fast. If they see what really happened, it could prevent this war.'

Alexandre seemed worn down by the events that had overtaken his life and his country.

'Megan, we're already at war. This isn't about genocide or democracy, it's about money and power, just like all of the wars that have been fought by men since the beginning of civilisation. There is no such thing as a righteous conflict, only a dignified defence.'

Megan was about to speak when the noise of jet aircraft split the sky high above the frozen fields and valleys. They all looked up to see four sleek fighter jets streaking across the sky thousands of feet above them. Megan had no doubt that they were American aircraft, and she grabbed Alexandre's shoulder.

'You're coming with us. It is no longer safe here.'

The old farmer offered her a wan smile. 'Is it safe anywhere?'

Megan sighed heavily and looked away toward the rapidly closing troops and armour.

'They may think that you and your wife were harbouring the enemy,' she said.

'They may,' Alexandre agreed, 'but they would know better. I am just a farmer and they know nothing of what I have concealed in that old barn. They think that they're fighting for something great, for something just, for their country or their honour or their future. They'll be past and gone with barely a look at Marin and I, or old Sergei.'

Megan felt a sudden pain in her eyes as she reached out and hugged Alexandre.

'I will not forget you,' she said.

Alexandre smiled. 'Nor I you. Now go.'

Alexandre turned and began hurrying back across the frozen fields toward the farmstead. Megan was looking at the rapidly advancing columns of rebel forces when a distant sound reached her ears. She hesitated, listening intently, sensing now as well as hearing the rhythmic thumping reverberating off the hills and seeming to rumble through the frozen earth beneath them. Callum lifted his chin and searched the skies above them like a bloodhound hunting for a scent. Lieutenant Cole's men began searching the heavens also. Megan listened with them, and the sound resolved into a deep bass *wokka–wokka–wokka.*

'Chinook!' Callum shouted. 'I'd know that beat anywhere on earth!'

Megan immediately understood and called out to Lieutenant Cole's men.

'The RAF are coming! Sir Wilkin's ride has arrived.'

The SEALS fanned out in a defensive formation as the distinctive double–beat of the Chinook's twin rotor–blades thundered through the cold morning skies. At that moment a sharp crack split the chill air and a peppering of bark pieces sprayed across the pure white snow as a rifle round ricocheted off a tree behind Megan.

'Enemy fire! Cover!'

Megan and Bolav lowered Amy's stretcher at the treeline as Callum hurried after them and ducked down. Megan looked out across the snowy fields and saw the rebels spreading out and heading in their direction. The SEALS were already laying prone in the bitter ice and snow, returning a crisp staccato fire.

A sudden horror filled Megan's chest as she watched. Alexandre was half–way to the farmstead, and his wife was standing in the doorway of the house, watching anxiously as her husband trotted toward her and their friends rushed from their own houses, weapons in their hands once more.

Megan lurched forward towards Lieutenant Cole.

'Cover them!' she shouted above the deafening sound of the incoming helicopter.

She could see the Chinook now, swinging between the towering valleys and aiming toward the farmstead, the RAF markings visible on the fuselage. Megan ducked and flinched as rounds of rifle fire whipped past her and churned the snow and soil at her feet.

'Get down!' Cole bellowed above the noise before returning to his weapon. He fired off two quick shots and a distant rebel soldier flipped awkwardly and dropped onto the earth, his weapon falling beside him.

'Mark the L–Z!' Cole shouted above the roar of the blades and engines.

Megan and Bolav began waving frantically at the huge advancing helicopter. To her right, Megan could see Alexandre advancing toward the rebels, waving his own arms and shaking his head. Closer, one of the SEALS tossed a smoke–grenade out into the field, the device spurting clouds of bright purple smoke onto the cold air.

Megan was about to try and scream something to the distant rebel line when the rattling sound of the rebel's small–arms fire cracked the frigid air.

'No!'

Megan's cry was drowned out by the sudden whining roar of a rotary cannon. A trail of heavy tracer–fire streamed like laser–beams from the side of the Chinook helicopter, massive rounds smashing into the frozen snow and earth and sending chunks of mud and stone flying across the rebel's lines. Megan saw Mordanian bodies scythed down as though by an invisible, lethal blade. Dozens of rebels threw themselves down onto the earth whilst others dropped to one knee and fired upon the helicopter.

'Alexandre!' Megan shouted.

The farmer was still waving his hands when dozens of rebels, streaming toward the farmstead and panicking under the withering fire from the Chinook, saw Alexandre coming toward them.

The Chinook fired a last few rounds as it turned and then it was settling down in the field fifty yards from Megan's position, blocking her view of the farmstead as the pilot used the helicopter's fuselage to protect them all from the rebel fire. On the opposite side, the Chinook's gunner maintained a steady and lethal hail of fire upon the rebel positions.

Megan ran with Amy's stretcher, Bolav struggling to keep up as the Chinook's loadmaster appeared at the swiftly opening rear–door and waved them urgently onward. Megan squinted against the whorls of snow and ice chips as she ducked under the huge spinning blades, felt the overpowering *wokka–wokka* beat of them as she led Bolav and Callum up into the helicopter.

The SEALS accompanied them as a group, moving and firing with lethal accuracy at the rebel positions, keeping their heads down as they helped protect the Chinook.

As Megan climbed the ramp she shot a glance out across to the homestead, and with a terrible cry that seemed to come from somewhere else she saw Alexandre lying motionless on the track beside the farmstead, and his wife Marin slumped against the door frame of their home as their friends fired their shotguns wildly at the advancing rebels only to be cut down themselves.

A sudden double–thump sounded above the rest of the noise, and Megan watched in horror as Bolav wavered on his feet before his legs collapsed beneath him, two blood–sodden wounds spreading across his chest.

'Man down!' Cole shouted to his men. 'Fall back now!'

Callum grabbed the other end of Amy's stretcher with his good arm, dragging it backwards into the helicopter as Megan dashed for the ramp again.

'Megan, no!' Callum shouted.

The SEALS piled into the Chinook, hauling Bolav's bloodied body with them. Cole grabbed Megan in a powerful bear–hug that almost lifted her off the ground, dragging her forcefully backward into the helicopter as it lifted off from the field amidst churning clouds of snow and purple smoke, the rear ramp closing as they flew away.

'Get down!' Cole bellowed at Megan.

Megan staggered, her arms aching in the soldier's iron–like grip, and watched as the fields moved away behind them, the snowy ground racing past below. In the distance, she saw the farmstead vanishing rapidly in the morning mists and with it the last forlorn island of peace in Mordania.

Fatigued and sick to her stomach, Megan turned to see Bolav lying on his back on the cold floor of the helicopter. The SEALS's medic was trying to staunch the flow of blood from the Mordanian's wounds, but it was clear to all that he would be dead within moments.

Bolav gestured to Megan weakly, and Megan dropped onto her knees beside the doomed translator as he spoke in a thin, reedy voice.

'There is something that you should know, Megan.'

Megan leaned close, hearing Bolav's words, and then sat back on her haunches in the Chinook as the Mordanian's life slipped away before her eyes.

***

56

'Bluebird One, in–bound. Vector for field landing.'

The voice of the Chinook pilot sounded distant in Megan's headset as she sat on a spartan fold–down seat attached to the fuselage wall of the helicopter. She stared vacantly out of the half–open rear ramp of the Chinook and watched the snowy fields and vast pine forests drift past below.

'Bluebird One, left to two–four–zero for descent, colours green, LZ secure.'

'Left to two–four–zero, descending now, Bluebird One.'

The powerful engines of the Chinook changed note and the helicopter began to descend toward Thessalia. Megan closed her eyes and with them her mind to the raw grief that poisoned her veins, swelling in her chest like a terminal disease. The image of the fallen farmer and his wife had become seared onto her mind's eye, as though her very soul had been branded with fire.

A hand touched Megan's shoulder, breaking her from her solemn reverie. She looked across to see Callum watching her, his jaw tense and his eyes strained. The Scotsman spoke loudly enough to be heard above the thumping engines above them.

'Not now. Think about Sophie – she needs you.'

Megan stared for a long moment at her friend, and then glanced out of the rear of the helicopter again to see the myriad snow–covered roofs of Thessalia, the streets and the people of the war–ravaged and scarred capital. She thought of Alexei Severov and suddenly the grief in her heart twisted into rage as she looked at Amy O'Hara and thought of what the police commander had done to her.

She looked back at Callum.

'You're going to a hospital,' she said.

Callum blinked, thrown off–guard by the comment. 'Okay.'

Megan unstrapped herself from her seat and carefully made her way to the cockpit, where the pilot and co–pilot were sitting behind the masses of dials and glowing computer screens as they brought the helicopter in toward the city. Megan placed a hand on the co–pilot's shoulder.

'How close will we be to Government House? It's important.'

The co–pilot thought for a second, and then spoke to the pilot. The answer came back an instant later.

'Two hundred yards, roughly.'

Megan nodded. 'Good, that'll be enough.'

The Chinook thundered over the city and through the cockpit windows Megan saw the vast refugee camps and, nearby, several rows of helicopters of various types, all United States aircraft and surrounded by hundreds of troops.

'The Yankee advance guard,' the co–pilot said, as though reading Megan's thoughts. 'Their marines are coming in from the carrier group one wave at a time. Even so, there are not enough to defend the city against Rameron's men.'

Megan smiled grimly.

'They won't need to if you get me down where I need to be. Radio anyone you can think of in the Red Cross who can deal with an immediate medical evacuation, and send a message to the British UN attache in Government House that Megan Mitchell needs to speak with him urgently.'

Megan moved back into the Chinook's fuselage, to see Callum regarding her quietly.

'You shouldn't risk going in there again,' The Scotsman cautioned.

'We can't let Amy anywhere near Severov's men, and that means Sir Wilkins is useless to us because he's in the same building as the secret police. We'll have to get her out another way and if I'm already in the building, Severov will no doubt be preoccupied with me.'

Callum nodded, and smiled weakly.

'I think I know what you're up to.'

'Not quite,' Megan said, 'and you're not going to like the rest of it.'

*

'I think that this is a most excellent idea. You will become my personal spokesperson and make your reports from the Thessalia Hilton, as before.'

Alexei Severov lit a short, fat cigar as he stood over Martin Sigby, drawing deeply on it and exhaling a thin stream of blue smoke into the air above his head.

Sigby slumped in a rickety wooden chair. His face was barely marked by the beating that he had received, but his entire body was battered beneath his clothes, bruised and bloodied.

Severov, his cheek patched with a crimson–stained medical dressing, looked down at him.

'You will ensure that General Mikhail Rameron is portrayed as we wish him to be; a war–mongering traitor who has slaughtered hundreds, perhaps thousands in his endless quest for power. And I, my friend, shall be the conquering hero who extinguished Rameron's brutal regime.'

'It will never work,' Sigby spat. 'Megan is still out there and she knows about you.'

Severov's smile grew broader still.

'I know that she is, and I know what she knows, and do you know what Mister Sigby? I cannot wait to see her again, for there will be much for us to discuss and she will enjoy none of it.'

'I wouldn't be too sure of that.'

Sigby looked away from Severov in disgust as the policeman leaned closer to him, those cruel eyes burning into his own.

'Oh, but you disagree, Mister Sigby? Perhaps you think that you might decide to take your chances, being away from my grasp, and tell the world that I am holding a French citizen hostage, no?'

Severov smiled, standing upright again and flicking his head at one of the guards behind him. The guard strolled to his side and reached down to a sheath on his belt, producing a seven–inch combat knife with a cruelly serated edge.

'You could,' Severov whispered, 'but it would make my friend here a very, very happy man. I would be destroyed, of course, by the Americans or the British, but that would not matter. Djimon here would be long gone, and your precious little friend Sophie would be gone with him.'

Sigby glanced across the room at Sophie's form huddling in the shadows as Severov spoke softly, clearly, letting Sigby think about every single word.

'He and his family and friends would use her for a few days, a few weeks perhaps, until they tired of her body. That would be when the real suffering begins, when they begin to use their knives to take her apart, small piece by small piece. I've heard that they can keep a victim alive for months in this way, quite literally eating them alive one bit at a time.' The commander took a last draw on his cigar, sucking until the tip glowed bright orange. 'Do not doubt their loyalty to me, Martin, even if I have fallen.'

Sigby looked up to see the Djimon's hand outstretched, palm up before Severov. The police commander ground his cigar–butt out on the huge, calloused palm of the soldier, who stood without flinching or complaining.

Severov smiled again.

'Come, Martin Sigby. It is time for you to make my name great.'

*

Megan jogged quickly across Petrevska Square, the sound of the Chinook's engines fading far behind her as she ran, dodging left and right past hordes of people, animals and vehicles all moving in conflicting directions.

Almost a dozen armed guards were protecting the vast gates of Government House and would not allow Megan in until they had received confirmation from Sir Wilkins that the British visitor was indeed expected.

'We cannot allow civilians into the building unescorted,' the NCO commanding the guards reported to Megan with a stern expression. 'Who knows what they might do?'

Megan had to wait almost ten minutes before she was allowed to enter the grounds, and she ran into the foyeur as Sir Wilkins hurried out to greet her.

'Megan dear girl! Thank God you're all right!' Then he saw the bruises and cuts on her face. 'My God, what happened?'

Megan wearily shook the attache's hand, managing a smile.

'I've a hell of a lot to tell you and very little time.'

'Of course, of course,' Sir Wilkins fussed, guiding her down a corridor past the bustling UN offices. 'Let me get you a good strong coffee and we'll sit down and discuss everything.'

Megan allowed herself to be led to Sir Wilkin's personal quarters, and an aide brought coffee and biscuits before Sir Wilkins closed the door and sat down opposite Megan with an eager expression.

'Now, please, for the love of God tell me what's been happening!'

Megan reached into her pocket and produced a digital memory card and a thick wedge of papers.

'First things first,' she began. 'Callum's hurt and he needs proper medical attention. I need your authorisation to have him airlifted out of the city. The UN and the RAF won't allow such a transfer without these legal papers they've given me being signed by someone of sufficient authority.'

'Of course,' Sir Wilkins said immediately. 'He will be all right, I take it?'

Megan tore off the last sheet of paper from the wedge and handed it to Sir Wilkins, who signed it hurriedly.

'It's a bullet wound, in the shoulder. He's not incapacitated, but he needs surgery to remove the shrapnel and bone fragments before the wound becomes infected. He's at the field hospital near Khobal Airport right now.'

'Ghastly business,' Wilkins said, quickly handing back the sheet of paper before calling out to his aide. The aide entered the room and Megan handed the papers over to her as Wilkins spoke.

'Ensure that this is acted upon immediately as a matter of utmost urgency. I want this individual flown out of Thessalia this very minute, is that clear?'

The aide nodded and scooted from the room.

Megan sighed a breath of relief and then turned to Wilkins.

'General Mikhail Rameron is operating his forces from a former refinery complex just north of Talyn,' she said. 'He was there last night and by now will probably have occupied Talyn.'

'Absolutely capital!' Sir Wilkins applauded in delight. 'First class, Megan. I shall inform the commander of the carrier group forthwith. They'll probably hit both sites to be sure.'

Megan frowned deeply. The attache was out of his chair and about to leave the office when he saw Megan's sudden change of expression. 'What is it?'

'General Rameron is not responsible for the events that are the main reasons for the launch of the military campaign here in Mordania. He probably did not launch any fighters against the American carrier, and his men certainly did not massacre the civilians near Borack. They were executed by the Mordanian Secret Police under the command of Alexei Severov.'

Sir Wilkins stood for a long moment, his gaze fixed on Megan's, before slowly retaking his seat.

'Go on,' he said.

'The murdered men were not soldiers but scientists were working on a device known as a Sterling Engine. They had perfected an existing design to the point where it was so efficient that it could be fuelled using modest amounts of helium to power motor–vehicles, aircraft and industrial machinery. Plans were in motion to gain energy from geo–thermal sources, providing clean, pollution free energy for the entire planet. They were on the verge of creating a global revolution in energy production.'

'Good God,' Wilkins uttered.

'Several international oil companies involved in the large–scale construction of piplines from the Caspian Sea to the Black Sea through Mordania, to bypass politically unreliable pipelines from Russia and Eastern Europe, found out about the engineering work and managed to bribe Alexei Severov to ensure that the work was brought to a halt.'

Sir Wilkins's eyes widened slowly.

'He murdered them for money?'

'Lots of money,' Megan replied. 'We haven't traced the transactions yet, but I have people on it. However, they did not know that the engines were being tested on vehicles of the Mordanian Air Force and Army, with assistance from General Rameron. Rameron no doubt learned who was responsible and why, and he rallied his forces into an attempted military coup.'

Wilkins leaned back in his chair and exhaled noisily.

'But he attacked the Americans,' he said in confusion.

'No, he did not,' Megan said. 'The Mordanian Air Force still has its full compliment of aircraft. The Migs involved in the attack were of a type no longer used by the Mordanian Air Force. I got someone to look into it, and they traced purchases of former military jets back to a company called Kruger Petrochemicals – two Mig–23 *Flogger* aircraft. We also found and photographed several devices here in Mordania used specifically for the remote–control of large pilotless fighter aircraft – American in design. The United States Air Force uses its old jets as full–size targets for its pilots to practice shooting missiles at in peacetime. Again, a check on the serial numbers revealed that they had been bought by Kruger Petrochemicals.'

Sir Wilkins shook his head slowly in disbelief.

'They flew them in as though the Mordanians were attacking.'

'In order to force a war with America,' Megan confirmed, 'which would support a government which would bend easily to the needs of American corporate demands, including Kruger Petrochemicals, because they have such influence within the administration. We no longer live in a democracy, sir. It's a dictatorship of corporate influences, capitalism run amok, international companies vying for control of government policies and the privatisation of foreign industries into American concerns. The deals are done to encourage total free–markets and capitalist profits at the expense of worker's rights, unions, even democracy itself. It's what the rebel NCO I spoke to meant when he talked about economic experiments. The West forces countries to convert their economies to capitalism at the expense of the people, creating huge debts for those countries as they receive loans from the World Bank to raise capital and even bigger profits for companies that take over those country's natural resources.'

Wilkins stood from his chair.

'The American attacks are imminent,' he said, 'but without proof none of this is enough for me to be able to call off the attacks.'

Megan smiled and waved the memory cartridge in her other hand.

'It's all on film, not just the remote–control devices, but the actual massacre of the scientists by Alexei Severov.'

Wilkins stared at Megan as though she had just informed him that she was God.

'No! That's the video you talked about?'

'Yes. He was seen and filmed, murdering the scientists, by Amy O'Hara.' Megan set the cartridge down on the table and looked at Wilkins. 'You need to get this to the UN and the Americans as fast as you can.'

Sir Wilkins stared vacantly at the cartridge for a moment, and then at Megan.

'Of course, but I don't know that they will be able to change the course of events that have been set in motion.'

'Then get it to Martin Sigby, and let him broadcast it all to the world.'

Sir Wilkins picked up the cartridge.

'Are there any other copies?' he asked. 'The more we have, the safer we are.'

'No. Make some, as quickly as you can,' Megan advised.

'And then we must get you out of the city,' Wilkins said. 'If Severov and his people learn of this, they'll do anything that they can to silence us. Is there anyone else whom we might need to get out of the country?'

'No. The only other person who knew everything was Bolav, the interpreter assigned to us by Severov. He was killed near Talyn this morning.'

'By General Rameron's rebels?' Wilkins asked.

'It was nobodies fault,' Megan replied sadly. 'He was just like all the other Mordanians trapped here under the yoke of conflicting governments, just like us, imprisoned by those who are elected to protect us. He was caught in the crossfire and there wasn't a damn thing that we could do about it.'

Wilkins made for his office door.

'Stay here. I'll get this to the copy room immediately, and then arrange a transport for you out of the city.'

'Wait,' Megan said, standing. 'Sophie?'

Sir Wilkins sighed, and offered Megan an apologetic expression.

'Sophie D'Aoust, as is her real name, was arrested yesterday and was flown out of the country this morning. She is to be repatriated to France to stand trial. I am sorry, Megan, there was nothing that I could do to intervene.'

Megan closed her eyes for a moment and nodded, before retaking her seat as Sir Wilkins hurried from the room.

***

57

'Stand aside.'

The stranger's accent sounded odd to the United States Marine guard standing in front of an officer's compound near Government House.

'No, sir, I can't do that.'

The marine peered at the man for a long moment, taking in the weathered, stubbled face and the bloodied shirt. The man leaned forward.

'You'll regret it.'

The marine did not alter his expression.

'You, a civilian, want me to interrupt a private briefing of my senior officers on a major strike mission and tell them that they've got the wrong target and that they should be running around searching for a missing television reporter instead?'

The man nodded and brightened his smile. 'That's the spirit.'

The marine's patience finally ran out. 'Get out of my sight before I kick your ass!'

'Can you kick that high, sonnie?'

The marine's eyes flew wide with incoherent fury and he swung the butt of his M–16 toward the man's bloodied jaw. The man side–stepped the blow, grabbed the rifle with his good hand as he shoved his right boot behind the marine's ankle. The soldier felt himself topple off balance and crashed onto his back on the snowy ground as the man yanked the rifle from his grasp and slammed his boot down onto the marine's chest.

'Now then. You'll be needing to learn a bit about manners.'

'Guard!'

There was a sudden commotion from within the compound and a handful of marine officers, all buzz–cuts and square–jaws, burst out into the chill air to see the bedraggled man standing over the fallen marine guard. Instantly, pistols appeared in the officer's hands.

The stranger turned, stepped up to the nearest officer and handing him the guard's M–16.

'Your recruits are no better now than they were back in '91.'

The officer, a General with two stars on the lapels of his flak–jacket, stared at the towering wretch before him with murderous eyes.

'And just who the *God–damned hell are you?!*

'Callum McGregor, sir, and you need to listen to what I have to say. I and two others have just escaped from the interior of the country. We have documented proof that the attack on your country's aircraft–carrier was faked and that the massacre that started this conflict was committed by the Mordanian Secret Police, who even as we speak are trying to do the same to those who are aware of the deception. Sir, I need your help to stop a war.'

The general stared at Callum in shock and glanced at his fellow officers, who seemed as stunned as he was. He turned back to Callum.

'I don't know whether to believe you or shoot you,' he rumbled.

'If you believe me now sir and it turns out to be wrong, you can shoot me later. The other way round, nobody wins.'

'Or I could just put you in the damned brig!'

'My friends, sir, would not appreciate that.'

The general turned as Lieutenant Cole's SEALS appeared from nearby. The marine officers recognised them as Special Forces soldiers the moment they laid eyes on them, and looked at each other in surprise.

'My name is Lieutenant Cole,' the SEAL's officer growled uncompromisingly, 'and you had better listen to this man, sir, because he knows what he's talking about.'

The general stared hard at Callum for a moment longer.

'You have real, hard proof of all this?'

'The best kind,' Callum said. 'But first, we urgently need to find somebody. You may be familiar with his name. Martin Sigby.'

*

Megan was sitting in Sir Wilkin's office when the attache's aide returned, poking her head through the door.

'Megan Mitchell?' Megan stood quickly. 'Sir Wilkins is waiting on the parade ground at the rear of the building. He has a transport waiting for you.'

Megan immediately made her way out of the office and back through Government House, walking to the main foyeur and turning right to pass beneath the towering staircases toward the rear of the building. Sir Wilkin's aide accompanied her to a long corridor that ran alongside the parade ground that Megan could see through the windows.

'There is a helicopter waiting,' she said. 'Walk to the end of the corridor, turn right and descend the staircase.'

'Thank you,' Megan said, hurrying along the corridor as the aide turned and headed back toward the UN occupied quarter of the building.

Megan looked out of the windows as she walked swiftly down the corridor, and saw a broad parade ground surrounded by tall razor–wired walls. A large Russian Mil Mi–24 helicopter sat in the centre of the parade ground, it's blades bowing under their own weight, ground crew fussing busily loading equipment aboard.

As she walked she looked down, closer to the base of the corridor windows. Large, heavy chain–link fences partitioned off one corner of the parade ground. Megan saw huge, muscular dogs standing in the cold air, alert and twitchy, eyeing the parade ground with hungry eyes.

Megan felt a sudden premonition of doom overwhelm her like a dark cloud passing overhead.

'Good morning, Megan Mitchell.'

A door opened in the corridor just behind Megan and Alexei Severov stepped out, a small, neat black pistol directed at Megan's chest. Three more doors opened and heavily armed secret–police appeared to aim Kalashnikovs at her.

Megan glanced at the end of the corridor, judging the distance, and as if reading her mind Alexei Severov tutted and shook his head.

'Not a chance, Megan,' he said, clearly relishing the moment. He took a pace closer until the tip of his pistol touched Megan's shirt. 'I believe that I owe you something of great importance.'

The pistol whipped up and across Megan's temple with a wicked crack, white stars flashing across her vision as pain bolted across her skull. Before she could react, Severov's knee slammed deep into her stomach, crumpling her legs and sending the breath rushing from her lungs as she collapsed onto the floor.

'Downstairs with her,' Severov snapped at his men.

Megan felt herself lifted roughly and half–carried, half–dragged along the corridor to a staircase that descended not toward the parade ground but down a narrow, dark passage of bare stone to a cellar or basement. Megan was roughly manoeuvered into an old wooden chair, thick hemp ropes securing her ankles and wrists to the legs and back of the chair respectively.

When she was securely bound to Alexei Severov's satisfaction, the troops moved back and let their commander stand before Megan, regarding her as though one might regard a work of art.

'Finally, Megan Mitchell, your interfering has come to an end.'

Megan did not reply, looking around her at the cellar. She could see the storage shelves and the stacked boxes, but she could also see dull, brown stains on the stone floor.

'A place for your hobbies?' she hazarded.

Severov smiled, leaning close to Megan. 'A place for my art,' he replied.

Megan looked at the bloodied medical patch on Severov's cheek.

'It looks like your art bites back.'

Severov's smile vanished as though the life had been pinched from it. He stood upright for a moment and Megan thought that the Mordanian might hit her again, but Severov turned away as he spoke.

'You are finished, Megan. This cold, damp and miserable place is a sight that you should savour, for it is the last you will see.' He turned to face Megan. 'An interesting thought – you will actually be dead in a few minutes time. How does that make you feel?'

A brief calculation flickered briefly through Megan's mind – *don't give the bastard the satisfaction.*

'Not fussed one way or the other, as it happens.'

'A shame, because before you die I wish to inform you of what has become of your accomplices.'

Megan tried to maintain a dispassionate expression as Severov indulged himself in a brief but graphic description of what had happened to Martin Sigby, and what would happen to Sophie D'Aoust if anything should occur that was not to Severov's liking.

'They have suffered, and they will continue to suffer for many years after your death, Megan.'

Megan managed to maintain her composure, smiling defiantly at Severov as she spoke.

'Unlikely. Even now people are looking for me, Severov. They know what you have done; the murder of the scientists, the payments made by the oil companies to you. The moment they realise that I am missing you'll be hunted by every soldier in this land. It doesn't matter what happens to me, you're finished now no matter what you do.'

The commander's expression had remained stony as Megan had spoken, and now he leaned close to Megan, his eyes hard and merciless.

'Oh, Megan, how mistaken you have become, how foolish you have been. There will be no witch–hunt in this country for me, nor any other, isn't that right Mister Wilkins?'

Megan's weary mind did not register what had been said for a moment. As though in a dream she saw Sir Wilkins step into the cellar from the darkness behind Severov, his face grave. Time slowed down as the attache approached Megan's chair, looking down at her with something akin to pity, perhaps remorse or regret, but no shame that Megan's addled brain could detect.

'My dear Megan,' Wilkins said quietly as Severov moved off to one side. 'You know, for my entire career I have felt such sympathy for the ordinary people who become the victims of political intrigue, of the great games that goverments play. Until now I had not known a single one of them. I am sorry that it had to come to this.'

Megan could feel her disbelief mutating grotesquely into unbearable rage.

'*Had* to come to this?'

'Yes, it *had* to come to this,' Sir Wilkins said. 'Your personal loss and suffering is incosequential compared to the stakes of this conflict. You, like so many others, are being sacrificed upon the altar of political expedience just like the civilians here in Mordania, those in Iraq or Afghanistan, those who lived in Vietnam or Napoleonic France or America during the Civil War. Believe me, Megan, it pains all of those who govern to know that millions of people died due to the *essential* strategies of countless governments over the centuries.'

Megan's eyes narrowed into thin slits of contempt.

'And who is *this* essential to?'

Sir Wilkins sighed, pacing slowly through the shadows before Megan as he spoke.

'Megan, you are but one person among hundreds of millions who are living out their lives as best they can whilst those who lead them manoeuvre and argue and debate and betray those whom they pledged to serve. People like myself also live as best we can, but on the only winning side that there is – the top. You ask why this was essential? Oil, Megan, and of course the money that goes with it. But it's also essential to maintain an American presence here in Mordania as a barrier against Russian influence in the Caucasus, which conveniently also provides a bulwark against Iran and China–supported Kazakhstan to the east. It is all part of the *Great Game*, Megan, protecting our way of life against the advance of others who might wish to change it. This is not the advance of democracy, my friend, but the eradication of everything that prevents capitalism and free–trade.'

Sir Wilkins paused in his pacing and looked at Megan.

'Your work is commendable, Megan, of the highest moral order, to uphold the democratic principle of a free press. It would also be a global catastrophe were it successful. It had to be stopped, Megan. I truly am very sorry that it has had to end this way.'

Megan looked away from Sir Wilkins in disgust.

'Saudi Arabia,' she said, 'the Gulf War. You were with the oil people there. I should have remembered, made the connection.'

'Why would you have?' Sir Wilkins said without a trace of irony. 'We were friends.'

'Were,' Megan agreed, and then looked up at Wilkins. 'Sophie, she has had no part of this.'

Sir Wilkins sighed heavily.

'Sophie D'Aoust may not be a threat to the political stability of the Mordanian government, but then again she possesses the same tenacity as you do, Megan, and cannot be allowed to leave this country again. Commander Severov here will arrange everything. Of course, Martin Sigby has been informed of this and will comply willingly to all of our demands.'

Megan swallowed as the rage within her threatened to burst out of her throat, as though she could spit flames and burn Severov and Wilkins alive. Sir Wilkins spoke again, his features still serious and his tone demanding.

'Where is Miss O'Hara?' he asked.

Megan laughed abruptly, then cut it short as she glared at Wilkins. 'Dead.'

Sir Wilkins smiled a brief, hollow smile.

'We know that she is alive, Megan. Bolav kept us quite well informed about the events that occurred whilst you were in–country, until his unfortunate death.' Megan's face collapsed as she realised the true extent of the betrayal. Sir Wilkin's tone turned sympathetic. 'There is no sense in causing further suffering for yourself in her defence. She will be found, sooner or later.'

Alexei Severov stepped forward keenly, his eyes bright with the anticipation of inflicting pain. Megan kept her gaze fixed on Wilkins, her voice clear and steady as she spoke.

'I really, truly would rather die than tell you.'

Sir Wilkins regarded Megan for a moment.

'You will be ready to die within a few minutes, after Alexei here as finished with you. Last chance, Megan. Tell us now, please.'

Megan squeezed her thighs together to try to still the sickening fear swelling in her bowels. She looked away from Wilkins and studied a spot on the floor as though it were the most important thing in the universe.

Sir Wilkins silently stepped back and Alexei Severov moved forward, standing in front of Megan and smiling with pathological delight.

Megan saw the police commander take a full overarm swing and smash his clenched fist into her face, felt her nose break as white pain gripped her head. The commander stepped back.

'Think on it, Megan,' Sir Wilkins said. 'One person cannot ever change the world. We will return shortly, and I do sincerely hope that by then you will have come to your senses.'

***

58

Martin Sigby, flanked by four secret–police soldiers, walked down a long corridor and was led out of Government House onto a large parade ground. Sigby saw the looming bulk of a Russian Mil Mi–24 helicopter dominating the area, a large troop transporter, and the dog–pens in the far corner. Ranks of hand–cuffed, hooded people were filing into the helicopter, prisoners of war for the exchange. He could see one of them lying on a stretcher being hefted aboard.

As they walked the helicopter's engines began to whine into life, the huge drooping rotors turning lethargically in the cold air and scything through the snow flurries falling from the dull and featureless overcast above.

The four police troops manhandled Sigby aboard a nearby troop transporter, sliding the heavy side–door shut and blocking out the already deafening noise of the helicopter engines. Sigby sat himself on a hard seat as the vehicle drove out of the parade ground and past the edifice of Government House. He ignored the slab–faced guards watching him with sullen eyes and instead looked down as they passed through Pevestraka Square, filled still with people but also now with American military transports and sentries.

So close, Sigby thought to himself, looking at the Americans swarming into Thessalia. Sigby sat back in his seat and closed his eyes, finally resigned to the terrible fate that had been chosen for him. His cause was finally lost, and salvation had escaped him.

The transporter approached a US Marine check–point, and as the vehicle slowed one of the guards sitting opposite Sigby leaned forward with a stern expression.

'Silence, Meester Seegby, no?'

The man demonstratively waved the serrated edge of a combat knife close to Martin Sigby's throat as the vehicle came to a stop and the correspondent heard American voices outside.

Sigby sat in silence, watching and waiting, when suddenly the rear doors of the vehicle were yanked open and a dozen heavily armed United States Marines poked their M–16 rifles into the cabin. The secret–police guards all raised their hands, their own weapons forgotten along with their courage.

Sigby sat like a deer caught in the headlights of a speeding car until one of the marines pointed at him.

'Martin Sigby?'

The correspondent nodded meekly.

'You're an important American military asset and you're coming with us.'

Sigby unbelted himself from his seat, and was about to stand when the commanding officer of the secret–police escort stood and blocked his way.

'We have our orders to escort this man to…,'

The marine officer raised his rifle at the Mordanian.

'And I have my orders to bring him with me. If you and your men would like to step out of the vehicle, sir, we can all argue about it right here, *right now.*'

The Mordanian looked at the marines, at their angry expressions and elite weapons, and he ducked back inside the vehicle without another word as Sigby leapt out. The marine officer led him by the arm toward the waiting marine vehicles.

'You need to stop that convoy!' Sigby said urgently. 'The government is holding people and if they find out I've left they'll be executed!'

'Don't tell us,' the marine officer replied. 'Tell him!'

Sigby turned, to see Callum McGregor sitting in a seat and smiling above the pain in his wounded arm. Beside him sat Robert, Sigby's cameraman. Sigby sat down next to Robert in disbelief before looking at the Scotsman.

'What the hell is going on?' he asked.

'You have work to do and not much time to do it,' Callum said.

'Sophie D'Aoust, she is being held by Severov right now!'

'Then only way to get her out is to do what I tell you.'

'Severov is expecting me to report in his favour, on the threat of what he'll do to Sophie should I choose not to!'

'Then trust me and she'll be safe.'

Martin Sigby closed his eyes and let out a long breath.

'Fine, but afterward you have to send me to Talyn,' Sigby said.

Callum stared at Sigby with a stunned expression. 'What?'

'There's no time to explain,' Sigby said earnestly. 'I have to go to Talyn, no matter what, do you understand? I absolutely *have* to go.'

Callum regarded Sigby for a very long time before he nodded slowly. Then he grabbed Robert's arm and pulled him close, so that he could talk to them above the clattering noise of the vehicle's engine.

'Now both of you listen to me, very carefully.'

*

'Sir Wilkins.'

'President Akim. What can I do for you, sir?'

The president glanced out of his window across the city.

'What news of the advance?' he asked.

'General Rameron's troops have extended their line from Talyn down towards Thessalia. We estimate that they will come within artillery range in less than an hour. The American build–up here continues, and I have it on good authority that a fleet of C–17 and C–130 aircraft with a further thousand troops will arrive at Khobal Airport within twenty minutes.' He paused. 'We are as prepared as we can be.'

President Akim looked out over the city.

'The people are confused. They do not understand what is happening. They cannot be sure who is the enemy, nor who is their saviour. Or even if there is one.' He turned to look at Sir Wilkins. 'Nor can I.'

Wilkins frowned and chuckled lightly.

'What ever do you mean, sir?'

President Akim smiled faintly.

'I recently offered a large sum of money to Martin Sigby, in return for which I requested that he report favourably toward my cause, that he accord this office the highest respect in his reports. Although he accepted the offer, he later returned the money and refused to be bought in such a way.'

'A noble stand,' Wilkins noted guardedly.

'But when my assistant logged the return of the monies to government accounts,' Akim went on without missing a beat, 'it gave her cause to recount the funds within. She noticed significant anomalies in the UN financial support moving through the accounts since your tenure began.'

'Anomalies?'

'Yes. You see Sir Wilkins, there was too much money passing through the coffers.'

'Too much?' Sir Wilkins laughed heartily. 'Well then, surely that's a good thing?'

'It would be,' Akim agreed, 'were the excess monies not filtered through accounts other than those of the UN, and vanishing afterward. I asked my assistant to investigate, and learned that the monies were being paid by Kruger Petrochemicals in America, and that they were being filtered out again to an account in London.'

Sir Wilkin's smile slipped slightly. 'I don't understand, sir.'

'No,' Mukhari Akim agreed, 'nor do I. Tell me, Sir Wilkins, about your accounts in London. Do you think that these mysterious sums of money would match any found in your own?'

Sir Wilkins stood in rigid silence for a long moment before trembling with indignation.

'Mister President, sir, any agreements I may have made in private with business associates are confidential and have no bearing either in this office or my own at the United Nations.'

The president did not speak, letting the silence draw out. Sir Wilkins flustered slightly, raising his hands palm outward as he spoke.

'I don't really know what it is that you're trying to say. That I have pilfered money from the accounts here? I have not, sir.'

'I did not accuse you of any such thing,' the president said quietly. 'Only that you are receiving more than one salary whilst you are here, and I would very much like to know why?'

Wilkins straightened his stance, raising his chin.

'We will discuss this at another time, sir. Right now, I believe I am needed urgently elsewhere.'

Wilkins turned and strode for the chamber door. President Akim's voice rumbled through the office behind him.

'If I discover that you have abused your position, I shall petition Brussels to have you removed from your role and immediately investigated. I have had copies made of the evidence.'

Wilkins left the chamber and closed the door without looking back. He walked quickly to the end of the long corridor outside, to where Alexei Severov stood smoking a cigarette as he watched the attache approach.

'He knows,' Wilkins said.

'Knows what?'

'About the payments.'

Severov smiled thinly. 'He knows about your payments, not mine.'

'Oh, my dear Alexei,' Wilkins chuckled, 'I can assure you that if you abandon me, he shall know about yours too.'

Wilkins felt something sharp plunge into his testicles. He shot up onto the tips of his toes as tears welled in the corners of his eyes. He looked down to see a combat knife in Severov's hand, the tip pressed against the most intimate part of his anatomy.

'Then we have mutually assured destruction, Sir Wilkins,' Severov whispered softly. 'Although I can assure you that yours shall be significantly more painful than mine.'

'We must work together,' Wilkins said quickly in a high–pitched voice, 'if we are to ensure our survival!'

'Yes, indeed,' Severov murmured. 'Martin Sigby is preparing to deliver a report, knowing that failure to describe Mikhail Rameron in anything but a terrible light will see the French girl die a horrible death.'

'Where is she?' Wilkins gasped as Severov jabbed the knife a little harder.

'In a very, very *unsafe* place,' the Mordanian replied.

Severov removed the knife and Wilkins almost collapsed in relief. The commander slipped the blade back into its sheath and took a last draw on his cigarette before grinding it out on his calloused palm.

'Meet me in my operations bunker, when Sigby's report is due to be broadcast. We shall invite our friend Megan Mitchell to watch with us, before she dies. It will be entertaining to observe her downfall.'

'What about the president?' Wilkins gasped. 'He cannot be allowed to remain in power, knowing what he does.'

Severov thought for a moment.

'He must remain for the time being, but once the war is over and the elections called he will have to suffer an unfortunate accident I'm afraid, most probably at the hands of Chechen seperatist terrorists. As you would say, a terrible business.'

Severov, apparently pleased with his decision, turned and strode calmly away down the corridor, leaving Sir Wilkins standing alone holding his crotch with one hand and wiping tears from his eyes with the other.

*

GNN (UK) Ltd, London

'The conference lines are connected, Mister Cain.'

Seth Cain sat in Harrison Forbes's former office and smiled coldly as the diminutive British woman backed out of the office and closed the door. He turned to a plasma screen that had been set up in front of the world map on one wall, displaying feeds from GNN offices in New York, Chicago, San Diego and Miami. Each held the uncompromising features of the GNN Board of Directors, the men who controlled the strings of one of the largest television networks on the planet.

'Good morning, gentlemen,' Cain said to the four elderly faces staring back at him from the screen. 'My apologies for calling you at this early hour.'

'What news?' one of the men asked. 'Bad news would be good news for us, you understand.?'

'Then I have terrible news,' Cain grinned. 'In a few moments you will witness the destruction of a terrorist movement in Mordania, the glorious victory of a democratic government supported by our very own troops, and all of it through the eyes of a GNN crew in Thessalia.'

There were a series of approving nods and murmurs.

'Live, I take it?' another of the greying heads hazarded.

'Absolutely,' Cain replied. 'Every moment of it in glorious real–time. Every news network in the world will be begging for the right to broadcast this footage. The entire world is waiting to see what will happen in Thessalia. We, gentlemen, have the world's attention.'

The oldest man on the plasma screen leaned forward, his penetrating gaze cast from thousands of miles away losing none of its potency through distance.

'I trust, Seth, that neither they, nor us, will be disappointed.'

Again, the lupine grin.

'Nobody will be left disappointed, I can guarantee you that.'

***

59

'I hope to hell that you know what you're doing?'

Lieutenant Cole watched as Callum McGregor patiently fiddled with a computer program in Martin Sigby's room in the Thessalia Hilton.

'Trust me,' Callum said. 'I was a very clever young man, once. Have you enough men to secure the building?'

'Only the section that you require. The rest of government house is too well guarded.'

'Fine, we will need only minutes for this.'

Callum made a last few adjustments as Martin Sigby and his cameraman appeared in the doorway.

'It's done?' Callum asked.

'Everything,' Sigby said.

'Good. Then we must go, immediately. There isn't much time.'

Sigby was about to leave when his satellite phone warbled its ringtone. He picked it up and answered.

'Martin! It's Harrison Forbes!'

'Harry? Listen, I'm sorry for the confusion and the…,'

'Shut up man and listen. I've been fired and so I'm firing you.'

'What? What are you talking about?! You can't just…,'

'I said shut up and listen, there's very little time! You know a man named Frank Amonte, correct?'

'Yes, I know of him – he was helping Mitchell in her investigation.'

'He is in possession of documents that could change everything. I have been fired because I refused to bow down before Seth Cain and GNN corporate pressure. Listen to me Martin, whatever you broadcast they will block. They will prevent anything you say that affects their agenda from reaching the news channels. You have to do your work a different way!'

'But we're about to go live!' Martin screeched frantically.

'Then listen, do it freelance. Call anyone you like, offer them your footage, anyone but GNN do you understand?!'

Sigby stood dumbfounded for a moment.

'You're giving up the rights to the broadcasts, to the story?'

'Exactly, all of them. This is more important than the rights, Martin, do you understand? Get that story out, sell it to whomever you please, just make sure it gets out and soon!'

Sigby nodded as he heard Forbes ring–off the other end.

Callum stood and was about to gather up the equipment and leave the room when Martin Sigby stopped him.

'I have to go to Talyn,' the correspondent reminded him. Callum made to pass Sigby, but the reporter stopped the big man with a hand on his chest. Callum stared at Sigby again, surprised at the force in the little man's expression. 'The moment this is done,' Sigby pressed.

'Why?' Callum demanded.

'Because..,' Sigby swallowed and then straightened a little. 'Because people are depending on me to do what I must.'

'You'll be shot on sight the moment you encounter the rebel lines. They'll..,'

'No they won't. They know my face now, just like everyone else. They'll take me to Rameron because that's what he wants, and it's what Severov wants to avoid. I want to show the other side of this conflict while there still is one. My broadcast won't go out on GNN – look for it elsewhere, okay?'

Callum shook his head.

'You people will die chasing your damned stories.'

Sigby smiled.

'Like you and Megan nearly died chasing Amy O'Hara? Besides, the risk I take is worth it. I have much to make ammends for.'

Callum sighed heavily. To his surprise, he felt a profound sense of melancholy to see the stumpy man before him filled with such determination.

'I liked you better when you were a selfish little sod.'

'So did I: life was easier.'

Callum glanced across at Robert, who was standing silently behind holding Sigby's camera. Sigby turned to him and shook his head.

'Not this time Robert, it's only my face that is safe amongst those people. Besides, the Great Highland Ape here will need your technical help with his crazy plan.'

Robert looked briefly at Callum, and then silently and obediently he slipped the camera straps from his shoulders and handed the heavy device to Sigby. Callum watched as the two men looked at each other for a long moment and then briefly embraced, and he wondered what dangers they might have shared in their time working together, just as Megan and he had done. Sigby turned to Callum and tapped his watch.

'Right on time,' he said simply.

'To the second,' Callum nodded. 'Now go.'

Sigby turned and hurried from the room. Lieutenant Cole glanced at Callum before speaking.

'The Chinook crew won't land him within firing range of the rebel lines. He'll be on his own.'

'Just tell them to do their best and get him as close as they can,' Callum said. 'He'll be all right once they realise who he is.'

'I'll be back to collect you in twenty minutes,' Cole said and shot out of the room at double–time.

Callum turned and looked down at Robert.

'I hope you like heights, son.'

*

The cellar door opened, and rough hands unbound Megan from her chair and dragged her from the darkness and up the steps outside into the light of the corridor. Although she had only been incarcerated for an hour or so, Megan squinted as she looked out of the corridor windows at the pure white snow outside.

Two soldiers guided her through the bowels of Government House, avoiding the busier areas, until they reached a large room on the west wing where Alexei Severov's personal quarters and command centre were located.

Megan's head ached and her face throbbed from Severov's blow, but she was clear–headed enough not to struggle against her captors, nor panic, for she may well have been being led to her death by firing squad. Instead she realised that she was being kept alive, for the time being at least, and she found himself wondering where Sophie and Martin were.

The command centre into which she was led was a simple affair, a large table with a map of the countries surrounding the Caspian Sea dominating the room, other smaller maps of Thessalia and other cities within the country, as well as enemy positions. A large, old television was set up on a table in one corner of the room.

Only Wilkins and Severov stood in the room.

The two soldiers bound Megan to a chair, and then Severov gestured to the door.

'Guard it and let nobody inside.'

The men silently obeyed.

'Still on Wilkin's leash?' Megan asked Severov.

Severov did not smile. Megan watched as he picked up a discarded flak–jacket from one of the tables, wrapping it around an ashtray and tying it before spinning his body, swinging the jacket violently and slamming the weighted end into Megan's stomach.

Megan felt as though her face was about to burst as she gagged, folded up at the stomach and wretched miserably. She felt Severov grip her hair and yank her head up.

'Welcome,' he snarled. 'We have something to show you before you die.'

Sir Wilkins was turning on the television set, which glowed lethargically into life as the screen warmed up. Slowly, the ancient cathode–ray–tube began to show moving pictures, in colour. Through her pain, Megan recognised one of the major American networks showing satellite television, the picture flickering occasionally due to the poor reception.

Beside him, Severov whispered enthusiastically into her ear.

'In just a short while, you're going to see a glorious triumph Megan; the moment where armed resistance to this government, in this country, falls beneath a military bombardment, where democracy prevails and where my men, on the front–line of the battle, return as victorious heroes.'

Megan, wincing against the pain, forced a grin onto her features.

'And while they're braving the front line, their valiant commander is hiding like a coward in his command centre.'

Severov did not reply, simply slamming Megan's face into her own knees and stalking away toward the television.

'Is it on yet?' Megan heard Severov ask Wilkins.

Megan watched as the familiar newsroom of an international network appeared, the sound of American voices filling the room.

'Ah,' Severov said cheerily, looking back over his shoulder at Megan. 'The sound of freedom, the good old U S of A!'

Megan felt the anger begin to drain out of her, to be replaced with a sense of hollow despair as she watched the news feed on the television, saw the opening credits rolling as the days main headlines were briefed to the world.

To her surprise an image of Sophie appeared on the screen, amid questions as to her whereabouts. Megan flinched as she heard the French Ambassador to Mordania demanding her return to French soil. Megan looked at Wilkins as a new and terrible fear and loathing crawled within her.

'What did you really do with Sophie?' she asked.

Sir Wilkins regarded Megan for a moment and then looked queryingly at Severov. The Mordanian grinned indulgently as he spoke.

'She is far from here, but nowhere near France.'

Megan felt sick, but before she could dwell on her grief Wilkins and Severov turned to the television screen as the main headline was announced by two immaculately attired anchors.

*

GNN (UK) Ltd, London

'Channels open, live feed running!'

Seth Cain turned to the speaker phone at his desk.

'Viewing figures?' he asked, as much of the benefit of the watching directors as anything else.

'Off the scale sir, massive global attendance. If anyone in the world isn't watching this, it's because they don't know what a television is.'

Cain grinned again and turned to the another, smaller television screen in his office, tuning it to GNN's News Channel as he glanced at the assembled directors on the larger screen nearby.

'Gentlemen, enjoy.'

***

60

'Hi, I'm Mike Weatherspoon.'

'And I'm Alice McKorvac. You're watching GNN International News.'

Megan Mitchell stared vacantly at the screen as the two Americans adopted deadly serious expressions; eyes steady, brows furrowed and only their mouths moving as they spoke, as though they were some kind of animatronic devices. Alice McKorvac's voice reached her as though from a great distance.

'At seven–fourteen Eastern Seaboard Time, the US Department of Defense announced that the USS Theodore Roosevelt carrier–group stationed in the Black Sea had begun military operations against the Mordanian terrorists of General Mikhail Rameron, acting in support of the democratic government of President Mukhari Akim.'

'That's right Alice,' Mike said sombrely as images of fighter aircraft being blasted from the aircraft carrier's decks appeared in the top–right corner of the screen. *'Troop transport aircraft operating from the Gulf region have brought a reported three thousand United States Marines into the Mordanian capital of Thessalia in order to protect the city from the advancing rebel forces of General Rameron, who is keen to cement his grip on the country by taking the government stronghold. Sources on the ground have reported that the entire city is in panic, with some in the Mordanian Parliament supporting the American presence and others denouncing it as an invasion force.'*

Megan watched as the image of launching aircraft and mass troop deployments disappeared, and Alice McKorvak's studied demeanour changed slightly.

'In a special report from our associate correspondent in Thessalia, Martin Sigby reveals the extent of the turmoil in the city, both amongst the people and its leaders, who are locked in what is fast becoming a duel to the death.'

Alexei Severov glanced over his shoulder at Megan.

'Here, Megan, is the collapse of everything that you have tried to achieve.'

The screen flickered briefly and Megan saw Martin Sigby appear, standing on the roof of the Thessalia Hilton. Behind him, the mass deployment of US Marines could be seen in action, along with helicopters and hastily erected artillery platforms. Martin began speaking, raising his voice slightly as a helicopter lifted off somewhere out of shot behind him.

'I'm standing here on the roof of the Thessalia Hilton, watching as a once proud and defiant city collapses into panic and confusion, as literally thousands of people either flee

south or barricade themselves in their homes. Thessalia has ceased to be a thriving trading centre of the Caspian Sea and is now officially a war zone.'

Megan could see Severov begin to smile as she was watching, and beside the commander she saw Sir Wilkins breathe a sigh of what appeared to be relief. The image on the television turned to people fleeing the city as marines guarded the roads at checkpoints, helicopter gunships circling in the cold skies above the exodus.

'With the deployment here of three thousand or more US Marines, the people of Thessalia have finally had to come to terms with the fact that the war that has raged in the north for so long has finally reached their homes. The Americans here have deployed with extraordinary speed, under the cover of air support provided by the aircraft–carrier stationed in the Black Sea, and their orders are nothing if not explicit.'

The image changed to one of a rigidly upright, steel–grey moustachioed four–star general speaking into the camera as a massive American C–17 Galaxy aircraft landed at Khobal International airport behind him.

'Our forces are being deployed as we speak in a protective screen around the north of the city and on the inshore flank. My men are at their peak, they are equipped with the finest weapons and ordnance that our country can provide and they are highly motivated to take this conflict directly to the enemy.'

A reporter shoved an oversized microphone just beneath the general's immaculately trimmed moustache.

'General, what do you make of the accusations from several European countries that this is simply another invasion of a sovereign country by American forces, that it's just another attempt at colonialism and the forced economic reform of a foreign country to suit American trade ideals?'

The moustache twitched briefly as though it had a life of its own.

'Sir, the American people and its government have a firm commitment to defending the freedoms and liberties of people the world over. We did not ask for this conflict, it was brought upon us by an act of war against our forces, and we as a nation cannot stand by and see such an act go unanswered. I have no knowledge or interest in economic policies. Democracy is the right of all nations, and America will not shy away from protecting that right.'

The reporter kept the microphone where it was.

'But Mordania is already a democracy. We've seen nothing to say that the rebel forces will not maintain democracy if they seize power.'

The American general smiled stiffly.

'Is that a chance you'd want to take with your country, son?'

The reporter backed off as four soldiers held back any further questions and the general strode with a dignified bearing to do his duty. Martin Sigby appeared again on the screen, and Megan's heart began to sink as she listened.

'There can be no doubt that the Mordanian President, Mukhari Akim, has allied himself and his country to the west and its ideals. His decision to make a stand against the tyranny of General Rameron's rebel forces here in Thessalia, with the Chief of Police Alexei Severov leading his men side by side with the Americans in valiant defiance of the impending attack, displays a conviction and belief in cooperation with the west that now makes his land strategically and uniquely important in this region.'

Megan saw Severov grinned broadly, his chest swelling as she watched.

'Pity you're not actually doing anything valiant,' Megan muttered.

Severov did not dignify Megan with a reply, simply continuing to smile as he watched the television.

'With the attempted air attack by Mordanian jets under the control of General Rameron, the cold–blooded massacre of civilian scientists near Talyn and the continuing brutality of the rebel advance upon Thessalia, there can be little doubt that in this conflict at least, western intervention is both required and justified. In the global war against terrorism, if the alliance can prevent General Rameron's forces from seizing Thessalia during the coming conflict, America and Mordania will have prevented a significant victory by the forces of terror and chaos over democracy and liberty.'

Megan watched as Severov began clapping slowly and loudly as he listened to Sigby's flag–waving speech. Standing beside the commander, Sir Wilkins was nodding approvingly, his florid features alight with relief.

Megan watched as Martin was speaking, and saw behind him American troops deploying from the rear of a Chinook helicopter. Behind them, she could see the church in the distance with its broad, round clock on the bell–tower. A line from days before flickered through her mind: *Mordanians say that you can set your heart by that clock.* Megan blinked, squinting at the clock as Martin Sigby began to finish off his speech and Severov continued clapping.

'Mordania and the USA have placed themselves at the forefront of what has often been called the most important conflict of all time, that between the forces of democracy and terror, and may have taken a bold step on the road to ensuring freedom and liberty not just for this tiny yet courageous nation, but for the entire world. Martin Sigby, Thessalia, Mordania.'

As the screen flicked back to Alice McKorvac and Mike Weatherspoon, Megan closed her eyes and slowly lowered her head.

*

GNN (UK) Ltd, London

'I can't see anything.'

Seth Cain stared at his screen, the two GNN anchors looking at each other in confusion as the feed from Mordania was lost. Alice McKorvak offered the cameras an apologetic smile.

'Er, well, sorry about that, there appear to be some technical difficulties with our correspondent's transmissons from Thessalia. In other news…'

Cain shot bolt–upright out of his chair and hit the button on his speakerphone. 'What the hell is going on out there?!'

A meek voice replied, sounding thin and reedy through the speakers. *'We've lost the feed sir.'*

'I can see that!'

Suddenly, Cain stopped speaking. Through the windows of the office, he realised that he could hear a transmission.

'Why can I still hear Martin Sigby's voice if GNN has no signal?!'

'Because it's not coming from GNN sir.'

Cain swallowed thickly as a sudden, dense ball of fear landed deep in his belly as he turned to look out of the office windows at the banks of plasma screens in the operations room.

*

Government House, Thessalia

Slowly, Alexei Severov stopped clapping and stared at the television screen with a vacant gaze, his skin slightly paler than before. Sir Wilkins was looking at the commander in confusion.

'What is it?'

The commander moved closer to the television, and snapped his fingers at a video–recorder set up on a table nearby.

'It is recording, no? Re–wind the tape.'

Sir Wilkins strolled across to the recorder and rewound the tape by a couple of minutes.

'There!' Severov snapped. 'Play!'

Megan slowly looked up and watched as the screen once again showed Martin Sigby talking, and Severov's jaw fell open as he pointed at the screen, trying to speak but unable to do so.

'For God's sake what is it man?!' Wilkins snapped impatiently.

'The clock,' Severov croaked. 'On the church tower.'

Wilkins looked at the clock far behind Sigby, and then glanced at his own watch before staring at the screen in sudden shock.

'It's thirty minutes behind time!' he gasped.

Megan, for the first time, allowed a grim smile to curl from one corner of her lips as she spoke softly.

'No, it's not. You shouldn't believe everything that you see on television.'

Wilkins looked at Megan, began to tremble, and then suddenly exploded in uncharacteristic rage as he hurled a fist down onto one of the tables, kicking chairs and screaming incoherently. He recovered himself enough to look at Megan with a furious expression.

'How? How did you know?'

Megan smiled.

'Keep your friends close and your enemies closer. Your man Bolav, you sent him to die out there and he knew it. Before he passed away he told me that Severov was not in charge, that somebody higher was in control of this deception. I just didn't know that it would be you.'

Alexei Severov approached Megan slowly, sweat sheening his brow and disbelief making his eyes wobble in their sockets.

'The people, on the television, they said it was a live feed,' he whispered.

'It was,' Megan said with defiant mirth. 'Right up to the point where Martin appeared.'

Severov, his fists clenched by his side and his jaw grinding in his skull, raised a finger to point at Megan.

'Where is Sigby?' he hissed.

Megan grinned, knowing what was coming to her but terminally delighted none the less.

'Telling the truth,' she said. 'The broadcast you just saw was a fake, seen only here in Thessalia. The real one is being broadcast across the entire globe and there's nothing that you can do about it.'

Severov clenched and unclenched his hands several times before letting out a wail of fury, like an animal carrying a hideous injury. And then he picked up a chair and swung it hard across the side of Megan's head, screaming as he did so.

Megan felt the solid side of the chair smack like an exploding bomb beside her ear, saw the room tilt as she was hurled onto her side. Pain bolted through her shoulder as it hit the tiled floor. She saw Severov, the veins in his neck bulging, his teeth gritted and his eyes filled with mindless rage, lift his right boot to bring it down on Megan's head. Megan closed her eyes.

'Severov!'

Wilkin's voice cut through Severov's rage and the commander, breathing heavily and seething with fury, looked across at Wilkins.

'Downstairs,' the attache growled. 'We don't want anybody to know what happened here, or hear what she might say.' Wilkins looked at Megan. 'Now it's your turn to disappear forever, but before you do we'll know where to find all of those people with whom you've collaborated.'

'It doesn't matter, Wilkins,' Megan spat. 'The whole world will know what both of you have done, especially you Severov. Do you remember the dogs, Alexei? The girl on the hill? The cigarette you smoked before setting those animals on her?'

Severov froze, staring at Megan in surprise.

'That's right,' Megan said. 'She filmed it, all of it, including the massacre of the scientists by your hand.' Megan looked at Wilkins. 'Everything was on film, and by now Amy and several copies of that film will be in the hands of the major networks.'

Wilkins stared at Megan in shock, his skin paling as though his heart were failing in his chest.

'She is alive, here?'

'Not here,' Megan said, enjoying her final moment of victory. 'I didn't send Callum home injured. It was Amy O'Hara you signed for, authorising her extraction from Thessalia. She had the original copy of the film on her. Yours, Tom, was a copy.'

Wilkin's shoulders slumped as he stared vacantly at nothing in particular, coming to terms with the depth of Megan's deception.

'You're finished, Wilkins,' Megan spat as Severov yanked her up from the chair.

Wilkins smiled as Severov pulled Megan away.

'This is politics Megan,' he said. 'Nothing is ever finished.'

The voice that rumbled from the doorway belonged to none of the men already in the room.

'It is now.'

President Mukhari Akim's broad shoulders all but blocked the doorway as Severov stopped short of his superior, his dark eyes wide with alarm.

Akim's gaze bore into the Chief of Police's with a terrifying intensity as he advanced.

'Release her,' the president said threateningly.

Severov hesitated, and then suddenly Sir Wilkins called out. *'Guard!'*

The two rebel soldiers guarding the corridor outside dashed into the room, weapons raised.

'The president is in league with the rebel traitors!' Wilkins shouted. 'Arrest him at once!'

The soldiers wavered uncertainly, until Severov snapped at them.

'Arrest him! He is behind the massacre of our people, with this woman!'

The two soldiers snapped their weapons around to point at the president, who glared at Severov with unrivalled fury.

'You have given your last command, Alexei.'

The police commander smiled cruelly. 'No – you have. Take him to the cells!'

As Megan watched in despair, the president was led away. Behind Megan in the operations room, Sir Wilkins picked up a phone and dialled a number, speaking quickly and efficiently.

'This is the president's office. Please inform the commander of the air package to begin an attack on *all* enemy positions immediately. Destroy Talyn!'

As Severov dragged Megan through the doorway, Megan caught the attache's eye.

'I hope you can live with yourself,' she muttered.

Sir Wilkins smiled quietly.

'This is the way of politics,' he replied. 'Governments survive, people die.'

***

61

'Steady son.'

Callum kept one hand on Robert's shoulder as the cameraman wavered unsteadily on the roof of Government House. Callum turned to look down at the SEALS far below them on the parade ground.

'It's done, now get in there and find out where Megan is!'

As the SEALS moved, Callum watched as Robert unplugged a laptop computer from the aerial array on the roof of Government House.

'Direct hack,' he said as he worked, trying not to look down at the parade ground far below. 'They've seen the recording that we made, not the live feed. Most of the Mordanian troops are on the same network and will have seen the same broadcast, but whether that's enough to protect this Sophie D'Aoust woman I don't know.'

Callum helped Robert down the steeply tiled roof and then down to the parade ground, where the SEALS had taken charge. Lieutenant Cole looked at him.

'This had better be worth it,' the soldier grumbled. 'My countrymen are under fire out there and I'm here with you doing damned television repairs.'

'If we find what I expect to find in there,' Callum replied, 'and we can inform the UN and your carrier fleet about it, your people won't be under fire for much longer. Let's go.'

Cole gave a signal to his heavily unit, and instantly the troops entered Government House and began spreading out, covering all points and clearing rooms as they went.

Callum followed the SEAL team in, Robert alongside him and filming as they moved.

*

Alexei Severov finished tying Megan to the chair in the cellar before standing back and regarding her for a moment as he lit one of his cigars. Megan could tell that the Mordanian would not make Megan's final moments long, for there was little time, but she doubted they would be anything less than unimaginably painful.

'I will hide,' Severov said. 'I will not be found in this land.'

'You will be found, and betrayed, by your own people as you have betrayed them,' Megan replied, strangely calm now.

Severov shrugged and reached for a knife sheathed by his ankle.

'Either way, you're not going to know about it, Megan.'

Megan rocked back hard on the chair before Severov could draw his blade, sending herself flying backwards and away from the Mordanian, who lurched forward. The chair hit the ground and one of the legs snapped. Megan kicked out hard at the commander's stomach, catching him a glancing blow. Severov span aside with a grunt of pain.

Megan rocked and jerked in the chair with frantic violence, felt the old wood break and splinter as she wrestled herself free. She yanked her wrists wildly and felt the remainder of the chair collapse around her, and desperately she staggered to her feet.

Too late. Severov lunge furiously toward her.

It was the punches that came first, sharp, painful jabs to Megan's eyes and nose, cutting her upper–lip and sending lightning bolts of agony through her skull as she staggered backwards into one of the cellar's stone pillars. She was about to lose consciousness after the fifth or sixth blow when Severov backed off, breathing lightly, and reached down again to the sheath at his ankle. Megan watched through fading, blurring vision as slowly, demonstratively, Severov drew the long bladed knife from its sheath and moved forward again.

'Enjoy, Megan,' he whispered malevolently, and the blade flashed toward her.

Megan ducked as a sudden crack of rifle fire and shouted commands in American caused Severov to whirl, moving away from Megan and staring instead at the cellar door with panic written across his features.

'In here!' Megan bellowed at the top of her voice.

Severov turned and ran, swinging the knife at Megan's chest as he did so. Megan staggered out of range of the glittering blade, tripped and crashed down onto a stack of empty crates near one wall as the cellar door burst open and a squad of Navy SEALS tumbled into the room, flashlights blazing into Megan's eyes.

'Son of a bitch!'

Lieutenant Cole rushed into the room, taking in the scene and with it Megan's bloodied, bedraggled form. Megan struggled upright.

'Get these bloody things off me!' she shouted.

Cole complied instantly, removing the binding from Megan's wrists as Callum burst into the cellar. The big Scotsman's face fell slightly as he took in Megan's battered features.

'Not *too* late then,' Callum said apologetically.

A door slammed somewhere in the back of the cellar, and Megan looked towards it before turning to Lieutenant Cole.

'Where does that door lead?' she demanded.

'It's an old supply corridor that leads out to the parade ground,' one of the SEALS replied for his commander.

'Sir Wilkins, the UN attache for Mordania, is behind all of this,' Megan said to Cole. 'Find him and arrrest him as soon as you can, and make sure that the US Navy guys out there in the Black Sea are watching television when Sigby's next report comes out. And find President Akim, he's in the holding cells somewhere in here!'

'What about Severov?' Callum asked.

Megan turned and dashed out of the cellar, climbing the steps outside two at a time.

The corridor was empty as she sprinted along it toward the nearest exit out onto the parade ground. She ran through the open double doors and out into the cold afternoon air.

The snow was falling again as she ran across the now deserted parade ground. She could hear the sound of artillery and small–arms fire in the distance as she ran, probably out on the fringes of the city.

Ahead, a narrow set of footprints had marked the thin layer of snow, spaced far apart in the manner of a running man. They had emerged from a side–entrance of Government House, crossing in front of Megan and heading toward the opposite corner of the parade ground.

Megan changed direction and saw that the prints led to a door that itself opened onto a corridor that led to the motor pool on the north side of the compound. Megan ran harder and sprinted through the open doorway.

The blow struck her deep in her stomach and folded her over as she ran, and she tumbled to the floor. She saw Alexei Severov lower his knee, slam the door shut and lock it with a bolt before he lunged at Megan, the knife in his right hand held low by his thigh, quick and lethal.

Megan rolled away and leapt to her feet as Severov whipped the blade in a quick back–handed slice toward her throat. Megan, off–balance and thoroughly winded, staggered backwards out of range, barely avoiding the silvery metal and giving ground toward the motor pool as she did so.

Severov's eyes glittered with malice as he nipped forwards, light and fast on his feet as he lunged and turned, the blade flickering and whispering on the air as it whipped and sliced toward Megan.

Megan ducked, falling back with each of Severov's attacks toward the end of the corridor and the closed door there. Her breath laboured in her chest and her stomach cramped painfully with each movement as she tried to avoid the rapidly flying blade whilst searching for a weakness in the

Mordanian's attack. Megan's addled mind struggled to think as the end of the corridor drew closer, Severov pushing her further backwards without relent.

Megan fixed her eyes on Severov's, behind the rapidly moving knife, and finally she found her balance and regained her breath. The Mordanian lunged forwards with a straight stab to the chest. Megan, continuously on the back foot, suddenly changed stance and moved into the attack. She turned aside from the wicked thrust as it flashed past her chest, gripped Severov's wrist in her left hand and upper arm in her right before driving her shoulder deeply into the Mordanian's chest.

Severov, caught off–guard by the sudden and aggressive forward move, span around and lost his footing, shouting out as he plummeted toward the ground on his back. As he fell Megan reversed her movement and turned away from the direction of Severov's fall as she twisted the Mordanian's wrist and yanked his arm upwards with all of her might.

Severov let out a howl of pain as he crashed onto the ground and his arm was wrenched out of its socket with a dull crunch. The knife toppled from his grasp to land beside Megan in the corridor. Megan let out a brutal shout of elation as she turned, lifting her right boot and smacking it down on the Mordanian's head.

Severov's head snapped to one side and he fell limp.

*

The SEALS watched in silence as Megan worked.

After a few minutes of observation, Lieutenant Cole gave a signal to his men. Callum watched as the soldiers melted away from the parade ground and the lieutenant turned to Megan with a serious expression.

'We were just guarding the compound. We saw nothing. Ten minutes and then we all vanish, okay?'

Megan nodded dispassionately and Callum walked away with the SEALS toward the nearest door, leaving the parade ground and closing the door behind them.

Megan waited for a few seconds until she was sure all of the soldiers were out of earshot, and then she lifted a bucket of icy water and dashed it across Alexei Severov's face. The Mordanian coughed and spluttered, coming awake as he lay on the snowy concrete, blinking and wincing as the pain in his head hit him. He looked around and saw Megan squatting nearby.

Megan did not speak, simply watching as Severov took in his surroundings, realising that he was bound at the wrists and that he was lying in the fenced–off corner of the compound: the kennels He looked at Megan for a moment, the chain–link fence separating them.

'We only have a short amount of time,' Megan said, 'and you have something that you need to tell me.'

Severov rolled and managed to get awkwardly to his feet. Megan watched him for a moment before speaking again.

'Where is Sophie D'Aoust?'

Severov returned her gaze for a long moment, and then his cruel smile reappeared.

'The dogs will not attack me,' he said confidently. 'They know my scent.'

Megan said nothing, gesturing instead to Severov's chest. The Mordanian looked down and then sharply up again, panic collapsing his features as he realised that Megan had clothed the commander in one of the old uniforms from the cellar.

'I rubbed the scent of the other, unwashed uniforms all over your body,' Megan said, and smiled, 'just in case.'

Megan watched with interest as the Mordanian swallowed thickly, his eyes searching for an escape from the compound. They could both hear the dogs now, sniffing and scraping at the solid doors of their kennels, seperated from Severov by a single sheet of thick wood. Megan gestured to the handle that lifted the door.

'Give me a reason not to lift it.'

'You wouldn't dare,' Severov said. 'You would be tried for crimes against humanity.'

'That's rich, from you,' Megan observed. 'But as it happens, we are completely alone for the next seven or eight minutes. Long enough for those animals to do their work, don't you think?'

Severov's bottom lip trembled and his legs bowed slightly at the knee.

'I don't know where she is,' he said.

Megan sighed, stood up from her squatting position and strolled across to the handle. She took hold of it and looked at Severov, who wailed in despair.

'How do I know you won't release them anyway?'

'You don't,' Megan replied. 'Although there are two good reasons why I wouldn't. Firstly, I am not the inhuman, murderous, hateful and cruel weasel that you are: and secondly, because I would rather see you serve decades in jail for your crimes than give you the easy way out of a painful, but short, death. It's your call, Severov.'

Megan gripped the handle tighter, and Severov glanced fearfully at the kennel door before speaking.

'She is in Talyn,' he said finally. 'I swear it is the truth, she is in Talyn with Rameron's forces.'

'What?!'

Severov mastered his mounting fear.

'To ensure the loyalty of Martin Sigby, I told her that the girl would remain in the hands of my men and would suffer untold pain should she be tempted to defer from my instructions. However, in reality such a plan is flawed as it is possible, no matter how remotely, that the girl might escape. I felt that it would be wiser just to have her killed, but why do it myself and risk arrest? Instead, I decided to let the Americans do it for me.'

Megan felt her heart plunge as Severov looked directly at her.

'Yes, Megan. You yourself supplied Wilkins and I with the location of General Rameron's headquarters. Now, she is part of the prisoner exchange and – how do the Americans say it – about to be bombed back into the Stone Age.'

'How?' Megan demanded. 'Exactly how?'

'We drugged her and put her on a stretcher, then flew her out of the city in a helicopter as part of the prisoner exchange. Her bandages disguised her identity. Nobody asked any questions. Now, she is in Talyn.'

Megan's face darkened with fury and despair.

'And right in the line of fire of the American bombers. You really have thought of everything.'

'You still have time to save her,' Severov pleaded. 'It is the truth I swear!'

Megan nodded. 'I believe you.'

Severov held her gaze for a moment, and in that instant he knew that Megan was going to betray him. His features twisted into an cruel grimace.

'No matter what you do she is gone!'

Megan covered her own anguish with a grim smile. 'And so are you.'

'No!'

Megan pulled the handle hard and the kennel door shot upwards. From the darkness within the huge North–Caucasian Mastiffs bounded out into the light, howling and snarling and baying.

Severov screamed and ran at the opposite fence, slamming into it with all of his might as though he might somehow pass through, but he did not. As Megan watched without emotion the huge pack of hungry dogs slammed into Severov from behind, dragging his screaming, bucking body away from the fence, huge fangs sinking into his body.

Megan looked away as she heard the sucking sound of tearing flesh and fabric, the crunch of splintering bones and the piercing screams of Alexei

Severov. She walked away through the snow, listening as the cries of pure, undiluted agony were slowly drowned out by the dogs as they literally tore Severov's body apart.

Megan hurried down the corridor toward the main foyeur of Government House, seeing the SEALS lingering there. Callum saw her coming.

'Is there time?' Megan asked. 'We need to call off the attack before it's too late! Sophie is with them in Talyn!'

Callum closed his eyes in disbelief and then opened them again.

'So is Martin Sigby.'

***

62

GNN (UK) Ltd, London

'What the hell is happening there, Cain?'

Seth Cain stood in silence as he stared out across the operations room. There, across the various plasma screens showing news channels from around the world, he saw Martin Sigby's image broadcasting.

Seth Cain was unable to reply as an unexpected horror slowly unfolded before him, enveloping him in its cold embrace as he watched.

*

The personal chamber of President Mukhari Akim was silent but for the large television dominating one corner of the room. Almost a hundred people, most of them administration personnel or members of the UN attache's staff, were crammed into the room and watching the screen.

Megan, her wounds temporarily patched up by the SEALS's medic, stood with Callum as the reports came through. She could see the BBC anchors and she could see the images of battles raging around Thessalia in the top right corner of the screen as the presenter spoke.

'There have been shocking scenes of conflict from Mordania this afternoon, and frankly the entire world appears to have gone into an uproar concerning the extraordinary coverage filmed by the British correspondent Martin Sigby from inside the Talyn headquarters of renegade insurgency leader General Mikhail Rameron.'

A female presenter took over the commentary.

'Government leaders of all countries have made calls for an immediate cease–fire in Mordania after these images were broadcast from Talyn just minutes ago by the BBC. We would like to warn our viewers that they may find some of the scenes in this report highly distressing.'

The screen changed to show a large military compound, with the ancient looking town of Talyn in the distant background dominated by a Gothic cathedral. As troops and equipment bustled nearby, Martin Sigby spoke to the camera above the sound of intense artillery fire.

'There have been so many reports of the events that led to civil war in the country of Mordania, from correspondents in all nations struggling to report on the conflicts here and also to understand how they came to pass, and why. It was not until this morning that I myself finally understood what had happened here, how it happened and how the media,

for so long the foundation of a free press in all democratic nations, have been undermined by the very capitalist successes that their presence protected.'

Megan felt a lump form in her throat, heard the whispers and murmurs in the crowd as she watched.

'This town and its people are under military attack from American forces attempting to prevent further conflict in the country, and yet it was by the hand of American corporate interference that the war itself began.'

Martin Selby's sombre personage was replaced by an image of investigative reporter Amy O'Hara. Martin Sigby's voice introduced her before telling her story.

'This woman entered Mordania on the request of a family friend, Petra Milosovich, a Mordanian scientist working on a government funded project. The project was successful in developing an advanced Sterling Engine, a device which operates on a closed–cycle and uses heat transfer as a means of producing useful work and thus energy. This engine, which is already used world–wide in its standard guises but until now had been unsuitable for use in aviation or automobiles, was now capable of powering cars, aeroplanes and generating potentially limitless electrical power from geothermal sources.'

A stylised image of a working Sterling Engine appeared.

'However, elements of the Mordanian government were already in negotiations with large petro–chemical companies for contracts to lay oil pipelines through Mordania to secure a reliable flow of oil to the west, avoiding politically unstable countries to the north. These deals were set to make a lot of people very wealthy, and the Sterling Engine was an obvious barrier to that wealth. General Mikhail Rameron, however, supported the use of the technology.'

Martin Sigby as he began to describe the terrible crimes committed in Mordania.

'Petra Milosovich asked Amy O'Hara to document their work before the government could shut them down. However, before she could do so, this happened. Some viewers may find the following images extremely disturbing.'

The scenes of the massacre of the scientists, filmed by the fleeing Amy O'Hara, were broadcast to the entire watching world. Megan watched as Alexei Severov murdered the scientists en masse, and then captured Amy O'Hara and let the huge dogs attack her before one of his own men intervened, at the cost of his life.

Gasps of horror and cries of disbelief filled the room as the images flickered grotesquely across the screen, across the world, and Megan saw President Mukhari Akim bow his head as he watched, unable to comprehend what had been done in the name of his government. Martin Sigby went on as the camera returned to him.

'The uprising of General Mikhail Rameron's forces was a direct response to the murder of dozens of Mordanian scientists by the secret police. With a clamp–down on the

free press, and with Rameron's forces thus isolated from the rest of the world, there was no way for him to counter the lies being broadcast from Mordania about rebel brutality against Mordanian citizens. Forced to fight back and attempt to take the capital and reveal what had happened, they were on the verge of succeeding when the American carrier group in the Black Sea was attacked.'

A new image appeared, this time of a Mig–23 fighter.

'This aircraft is a Mig–23, a Russian built fighter that has been sold to many nations across the east; the aircraft that attacked the carrier group and were shot down by American F–18s. However, the Mordanian Air Force has not lost any of its aircraft. This is because the jets that attacked the American fleet were not Mordanian. Three months ago, two former Ukrainian Mig–23s were bought by an American 'collector' but were never delivered to his Texan home. Instead, the jets were transported covertly into Mordania and adapted for an advanced remote–control system similar to the ones used by the United States Air Force to control target–drone aircraft. These systems were bought by the same 'collector' and sent to Mordania. The buyer of both the jets and the control systems also happens to be the head of Kruger Petrochemicals, the same company due to build the oil pipelines in Mordania. The record of purchase of these devices and aircraft has been made available to the United Nations for investigation.'

'Sone of a bitch!' someone shouted in the room.

Megan could see heads shaking, gasps of shock floating through the air around him.

'The attack on the carrier group, organised and conducted by those in the pay of Kruger Petrochemicals, resulted in American involvement in the conflict, a swift resolution to the Mordanian problem by virtually ensuring the complete destruction of General Rameron's forces and the devices that they have been trying to protect. In all of this, they were aided knowingly by one Sir Thomas Wilkins, the UN attache to the Mordanian Government, who orchestrated the entire affair from within the country due to his strong links to the oil industry.'

More gasps and shouts of disbelief, but Megan could no longer hear them, for a swelling premonition of doom was blossoming darkly within her mind. Behind Sigby, she could see troops suddenly running, civilians in chaos, panic gripping the town of Talyn.

In the distance, an air raid siren could be heard as Martin Sigby continued.

'This entire conflict was started by the interference in politics of major oil companies and big business, desperate to ensure their continued survival and profits in a rapidly changing world. Its success was aided by the sheer scope and dominance of the major news networks, often largely owned by individuals with their own agenda, who have chosen not to use the news as a medium for informing people of events in the world but as a weapon to control what we think, what we see and what we think we see on our televisions around the world.'

In the city behind Martin a building suddenly vanished amidst a brightly swelling ball of smoke and flame as a thunderous explosion rocked the city. The camera vibrated and Martin Sigby ducked, one hand instinctively covering his head as he spoke over the noise of passing fighter aircraft, explosions and screams.

'Our world, our freedoms, our way of life depends not on the military strength of our forces nor their dominance of countries with differing ideals and values to our own. It depends on the population of our planet being informed honestly of what is happening in other countries, of being free to make choices based on truth and evidence, of being able to see how lucky we are to have such information at our fingertips.'

Another, closer, explosion rocked the city, and Megan saw chunks of masonry and shards of glass fly past somewhere behind Martin Sigby as he began to shout over the devastation surrounding him.

'These people are dying, right now, because of the greed of already rich men, because of the lies that we see on our televisions every night, the media used to justify wars that should never have been fought, used to enforce laws that infringe on privacy and curtail freedom, used to brainwash us into believing that every culture other than our own is unstable and likely to destroy us. We are being lied to, day after day after day and we don't even know it.'

A huge blast sent an apartment block crashing to the ground a mile behind Sigby, followed by the sound of jet aircraft thundering overhead in the skies, anti–aircraft fire rattling in response. Sigby raised his arm from his head and pointed behind him to where the torn, bloody corpse of a young woman had landed, crumpled in a heap with limbs bent at impossible angles.

'This is news! This is truth! This is what happens when governments lie and the media supports them. This is what war really looks like, and someone, somewhere, is smiling to themselves and becoming extremely rich. We are told that wars are fought for oil, but even that is not true – these wars always push up the price of oil, because the percieved instablilty in supply causes concern in the stock markets, pushing up prices and making the oil companies even wealthier. The longer there is a war in an oil country, the happier the money–makers are, the happier the weapons companies are and the busier the news networks are, telling you how important it all is.'

Chunks of debris arced across the sky, car alarms screaming as loudly as the cries of the injured as Martin Sigby continued to point behind him.

'Are we not more than this? Haven't we got something called democracy, that allows us to prevent such things as this? As long as we all sit in our cosy homes, safe in the knowledge that we're all right, there will be those who will orchestrate wars like this to enrich themselves at the expense of those who are not as lucky as we are. Those people are dying, and you're being told that it's for the best.' Sigby stared at the camera for a moment in genuine despair. *'Best for who?'*

The blast came from the right of the screen, tearing the concrete beneath Martin Sigby's feet apart. The reporter's body was flung aside amidst a cloud of supersonic debris with a violence that no human being could survive.

The screen went abruptly black and the feed cut back to the two presenters, who both stared dumbfounded at the cameras for a moment.

Megan closed her eyes, felt the ball in her throat tighten unbearably. One of the anchors finally recovered his voice and his senses.

'The leaders of several countries have already condemned the American attack on Talyn, although we're getting reports that the full force of the airstrike has been called off directly by President Baker himself.'

'That's right Mike,' the other presenter said, *'and I've just heard that UN attache Sir Thomas Wilkins is in the custody of US Navy SEALS in Thessalia, while both Sherman Kruger and Seth Cain of GNN International are to be issued with subpoenas by Congress in order to ensure that their role in these events, if any, is properly explained.'*

Megan stared vacantly at the screen as the two reporters began filling in the details of the American attack on Talyn. The room slowly emptied of people as they walked away in sombre silence from what they had witnessed.

Megan turned and walked with them. Outside, she could hear that the guns had stopped firing.

***

63

Megan stared down at Talyn from a low ridge of hills that stood just north of the town. In the early morning light she could see the bombed military compound nearby, its buildings now crumbling heaps of shattered masonry, the burnt carcasses of vehicles still smouldering amongst the remains.

In the town beyond, pillars of oily smoke obscured the sun rising into the powder–blue sky. Large buildings were peppered with shrapnel holes and deep wounds from bombs dropped the day before. She could see people moving about through the debris filled streets, rescue teams and ambulances, civilians and passers–by watching as they struggled heroically to liberate those poor souls trapped beneath the rubble of what had once been their homes. Amongst them, the ever valiant aid–teams and volunteers laboured alongside Mordanians to alleviate their suffering.

A jeep drove up the hillside from the nearby military compound, Callum at the wheel. It pulled up alongside Megan, Callum switching off the engine before climbing out and joining her to look out over Talyn.

'President Akim has fully endorsed the cease–fire,' he said. 'The Americans are to stay in the city until order has been restored, then they'll most likely bug out.'

Megan nodded, not saying anything. Callum sighed before speaking again.

'Martin's dead, you know that don't you?'

'I know.'

'General Rameron was also killed in the bombardment, along with most of his staff. The UN teams are sifting through the debris now, trying to find any others lost during the attack.'

Megan took a deep breath. 'Sophie?'

Callum swallowed thickly before speaking.

'Sophie D'Aoust's body was recovered by President Akim's investigators from a building in the south–west of the town. I'm sorry, Megan.'

Megan did not reply for a long time, watching the various news crews down in the town reporting on the devastation that surrounded them. When she did, her voice sounded hollow, devoid of feeling.

'I want to see her again.'

Callum looked briefly down at his boots before speaking carefully.

'Megan, the safehouse she was in was hit directly. She was identified only by fragments of clothing and hair. You've got to let this one go. You saved one lost soul but you can't save them all.'

Megan's jaw tightened slightly.

'We didn't achieve much, did we?' she said quietly.

'We found Amy, that's enough. They're saying on the news that the American president is going to seek new laws through Congress that will limit big corporations and banks from using lobbying to influence media networks or government offices. If they pass half of what's being talked about, things like this will never be allowed to happen again. It's a revolution all of its own.'

Megan seemed unmoved by the magnitude of the aftermath of the conflict.

'Too many people lost their lives for this, Callum.'

'They always do, you know that. Governments never act until they're forced to, often due to exposure of their own flaws by the media. We've made that easier now, for the media to act freely. Come on, let's get out of here.'

'There's nothing much else left for me to do anymore.'

'Except live,' Callum said, and gripped Megan's shoulder. 'You've spent so much of your life looking for other people, I reckon you've lost yourself. One person can't change the world on their own.'

Megan smiled faintly as she remembered Sophie D'Aoust's words.

'They can do more than someone who does nothing.'

Callum let his arm drop in silent exasperation. Megan turned to look at him, and smiled faintly.

'But you're right, we'd better go.'

They turned together toward the jeep, leaving the smouldering rubble of Talyn behind them.

***

64

London

Megan Mitchell liked mornings in the city. There was nobody else around.

The sun had just risen in watercolour over the glassy surface of the Thames as she jogged along the side of the river, the towering edifice of Big Ben and the Houses of Parliament peering through the light mist hovering above the water.

There was no headache this time and the morning air smelt fresh and clean.

She was back in St Katherine's Docks before the first of the other residents had left their apartments for their offices and banks, their garages and bakeries, supermarkets and estate–agencies. She jogged up the steps to the Penthouse suites and walked to her door, opened it and stepped into the apartment.

It had been two weeks since the flight back from Mordania and her various, indeed numerous bruises, cuts and abrasions had healed nicely enough for her not to feel like an outcast in public. Which had been just as well, for the mention of her name upon the news networks, when her disappearance in Mordania had caused Martin Sigby to alert the world to her plight, had provoked a rash of interview requests from networks eager to learn of what the celebrated correspondent had experienced in his final days in Thessalia.

Megan had given only a single, two–hour interview to a journalist whom she trusted. Likewise, Amy O'Hara, herself now a media celebrity in America, had agreed only to one comprehensive interview in which she furthered Martin Sigby's final reports with greater details of the engineering works of her uncle and of the brutality of the secret police in Thessalia.

Megan flicked the television on as she slipped out of her T–shirt and began her *Shotokan* form routine. Reports on the news channels detailed the decision by incumbent Mordanian President Mukhari Akim not to run for office in the elections that had been promised for the following year, despite a surprising percentage of his people showing great confidence in his dignified handling of the aftermath of the conflict.

Megan changed channels and saw an image of Sherman Kruger, the oil baron whose immense corporation had come under the spotlight following the revelations that he, along with media tycoon Seth Cain, had deliberately engineered the conflict from the very beginning. Megan watched as Sherman Kruger's representative spoke to the cameras, a huge white luxury yacht floating on crystalline waters behind him.

'…and I say again that these vicious conspiracy rumours are nothing more than the figments of the imaginations of journalists with nothing better to do than orchestrate smear campaigns against the energy companies of this great country. Kruger Petrochemicals is proud to be an American, patriotic and democratic company. It is not, and never has been, the policy of Kruger Petrochemicals to allow profits to hinder the advancement of the human race.'

A reporter aggressively shoved a microphone beneath the representative's nose.

'And what about the allegations that the company purchased the aircraft responsible for the attempted attacks on the American carrier fleet stationed in the Black Sea during the conflict?'

The young man smiled slickly at the reporter.

'Sherman Kruger is and always has been a fan of aviation. The aircraft were bought legitimately but were hijacked on their passage by road from the Ukraine to Europe. Of the equipment alleged to have been used to control these aircraft in their henious attack on our servicemen and women in the Black Sea, we know nothing.'

Another reporter jostled his way to the front.

'Then perhaps you could explain these sir,' he said, showing the papers to the camera, each with a clear example of the old man's signature at the bottom. *'These are the purchase papers for both the radio equipment and the aircraft, signed by Sherman Kruger's own hand sir. They were obtained by a journalist in New York.'*

The representative's face collapsed in upon itself and one hand shot out for the papers. The reporter whipped them out of his reach as a barrage of questions fell like rain upon the young man.

'What of reports that Sherman Kruger's assets have been frozen, and that he is now to be charged by the United States Government for treason?!' asked another reporter. *'How do you think he feels now, to be effectively penniless?'*

The aide hurried out of sight onto the luxury yacht, followed by the ranks of reporters and shouted questions.

'Well done Frank,' Megan smiled to herself as she remembered the tenacious New Yorker who had first approached her.

The image changed to one of American President Baker, who was addressing a press conference from the White House and had just been challenged to explain how his administration had been duped by the media into entering a war.

'There can be no excuses for the conduct of those who would use the power of their organisations to influence politics or public opinion for their own gain. However, we are a capitalist nation – there are those who will rise to positions of immense power outside of politics as well as within. We must learn to strike a balance between what is acceptable in our society and what is coercive. The people did not want this war – people very rarely do want war. Only governments seem unable to avoid it. Yet we cannot avoid our own place in time and the duties of office in which we are expected to succeed by the people who put us there. You.'

The president looked up from his notes, speaking without an auto–cue.

'We must survive. We must bear the burden, undertake the responsibility to rid our world of terror, of deceit, of senseless conflict and of wars without reward. There are no winners and we know it, and yet still we continue to choose bloodshed over public opinion, time and time again. People think that the president of the United States has no superior. Well, he does. You. That is what a democracy is: a politician should not be a leader of the people but a servant of the people. We were challenged to defend a democracy in danger, and we did so. Had we not, we would have been criticised. We did, and still we are being criticised. Damned if we do, damned if we don't. Our freedoms are not free, as well you know. Generations past fought and died to defend our way of life, and I have no doubt that future generations will do so too. It is up to us – not just me or just you – all of us, to ensure that if they go into battle again it is for the right reason, and not for those who would wish to gain financially.'

The press conference erupted into applause as a small knot of presidential aides wrung their hands and bore worried expressions at the extent of their president's candour.

Megan turned off the television and walked toward the shower just as she heard the mail drop into her safety box. Megan opened the box and lifted out a handful of letters. She was about to drop them onto the sofa when a postcard caught her eye. A picture of the northern Mordanian city of Rhocha in summer was on the front, and the postmark was Mordanian. Megan flipped it over.

Everyone wants to be found, but not everyone wants to be located.
Rameron's men protected me, Akim's men liberated me
and Callum's false news has freed me for life.
One day I hope to see you again,
SD

Megan blinked in surprise, felt a sudden stinging in the corners of her eyes as her throat ached. Smiling like the idiot she sometimes felt she was, she stood the postcard on a narrow shelf beside the television. She looked at the calendar and saw that it was Monday. Still smiling, she walked across to her answering machine and pressed the message button.

'You have two–new–messages. Message one.'

'Hi Megan, it's Tom from the office. Heard you were back in town and got your number from Harry. Give me a call back if you fancy a drink or something.'

Megan was about to say 'delete' when she hesitated, turned, and grabbed a piece of paper to write Tom's number down.

***

ABOUT THE AUTHOR

Dean Crawford is the author of the internationally published series of thrillers featuring *Ethan Warner*, a former United States Marine now employed by a government agency tasked with investigating unusual scientific phenomena. The novels have been *Sunday Times* paperback best-sellers and have gained the interest of major Hollywood production studios. He is also the enthusiastic author of many independently published Science Fiction novels.

REVIEWS

All authors love to hear from their readers. If you enjoyed my work, please do let me know by leaving a review on Amazon. Taking a few moments to review our works lets us authors know about our audience and what you want to read, and ultimately gives you better value for money and better books.

7818831R00207

Printed in Great Britain
by Amazon.co.uk, Ltd.,
Marston Gate.